Viv pinched her lip

"Neither have I

She laughed in  ou have in mind for proving your abstinence this evening, you could never prove that."

Miles leaned closer until she could feel his warm breath. "You're going to kiss me," he said, his words a delicious, rumbling promise.

"Hardly."

"You are. And you're going to use that delectable pink tongue of yours and taste me."

Viv shivered. She looked for any means of escaping his seductive ease, but her feet wouldn't move. Her knees had turned to porridge.

"And when you taste nary a drop of whiskey nor a hint of cigar smoke, you'll have to believe that I've kept my word."

"Tonight, perhaps."

"Is that an invitation, my dear? Because I could come back again and again." He placed the gentlest kiss on the apple of her left cheek. "And again." Then the other. "Until you believe me."

Viv closed her eyes. His voice, the rich scent of him, conspired like an opiate to muddy her thinking. She breathed past a hot ache that radiated out from her belly. Only the wall held her upright.

"Vivie," he whispered against her mouth. "Kiss me."

This title is also available as an eBook

Flawless

The Christies, Book One

CARRIE LOFTY

Pocket Books

New York   London   Toronto   Sydney   New Delhi

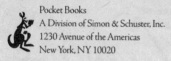

Pocket Books
A Division of Simon & Schuster, Inc.
1230 Avenue of the Americas
New York, NY 10020

This book is a work of fiction. Names, characters, places, and incidents either are products of the author's imagination or are used fictitiously. Any resemblance to actual events or locales or persons, living or dead, is entirely coincidental.

First Pocket Books paperback edition October 2011

POCKET and colophon are registered trademarks of Simon & Schuster, Inc.

For information about special discounts for bulk purchases, please contact Simon & Schuster Special Sales at 1-866-506-1949 or business@simonandschuster.com.

The Simon & Schuster Speakers Bureau can bring authors to your live event. For more information or to book an event contact the Simon & Schuster Speakers Bureau at 1-866-248-3049 or visit our website at www.simonspeakers.com.

Designed by Jacquelynne Hudson
Cover illustration by Jon Paul Ferrara

Manufactured in the United States of America

10 9 8 7 6 5 4 3 2 1

ISBN 978-1-4516-1638-5
ISBN 978-1-4516-1640-8 (ebook)

To Keven
For all the reasons I can't mention.

Acknowledgments

Thank you to Patti Ann Colt and Kelly Schaub for early reads, and to the members of Chicago North who critiqued a very rough draft. In particular, the comments provided by Blythe Gifford, Courtney Milan, and Nancy J. Parra set me on the right course.

I am deeply beholden to Cathleen DeLong, who offered continual support, incredible friendship, and keen insights on various incarnations. I'd quote a bunch of lyrics to show my appreciation, but you already know them by heart. #truths

As always, I am grateful for the encouragement of good friends who keep me relatively sound of mind. Many, many thanks to Ann Aguirre, Zoë Archer, the Broken Writers, Jenn Ritzema, and my family: Keven, Juliette, Ilsa, and Dennis and Kathy Stone.

Two additional individuals, Kevan Lyon and Lauren McKenna, have earned my undying gratitude for taking such a tremendous chance on this story. The support I received from both of you, as well as from the incredible team at Pocket, has resulted in the most creatively satisfying experience of my life. With utmost respect, I thank you.

Prologue

*V*ivienne *stared at the portrait* of her loud, arrogant, bombastic father and stifled the grief that had yet to ease. Captured by deft strokes of color, Sir William Christie's patented scowl glared down from above the library's austere marble fireplace. Even three weeks on from his rain-drenched funeral, the truth of his passing had yet to sink in. But there she waited in his brownstone mansion for the reading of the will.

She waited to breathe again.

Her gloved hands wouldn't stop their restless dance across a pleated ruffle at her waist. Had she repaid her debts to him when she'd been nothing but a dead Frenchwoman's brat? Had she masked her resentment when he'd held back his approval, expecting her to rise above the circumstances of her birth?

Harsh, her father. Always harsh. But never had there

been a man more true to his word. He had claimed her as his daughter. The details of the bequest, however, had been kept in the strictest secrecy. Anything less than a substantial share of the estate would mean a return to England—to her husband. The rabble and grime of her childhood in the Paris slums held more appeal.

At least then she'd been cherished.

Viv pressed unsteady palms between her breasts and breathed once, and again, until her fears quieted. She needed to keep her best face in place. Instead of more fretting, she reinforced her courage with memories of those first few monstrous months after her betrothal. Wealthy Sir William's knighthood, bestowed by Her Majesty for his contributions to British rail facilities, had only permitted Viv entrée. The remainder of the steep social climb had been hers to undertake. On the cusp of marrying into the aristocracy, she had succeeded in becoming a vital, respected member of London society.

The greatest challenge of her life—a challenge met and conquered.

Whatever the will held in store for her, Viv would persevere. She believed that of herself, as had her demanding father.

The door behind her opened. She turned to find the butler ushering a tall, stoic man into the library.

"Alex," she breathed.

Only upon seeing her older half brother did Viv realize she'd been counting the minutes until her siblings' arrivals. Their laughter and unflinching devotion had laid a bedrock of strength atop memories of her mother's love. Alex's embrace was strong and sure. When sleep had eluded Viv as a child, he had been the one to read aloud the mythological stories she loved—no matter that he examined life with the analytical detachment of a gifted scientist.

He drew back and gave her shoulders a squeeze, as if making certain she would remain standing when he let go. The library hardly seemed so gloomy with his steady support. "How are you holding up, Viv?"

"Well enough." She shrugged slightly, studying him. Five months had only just started to ease the grief of his wife Mamie's death. Weariness still tugged his lips downward and deepened the creases fanning toward his temples. "And you?"

"I've been better." He offered a tremulous smile. "But I've been worse, too."

Like a verdant breeze in spring, Gareth and Gwyneth arrived next—together, of course, and as stylish and noisy as always. Chatter from Gwen. Snickered replies from Gareth. And laughter enough from both to prompt a full grin from even Alex.

Aside from those final days of their father's demise and burial, Viv hadn't seen the twins since August, when Gwen had debuted as Gilda in *Rigoletto*. Her younger half-sister's star was on the rise in the world of opera, with Gareth there to manage her career.

Holding themselves with the matched confidence of youth, wealth, and expectation, they harbored no outward doubts as to their share of the Christie estate. Neither did

Alex. After all, her siblings were not bastards. Viv was, with her misbegotten origins hidden by an adoption's paper-thin veneer of respectability.

If their father had needed to disclose her true origins to his attorneys . . .

Gwen and the boys knew. But Viv's place in Society would be lost forever if anyone else learned the truth.

"It had to be the library," Gareth said, shaking Alex's hand before the men pulled one another into a quick embrace. "I always hated this polite dungeon."

After receiving Gareth's affectionate kiss on the cheek, Viv embraced her sister. Gwen, all sunshine and champagne bubbles, always held on a little longer and a little tighter than anyone else, so Viv closed her eyes. Comfort eased deep into her bones. "Good to see you, my dear," she whispered.

"And you, Viv. I don't know how I'd manage all of this bother without you and Jonesy to see me through," she said, using her twin's childhood nickname.

"Don't worry. All will be well."

Gareth dropped onto the nearest settee. "Are we still gathering in Newport?"

"Packed and ready," Viv said. The Christies' palatial summer home, dubbed Calton after Sir William's birthplace, would be less hospitable at that time of year. But they'd anticipated the need to escape Manhattan Island and regroup in private, no matter the will's contents. They would protect one another as they always had, banding together beneath their father's long shadow. "Alex, is Edmund well enough to travel?"

Dressed in an elegant yet practical woolen suit, Alex appeared every inch the celebrated astronomer. But he was also the exhausted father of an infant son born prematurely. "I do hope so. His nurse is keeping him comfortable, but the croup has yet to leave him be."

Forever the first to offer comfort, Gwen followed Alex to another settee and held his hand. "Here's hoping this won't take long," she said.

"Little likelihood of that," Alex replied. "You know how Father was. Such an opportunity for grandstanding won't go unnoticed, even from beyond the grave."

Viv resisted the urge to flick her gaze back to the portrait, as if Alex's skepticism might deepen that scowl rendered in oils. Their father's severity had been just as fixed while he lived. To his last breath, his mind failing and his body succumbing to pneumonia, he'd required only a frown to reduce her to the child she'd been, plucked from a grim Parisian prison and whisked to a pristine new life. She'd long ago forgiven his sternness because of the gifts his kindness had bestowed, her family being the foremost.

Alain Delavoir, the estate's hawk-faced executor, arrived without fanfare. He settled into the leather wingback behind a massive mahogany desk, his bony frame dwarfed by furniture crafted to suit Sir William Christie's robust Scots build.

"Everyone, please have a seat," he said.

Momentarily beset by her fears, Viv swayed. Somber oxblood walls tightened. Dust and a trace of mold leeched out of countless books on sober, orderly shelves. But that smell only stiffened her resolve. This was her father's domain. And she would rise to his expectations—surpassing them, if possible.

As she settled onto the dark room's third settee, she thought of her little brownstone some three miles north. The chrysanthemums were in bloom, while spring would rejuvenate her beloved lilacs. Her home. A place of refuge she'd purchased with hoarded resources. Granted, that refuge had rotting shutters and a leak in the cellar, with walls in need of paint and a roof that let in bats. But it was hers and she loved it. She hoped for money enough to maintain it properly. Nothing was more important than keeping the property that represented her independence.

"The good news is that the estate will not be subject to probate," Delavoir said, his accent a discordant hybrid of Paris and Westchester County. "The entirety of the Christie fortune has been duly allocated, or else stored in trust. My duty today is to outline the nature of these arrangements."

Alex's expression was dubious. "Father never said anything about trusts."

"Nor did he intend to," Delavoir replied. "He'd hoped discretion would minimize speculation and protect share prices."

"While keeping us in the dark," Gareth said with a grimace. "No surprises thus far."

"Jonesy, he probably had his reasons." Not only the most empathetic, Gwen was, inevitably, the most stalwart defender of their father's actions. Thus she and her twin maintained staunchly opposing natures. "No use second-guessing them now."

"Of course he had reasons." Grinning, Gareth ticked them off his fingers. "Reexamining our reprehensible life choices, admitting he was right all along, and thanking him for the lesson learned."

Viv laughed behind her gloved hand. Even Alex smiled. Much of the tension dissipated, lifted by shared mirth. Yes, they would persevere. She believed that with all her heart.

A tall man barged past the sputtering butler and strode into the library. Cigar smoke swirled around him like a sickly fog.

Viv's stomach twisted. *Dear God, he came.*

Miles Warren Durham, 9th Viscount Bancroft. The man she'd married to please her father. The man she'd fled to save her dignity.

Ribs straining, she felt her heart trying to escape the confines of her body. The moment he would look her in the eye dangled between them like the blade of a guillotine. It would be lurking there in his languid gaze—the confrontation they'd delayed for over a year.

Without acknowledging anyone, Miles strode to the sideboard and opened a decanter with sloppy haste. As if by some dark magic, he didn't spill a drop of liquor on the plush Turkish carpet.

The sight of him stripped Viv of the hope that time might blunt her response. He remained just as imposing, in possession of height, brawn, and negligent grace. Coffee-colored hair curled just at the edge of his collar. And his face. She'd always been a fool for his face, especially freshly shaven as he was just then. All symmetrical and strong, his chin, nose, forehead had been crafted from the very best of his aristocratic forebears.

Seeing him again left her lightheaded, just as recalling the Saunders' gala still lit a fire in her chest. Miles had conjured such rough pleasure on their last night together. A swift heaviness settled in her breasts and between her legs, which she tried to ease by sitting straighter, by clamping her knees so tightly that bone ground against bone. Memories made her blood bubble and roll, tingling under skin that had yet to forget his touch.

But the following week, after discovering the real reason behind that passionate seduction, she'd departed for New York.

Unable to look at her siblings, Viv feared what she would see on their faces. Confusion, maybe, or disapproval. Outright pity. She had weathered such censure in London by adopting a placid, tolerant demeanor, but that falsity never felt right when facing her family. She'd hoped Miles wouldn't bother to come—too intent on debauchery to make the tedious transatlantic crossing—just as she prayed he wouldn't choose that moment to lay bare their private war.

"Don't let me interrupt." He collapsed beside Viv and draped an arm around her shoulders. Cigar ash flicked onto one of her cream-colored kid gloves. Yet he remained perfectly at ease and perfectly groomed. A blue-and-white silk ascot hugged his throat as he swallowed scotch. His highborn English accent slurred around sloppy consonants, but his actions spoke of clear-headed antagonism. "Let's have done with this."

Miles's warm breath slid along her nape. Viv hated herself for shivering, for aching, for indulging him with even an ounce of her attention. He'd always been so unpredictable. Temptingly reckless. But she could only apologize for his behavior so many times. The esteem he'd squandered with each fresh disappointment tempered her desire. How could she give herself into the keeping of a man she did not respect? A man who disdained his title and squandered the wealth her family had worked so hard to attain?

Never again. She found strength in those words. *Never again.* The mantra throbbed in her mind as she shrugged from under Miles's hold, one as casual as it was meant to intimidate.

Delavoir adjusted his monocle and cleared his throat. His blatant impatience drew Viv back to the gravity of what he would reveal. The will. Her future. A chance to be free of the dangerous man at her side.

Retrieving a document from his patent folio case, Delavoir said, "The majority of Sir William's liquid assets have been endowed to Crittenford, the academy for immigrant children he founded some years ago. As for the remainder of Christie Holdings Limited, the railroads, and the newspapers, he relinquished his own shares back to their respective companies."

Viv's fingertips turned to ice. Puzzlement slid toward sick understanding. Even Miles perked up at the news. "Of all the bloody cheek," he said, grinning. "He's entitled it all away."

Gwen had gone white. Her chin trembled. "But . . . he wouldn't!"

"He has," Delavoir said firmly.

Miles snickered before returning to the sideboard. "Then I believe I shall refill my Hennessey before we're all turned out."

"And what remains for us?" Alex asked.

"You are to be offered managerial positions, each with a different subsidiary company. These companies were acquired through the years by Sir William. For some reason or another, all are on the brink of collapse."

Delavoir produced four folios. When Viv saw her name emblazoned on the topmost one, she stifled a relieved smile. No matter her father's intentions, she hadn't been left out. He'd kept his word, just as she knew he would.

"If, at the end of a two-year contract, the company you've managed is worth more than its value upon Sir William's death, you will be awarded a substantial bonus and the option to purchase a controlling interest in your enterprise. In the meantime, the businesses will remain property of the shareholders."

Gwen's hand fluttered up to her throat. "We would be . . . *employees?*"

"Precisely," Delavoir said.

"Father always did want us to take after him," Gareth said sardonically. "Now he gets to make sure that happens."

No easy smiles anymore. Only then did Viv notice the

dark circles beneath his eyes—eyes the same deep hazel shared by four children born to three different women.

"What if we decide to refuse this offer of employment?" Alex asked.

Delavoir tapped the folios with skeletal fingers. "Then your proposed contract is nullified, and your inheritance will be a single payment of five hundred dollars."

Viv's voice wavered a little when she asked, "And if we fail?"

"Again, a single payment of five hundred dollars," Delavoir said. "Nothing more."

Goose bumps pocked her skin. She had learned a great deal about her father's enterprises—far more than the others, who had indulged in the license of legitimacy by rebelling in little ways. But to run a whole company!

With her head listing toward Alex's shoulder, Gwen looked as ill as Viv felt. But even Alex, the calm, stalwart center of their family, drummed his fingers along the armrest. Gareth shook his head with a rueful chuckle, as if to say, "I told you so."

Only Miles appeared amused, leaning carelessly against the sideboard. His slipshod posture contrasted with his perfectly tied ascot and the sharp line of his dark gray suit. The smirk marring his fine mouth would've been more appropriate for telling a bawdy story. The afternoon had turned nightmarish, but Viv's husband retained a detached humor she dearly resented. And envied.

"I'd have thought at least one of you would inquire after the reward," he said with a slight sneer. He skewered

Delavoir with an expression that attested to generations of power. "So tell us, man. What is the bonus?"

"One million dollars."

"Each?" Alex asked, mouth agape.

"Potentially, yes." Delavoir picked up the topmost folio. "Lady Bancroft, would you care to know the details of your position?"

Viv's brain was still grappling with that sum. One million dollars. "Yes, I would."

Miles returned to sit beside her. With a half smile on the only lips she'd ever kissed, he seemed almost . . . *eager*. Her muscles twitched with the need to take his hand and draw from his unexpected strength. She'd yearned for exactly that across two years of marriage, only to be refused and, eventually, disillusioned. Physical pleasure entertained him, but the unruly viscount had never sought more, never offered more. The trial of adoring two selfish men—her father and her husband—had taught Viv that some mountains weren't meant to be scaled.

She firmed her spine and faced Delavoir. If she would do this, she'd do it alone.

"Vivienne, Viscountess Bancroft," he began, "adopted daughter of Sir William Christie and the late Mrs. Catrin Jones Christie."

Gripping the armrest, she offered silent thanks for another gratifying reprieve. Even in death, her father had kept the façade of her adoption in place. She was a Christie. And she'd prove it. If her father believed her as capable and deserving as her half siblings, she would not fail him.

"You will manage the Christie Diamond Brokerage House in Kimberley, Cape Colony."

"Cape Colony?" Her mind blanked. She swallowed past a dry lump. "Where is that?"

Miles laughed—a thin, malicious sound. He leaned back and puffed once on his cigar, meeting Viv's gaze for the first time. Through a sallow cloud of smoke, his earthen brown eyes blazed with a sharp intensity that made her tremble.

"My dear lady," he said, "you are bound for the south of Africa."

One

Cape Town
March, 1881

Although Miles *stood well back* from where the *Coronea* had docked, the push and crush of humanity threatened even his studiously crafted calm. Hordes of disembarking passengers wrestled with their belongings as they forged toward land, a never-ending snake creeping down off crowded decks.

The ripe stench of coal fires, harbor rot, and hundreds of bodies overpowered the clean salt of the ocean. Seabirds circled and swooped in a chaotic dance. Beyond the prickly masts of anchored ships, the sky had lost the garish colors of dawn, given over to the glare of midmorning. Miles touched the back of his neck where a light wind teased his hair. The cool seaside air reminded him of Southampton.

I watched thee on the breakers, when all was storm and fear.

But Lord Byron's words offered Miles no comfort, only an odd sort of foreboding.

Four months had lapsed since the will reading, when Viv's siblings had also learned the details of their assigned companies. There in the library, Miles had passed the time glaring at his wife's exquisite neck and marinating his lustful, resentful thoughts in Hennessey. He'd awoken to find himself alone in a guest room in Old Man Christie's brownstone.

He grimaced and shifted his gaze across nearby faces, baffled by an embarrassment he rarely suffered. But the emotion refused a lengthy stay. Anger took its place. The whole Christie clan had decamped to their mansion in Newport. Holidays with the family, but that hadn't included Miles.

Viv had left him a note. Yet another elegant, prissy note to say she was leaving.

So he'd sobered up. And made a decision.

After catching the first steamer back to England, he'd evaded his father long enough to gamble his way into a bit of ready cash. Then it was off to Cape Town. But damned inconvenient timing, the war against the Boers. Passenger traffic had slowed to a trickle, with Viv stuck in the States until the February armistice. The ink had yet to dry on the official peace accord. Time wasted, yes, but also time spent resolving how to get what he wanted.

Vivienne Bancroft would come back to him. Willingly.

With a hand to his brow, he looked toward the luxury clipper's topmost deck. Viv would be up there among that tangle of people, along with the manservant he'd sent to intercept her luggage.

Intercept . . . and then hold hostage.

Impatiently swiping at a cluster of midges, he craved a drink—not just any drink, but a long, stinging, obliterating swig of cognac. But he hadn't touched a drop since leaving New York that fateful morning. A good game required sobriety, which few of the world's casual card players understood. And Vivienne was anything but an easy mark. He would need all his wit and wile to keep from falling under her spell like a bloody fool.

Again.

Miles found himself twirling his wedding ring. That little hypocrite—all decorum and indignation until her mouth met his.

Had beastly Sir William given his daughter a plump dollop of cash, she would've had the financial means to end their marriage. Miles would've gone back to London, alone, solvent enough to keep the family estates intact. But little else remained of her dowry.

Instead, the challenge of Old Man Christie's bequest offered an unexpected one-million-dollar reprieve. Stretching his arms, Miles stood away from the crate and sucked in cooling gulps of air. *Damn and blast.* Far, far too much money to ignore.

His scant head start aside, during which he'd secured accommodations in Kimberley and completed banking transfers, he and Viv would need to learn quickly: every major player, every aspect of the diamond trade, and even the bloody weather. They were starting near to zero. He should have been terrified but a sharp thrill sped the beat of his heart.

Beyond the challenge of earning that rich sum, he had a score to settle. Viv had *left* him. The surprise of finding their London town home abandoned still made him shake. One year spent fending off polite rumors about his marriage had been one year too long.

The crack of a whip snapped his attention toward a man sitting atop a heavily laden wagon. The road leading away from the docks, clogged with dark bodies, permitted no room for the vehicle to pass. Burly and dough-faced, the wagon master wasn't directing his whip at the donkeys straining against their tethers, but at people.

"Get off there," the driver shouted. He threw his weight into the next strike of braided leather.

A young woman screamed and fell. Those nearby snatched her arms and hauled her upright, saving her from the crush of feet and hooves. Blood streaked along her shoulder, and her worn homespun dress was torn and covered in dust.

With relentless clarity, the Cape's autumn sunshine illuminated every face twisted by concentration and fear. The donkeys continued to bray. The wagon master raised his arm again. Leather sliced through the air, this time striking a tall shirtless man whose dark, scarred back had already suffered the bite of a whip.

"Out of the way, you kaffir scum!"

Across three months, the colony had subjected Miles to many such scenes. Perhaps the difference, on this occasion, could be traced to the bitterness Viv churned in his blood. His arms ached with the need to pummel his fretfulness into submission—or pummel *someone*. The lawlessness of the colony, the otherworldliness of it, gave him permission to do what his tedious title had never permitted: take matters into his own hands.

"Oh, bloody hell."

He strode into the crowd, abandoning his role as a mere bystander. Fully a head taller than most of the hunched, scrambling people, he fixed on the wagon master. Every successive crack of the man's whip filled Miles with sizzling indignation. Like most of the British Empire, Cape Colony hadn't permitted slavery in almost fifty years. That didn't stop some colonists from treating Africans as they would the lowest animals.

Miles didn't consider himself a do-gooder, but such a flagrant abuse of power assaulted his most basic principles. It wasn't sporting and it simply wasn't British.

He elbowed his way through the throng until the wagon master loomed above him on the bench. Miles quickly climbed aboard, senses centered on his target. The wagon master turned just as Miles balled his fist and let it swing. A satisfying crack of bone rewarded him as his opponent's nose gave way.

Blood streaked the man's mangy beard with crimson. Narrow-eyed anger replaced his stunned grimace. He reared back the butt of his whip and brought it down like a cudgel. Miles used his forearm to deflect the blow, then retaliated with a flurry of jabs to the gut.

Foul exhales accompanied the wagon master's sharp grunts, but his flab seemed to absorb the impact of each punch. Winded, he tottered slightly. His guard dropped. Miles snatched the whip. When the man's expression bunched around the need to continue the fight, Miles jabbed the butt of the whip against that bloody, broken nose. The wagon master howled and clutched his face.

"Are we quite through?" Miles demanded, his throat stinging.

His opponent sank onto the bench and nodded once. Rage still flared across his expression but his shoulders caved forward.

"Good." Miles slowly, deliberately coiled the whip. "Now I suggest that you notice the situation here on the docks. Too many people, for one. Laughably poor engineering. But that's no excuse for whipping people."

"They're bloody kaffirs," the man said, his voice muffled behind his hands. "Beasts like these here donkeys."

Miles glanced across the sea of faces, more dark than light, and wondered again at the state of the Cape. Ripe, vital, raw, it perched continuously on the edge of violence. He tasted its bitterness in the air and felt it itching under his skin—a shocking sort of awakening.

"No more beastly than the rest of us," Miles said.

He hopped down from the wagon, not so negligent as to disregard a defeated opponent. He'd often seen desperation or pride draw out a confrontation, and harbored no compulsion to go another round. Too much animal in that man.

As the immediacy of the fight seeped from his body, Miles shivered. He eased back into the crowd on legs just shy of steady, intent on returning to the machinery crate. Surely Viv had found her way off that damned clipper by now.

He bumped into a solid wall of ebony flesh and found himself looking up at a man—a rare occurrence. Before him stood the same shirtless African who'd taken one of the wagon master's cruel strokes. His shaven head gleamed.

"Pardon me," Miles said.

"Thank you." The African's deep bass was melodic, like the notes of a bassoon. Across his back would be those old silvery scars and a fresh line of split skin, but his expression was none so grim. "Boggs is a scourge."

Miles raised his eyebrows. "A scourge? Nice word."

"I speak the truth."

"And I believe you. My hope is that I won't require his services."

"Hire a wagon," the man said. "I'll drive for you instead."

Miles studied that dark African face. Every feature was as he'd seen in caricatures and even so-called scientific journals: the wide, flat nose, the large lips, and the fathomless black irises surrounded by white. Those demeaning illustrations hadn't captured what it was to look upon such a man. Miles found intelligence and a rugged, hard-edged dignity—a refreshing change from the feckless gentlemen who'd comprised his social circle in London.

"You need a work pass," Miles said.

"Yes, sir."

Without a work pass, Africans could be subjected to police harassment or even expulsion from the city limits. In

Kimberley, the constant threat of diamond theft tainted all manual laborers, regardless of skin color, but Africans bore the heaviest burden of suspicion.

"Good, because I need reliable workers. I'm returning to Kimberley, if you're interested." He held out his hand. "Call me Bancroft," he said, omitting a significant part of his identity—namely, his title.

The man stared at Miles for a long moment, then shook hands. His grip was strong, his expression intent. "I'm Umtonga kaMpande. But you English seem to find that a challenge."

"No argument here."

"Because you have shown the kindness of a friend, I ask that you call me Mr. Kato."

"That is a kindness in itself, Mr. Kato. Any woman? Any possessions?"

"No, sir."

Miles nodded. "Good."

With nothing more by way of niceties, he turned and strode back toward the *Coronea*, toward Viv, glad to know that the tall African would follow.

Viv brushed a gloved hand across her forehead and pinned the porter with a hard look. "What do you mean they've been *taken care of?*"

The short man, bulky and rippling with menacing muscles, simply shrugged. "Your baggage has been taken care of, ma'am."

Fear brushed up her spine. Had her things been stolen?

Hardly on African soil for five minutes and already a snag. She took a quick breath. "By whom?"

"He said he was your husband, ma'am. Lord Bancroft."

Viv blinked.

He's here?

She locked her knees against the impulse to sink onto the foot-worn planks of the dock. "My husband," she whispered.

Of course he would come. She'd been willfully naïve in believing her trip to Newport would signal her intention to remain separated.

Miles indulged every vice that caught his fancy. His passion for gambling reigned supreme over alcohol, women, and even his blasted cigars, but perhaps his uncanny luck had run out. He must truly need money if he had come to the Cape, ready to make himself a nuisance in exchange for a portion of her earnings. And if he held her possessions, then he awaited the confrontation she'd evaded in New York.

This time he'll get it.

She needed her belongings. Every last item would be necessary if she were to endure the twenty months that remained of her contract.

No, more than a year and a half was too much to consider. She wouldn't dwell on the immensity of her task, choosing instead to relive the lessons of her father's many successes. One day at a time. One foot in front of the other. Piece by hard-earned piece. She could prop her hopes on no more complicated buoys. In doing so she would find the strength to survive this trial. Deep inside, she would rediscover the tenacity of an urchin who'd once stolen a dying vagrant's dinner just to quell her own aching hunger—and the resilience on which that quiet girl had depended when her mother was jailed and hanged.

But at the present, she simply needed to find her husband.

She signaled to Chloe Tassiter, her maid, who handed the porter a shilling. "Can you take me to him, please?" Viv asked.

"This way."

As nimble as a fleeing rabbit, he ducked into the crowd, navigating passengers, porters, and incalculable bags and trunks. He jostled to clear a makeshift path. The same foot journey without his aid would've been terribly difficult, two women consumed by pressing bodies.

Unlike her siblings, Viv had endured the grueling burden of an impoverished youth and the secret knowledge of her illegitimacy. That meant balancing the strictures of good society with the example of Sir William Christie's limitless ambitions. She never failed to appreciate when her way was made easier by the privilege she now enjoyed—privilege she would labor ceaselessly to keep.

Good heavens, a million dollars! She'd be able to return to her home in New York, to her gardens, to her life. And she would finally be free of the title she'd learned to wear like a horse harness across her shoulders. But she could take nothing for granted until she'd dispensed with her father's assignment.

Viv bumped a coop full of clucking hens and bruised

her hip. She and Chloe didn't so much walk as gush toward some unseen destination. Children struggled to haul crates twice their size, kicking scrawny dogs that nipped at bare feet. Men who may have been fathers to those children—or worse yet, their keepers—waited at the wagons and loaded the possessions, always pocketing the coins.

Chloe took Viv's upper arm and offered a reassuring squeeze. "Courage, my lady."

Although a servant since her youth, Chloe had never lived as roughly as this. Raised on Lord Bancroft's ancestral estate, she knew service and she knew her station, but her blue eyes were wide and she sucked on her lower lip. On those crowded docks, Chloe Tassiter may as well have been royalty.

Viv, however . . . Her body ached with a deep recognition. She had once hidden in the shadows of a similar world, her days marked by stealth, fear, and hunger. She breathed its filth and knew its secrets.

"My lady, do you know where we're going?" Chloe asked.

A shudder wiggled through Viv's stomach—that sudden, queasy feeling of being taken advantage of. The porter could be leading them anywhere. Suddenly, her husband's volatility held more appeal than those beastly unknowns.

"I say." Viv lifted her voice above the din. "Where are you taking us, man?"

"Just there." The porter nodded toward where a wagon waited along a footpath.

Viv stopped short.

Miles, Lord Bancroft, leaned against one large wheel.

Only, she'd never seen him in such a state. Gone was the snide aristocrat, preened to perfection. In his place stood a taut, muscular man whose waistcoat gapped open along a lean abdomen. His neck was bare, the collar undone. He'd rolled his shirtsleeves. A coiled whip dangled from his belt and rested against his hip.

Blinking back the grit and sunshine, Viv struggled to assemble the jigsaw of new impressions. Thick hair he normally tamed with pomade stuck out in spiky disarray. The coffee-dark color was streaked through with lighter strands, kissed by bright midday. Every indecently exposed inch of flesh had assumed a luscious caramel shade. Too much time spent in the sun, her mind argued. But the color suited him—much better than the pallor of genteel boredom and too much time spent in gambling halls.

A taunting grin turned him from merely handsome to maddeningly so.

Miles . . . wearing a whip. He'd turned positively heathen.

Viv tried to tell herself that she didn't want to see him there, obviously pleased to have taken her by surprise. Yet she could not deny a flush of relief. Twenty minutes on the docks had stripped away months of preparation, when she'd waited out the Boer War by studying all she could find about the diamond trade. Confronted with the stomach-sick shock of the Cape, she realized that her will alone would not be enough. Never had she felt more gallingly female.

She needed him. He knew it. And her pride would suffer.

For the sake of that bonus, however, Viv met him at the wagon. "My lord," she said simply.

"My lady." Miles bowed, more sarcastic than respectful. "Surprised to see me?"

She ignored his gloating question and nodded toward her possessions. "Is everything accounted for?"

"Mr. Nolan tells me as much."

Glancing to where Adam Nolan sat among her crates and trunks, Viv allowed a tight smile. "Good. I trust him."

"Meaning you'd count everything twice had I been in charge of the matter," Miles said.

The hard emotion in his eyes tempted her to recoil. She remembered that afternoon in the library and the silent anger he'd turned her way. Yes, she'd left him. And she'd left all over again, preferring her siblings' loving company to his unpredictability. Her reasons remained strong and valid. No glare, no matter how intimidating, would change her mind.

A fine spray of dried blood formed a ghastly constellation across his rumpled white shirt. That he'd already found trouble was hardly a surprise. Trouble and company. A massive African wearing breeches and little else sat on the wagon bench, reins in hand.

Her attention returned to Miles, to his shirt, to his tanned neck and forearms. To the vigorous width of his shoulders and the ready strength of his thighs. This version of her husband was new. All new—at least on the outside.

Just how long had he been here? Had he arrived when the peace concluded in February? Or even earlier?

"We have tickets for the train to Kimberley," she said, banishing her fascination. "Can your man take us to the station?"

Miles's grin returned, that reckless expression so out of place in polite society, but so startlingly at home on the Cape Town docks. "We're all yours, my lady . . . for a price."

Tender skin chafed beneath her elbow-length gloves, and the cleft between her breasts flared with heat. Better than anyone, she understood that apparent courtesies from her husband would be met with a reckoning. The gleam in his dark eyes told Viv that the last thing he would demand of her was money.

Two

*M*iles *shifted his weight, suddenly* restless and hot. The impact of seeing Viv after four months—while sober this time—was more crippling than he'd wanted to believe.

Dear God, she was beautiful.

Ringlets of sunshine-blonde hair framed regal cheekbones and accentuated the sleek line of her jaw. Lush lips that rested in a perpetual pout hid sins and secrets. But her eyes . . . Miles had fallen into them once and had yet to break free of their magic. A distinctive hazel, her irises blended moss and gold until neither held sway. An ingenue's curiosity layered over a woman's keen understanding of how the world worked.

Miles searched for clues that she could be bested. Her face had taken on a great deal of color, which suggested she'd spent time strolling the *Coronea*'s promenade deck. Her figure remained trim yet curved in all the right places, meaning she hadn't indulged in the never-ending array of delicacies available to first-class passengers. All rather innocuous.

But telltale circles beneath those remarkable hazel eyes—

circles not entirely obscured by a careful dusting of talcum powder—revealed restless, perhaps even sleepless, nights.

He exhaled. He relaxed his shoulders. And the enmity he had every right to feel eased his lacerated pride. True enough, he had another man's blood on his shirt and he craved a steadying drink, but he understood his goals. He wanted Viv out of his system before they parted once and for all. And he wanted her to regret it with every aching, lonely fiber of her body when he was gone.

She stood like a silk-encrusted statue. Never a crack, no matter how many whispered rumors. Only his touch had ever revealed the passion lurking beneath. Rare moments when she'd lost control, gasping his name, were more precious than all the diamonds in the Cape.

Miles planned to seduce her, just for the fun of proving that she loved it.

"Make your demand," she said. "I expect I know what you'll say."

"Not at all, my dear. I don't want your money, and I don't desire marital privileges—well, not yet. Not here on the docks."

Rosy lips parted on a quiet sound. Her expression sparked with something very close to hatred. More like a cousin to hatred, perhaps, because he'd seen her well and truly angry. This little farce of a reaction meant they were only getting started.

"Out with it," she said.

"I want you to ask."

After a flicker of surprise, her composure returned.

Miles wanted to retrieve his pocket watch and measure the span of time between *flustered* and *restored*. He'd place heavy wagers on her abilities, if anyone dared take him up on such a bet.

"Ask?"

"That's all. Ask that I instruct Mr. Kato to take your bags to the train station."

"And then?"

"Then we'll take your bags to the train station," he said, as if to a child. "The concept is not a difficult one, Vivie."

"Don't call me that," she snapped.

"Why not?" He touched a lock of shimmering blonde hair where it curved along her ear. "Remind you of something?"

"You know it does."

"Yes." So much time had passed, yet her warm floral scent still left him ready to beg. "Nights to remember."

"To forget, you mean."

His ardor chilled. Memories, both fervent and tender, flayed him with the mistakes of their shared past. The intensity of her passion had been the one great surprise of his utterly predictable life, and her constant need to deny it had been the undoing of their marriage. He'd always wanted what she refused to offer.

If any begging were to be done on that morning, it would be her task.

Miles scraped his gaze down along her body, then climbed into the back of the wagon with Adam and the maid. Every bit of his wife, from her ire to the frown that drew a line between her brows, was busy shocking frozen pieces of him back to life. But he would bend her, bully her, bed her—on his terms, not shaking and frothing like a servile dog.

"Ask, Vivie, or I'll unload it all into the harbor."

"You wouldn't!"

"Indeed, I would." He spread his arms wide. "I don't back down from bets and you know it. Or was it some other Viscount Bancroft who swam naked across the Thames?"

"Then I'll inform the police!"

"They'll only remand you into your husband's custody," he said, feeling giddy and mean. "Oh, wait . . . that's me. And all the while, your bloomers will be floating out to the Atlantic."

"You're disgusting."

"Perhaps, but I'm also a Peer of the Realm. Hard to believe, I know, but I do have influence." He tugged at his bloodied shirt, buttoned his waistcoat, and stared her down. "I can make the success of your daddy's company more likely . . . or bloody near impossible."

Genuine hurt stole the luster from her eyes. But the remorse he should've felt didn't come. Instead, as loose and lively as a freed prisoner, he breathed the fetid dockside air. His captivity was at an end.

"Very well, my lord," she said.

"Call me Miles. You used to."

"When I held out some hope for your worth in this life."

"You once held such hope? My dear, that was nearly generous."

"You deserve a *great* deal more," she gritted out.

Her anger was back, pulsing from her in billows. Porcelain cheeks flared with bright, hot color. She leveled a glare that deemed him an insect to be squashed. Miles merely grinned. Aside from the petty fun of her indignation, he could trust her body's reactions, from the innocent to the erotic—bare truths in their false world.

"All the same," he said. "You'll address me as such if you want my cooperation."

She didn't move, as if gathering the strength to even breathe. Then she swallowed and held up her hand. "Miles, my lord, will you deliver us to the train station? Please?"

He'd expected to hear defeat in her voice, something beautiful stripped of its grandeur, but she sounded decidedly too self-possessed. Beneath the sweetness of her smile waited venom.

Her father's daughter.

But for now, a win was a win. He reached for her hand.

Vivienne sat alongside Mr. Kato, the huge, silent African, as he skillfully guided the wagon toward the train station. She wished to continue nursing her dislike for Miles, but Cape Town held her mesmerized. Harsh blue-shadowed mountains angled along the horizon, holding the entire settlement in a hand ready to clamp shut. She'd half expected the blooming branches of her spring garden, but of course, March was the same as September in the north. Autumnal shades already dotted the foothills and lined the limbs of unfamiliar trees. The fertile smell of loam found her in warm, welcome bursts.

But the city wore a mask. Ostentatious homes, rich with

color and layers of fresh paint, could only brag from behind the safety of high ornate fences. They loomed over decayed shantytowns, tumbledown tents, and countless squatters. Ugliness gathered in the shadows like a cache of weapons, waiting to do violence.

While running on pure determination, Viv had been able to retreat from her dark childhood. Now those destitute years crawled over her skin and down her throat. She squeezed the wooden handle of the portmanteau in her lap—squeezed until her pinkie finger jerked.

The train station was a picture of barely controlled bedlam. Wealthy colonists strolled toward first-class accommodations, while servants dragged luggage in their wake. Rougher folk flocked toward the overburdened rear cars. A woman, great with child, followed a tradesman with a full blond beard whose back bowed under the weight of a massive trunk. She gripped the hands of two young boys, their little legs pumping to keep pace with her determined waddle. The crowd gobbled them up as a whistle announced the train's impending departure.

A baby wailed and Viv knew its terror.

She eased down from the wagon bench, having lost feeling in her rear. Miles was busy directing Adam and the African in the care of her possessions. "Take Lady Bancroft's girl with you," he said to his manservant. "Here are your tickets, plus money enough to make sure Mr. Kato is fairly accommodated. He cannot lose his pass, understand? And for God's sake find a salve for his back. And a shirt. One of mine, if you must."

Viv watched the exchange, curious. She had always known Miles to be fair with regard to servants and tenants on his family's estates. She just never recalled him . . . caring. He had treated such matters as just another responsibility to be mocked.

Adam offered Chloe his arm and a friendly smile. He was exactly as Viv remembered, his master's opposite in so many ways: shorter, fair, genial, and thoughtful. How he'd managed such a lengthy working relationship with Miles, loyal even to the back of beyond, was a mystery she had reconciled herself to never solving.

"Alone again," he said as the trio walked away. "It's been, what—a year? Two? I honestly cannot remember back that far."

"An entire naval crew's ration of liquor each night will do that to a brain."

"Especially one as stunted as mine?"

"Quite." She peered at him, as if doing so might reveal his deeper intentions. "You're determined to make this difficult. Tell me why."

"A gentleman does not air his laundry in public."

"No, he threatens to toss his wife's laundry into the harbor."

"New money insists on showiness," he said with a slight sniff. "Seems a shame not to display what frilly bits of lace and satin the Christie fortune can buy."

Viv smiled sweetly. "Perhaps I'm fresh out of lace and satin."

"Oh?"

"If you recall, shoring up your father's bankrupt estates permitted little allowance for niceties."

His lips lost their teasing tilt. "Sounds a great deal like our marriage."

She stiffened. Mussed clothing and chaotic hair made him appear more rakish, and yet he was the same man underneath. If only that weren't the case! She couldn't take her eyes off the brawn he'd acquired in only a few months. Wider shoulders. Thicker arms. His haphazardly buttoned waistcoat strained over his more muscular chest. What, exactly, had he been doing?

And why did her body insist on reacting so contrary to good intentions?

Because it always had. *She* always had. With Miles.

"Tell me what you intend. Please," she added for good measure. Even her father knew the value of pleasantries during business negotiations.

"When you sit with me on the train."

"You seem certain I'll do just that."

"Yes," he said. "Because you think you can best me. Admit it, you can't wait to take me on again. You've been bored stiff."

"At peace, more like."

"Peace isn't meant for the living."

The tips of his fingers graced her corseted waist as he guided her toward the first-class car. What should've been a gesture of affection or support felt as if he'd wiggled under her crinolines. Hot-faced memories layered atop her restlessness, softening her guts to glue.

And blast, she was simply *aware* of him again. Tiny flecks of gray at his temple blended with sun-streaked strands, while matched creases on the insides of each brow were more pronounced. She'd never noticed the scar behind his left earlobe, never truly appreciated the shape of his Adam's apple. Proper dress had always concealed such tiny details, heightening their intimate appeal.

"What, no more sweet venom?" he asked near her ear.

"How do you mean?"

"I've been touching you for roughly thirty seconds and you've yet to protest."

"I never did protest, remember?"

"Yes, quite the good little wife," he said genially. "When we lived on the same continent."

He ushered her aboard the train. Close confines pressed the front of his body almost indecently against her back. Or maybe that was just more of his baiting. She shivered either way.

The first-class carriage smelled faintly of leather and strongly of cigars. Sunlight shimmered across carved wood, gleaming brass railings, and beveled, gilt-trimmed mirrors. Richly upholstered benches faced each other along the right bank of windows. Three double-wide sleeping berths stretched along the left, their fine white coverlets peeking from behind parted, dark blue velvet curtains.

Viv stood in the center aisle. She hadn't thought to find such sumptuous amenities, nor so few people. Well-dressed men read newspapers, with tumblers of liquor at their fingertips. The only two women in the carriage sat together, their coiffed heads angled over a fashion catalogue. The contrast between the glut of passengers outside and the calm decorum of the carriage left her light in the head.

"Only the best for the world's wealthiest colonists." Miles's murmur sounded equally derisive and bored.

"Then we're in the wrong car."

"Because you're no longer a well-heeled Christie?"

"No," Viv said. "Because I am no colonist. I have no intention of staying here a day longer than necessary."

They took seats across from one another. Miles's long legs brushed her skirts, but she was ready for him this time. No flinching. His old patterns were remarkably unchanged. Taunt. Tease. Unnerve. Until she was so topsy-turvy that his certainty was all she could cling to.

She knew how to fight back now. By ignoring him, to start.

After the whistle bellowed again, the conductor shouted, "All aboard." The wheels squealed and the train car jerked.

So strange to think that she would've remained in London had he been humorless, ignorant, physically repellant—an arranged marriage without complications. She would've endured no disappointment when Miles drank a sailor's ration or smoked like a Bowery chimney, nor would memories of mutual passion haunt their shared past. But despite his disheveled clothing, he held himself as every inch the fine gentleman and could produce a flash flood of charisma.

That he could charm every other female with the same

precision made her stomach burn. And after what Viv witnessed on the morning after the Saunders' gala, she'd been forced to admit that she could no longer rely on him. Not even for discretion.

He lit a cigar. "You're staring."

As the station slowly crept out of sight, Viv forced herself to confront him directly. "Why are you here? I can understand why you'd attend the reading of the will. That could've meant easy money."

"Is that what you'd expected?"

"Maybe," she said softly. "But you should've stated your intentions, rather than trying to unsettle me."

"Did I? Unsettle you, that is?"

"You know you did."

"Frankly, someone needed to get a jump on this two-year contract."

She frowned. "When did you arrive?"

"Early January."

"But the war was on!"

"It hadn't been when I departed England. A lot can change on that blasted long journey." His expression hardened. "Besides, I had no intention of being the one left behind this time."

Viv didn't reveal what she heard in his voice—something close to hurt. She didn't dare believe that her leaving had affected him, but a nasty worm of guilt left her shaken.

"What do you have in mind for our future?" she asked.

"I find that an interesting question because, until very recently, there hasn't been much *our* to speak of."

"I want that bonus, Miles."

"Ah," he said, leaning forward. "Now we're getting somewhere. Why?"

"My brownstone requires maintenance."

"Where you live in New York?"

She lifted her chin. His lush, deep brown eyes had always been the gateway to temptation. He thought all the things she could never think, and dared her to come along on his adventures. She'd tried. For almost two years. But audacity was outside of her nature.

"Yes, in New York. Where I'll return when this matter is concluded." She took a deep breath. "I want our separation to be permanent."

But rather than react with scorn or anger, he maintained a quiet intensity. A silent showdown.

When she could take no more, Viv tried for a lighthearted tone. "Now that we know what I want, it's your turn."

He unleashed a slow, devastating grin. "I want you in my bed."

Of course he would. She'd known there on the docks, reading the heat in his avid gaze. But the blunt truth of it grabbed her insides and twisted. He'd make her beg and shiver, only to leave her wanting a place of refuge he'd never provide.

And if he harbored resentment because she'd left . . .

"Will you force me?" she asked, her mouth parched.

"What sort of gentleman would that make me?" He smiled a bland sort of business smile. "Now, let me share a story with you. Last summer, in a bizarre yet not unexpected turn of events, I won a woman in a card game."

No matter the truths she repeated until her head burst, she still recoiled from the idea of Miles in another woman's arms. "How very . . . *you*."

"As I said, not unexpected. The most fascinating part, however, was that the woman seemed resigned. She'd been part and parcel of a losing hand before. It took the edge off any sort of enjoyment I might have found." He exhaled a stream of silvery smoke. "So I sent her home."

Viv didn't want to feel relief, but it cooled the jealous heat in her veins. "Make your point."

"You asked what I want, so I'm telling you. I want your enthusiasm, Vivie."

He'd whispered that name in their bed, holding her and kissing her, bestowing an endearment no one else had ever used. He'd also called her that the night of the Saunders' gala. Fueled by alcohol, he had seduced her behind a wide spiral staircase. Anyone could have seen. With passion and shame fighting for dominance, she'd bit the muscle above his collarbone to keep from crying out. Never had she dipped so near to what she truly was: the bastard daughter of a whore.

But never had she felt such treasured hope. She had viewed the aristocracy with the same awe as any of New York's best. To secure a title was an accomplishment managed by only the richest families and choicest offspring. Learning her fiancé would be the dashing Viscount Bancroft had been a day of utter joy. All her dreams and hard work conspired to her advantage.

The drinking. The gambling till all hours. The hideous gossip that always followed. Miles was not dashing; he was a disappointment. The night of that gala, she had thought otherwise. Maybe, just maybe, he could change.

He'd proven those hopes unfounded by dawn.

"You ask too much," she whispered.

"Do you want that bonus?"

"You know I do."

"Then you will summon as much enthusiasm as you possibly can," he said, his voice hard. "Only then will you find me a willing partner in this little venture."

"A partner? You are a rake who lives for the next hand of cards. You have no skills, no patience, and every rankling syllable you utter is designed to divide people from their sanity. I could *never* depend on you."

He lifted his dark brows. "Perhaps, but I've been living here for nearly three months. That's a great deal of experience in a place you've never even seen. So, my dear, you can do this alone, peddling your lovely wares to men here on the Cape. Or you can share our marriage bed with me."

Deflated despite her simmering anger, Viv forced herself to be practical and accept the truth. He was a man, he was a peer, and he'd amassed a tremendous head start. She would never be able to command his overt influence, which he could turn against her if he chose. His smug smile made that threat.

"And the money?"

"One third."

"Hmm . . . Debts, my lord?"

"I'm a better gambler than that. You hit the nail on the head earlier. Your dowry made my father's estates solvent, but hardly enough remains to accommodate my lifestyle."

"Debauchery is deuced expensive," she said, affecting his accent and lackadaisical attitude. "Vivie, love, be a dear and ask daddy for more."

Miles swallowed and looked away. *Odd.* Perhaps being confronted, while sober this time, with his oft-repeated request caused a little shame.

But he was the master of quick emotional recoveries.

"I would rather the privilege of debauchery than your starched half-life. Always so prim." He leaned forward in his seat. "Always . . . trying so hard. Such a *nouveau riche* mistake."

"Your parents didn't think so. What did your mother say to me on our wedding day? I believe it was, 'You deserve better than my son.'"

"She was as good at pretending as you are."

Viv hoped she hid her flinch, but he rarely missed a clue of any kind.

"But I won't quibble about money, my dear," he said. "Should we wish to be uncouth, we may as well shed all reservations and return to discussing sex. After all, money is little compared to the gusto you can deliver. So, do we have a deal?"

"I only want what I'd sought upon leaving Manhattan. A life without you."

"Then you know how to earn it."

If giving her body to Miles, to her husband, would ensure

that unthinkably large bonus, so be it. After all she refused to surrender anything more dear: her trust, her dreams, her heart.

Decision made, Viv stood and found her balance in the swaying train car. Looking down at him strengthened her resolve. "No drinking," she said tightly. "No other women. And none of your bloody cigars. Are we agreed?"

He was fidgeting with his wedding ring. Their eyes met and he tucked his left hand out of sight. "Agreed."

She savored her rare moment of authority. "Then I'm all yours."

Three

*M*iles climbed out of the stagecoach. He wove his fingers together at the back of his neck, stretching tired muscles. For three days they'd been traveling, first by train to the terminus at Beaufort, and then by coach since early morning. The steep incline of the Table Mountains had given way to the Karoo, the arid plateau over which they rolled for endless hours.

Staring across the grassy flats, he tried to avoid comparisons with his ancestral home in the cheerful, pampered greenery of Hampshire. London, too, with its grand architecture, leafy parks, and even its dire slums, would not produce a fair outcome. By either of those standards, the Karoo was a huge expanse of *nothingness*.

He pulverized a clod of yellow dirt with the heel of his boot. He kicked another just to watch it burst. A hot wind took the loosened earth and spread it eastward in a fine, gritty spray. Only when he took the time to look closer did he see individual features. Scrubby acacia trees offered little shade. Their narrow leaves, needles, and gourdlike seedpods only made the lack of greenery more apparent.

Miles nodded once, paying his respects to the magnificent wasteland that stretched to each horizon. *My name is Ozymandias, king of kings.*

Adam climbed down from the luggage hold atop the coach. He squinted into the high, sharp sun. Already his fair complexion had been reddened by the elements. "How do we fare?"

"Another day at least."

"Marvelous, my lord."

Miles exhaled his frustrations. "What have I asked? I don't mind the sarcasm, but for now forget proper address. We both know this place isn't all fine company and businessmen." He brushed his gaze across the wide stretch of the plateau and grimaced. "I won't relax until we reach what passes for civilization. Keep close to the women and keep your eyes open."

"Trouble?"

With a shift of his brows he indicated the armed man atop the stagecoach's high forward perch. "Our guard hasn't climbed down to take refreshments with us. None of them has."

Adam followed his line of sight, appraising the six motionless stagecoaches. A shimmering gleam of excitement hastened over his deceptively youthful features. He appeared almost as predatory as Miles felt. "I understand, my lord." He clapped his mouth shut, then grinned. "Sir."

"You did that on purpose."

"Only a little."

"That will do, Mr. Nolan," Miles said with a slight grin. "Refresh yourself while you can."

Acknowledging his dismissal with a much brighter smile, Adam headed for the small way station where passengers congregated. There existed no prohibition against shouts or laughter, but everyone kept their voices low, close, hushed. Men refilled canteens and smoked, while a few ladies in fine clothes huddled together in the meager shade of a ramshackle porch.

Miles lifted his foot and tapped the butt of his purloined whip against its sole, smacking off the filmy loam. So much space. The vastness of the Karoo made his family's estate and even broad stretches of English countryside feel tight and tiny. This was the entire heavens above and the whole world at his feet.

The British Empire had only just come to an armistice with the Boers. What had Old Man Christie been thinking, sending his daughter to a place that had pulsated with tension for more than a decade? And was Miles doing her any favors by encouraging her to continue? He could've pressed his hand and, as her husband, insisted on their return to England. Three months of colonial life had shown him what to expect. But no. He'd been caught up in that bonus and, to be even more blunt, in Viv. Now any return trip would be as trying as the journey onward.

Look on my works, ye Mighty, and despair!

All well and good, Mr. Shelley. But poetry wasn't getting them to Kimberley.

Viv stood on the top step of the stage, slowly surveying her domain. Grinding miles of travel had dimmed the spark of her antagonism, or perhaps she was hoarding her resources against his next foray. Her stamina for ignoring his attentions had increased greatly since they'd lived as husband and wife. She'd looked out the window for hours at a time, just as she stared now at the way station, examining the scrubbed, bare plateau as if it held the key to understanding the universe.

Miles didn't merit a glance.

Three days.

Three days of sitting across from her, eating with her, watching her. Three days of coming to grips with the magnitude of what they'd agreed to: twenty months as partners. He was awed and humbled by that prospect, even more so than by his marriage vows—likely because he hadn't spoken his vows in earnest. This bargain was beginning to feel as if he'd staked his soul.

He flicked the whip. Its woven tip licked the earth and snapped with a satisfying crack.

Viv flinched. Her glare burned a hole in his head, but at least he'd claimed her attention. "Must you?"

"I absolutely must. Practice, you see."

Although Miles presented a hand to aid her descent, she ignored him and slid past in a rustle of silk and lace. Both feet planted on the ground, she gave a little hop to right her bustle and straightened her hat—some monstrosity of fashion that dared the rising wind to rip off its feathers and bows.

If her intention was to prove that she was as *au courant*

and senseless as the rest of the moneyed travelers, she was succeeding. But then, she always had when it came to keeping up perfect appearances. In tight, exclusive groups they critiqued their surroundings with obvious distaste, wearing their success and wealth like medieval crests. The lesser folk crowded into the scant shade of the rear coaches, a new sort of peasant to be consumed by a new breed of empire.

The first-class passengers watched Miles with obvious curiosity. Although he should've taken part in that show, cultivating the relationships that would aid in making Viv's brokerage a success, he didn't feel like relinquishing his anonymity just yet. Once he returned to Kimberley, he would become Lord Bancroft again. For now he was just a man in the desert holding a whip.

Another day and then back to playing Society games. But Viv would be his solace.

Sidling up beside her, he gently encircled her nape with his fingers. "Such a marvelous day for a walk in the park, darling. Aren't you glad we came?"

She stiffened. The man and woman with whom she'd been conversing both gawked, then made excuses to leave. For his part, Miles couldn't take his eyes off his wife. The angle of her dainty chin made it appear as if she looked down at him. But in doing so, she revealed the sleek, pale line of her throat. What would she do if he nuzzled her there, right now, for anyone to see?

Slap him. And he'd grin.

But such uncalculated folly would run contrary to his

purposes. He wanted her willing and eager, not on the defensive. So he forced that rogue thought away.

"Walk with me, Viv."

She slowly pried his hand off of her skin. "Where?"

"Anywhere."

"No."

"Afraid?"

She sniffed. "Hardly."

"All very proper, I assure you," he said, leaning as close as he dared to the tempting arch of her throat. "I have no intention of accosting you behind the stables." He straightened and tucked her arm through his. "Besides, my back aches. If you've suffered as much as I have in that coach, you'll appreciate the chance to move."

She regarded the other passengers, then Miles, as if weighing the relative digestibility of two equally rotten piles of food. "Very well. But put that beastly thing away."

As Miles coiled the offending whip, she claimed the opportunity to precede him. She turned away from the corrugated iron way station and strolled into the sun. A matched trio of peacock feathers waved like a colorful flag atop her hat. Miles shook his head and followed.

They climbed a small bluff. Bent and warped acacias littered the plain, so infrequent and so isolated—an afterthought from God. Bushweed and devil's grass pocked the dirt with splotches of dusty brown and gray-green. The afternoon sun stripped them of detail. Lizards darted across the scorched ground and warblers sang from hidden places. Miles squinted but found no animals, other than a few high-soaring birds of prey. Likely at that hour, beasts such as steenbok and topi—both antelopes of some kind—were sensible and sought shade.

Far, far to the north, a string of clouds the color of fading bruises stretched over a decadently blue sky. Another thunderstorm, it seemed. The unbearably hot months of summer also made up the rainy season, with afternoon cloudbursts a common occurrence. At least he'd learned that much already.

"We are not in England," he said.

"Nor New York." With a slow turn of her head, Viv traced the horizon from east to west. A sheen of sweat dampened the divot above her upper lip, while her mouth curved into a look of wonder. Sunshine turned her skin to lustrous gold. "What a startling expanse."

The camaraderie of that moment, sharing such an unimaginable sight with his cloistered wife, took Miles by surprise. He wanted to ask if she felt it, too—the potential— but that was far too personal. Better if he just left their stalemate as it was, at least until they found some privacy. Then her frozen demeanor would have to go.

Catching her profile out of the corner of his eye, he banked the greedy impulse to toss the bonnet from her head and ravish her down-turned lips. To stand so near after such tedious months tempted him in ways he was unused to resisting, like licking the condensation off a glass rather than drinking the cool water it held.

"I saw her at the train station," Viv said softly. "That woman and her boys."

Reluctantly, Miles followed the line of her gaze and found the woman, large with child, seated next to a wagon wheel. Deep lines of exhaustion marred otherwise pleasant, rounded features. A blond bearded man of indeterminate age stood next to her in the wagon's shadow and handed her a tin cup. Two young lads with their mother's dark hair chased a lizard through the scrub and thistle, the object of both parents' unflinching attention.

A thousand questions came to mind regarding their circumstances. Yet Miles's responsibility was to aid in managing a diamond brokerage, and his desire was to subject Viv to an unhealthy degree of sexual intimidation—neither of which included caring why a family would undertake such a hazardous journey. He snuffed out his curiosity like pinching the flame off a wick.

The last pair of replacement horses was brought out by two burly stock tenders, men who could've been striding along the warp of an unfinished schooner in a Liverpool dry dock, knocking lumber and metal into a seafaring vessel. They appeared every inch British laborers, a disorienting contrast to the alien landscape that surrounded them. Only here, in seeing those men, did Miles begin to understand the extent of what it meant to claim the world for Victoria.

Claiming. Just as he wanted to possess his wife.

"I found myself surprised by the appeal of this place," he said, voice low.

"I wouldn't go so far as to say it has . . . appeal."

"Grandeur? Majesty? Pick a word, Viv."

"Perhaps I would, if I didn't believe it prelude to a jest of some kind."

"No jest." Never a man to be denied anything he set his mind to having, he caught her chin. "I just want to know what you think of our new home."

"It's menacing."

He grinned and touched a lock of hair nestled around the lobe of her ear. "No, my dear, you're thinking of me."

A startled gasp puffed her sweet breath against his skin. With the conditions so harrowing, he hadn't shaved in three days—three days when she hadn't even acknowledged his presence.

She would now. And he would damn well enjoy her while she still belonged to him.

Tension that constricted his ribs, building across days and months and an entire year, flooded into his kiss. Heady, succulent pleasure swept through his brain before settling in his blood. Fire lit him from the inside out. She pushed flat palms against his chest, but he was not done *taking*. Soft lips molded beneath the pressure of his mouth, then to the press of his tongue. She tasted saltier than he remembered, not so sugar sweet and untouchable. This was a woman who would fight him, and on that high desert plateau with the hot wind on his face, he craved her vigor.

She gave it to him, almost reluctantly. Slender fingers slipped from his chest to his biceps and squeezed. Miles seized that invitation and pulled her flush against his aching body. The elegant arch of her back was meant to be held—to be caressed while lying naked across the finest, softest sheets. He crisscrossed his arms up along her spine. The rigid whalebone of her corset kept him from the bountiful female flesh he desired, just as surely as her manners hid the vibrant woman who kissed with such passion.

He wanted rid of all of it. Strip her bare of every defense. Make her regret that she'd ever thought to leave.

"Miles?"

The breathy quality of her voice quickened his pulse. His rigid cock throbbed with wanting. He desired only to grab a handful of her backside and grind their hips, to make her feel the power of his desire, but her blasted bustle covered her curves like a wire cage. Instead he slipped his tongue along hers, relishing the sharp sensation of her teeth as he dove deeper. Mysterious and hot and sinful, she let him in.

A jolt of victory added strength to his arousal. Viv's tentative surrender made him feel as if he'd already won the battle, barging past her forged defenses. All for just one kiss—one kiss more than he'd seduced out of his wife in a year.

But then another hard shove.

She edged from his hold, when he'd thought himself capable of holding on to her until evening fell, until her inhibitions gave way beneath cool night shadows.

"Miles!"

More desperate this time, a note of hysteria chilled his aggression. Viv's face had turned ashen, hazel eyes flaring wide. Had his kiss fostered such a look of horror? He liked that idea no more than he liked caring what she thought.

"What is it?"

Although her reddened lips glistened with the slick aftermath of their kiss, her expression did not lose its dismay. She lifted a gloved hand and pointed to the north. "There."

A blast of prescient fear hit him like a furnace door yanked open. The purple stain across the northern sky that he'd assumed to be a cloud formation was, in fact, the dust kicked up by a dozen men on horseback. They rode at full gallop toward the way station. Splinters of sunlight flashed off drawn weapons.

"Run, Viv. Now!"

He grabbed her hand and tugged her down the shallow bluff. Her boots, hat, bustle, and corset—none was meant for a hasty retreat, but she kept pace stride for stride.

"Men on horseback!" Miles shouted over the wind and blood in his ears. "Due north!"

Guards atop the six coaches stood and peered toward the horizon. Understanding flashed across each face with the speed of dry brush catching fire. Armed with a shotgun, the man at the front of the procession began issuing orders. "All passengers, back in the coaches! Now! Men, take positions. Pickford, tell me who the hell those riders are!"

A short ragged-looking youth with ginger hair scurried up a ladder and onto the roof of the way station. He lifted binoculars, but Miles didn't waste time waiting for the boy's conclusion.

"Mr. Nolan," he called. "Your assistance, if you please."

Adam appeared in an instant. He sighted the loaded chamber of his revolver. "Here, sir."

Viv was breathless, and she still held fast to Miles's hand. "Where's Chloe?"

"Inside the second coach," Adam said, pointing.

"Find Mr. Kato and come right back." Gratified by Adam's lack of hesitation, Miles hurried his wife to the awaiting vehicle.

He elbowed three well-groomed men of means out of the way to push her to the head of the queue. Grumbles were his reward but offered no deterrent. She turned to face him from the coach's top step. The perfect array of hat and hair had been jostled to the point of ruin—nearly as disheveled as he had desired while they kissed. But that moment had shattered.

"Miles, what are you going to do?"

"Later I'll tease you about your uncharacteristic concern for my well-being. Now, stay inside." With the other gentlemen safely aboard, he slammed the door. Adam and Mr. Kato stood waiting. "Come with me."

Beside the lead coach, the guard with the shotgun was instructing a trio of similarly armed men. Miles recognized them as the brawny stock tenders. "Pickford says they're renegade Boers. Mismatched uniforms and weapons from the Transvaal's army. Raiders. Fifteen of them."

"How many men do you have to defend these coaches?" Miles asked.

Cool blue eyes narrowed as he took in Miles's appearance. "Who are you?"

"Miles, Viscount Bancroft. You?"

Suspicion slid off the man's face, replaced by awe. "Wilkes, my lord. Hanford Wilkes. I'm head of security."

"Former military?"

"The 15th Hussars, my lord."

"A cavalryman without a horse. Excellent. Now answer me, Mr. Wilkes. How many men do we have at our disposal?"

"Nine, if we count young Pickford."

"I said men, not children. And I loathe those odds. Do you have weapons enough to arm my men here?"

"Weapons aren't the trouble, my lord." Wilkes pointed to the way station. "We're always fully armed. Probably another dozen rifles in there. It's manpower we lack."

Miles nodded, easing his nerves with every crack of his knuckles. But when his thumb touched his gold wedding band, his trepidation redoubled. He wanted to protect Viv, but how the bloody hell was he going to manage that?

By doing whatever it took.

"I'll find enough fingers to pull triggers," he said tightly. "You determine the best position for the coaches and the guards. Mr. Nolan, Mr. Kato—with me."

Four

Viv gouged her nails into the velvet upholstery as the stage lurched. Chloe gasped and clutched tighter to Viv's arm.

"They're moving the wagons into a defensive formation," said one of the four other passengers. He was in his early fifties and wore a bowler hat, a fine twill suit, and a smirk. "These raiders try everything to keep prosperity and progress from coming to this land."

"Your pardon, sir," Viv said, "but at the moment, they are keeping *us* from progressing. That should be our sole concern."

"A mere delay." He waved his hand and set about stuffing tobacco into a carved ivory pipe. "Besides, should the worst happen and we never make our destination, Her Majesty will have no recourse but to wipe out the entire population—Boer or bushman, whoever they are."

Viv's mind was still twirling. One minute she'd stood with Miles atop a bluff that overlooked what felt like the entire Earth. Kissing him. Holding him again. Wanting his bare skin pressed against hers. The next minute she huddled with her maid in a well-appointed coach, its shades drawn and its male occupants unbelievably resigned despite a cloying atmosphere of sweat, dust, and fear.

"Such retribution is your comfort?" she asked the man in the bowler.

He didn't reply, not when the coach jerked to a stop and feet pounded on the roof. Chloe buried her face against Viv's upper arm and muttered a breathless, indistinct prayer.

"It's the guards with the shotguns," Viv said close to her maid's ear. "Raiders would be shouting or firing."

"Quite right. I'm Charles Haverstock, by the way." He removed his bowler and smoothed a sallow hand across a bald head shiny with sweat. "A pleasure to meet you, Miss . . . ?"

"Viscountess Bancroft," she said coolly, adding the slightest emphasis to her title.

His eyes, made narrow by heavy wrinkles and drooping upper lids, opened painfully wide. "My lady," he stammered. "Forgive me, I—"

"I doubt this is the appropriate time, Mr. Haverstock."

A gnawing sense of claustrophobia made her want to rip out her hair and run screaming from the prison of that stagecoach. The elegant high lace neckline of her gown choked off what little hot air she managed to inhale. Needing relief—and her curiosity like a tick gnawing in her brain—she eased aside the window screen.

"They'll see you!" Chloe hissed.

"Nonsense." Viv managed a sense of detached composure. She had endured every day in London with just such fortitude. "They'll be watching the men with guns, not the passengers cowering in here."

Shouts continued as the guards moved into place around the circled coaches. Nine men carried a variety of armaments, their expressions honed of determination. But where was Miles? And what under heaven could her wastrel husband do against armed horsemen? The surprising, protective sense of panic skittering across her nerves left her dizzy.

If he died today . . .

She shook her head, dislodging her hat. She unpinned it and handed it to Chloe, who promptly began to worry the beadwork off the flared brim.

Time melted around them, slowing and lengthening until Viv heard every whorl of wind, saw every restless shuffle of men's boots, heard every thump of oncoming hooves against packed ground.

Fierce cries broke her trance. Shots exploded. A dozen raiders vaulted over the bluff, down toward the wagons. Smoke from gunfire and the quick kick of dust smoothed distinct bodies into a gauzy mass of movement, shadow, and muted color.

From out of the cacophony came a low, loud command. "Hold steady! Wait for Wilkes's signal!"

Miles?

Viv peered through the disorder and found him kneeling behind a wagon wheel, sighting with a leveled rifle. Adam,

Mr. Kato, and even the blond tradesman occupied various points of cover. Each was armed. Their deadly expressions matched those of the hired guards.

"Ready?" came a distant command. "Fire!"

The raiders' gunfire had been sporadic, but the barrage from the coaches' defense came as a unified blast. Masculine screams answered, as did the squealing pain of downed horses.

"Ready again! Fire!"

Another barrage followed. Chloe shrieked, clamped her arms around her ears and doubled over, sobbing. But Viv could hardly comfort her maid, not when she watched her husband fire and reload. Hunting trips with his noble kinsmen had provided him with certain skills, but this was calm, collected violence done to protect innocent people. With her palm flat against her breastbone, she pressed to keep her frantic heart from bursting.

"Fire!"

At first Viv thought the shout was yet another command, one to bolster that unified defense. But cries strengthened. Then came the stench of smoke—not cigars or gunpowder, but burning cloth and leather.

The coach is on fire.

She choked on words that wouldn't come. Even swallowing wouldn't help, her throat feeling blistered and tight. She gave up on speech. With a fierce tug, she yanked Chloe upright and shoved the mauled hat out of her lap. The copper handle wouldn't budge. Viv rattled the door and even conjured a few long-buried French curses.

Haverstock pushed Chloe out of the way to get to Viv. "Let me."

But he hadn't touched the hot copper before the lock finally gave way and swung outward. Miles stood ready to receive her.

"And here I thought these accommodations were first class." He hauled her down with one arm firmly encircling her waist. Whip held with his other hand, he'd slung a rifle over his shoulder. "Miserable is what they are. I fully intend to lodge a complaint."

They turned as one—as a raider charged their position. The world at the edge of Viv's vision grayed, but she clearly saw the attacking man's virulent expression. Teeth bared. Eyes narrowed. Pistol raised.

She was going to die.

Miles snapped his arm to the side. The whip snaked through the air with a crack as loud as the nearby gunshots. Again and again he flicked the coiled leather. The attacker's horse reared back on its hind legs, throwing off the man's aim. A bullet shot from his pistol but flew high overhead.

Before Viv could protest, Miles pulled her to where a group of women and children huddled behind a boulder. "No, wait! Chloe!"

A frown knotted his brow, then he nodded. "Promise you'll stay here."

"I promise."

Of course he would grin. Even at a time like that, as if she'd consented to sharing the next waltz. But this Miles was a feral cousin to the man she'd married. He gave her waist one last squeeze before rejoining the fight at a full run.

Viv remained by that boulder but kept him in sight—as if watching him would keep him safe. Another onslaught of raiders barred his way back to the carriage. With whip and pistol and hoarse shouts, he blended seamlessly with the trained guards. The head of security directed his men, while Miles organized the ragtag band of volunteers. He knelt beside Adam, shoulder to shoulder, and aimed a rifle. They fired in unison.

What about Chloe?

The burn of smoke and bitterest guilt throbbed in her lungs. If anything happened to her maid, how could she forgive herself?

Rarely had she felt confidence in Miles. Maybe not ever. At that moment, however—unable to do anything else— she put her faith in her husband.

Please, Miles. Save her too.

As if hearing that silent plea, Miles handed his rifle to Adam. Bent low, he skittered through the fighting and returned to the carriage. Frenzied flames ate through canvas and leather and wood. Opaque smoke billowed heavenward. A raider without a horse charged behind him.

"Miles!"

But her warning went unheeded. The raider launched onto Miles's back. A wickedly curved knife flashed in the sunlight. Viv's heart lurched. She sank into the dirt, all strength gone from her trembling thighs.

Menacingly huge but wearing a placid expression, Mr.

Kato grabbed the raider with the ease of a mother lifting a newborn. He handled the man with no such care, flinging him against the carriage where he landed in a dusty heap.

Miles was safe. For now.

He reached the carriage door just as Chloe tumbled out. She hit the dirt on all fours, covered in soot and ash. Sparks and debris from the coach rained down and ignited Chloe's dress. Miles simply swatted the flames, then rolled her onto her back. Mr. Kato stood nearby with a wide stance, his fists at the ready. Adam and the blond tradesman joined him as Miles gathered Chloe in his arms. The trio covered his retreat toward the safety of the boulder.

Viv couldn't breathe as they crossed the field of battle, just willing them to be safe. Her tongue tasted sour, like unripe plums. But her gaze alit on a sight that exchanged fear for vitalizing anger. Haverstock, that fawning toad, cowered beneath the luggage wagon. Had he really been so spineless as to abandon the coach before a woman? Was that what constituted civilization in Cape Colony?

Not for every man, because Miles arrived at last. Breathing hard, eyes wild, he handed Chloe into Viv's awestruck keeping.

"Stay low," he said simply. "I'll come back for you both." The raider must have made use of that curved knife, because blood trickled from a gash on Miles'ss collarbone.

She smoothed hair back from her maid's black-streaked face, but Viv couldn't look away from her husband's injury. "You're hurt."

"When I'm done pretending to be a soldier, you can pretend to be my nurse." He turned back toward his peculiar little army. "Capital work, men. Now we end this!"

Viv stretched, arching her back as far as her corset and stiff muscles would permit. She smelled of smoke, sweat, and the primal perfume of a hard, hot wind. Two other women sat with her in the lengthening shadows behind the way station. Each tended to patients injured in the skirmish. Coated in dust and soot and muted expressions of shock, the women appeared unnaturally identical. Viv assumed she would look little different.

Chloe lay curled on her side against the corrugated iron wall, head in Viv's lap. Disheveled brown hair lay against her ashen cheek. A good, sweet girl, she deserved a life among people who cared for her, protected by a system of rules that meant never needing to dive from a burning stage in the midst of a gun battle.

Whatever morbid thrill Viv had experienced in surviving their ordeal was gone. Only lethargy remained. Her whole body felt sloppy, reeling in this quiet moment after a storm of violence. One coach was burnt and another lay tipped on its side, its axle cracked in two. Fatigued resignation slackened the survivors' faces as they slogged through appointed tasks.

Exhausted, she watched Miles help redistribute luggage and passengers to the four remaining vehicles. His ragged shirt was a mess of dirt and blood, open at the neck, sleeves jerked up to his elbows. Sweat gleamed on his tanned skin. If she stood closer, would she see little rivulets dripping down the hollow at the base of his bare throat?

Even more surprising than her lewd daydream was the fact Miles worked alongside Mr. Kato. The nobleman and the African, both laboring toward a common purpose as they had done in battle. Now they restored order and maintained calm.

A fantasy, to be sure. A mere trick of this challenging land and its dry desert mirages. She knew him too well. Only a fresh deck of cards and his other numerous vices held the power to drag her husband out of bed each afternoon. That he'd crossed the Atlantic was distinctly out of character. That he'd behaved like an avenging hero was like watching a myth become reality.

The blond tradesman's wife approached the way station, her face drawn and flushed. "Pardon me," she said softly, arms crossed protectively over the bulge of her belly. "My husband . . . Can you spare some bandages?"

"Of course." Viv glanced at the other two women, who were busy with their own wounded charges. "Chloe, you stay here and rest," she whispered.

Her maid only nodded and curled into a tighter ball. Viv hated to leave her in such a state, but the girl would survive until the worst had passed. No one had the luxury of extravagant choices on that morbid afternoon. Carry on . . . or quit.

Viv had no intention of quitting.

She stood and scooped up the makeshift bandages and medicines they'd scrounged from among the luggage.

"I wouldn't want to trouble you."

"No, please," she said. "Let me do what I can."

The woman nodded and led the way to the last stage-coach. Whereas Viv's had contained no more than six people since setting off from Beaufort, the train line terminus, this coach held twelve. The passengers' bodies were thinner, their clothes less ostentatious and bulky, and their possessions fewer. Four of them were children, including the woman's young boys. In the shadow of the coach the two lads sat like bookends on either side of their father, who reclined on his elbows with his legs stretched out. The fabric of his trousers had been torn at the knee, revealing a huge gash.

"You've brought reinforcements to fuss over me, eh, Alice?" he said.

"I need reinforcements, you stubborn fool." Alice knelt beside him and shooed the boys away. "David, John, go find trouble. But don't touch anything, you hear?"

Viv grinned at the contradictory advice as the boys sped off toward the bluff. Although Alice turned to the task of cleaning her husband's injury, he never took his eyes off their sons. Viv had done the same when watching Miles, as if will alone would keep them safe.

She shook free of her maudlin mood and prepared the bandages. "You're bound for Kimberley, then?"

"That's right, ma'am. The name's Ike Penberthy, from Cornwall." He tipped his head toward his wife. "You've already met Alice."

"Actually, we hadn't got so far as introductions. I'm Vivienne Bancroft." She wound the bandage around his knee as

Alice supported his foot in her hands, holding the injured leg just off the ground. "I'm grateful you took up arms to defend us, Mr. Penberthy."

"Couldn't stand by and let them hurt me and mine." He grimaced when Viv tied off the strip of linen.

"Sorry."

"Don't mention it." Alice edged around and wiped his forehead with a damp rag. He smiled up at her. "Heaven, my angel."

"This is hell if ever there was one on earth," Alice said, her wide mouth drawn tight. "And I thought the mines in Cornwall were bad."

"You say that now, but wait until you're wearing diamonds from head to toe."

Viv had to look away. Could the diamond fields really hold such riches? She'd been so intent on the terms of her father's will and the bonus it offered. The thought of actually pulling handfuls of diamonds out of the dirt struck her as fairy-tale talk. Yet this family had traveled for months, uprooting their lives and risking the safety of their sons on just such a promise.

Her curiosity was too great. "What brings you this far from home, then?"

Ike rubbed the back of his neck. His buoyant, confident expression waned, and a quick glance toward Alice tempered his jolly personality all the more. "We left Cornwall thinking we could work our own piece. But word on the Cape Town schooner is that the claims are all consolidated now."

Alice rubbed his shoulder. "He's skilled, my lady. And educated. No matter the outcome, Ike will see us through."

"Oh?" Viv smiled. "What sort of background? If you don't mind my asking, that is."

"I know rocks and the like—assaying. I graduated from the Miners' Association school in Camborne."

Footfalls behind Viv caught their attention. Both Ike and Alice squinted up to face the approaching man.

"Penberthy, how many dead from this wagon?" Miles asked.

Viv arose with some semblance of grace, even though her muscles had stiffened with fatigue. Never had she seen him look so capable and electric. His sun-touched brown hair had been coated with pale dust, but his face was freshly scrubbed.

"Only one," Ike said. "The others have already collected his body. A lad of seventeen, down from Glasgow way. Dead now."

Miles took her elbow, offering silent, unexpected support upon hearing such news. The sarcastic comment or lewd expression she'd learned to expect throughout their marriage never came. That was nearly enough to unbalance her anew.

"Help me up, Alice." Ike waved away her protests. "This is the man who made it happen, and I'll stand to greet him properly."

"Nonsense," Miles said. "Hanford Wilkes was in charge here. I merely found him a few more able soldiers."

Viv made the introductions. She couldn't help but

admire how Miles's firm handshake and relaxed charm seemed to instantly earn the man's respect. It shone on Ike's face, bright as a lamp.

"You'd better get that tended to," Ike said.

Miles glanced down at his collarbone. Then at Viv. "I intend to."

She tried for a noncommittal smile, despite shivering at the thought of touching this new, more primal version of the man she knew all too well. However, she was not convinced she was out of danger—at the way station or with Miles. "But what happens now? Is there room enough for everyone to continue on?"

"Wilkes sent a runner back to Beaufort," Miles said. "Additional stagecoaches will arrive later this evening, if we're lucky. Maybe even a military escort."

"Then why weren't we escorted in the first place?" Alice's pinched mouth revealed her displeasure even more eloquently than her words.

"An astute question, Mrs. Penberthy." Miles appeared tired, his customary grin forced. "One that I'll be sure to ask people more sensible than myself. Now, if you'll excuse us. A man wounded in pitched battle deserves the tender mercies of his wife."

Five

Miles walked Viv toward the bluff where she had first spotted the incoming raiders. She carried bandages and a skein of water, collected after having checked on her maid.

The sun would not set for another few hours, as the long, long summer day dragged toward twilight. Deep orange burnished her flawless skin and turned wheat-blonde strands of hair the color of bronze. She must've scrounged some manner of toiletries because her face was clean and her hair had been wetted, combed, and fashioned into a simple bun at the base of her neck.

Without a word, her hands steady, she sat facing Miles on the bluff and began to dress his gash—as if they hadn't kissed earlier that afternoon. As if tending wounds constituted part of her duties as a viscountess. A little crease tucked between her brows as she concentrated. He could almost believe she was as cool as she appeared, when he needed her to be otherwise.

Only problem was his fatigue. The skirmish had taken

a hideous toll on him, though he didn't know why. Mortal danger, maybe? Was this the natural reaction to walking away from such violence? He was simply too tired to bait her, wanting only the moment of comfort she seemed willing to provide. The rest could wait.

"I've hired Mr. Kato," he said by way of neutral conversation.

"Without consulting me?"

"He stood over me, armed, while I saved Chloe's life. I hardly thought you'd mind."

"No, I shouldn't think so."

"Besides, he used to work for the Barnaby Mine until they were bought out. His worth is hard to overestimate. Brawn, obviously, but also a potential link to local habits and enterprises—languages and the like. He says the men who attacked were renegade Boers who have yet to accept the terms of surrender. They harass English travelers for revenge. Maybe for profit. But either way, Mr. Kato seems a good man to have on our side."

"You spoke with him?"

"I didn't read his mind, if that's what you mean." His stomach flipped, *hard*, when she smiled softly. Miles soaked it up. To see Viv happy and smiling. God, how long had it been? And how long had it been since he'd been the cause?

"I suppose," she said steadily, "that entering an unknown situation with a ready ally cannot be a mistake."

He enjoyed her acquiescence. However, if Viv started to agree with him and think him a dependable, prudent partner, he might need to remain as such. He found the Cape appealing but not so dearly as to become a responsible human being.

She had returned to washing the blood and grime from his collarbone. Miles bit his back teeth together. The stinging pain was bad enough to distract him from her soft, soothing touch. For that alone he resented the injury, even if it had brought her this close. She bent low to inadvertently reveal the back of her neck. Pink skin. Slightly sunburned. Stray whorls of silken gold curled there, taunting, teasing him with the need to sink greedy fingers into her hair and pull her mouth to his once again.

Bloody hell. He was a viscount and a married man. He shouldn't need to suffer grievous harm to earn the privilege of his wife's hands on his skin. But that's what it felt like—a privilege after all this time.

"And you managed these negotiations while I tended Chloe?"

What was it about her tone of voice that shamed his past behavior as much as it inspired him to keep doing good? He grabbed at levity to keep such thoughts at bay. "Just making myself useful."

"That was quite a feat you managed, Miles." Her voice was rough and soft, as if she'd recently recovered from an illness. "Gathering those men as you did."

"A perfectly good resource going to waste. I hadn't thought to do the right thing. Or any thing at all, really. But dying here had been the only other option, one I absolutely refuse to entertain. Think of the indignity, Vivie."

He feigned a shudder to cover a deeper dread. Seeing her hurt was simply . . . unthinkable—even though he knew he'd caused his fair share over the years.

"But who knows how many lives you saved today."

He chuckled. "Is that a thank you?"

She lifted her eyes—those magnificent hazel eyes that concealed so much. How did she keep it all locked away? He'd been born to title and knew less about dignity than she managed with that simple sweep of her gaze.

Sweet Lord, he wanted to taste her again. To feel her surrender.

"No," she said softly. "This is. Thank you, Miles."

He searched his mind for a crude, leveling comment to counter her earnestness, but none came. His brain was a blank. All he could do was stare into eyes made to glow by the fire of a sinking sun.

Viv blinked and ducked. Still gentle, she patted his wound dry. "Chloe isn't going to fare well here," she said, almost a confession. "I shouldn't have brought her."

"She'll adjust."

"She shouldn't have to. This was my endeavor, but now . . ."

He couldn't help but touch her then, just under the chin. Viv wanted a confidant, apparently, but he wanted her skin beneath his hands. A fair trade. "But now?"

"What are we doing here?" For a moment he could almost believe she meant them. What were *they* doing? In truth, they'd been on the verge of an irreconcilable implosion since stepping up to the altar. "What if this is a place where we won't ever be safe?" she asked, dispelling his fanciful notions. "What if these hard-working people have been utterly duped by tales of easy riches? I—"

She swallowed and Miles dropped his hand. Even worse than fatigue, there was danger in her vulnerability. Any doubts would be shadowy mirrors of his own, and he didn't like having that in common with Viv. He desired a much baser connection. Fighting for their lives had only exacerbated the hum and thump of need that shuddered through his body.

This wasn't what he'd planned. It certainly wasn't why he'd traveled across the width and breadth of the Atlantic and weathered life in a hellish camp on the edge of war. Adventure aside, his goals remained as simple as a man could possibly manage. Earn the money. Bed his wife. And this time, be the first to leave.

"Seems to me, Vivie, that you have two choices." Miles dragged to his feet and dusted off his trousers. Viv flinched as the grit flew into her face. His only apology was a grin. "You can climb aboard one of these delightful coaches and discover what Kimberley holds in store for you, or you can say the word."

"Say . . . *what*, exactly?"

"Say the word and we can go home." A familiar meanness reinvigorated his sense of purpose. "You remember home, don't you? The view of the park in spring bloom from our bedroom window? The sheets we tangled into knots on our wedding night? Oh, and I'm certain we can snag an invitation to the next gala Lord Saunders hosts.

He enjoyed my company last time, I'm certain of it, and I enjoyed you."

Fire sparked across her expression. "At a time like this you decide to taunt me with that night? We could've died today!"

"All the more reason to enjoy each other when the opportunity is presented."

He grabbed her hands before she could object and hauled her up. She steadied herself with both palms on his forearms. Her breasts brushed his chest, which was bare to the sternum. They stood so close that when Miles licked his lower lip, he tasted hers with the same quick sweep of tongue.

She inhaled sharply. Perhaps she read the untamed hunger in his eyes because she pushed out of his arms.

Miles tensed and hissed. "Good God, that hurts."

He'd expected more anger, or even the vulnerable fear that could wear away at him like the slow drip of water. Instead she'd replaced her protective mask, the one that said his comfort and teasing were equally unwelcome.

"Then hold still while I finish, you fool. Shirt off."

With more economy than sensuality, she helped remove the battered garment. Thus was the moment when Viscount Bancroft stood bare-chested before his own wife in the middle of a desolate African plateau. He nearly shook his head at the dizzying wonder. Boredom had been his lifelong curse. Body alive—both pain and pleasure—and mind alight with sensual imaginings, he was anything but bored.

He studied her as she wound bandages over his shoulder

and around his collarbone. It was either that or succumb to the potent need gathering in his cock. She smelled of sweat and dust and Vivienne. He'd endured enough pretty detachment and polite façades to last ten lifetimes.

This was real. And he loved every moment.

She finished the dressing and stepped back, hands clasped at her stomach. Her expression, however, was not so demure. If he didn't know better, Miles would've sworn that his prim, proud wife was drinking in the sight of his bare chest. Was it possible she would make this game so easy?

Not a chance.

"So," he said, rolling his shoulder against the dressing. She'd tended him well. "Here are your choices, Vivie. Push on or return to jolly old England." She held her ground as he closed in, which made him smile. The fading warmth of the sun was nothing to the heat of her body defying his. "However, if you insist on reconsidering your position with every new challenge, we will endlessly repeat this conversation. I'll lose my patience."

"You have no patience to lose." Her chin lifted and her gaze plowed into his. "And we won't have this conversation again. I'm here for the duration, Miles. I *will* have that bonus."

"Good. Here I was thinking you'd nullify our little arrangement. There would be consequences."

"You won't force me," she said.

As if he would. As if her words would stop him if he wanted to.

"Just because I've decided to keep from seducing you on a public train," he said, "or in the midst of a surprisingly violent desert, doesn't mean I've forgotten the terms of our cooperation."

"Neither have I."

"Good." He swiped along her cheekbone, smoothing a streak of dirt she'd missed. Dragging downward, he tugged softly at her lush lower lip. She opened her mouth. No pouting now. Just expectation. Sparks fired in his blood—sparks that matched the fiery challenge in her luminous eyes. He pulled away, the pad of his thumb wet. "Tomorrow we'll arrive in Kimberley and we'll get to work. Then, Vivie, I will have my reward."

Thirty hot, long, miserable hours after the arrival of an army escort, the string of coaches and supply wagons rumbled within sight of Kimberley. Viv sat next to the window, with Chloe at her side and Miles on the bench opposite. Chloe had yet to speak beyond the bare necessities of communication, but at least she'd nibbled on a few pieces of dried fruit and a biscuit. Although the heat inside the coach edged toward unbearable, she curled along Viv's arm and clung tightly, as if to a sunken ship's last piece of flotsam. Her dark hair lay slicked with sweat against her temples and along the nape of her neck.

Viv choked back her concern, as the girl's misery became a physical mirror to her own internal struggles. Here was Kimberley, a speck of nothing in the middle of nowhere, yet a town that boasted unspeakable wealth and potential. Here would be Viv's home for twenty months. Miles had done her a service by reinforcing her options in the clearest possible terms: survive and prosper, or return to him a failure. She would need to submit to her marriage without even the leverage of wealth—subject to his impropriety, his wildness, his whims.

Unlike Chloe, who had no recourse, Viv at least retained the luxury of choice. She would simply need to make the same choice every morning, every evening, and every time circumstances urged her to relent. Her father, born in the slums of Glasgow, had provided her with no other example. Neither had her mother, dignified and proud even on her last day drawing breath.

"We'll get her home and make a room to her liking," Miles said, his voice unimposing. "Once she sees it's not all dirt and violence, she'll come to."

Wary of his concern, and worse still, of how he'd correctly guessed her unspoken worries, Viv only nodded. She was so used to enduring his polite provocations.

He shrugged gingerly in return, his injured arm none so vigorous as its twin. Eyes closed, utterly indifferent, he behaved as if the sight of Kimberley rolling into view held no special appeal. Was he really so confident in their ability to succeed? Or would his arrogance be their undoing? Against all reason, she wanted it to be more than arrogance. She wanted him to be the man she'd seen at that way station—calm, quick, in command.

His success will be mine.

Then he'd claim his reward.

A shiver wiggled down her back, its heat like fingers slowly stroking from her soles to her scalp. How did one defend against a man who already believed victory a foregone conclusion? If they were to survive and, indeed, to prosper, she would need to establish a few guidelines and erect a few dozen walls. Letting him nettle her for the duration of her stay would only drive her mad. Letting him back into her heart would break her in two.

The coaches rattled down the central thoroughfare as townspeople paused in their activities to watch. Some pointed at the mounted soldiers. Multistory buildings lined both sides. Although new and well maintained, the siding and wooden walkways had been bleached by the wind and sun. Only the signs above each business remained bright with fresh coats of paint, eagerly proclaiming invaluable services or goods.

"Chloe," she said. "Chloe, my dear, sit up. Look. We're in town."

Her maid reluctantly roused. The side of her face was creased where she'd burrowed against Viv's satin sleeve.

"See?" Viv pointed to one of the garish signs. "A blacksmith, a mercantile, a tea parlor, a dressmaker. There's the telegraph office and a dry good's store. Even a jewelry appraiser . . . and another . . ."

She frowned slightly, regarding the scene as she would a child's scribble—something she was meant to understand but could not. Kimberley was no bigger or smaller than any American frontier town she'd read about in her father's newspapers, full of cowboys and entrepreneurs and fallen girls. But along that street she counted four jewelry appraisers and eight gemstone brokers.

Miles had perked up. His unexpectedly eager expression matched the one he'd worn on that distant afternoon in her father's library. His instinct for the unnatural made him a magnet for trouble. Apparently his feigned disinterest could not compete with such prospects.

"Amazing, isn't it?" he asked, catching her eye. "I'd wager that no street in London boasts as many jewelers in such close proximity. You'll find it's quite a town, Viv."

"So it's true then, about the diamonds? This isn't some malicious fiction trumped up by ambitious colonials?"

He smiled broadly. "All true. You'll believe it when those jewels are out of the shop cases and draped around your neck."

"We're here to work."

"But diamonds are our work." Leaning back against the padded bench, he appeared far too relaxed in that confined coach. "Wait until you see the Big Hole."

"The Big Hole? That hardly sounds promising."

"Like I said, wait and see. It's . . . staggering."

Upon arriving at the coach station, Viv stepped out and surreptitiously stretched her stiff legs. Chloe limply followed her into the open air, and Miles waited by her side as the coach's other occupants bustled away to resume their lives in Kimberley. Adam and Mr. Kato appeared, the former taking charge of Chloe and directing the latter in the collection of Viv's luggage. Mr. Kato smiled and greeted two other Africans, their language so entirely foreign, full of clicks and sharp consonants. Miles was right. They would pay the man well, not just for his strength but for what he could teach them about the Cape.

"Take everything on to the house," Miles called to Adam. "We'll join you shortly."

Viv raised her brows when they were alone. "We have a house?"

"'House' makes it sound insignificant. It's not small." He leaned nearer. "Just remember that without me, right now, you'd be asking that coward Haverstock for more than just directions to a suitable hotel."

"Don't be facetious. It has no appeal for me, Miles. Never did. I appreciate that I'm beholden to you and that I require your help. Now please, stop beating me with it."

He tipped his head. "That frustrates you, doesn't it? Being beholden to me."

"Yes."

He smiled, cool and distant, and donned a functional bowler. "Find a way around it, Vivie."

She licked her bottom lip and tasted salt and dust. He would push and prod, she would fend him off, and they would start all over again. Their months together stretched out like a road dressed with barbed wire and explosives. And after each encounter, she would need to shake off her anger and get on with the task at hand.

One step at a time.

Miles only offered his arm.

She breathed through her nose, as if breathing past a sharp pain, but his heat still made her tense. They'd touched while completely nude. They'd kissed and made love. They'd done things—dizzying, splendid, *filthy* things—for which she had no names. Those images rushed in, leaving her short of breath. Miles flicked his eyes to where their bodies entwined. His smug half smile spoke volumes. Such an innocent thing, he seemed to say. Just a man and wife standing arm in arm. But Viv felt stripped and vulnerable.

"Now," he said, as mercurial as the weather, "on to the Big Hole."

Six

They had a hundred tasks to accomplish in a very short span, but Miles wanted her to see where it began. Where the earth opened beneath the hands of men and gave over untold wealth. The rest was simply the tedium of business. He wanted Viv to understand where the diamond trade started so they could both know it and taste it and smell it. Then they could figure out how to make their business grow.

He led the way through to the north side of town. Viv kept pace with his strides. "You trust me with this?" he asked quietly.

"Leave it."

"No, I don't think so. You could manage your father's business affairs perfectly well without seeing where the diamonds originate. Why humor me?"

"Because you said it was staggering. I want to know what impresses you."

Like the busiest roadways in London, Kimberley's streets boasted the breadth of humanity, from the poorest itinerant tribesman to the grandest dandy. Miles never would've expected to see men wearing this year's fashions while strolling through such a rough town.

"Besides, my father sent me here. He must have known what it would be like, which means he had faith enough that I might give it a go."

"There's always the possibility that he had no intention of your success—for you or for your siblings."

"Don't ever do that again," she said evenly.

"What, contradict you?"

"No. I don't mind contradictions, if your advice is offered in all seriousness and for the benefit of our enterprise."

Miles adjusted the set of his hat, angling it against the sun's strident gold. "Then what shouldn't I ever do again?"

"Suggest that my father set me up to fail."

"A bizarre request," he said. "You can doubt yourself, wonder if you're up to this challenge, but you can't stomach thinking that Old Man Christie believed the same."

"He was a right bastard, but he wasn't a liar or a cheat." She kept her face rigidly forward. "I'm through doubting, my lord. And if you're prepared to use my every admission against me, then consider my ill-advised need to confide in you at an end."

"I never asked for your confidences, Vivie," he said, his voice roughened. "In fact, we both know what I desire from you."

But to Miles's dismay, she didn't react. No sharp retort. No telltale twitch of her arm. Panic sent a shiver of fire up through his chest. He could stomach her disdain, and he positively thrived off her anger—but her disinterest?

As a carriage passed, he took the opportunity to look at his wife. Men turned to watch her as she passed, so why shouldn't he take in his fill, too? Viv sported a navy blue gown with few drapes, pleats, or adornments—one that, despite its practicality, clung to her figure with the diligence of a lover. She tipped her neck at such an angle as to appraise the busy street from beneath the rim of a functional sun bonnet. He could only see her bow of a mouth and the reddened bridge of her nose.

Through the years, he had observed with detached amusement as even the wealthiest and most polished New York socialites were eaten alive by the petty cruelty of London Society. Viv had managed that transition with unaccountable ease. Never a glance or ruffle or hair out of place, unless he tempted her to it. And then she was *glorious*.

He would have that again—rip away the mask she kept in place for every other man. Because Miles was *not* every other man.

"Please stop staring," she said.

"You're beautiful."

"You're a fool."

"Ah, but you're enjoying yourself."

He knew no such thing, of course. Not that it mattered. No sense hoping other stars might align, that they might actually find common ground outside of physical pleasure. They'd never had that much luck.

Walking on, the appearance of the town altered from functional, neatly planned rows of businesses to the disjointed mob of mass housing. Not houses, in truth, but shanties and tents that stretched from horizon to horizon. People of all colors scurried like ants through the fierce maze of corrugated tin and tar paper. Around each campsite women tended fires and watched wayward children. The homey scent of their cooking was overpowered by the stench of humanity piled on itself like heaps of garbage. Flies buzzed, a second noise above the muttering hum of a thousand conversations.

They arrived at the Hole.

Silent now, Miles's chest filled with foreboding awe. That same sense of wonder overcame him as it had the first time he'd walked to this spot. The crash-pull sound of engines layered over the clamor of the settlement. The strike of metal against rock became a constant throb in his bones. He stopped fifty feet from the drop-off, knowing he'd need to approach the very edge to peer down to the bottom. The tremendous pit looked like a meteor's impact crater or a great, gaping chasm wrought by an angry god. But it was man-made, where once had been an otherwise nondescript swath of land.

"It's . . . indescribable," Viv whispered.

"And it's where our future begins."

Viv was looking at what could only be described in biblical terms. It was hell. It was a medieval cautionary tale about sin and the apocalypse filled with plodding, lost souls bent on tasks as unavailing as those forced on Sisyphus.

Crews urged man and horse and donkey to turn pulleys that looked like huge wagon wheels tipped horizontally.

With every cranking turn the chains screamed as would patients in Bedlam. Men swarmed around raised buckets and disgorged the mundane contents into dozens of wheelbarrows.

"For twenty years they've been lugging dirt out of this hole." Miles watched her with an attentiveness that itched along her skin. "They take the soil to sifters to sort for the diamonds."

"How many does it produce?"

"Couldn't say, in truth. Some say fifteen thousand carats per year." He pulled off his bowler and scrubbed the back of his head with quick, agitated strokes. She fought the reflexive urge to smooth those tufts back into place. To simply . . . touch. "Bloody amazing, isn't it, Viv?"

"You're impressed." She watched him for signs of his customary disdain but found none.

"Why wouldn't I be? Ingenuity and sweat and greed made this place."

"Says the man who was born in a seven-hundred-year-old manor home."

"Yes, and a man who's never worked a day." He smiled into the setting sun. "I know the extent of my sloth. But whereas my ancestors secured my birthright by toil and sweat, so do these men. Only now, we get to see it as it happens."

Feeling buoyant and scattered, she couldn't help a smile of her own. "As opposed to contending with the wastrels who will be born to it in generations to come."

"Precisely. This is the moment of glory, not what comes after."

This was unlike any sight or experience she'd ever thought to have. For the moment she simply soaked it in. Tomorrow would come the hard work of assessing the state of their financial foundation—firm, wobbling, or fatally pitted with mold.

She toed forward a step, then another, until only a body's length separated her from a five-hundred-foot fall. Loops and swirls of roads cut by hundreds of wagon wheels decorated the bottom like hopelessly knotted strands of yarn. Men of all colors urged donkeys to pull the carts toward the circular edge, where some roads climbed up in a tedious spiral. When the spiral became too steep for progress, buckets topped by the wagon wheel pulleys waited to complete their strong work.

So many bodies. So many lives. The endlessness of that work slid over her like an airless blanket.

"Is it safe?"

"A side collapse is probably the danger that strikes me as most dreadful."

"Side collapse? Is that what it sounds like?"

Miles nodded. "Just like. Money gets too tight to buy timber, or men get lazy. They don't shore up the mines' sides. Rocks knock loose. Too many and it's an avalanche without the snow."

To be pulverized beneath a falling wall of solid granite was worse than anything she could imagine. A ghostly shadow of that crushing pain pinched her ribs. She clawed at the bonnet ribbon tied beneath her chin, needing air.

Miles caught her under one arm and walked her away

from the crater. His palm pressed flat between her shoulder blades. The innocent touch was so very different from the passionate kiss he'd demanded while standing atop the plateau bluff. Breathing deeply, she let herself accept the comfort he offered. Just for a moment.

She straightened her hair and huffed out the last of her flustered response. The tangy air smelled like the charge of a dry lightning strike. "All very impressive, but we don't control the mining interests. Ours is a brokerage house."

"Correct," Miles said, arms crossed over his chest. He'd let her go. But when had he rolled up his sleeves? Shadowy hair dusted over cords of muscle and lean tendons. "Yet it all begins here. In order to understand the diamond trade, I've found that understanding its origins is very important."

"Why?"

Her wayward husband's dark eyes had taken on an unfamiliar cast. "Because this wound in the earth was made by digging out one bucket at a time. Countless hands. Years and years of toil. And for what?"

"All for diamonds."

"This is no ordinary business, Viv. We must remember that."

A sinister sort of comprehension came over her like a bad dream. Then, at the far side of the Hole, a whistle sounded—followed by another and another, all at different intervals.

"Quitting time," he said. "Each company insists on keeping their own hours and sounding their own whistles."

"Charming. And grown men stand at the helm of these companies?"

"They make me look mature."

"Never say," she said, but not without a slight smile.

Workers at the pulleys didn't stop urging their animals into unending circles. One bucket at a time, they rescued their brethren from the planet's bowels. Only when the last man had scrambled out of that daily hell did Viv shake free of her hypnosis.

She needed out of her corset, needed a bath and a year-long sleep.

One batch of several thousand men was soon replaced by half as many, all of them carrying weapons instead of axes, shovels, and buckets.

"Guards," Miles said as if to himself. "All those undiscovered diamonds. Such a charming place Old Man Christie picked for us, isn't it, Vivie?"

Mention of her father's challenge returned her thoughts to her siblings. How were Alex, Gwen, and Gareth faring in their distant destinations? All had been assigned such differing tasks, in places as far away and unfamiliar as Kimberley. Mail could be months in coming to Cape Town, then weeks again before reaching her eager mind and lonely heart. Her family, all so inaccessible.

She was almost thankful, then, for Miles. No, she *was* thankful. Nothing would prevent him from transforming back into an insidious fiend once they reached their accommodations. But right then, when he remained both spirited and contemplative in the face of that marvel, she was terribly glad of his presence.

"Come, before it gets too late."

With the poise of the nobleman he was, and in contrast to his unkempt appearance, he again offered his arm. Viv walked with him back toward town, where he hailed a hackney. The driver turned north. Ambitious stars and a slice of moon shimmered overhead. Night-blooming flowers—she hadn't realized how greatly her ignorance of the local flora would bother her—offered up the gift of their sweet perfume. Perhaps when all was settled, she could begin a garden in this unusual place.

Anything to make it her own.

On the opposite bench, Miles's mind was elsewhere. He concentrated on the blackened eastern horizon like a weathered pirate assessing blue Caribbean waters. Where was the spoiled nobleman who'd fed caviar to his hunting dogs on a bet? Or who, at his cousin's engagement gala, had spent the evening introducing Viv to every foul term for a woman's intimate places? His whispers. Her answering anger and arousal. Never had an evening dragged on with such anticipation. Alone together that night, he'd repeated those words all over again, but with his mouth nestled between her legs.

And yes, she'd *shattered*.

Soon his focus would return to her, always for his own amusement. He had sparked her to life, every nerve ending bright and awake. Perhaps that explained his innate skill at cards: his opponents simply lost the will to compete.

That evening, they would sleep beneath the same roof for the first time in more than a year. Would he come to her? So soon?

Would she let him if he did?

The cab pulled to a stop. With her fingers in Miles's palm, she descended and caught her breath. A white manor home gleamed beneath the scant moonlight. Dark shutters—maybe blue, maybe black—bordered a dozen windows, each with six panes of leaded glass. Candles brightened the rooms with glittering friendliness, just as torches lined the perimeter of a gated front garden. On the second story just above the entryway, two French doors opened to a balcony that stretched the entire width of the verandah. Sheer, pale curtains fluttered in the cooling breeze.

"This is home?" she asked.

They stood side by side, his hand on the latch to open the whitewashed gate. "Yes, this is home."

She hadn't expected this, the closeness of it all. His softly spoken words were an intimate promise. He didn't touch her now, but the idea of him twinkled and twisted under her skin.

She swallowed. "Lead on."

His boots crunched on the gravel walkway. Dark foliage hid in shadows along either side of the path to the front door.

Adam greeted them. He sat on the wraparound porch with a rifle across his lap. "Chloe has been installed in the quarters adjoining your room, my lady," he said. "And the housekeeper, Mrs. Shelby, has prepared a supper for you. A bath will be ready when you require it in the morning."

Relief made her weariness even heavier to bear. But she was never the kind to let such weakness show, not when hard-earned manners helpfully took control of her tongue. "Thank you, Adam. Your efforts are much appreciated."

"His Lordship's orders, my lady."

No platitude could rescue her when Miles gazed at her with such utter absorption. She licked her bottom lip. "Then . . . I'll bid you both good evening."

"Your bedroom is up the stairs, first door on the left," he said quietly as she walked away. "I'll join you there shortly, Vivie."

Miles had no intention of letting that be the end of their day. Despite the last time he'd overcome her defenses, behind the staircase at the Saunders' gala, he wanted their next encounter to be entirely private. Her gasps and breathy pleas would be for him alone. And very soon.

The darkness disguised Adam's typical blushes and smiles, rendering him the blunt, toughened bastard Miles knew him to be. Therein lay his unspoken value—that, and his gratifying loyalty. Few would ever assume a viscount's manservant to be a soldier's son, or that Adam had proven so adept at learning his father's countless techniques for defense.

"Any problems?"

"None, my lord."

"Good," Miles said. "But you need rest. Where's Mr. Shelby?"

"He'll be along shortly. He's . . ." Adam hesitated. "He's bidding Mrs. Shelby a good night."

"I envy the man." Only at Adam's raised brow did Miles realize he'd spoken that damning doubt aloud. "No matter. The night is young, Mr. Nolan."

On a gruff farewell, he pushed through the front door and down the corridor. The air inside was slightly warmer. The scent of an extinguished stove—woodsy, tinged with stale cooking smells—invited the return of his fatigue. Up the stairs and down to his bedchamber, Miles pushed the tiredness away while he grappled with the bigger matter.

Vivie was home. His hellfire ridiculous brain couldn't think anything else. Now . . . what to do with her?

Keep her.

He shook his head once, hard, angrily, and cursed himself a hundred-fold fool. Keeping her wasn't his objective. If he was going to knock his darling Vivienne down a few pegs, he needed a clearer mind.

He cracked the knuckle of his right thumb, then poured water from a pitcher to quickly wash. For a man used to sleeping until noon and enjoying every sensual pleasure available in England, the demands of the previous few days—nay, months—had taken an insidious toll.

But more than he craved his vices, he wanted to *conquer*—an echo of the medieval warrior who'd wrested ancestral lands from dastardly cousins or half-bestial Celts in order to found his noble line.

There were diamonds to be yanked from the ground, diamonds to be assayed and graded, diamonds to be sold. A list of competitors as long as his leg awaited their subjugation. There was a future to be won. Unlike everyone else in Kimberley, he and Viv didn't need to earn much—just a penny of profit and they'd secure that million-dollar bonus.

But Miles wanted to win big.

Why? Why this urge? It was as irrational as the urge to take off at a run. Gentlemen didn't run. They didn't sweat and they didn't get dirty. They didn't concern themselves with the workings of mines and counting houses and the trade of precious gems. But *here* they did. Maybe that was the appeal, as much as the freedom and the danger. Here in Cape Colony, the rules had been turned upside down. He enjoyed the vertigo.

And Viv.

Toweling off and donning a clean shirt, he promised to win big with her as well. Yes, they would prevail against her father's posthumous scheme, but Miles wasn't going to hand her the independence she craved, not without fair compensation. When it came to what her body desired, she was one of the most hypocritical people he'd ever met. He planned to remind her of that, repeatedly, until she ceased to be the needle gouging his chest.

Starting tonight.

Seven

Viv perched on the edge of the settee in her bedroom. She knew she should move. But she remained very still and, as if watching herself from afar, silently laughed at her absurd situation. Once she might have been considered one of the most capable children in Paris. And she had certainly been regarded as an accomplished addition to London Society, a feat quietly acknowledged as all the more impressive because of Miles's rebellious ways. That she could host a splendid tea for the Duchess of Colemont, her smile never wavering as they discussed his latest all-night card game, had deserved all the celebrations due a conquering hero.

For fifteen years she'd labored to learn the rules of propriety, etching them onto her person—the very essence of what it was to be Vivienne Christie Durham, Viscountess Bancroft. The strictures had pinched and strangled at first, like a corset laced to the point of pain.

But what would she be without them?

The fact of her shameful parentage would escape the vault of family secrets. Her dear siblings knew, and they'd rather die than do her harm. Otherwise, with their father's death and with the death of his second wife, Catrin, four years earlier, the door to Viv's true past had closed. To everyone else who breathed, the simple story was best left unquestioned. In the summer of 1863, during the tumult caused by the War Between the States, William and Catrin Christie had decided to adopt an eight-year-old girl. Perhaps Catrin could no longer bear children. Perhaps they did so out of Christian charity.

No one dared suggest that they did so out of obligation to a condemned French can-can dancer and her bastard daughter. With the largess of the dowry they'd received, even Miles's parents had never asked. But as an adopted child, she had always been the object of speculation. What blood did she carry in her veins? As a result her efforts to blend in—no, to excel—held a sharp edge of desperation.

Don't be found out.

She'd almost told Miles. Once. Her desire to believe in him ran that deeply. On the night of the Saunders' gala, he had waltzed her around the ballroom until she couldn't take a breath without pulling his dizzying scent into her body.

Whisking Viv behind the grand staircase, he had pushed her against the cool marble wall and lifted her skirts. His warm, smooth palm had muffled her sounds of pleasure. Inside her, around her, whispering harsh, blunt words, he had taken what she willingly gave.

Viv had only needed his love.

Had Miles spirited her home to continue that fiery

seduction, she would have been his. Forever. No matter his failings. She would have confessed everything.

But he merely slicked errant strands of coffee-dark hair into place and returned to an all-night game of cards. Viv made her own way home, numb yet aching, only to awaken to rumors that Miles spent the night in a whorehouse.

The next time he spoke to her, he had asked for money. A remarkable gambler when sober, he was a sieve when drunk. No apologies. No penitence when he admitted the need for ready cash had prompted his seduction. Viv wrote a letter to her father, but not to request an additional allowance. She was returning to New York.

A quiet knock sounded on her door. "Viv? May I come in?"

Her heart jumped. She'd been waiting for him. This was the reckoning she'd delayed for days—the confrontation they'd avoided for over a year.

The floor felt spongy and vague, as if she floated through a hazy dream. What would he do? And on what grounds could she refuse? Her fingertips touched the doorknob but she didn't feel it.

Miles stood at the threshold wearing a clean shirt. Open at the neck. Sleeves rolled up. Had he completely forgot how to dress? Or did he do it to tempt her wayward impulses? Water darkened his hair. One fat droplet still clung to his earlobe. The murky circles beneath his earthen brown eyes were like tribal tattoos, but he wore the expression of a man who would not be deterred by the mere need for sleep.

One bared forearm propped over his head on the doorframe. Dark hair decorated his tanned skin—a contrast of colors and textures that begged for exploration. He'd never been an unfit man. Too many dares and lost wagers, from polo matches to pugilism, required physical readiness. Now his muscles were long and toned, like taut, sturdy ropes. What else had changed? What of his body would be new territory?

Miles laughed softly. Even the slope between her breasts flared hot and prickly as she blushed.

"Yes, my lord?"

"I said, may I come in?"

Close the door. Close it smack on his face.

But he would only return again, either that night or the next. And despite how dangerous this encounter might prove, Viv wanted to have done with it. Maybe then she could remember her reasons for leaving. Yes, he would say or do something to make her stomach turn over. He always did.

Despite wielding a whip and motivating an impromptu militia, Miles, Viscount Bancroft, was no hero. But he was her partner. No denying that they needed to clear the air.

"Only because you asked."

"I'll remember that for the future." He flashed a cocky, disarming smile—one that, coming from any other man, would've elicited a disgusted sniff. Instead her blush deepened.

He glanced around the room as he entered, then slumped into the nearest chair. The floral brocade and stuffed cushions only accentuated the long, angular lines of his negligent posture. He pulled an oblong scatter pillow from behind his back and tossed it aside.

"Like your accommodations?"

"Quite," she said by rote.

In truth she'd hardly paid the room any mind, so occupied had been her thoughts. A pale yellow wood, polished to a high sheen, bordered the door and every window casing. Gilt trim touched the edges of the room's two mirrors and four picture frames, all of which lent the interior a sunny disposition. The luxurious details continued: cream lace curtains, a table and chairs embellished with quatrefoils of the Gothic style, and two matched wardrobes wrought from some exotic tree, perhaps teak—a dark contrast to the brighter accents. A feather duvet covered in white brushed cotton stretched across a four-poster bed, with decadent, colorful pillows strewn along the curling brass headboard. Mosquito netting draped in neat swoops from floor to ceiling.

And her astonishing balcony! How enticing to sleep with the whispers of an exotic land lulling her to sleep. Now it was hers, the doors open wide to a night like she'd never known: calm yet exhilarating, filled with unfamiliar sounds and all-too-familiar impulses. From her balcony, on the crest of the bluff upon which the manor looked down over Kimberley, she could see the city's more extravagant homes brightened by electrical lighting.

Was Miles due the credit for her beautiful bedchamber? So tasteful and comforting, it could've been pulled from the place in her mind that most desired a safe, luxurious space of her own. She hardly wanted to ask, dreading how poorly her pride would endure expressing her appreciation.

With Miles still silent, she crossed to sit on the settee, where they faced off like polite gladiators. *Get on with it,* she thought—screaming the words in her mind. *Get this over with.*

But he stretched his legs and crossed his ankles, settling in as if he had no destination, no purpose. The cocky smile turned taunting.

She pulled her arms into the shelter of her abdomen. "I cannot get used to this place."

Miles raised his eyebrows. He seemed as taken aback by her words as she was. "The contradictions, you mean."

Again Viv was disconcerted by how accurately he was able to judge her moods. That hadn't happened back in England. Not ever. She could have written detailed explanations on every inch of expensive French wallpaper in their town home and he would have missed the point entirely. Perhaps even intentionally. Here, his uncanny ability was becoming habit.

"Yes," she said hesitantly. "That's it exactly. As poor as any hovel in the London stews and then . . . *this.*"

"I quite like it. At least here we can't ignore those who finance our livings. We can avoid making eye contact when we pass them on the street, but they're a constant reminder of the human toll of mining."

"You like that reminder?"

"It keeps a man humble."

She couldn't help but snort. "Hardly."

His teasing expression faded. "And any man it doesn't humble . . . Well, then we'll be better able to understand the high-end bastards with whom we're competing."

Even while sparring, he was assessing this place. Viv wanted to think of the process as an extension of his passion for gambling. Did that explain the dedication with which he approached each uncharacteristic task? Just a series of dares?

"Enough of this sad-sack talk," he said, rising with more grace than a man should possess. "Stand up."

Viv flinched. "Really, Miles? You're going to play this now? I haven't bathed, for God's sake!"

"And you're probably exhausted."

"Yes, I am."

"Which is why I thought you might need help removing your dress." He said it so matter-of-factly, as if seduction weren't his aim. "Now, do you want out of that corset or not?"

Miles waited. He should have felt conspicuous or ashamed of his imposition. But he didn't. At the end of a long and strenuous day, Viv was exactly what he needed.

Not that he expected to bed her that evening. She was filthy, as was he. His collarbone throbbed. And he doubted his wife's ability to do more than lie on that deliciously white duvet and accept his body's unwelcome invasion.

Yes, Miles wanted to win big. Their deal had been for her enthusiasm. Lovemaking on this, their first night together in the contradictory wilds of Kimberley, would result in more resignation than vigor. Her posture practically shouted, "Have done and leave me be."

Too bad. Twenty months awaited her slow but certain capitulation.

Not that he expected to wait *that* long. God above, to live in close proximity to her for that many months, weeks, days—nights. He hadn't come to Cape Colony to go mad.

"How does Chloe fare?" he asked.

A flash of surprise broke through her wariness. Then it was gone, leaving only the silvery memory of it, like the burn of a lightning strike on the back of one's eye.

Miles took note. Flies to honey and all that. Another technique to save for the future. But merciful Christ, did she find concern from him so unlikely? Probably. He couldn't remember the last time he'd inquired after her well-being without ulterior motives. Like now. He flicked his wedding ring with the pad of his thumb but forced himself to stop.

"She's resting," Viv said. "I found an empty tray of food outside her door, so she must have eaten."

"Good, good. And you don't want to wake her up, do you?"

"No."

"I thought not. Up, then."

With the hesitancy of an invalid standing for the first time in years, she arose from the settee. "You don't have to do this," she said, her voice catching.

"Does that mean you want me to leave?"

"Yes."

He trailed his index finger up her forearm. Goose bumps followed his progress. "That wasn't our agreement."

Her eyes rolled closed. Desire slid straight to Miles's

groin. But her expression had nothing to do with succumbing to passion. Hypnosis or an out-of-body experience appeared to be her aim—anything to escape that moment, standing there, being touched by her husband.

Miles watched, fascinated, as the side of her neck fluttered with a fervent pulse. She seemed so outwardly calm. He remembered her first introduction to his parents, the Earl and Countess of Bettenford, at their ancestral home in Hampshire. *Regal* had been the only word his stuttering brain had summoned. That Viv's astonishing beauty had swayed his father was no surprise. That her tranquil grace and immaculate poise had even managed to charm his mother remained one of the seven modern wonders.

That Miles had wanted her as much as his parents coveted her dowry . . . Trouble.

How often did she confront the world that way, with her body and her words so perfectly composed, yet her insides churning in revolt? Perhaps he should've been pleased that he merited such an effort, but Miles wanted to shake her until she cracked open and spilled out all that was ugly and true.

"What's so amusing?" she asked.

"I was just thinking of . . . true things."

"We can do this if you wish, but my enthusiasm will be sorely lacking."

"Not to worry. I have decided not to bed you, Viv. Not tonight. Not tomorrow night. I'd like to say that I'll wait until you want it as much as I do, but I despair for delaying that long."

"Ah."

What an odd noise. Perhaps it was a sign of relief, but Miles couldn't be certain. He enjoyed knowing that he had her so keyed up and ready to anticipate the least little imposition.

"Turn around," he said.

She met his gaze and held it. Her eyes, that startling shade of green and gold, had dulled to a mossy gray. They were bloodshot. Flecks of dust from the wickedly crude streets still clung to her hair, sullying the vibrant gold. Everything about her had dimmed. Strange, when he felt so charged and alive.

Miles'ss certainty faltered. What if this bedeviling colony held no magic for her? How could they be so mismatched when he wanted her so badly?

At last she complied, briskly, without another word. Miles found himself looking at the exquisite arch of her neck. Sweat had tightened the swirling curls at her nape. He needed to kiss her there. That was the compromise his mind made with his body. He would kiss her there and leave her be. After removing her gown.

He bit back a groan.

It didn't take much, just the tilt of his head and the brush of his lips. She smelled as elemental as he did, all dirt and sweat—more of the ugly truth that held him so enraptured. At the first touch of skin to skin, she gasped and he hardened.

Viv spun and backed away. "Stop."

"All right."

"Stop all of this!"

"Well, that I cannot do." He grabbed her by the shoulder and turned her back around, quickly unlacing her gown before she had the chance to second-guess his intentions. Metal spikes were more pliant than her spine. "Now, tomorrow morning we can visit the clearing house and I'll acquaint you with the fundamentals of our enterprise. I expect you'll fare much more soundly than I, what with your father's example to draw from."

"Why are you doing this?" she whispered.

"Then some evening soon, I'll visit the Kimberley Club. I fear I must, seeing as how no women are permitted. It must gall you when you realize I'm a necessary part of this venture."

"What is so necessary about a smoking club?"

His fingers still shook and blood hammered in his shaft, but Miles found the presence of mind to talk about their schedules. He deserved a curtain call for putting on such a show. "It's where the rich and powerful men of Kimberley brag about their new wealth. Mr. Nolan mentioned that Neil Elden is back in town. I've never met the man, but I suspect I must."

"Who is he?"

"Owner of the Lion's Head Mine and one of our board members. He splits his time between Kimberley and Cape Colony, where he sits on the provincial Parliament." He smiled next to her ear. "Luckily I sit on Her Majesty's genuine Parliament, so you'll be pleased to know he doesn't intimidate me in the least."

The laces gaped open. Viv shrugged and the gown slipped down her arms. His wife turned to glance over her shoulder. Since when should she be smiling? She lifted her chin, not like a minister's bride on her wedding night, staring at the ceiling and awaiting the worst, but a warrior planning a counterattack.

"And the corset, please."

Miles froze. Breathing deeply through his nose did nothing to calm his ticking pulse. It seemed she was finally raising the stakes. He made short work of the remainder of her stays and laces, hoping that haste would ease the tremors in his fingers.

Free of her encumbering clothing, Viv stepped out of the pile of silk and satin and lace. She wore nothing but her shift, drawers, and stockings, her dust-streaked hair still bound up in a bouquet of curls and pins. Her long, graceful legs didn't falter. Her spine didn't lose its majestic grace.

But something had changed. He would've sworn that the faintest wiggle of her hips was designed to drive him to the brink of his control. He transformed into a statue, unable to do anything but watch as she crossed the room, selected a silken wrap from among a pile of filmy female garments, and slid into it.

The room had turned hot, exacerbating his temper. "You have one month. I'll concede exactly thirty days so that you can settle and relax and whatever else you need to do. That gives me thirty days to prove that I'm in earnest: no cigars and all that. And don't delude yourself that such a bargain will be simple to uphold. Habits are habits."

That was the closest he would come to admitting her particular stipulations might be more than he could deliver.

But he would not relent. More determined than he'd ever been amid the softness of a nobleman's life, he would not lose this test of wills.

"Then, Vivie, you will submit to our terms."

With the movements of a creature hewn of iron, not flesh, she sat primly on a wingback chair. "I understand. Good evening then, Miles."

Before he could think, before he could feel too deeply, he crossed to where she sat. That trembling in his fingertips increased, like a thunderstorm gaining strength with every mile of drenched earth. He felt blustery and wind-tossed.

Pressing his palms along each armrest, he leaned over. "Lift your chin," he said hoarsely.

"Pardon me?"

"Like you did just a moment ago, daring me to strip off your corset. Lift your chin."

The apples of her cheeks turned rosy, but she obeyed. Heavy-lidded hazel eyes snapped and sparked with an energy to match his own.

There was his Vivie.

The unconscious hauteur. The disdain and fire. The animosity that could flip so easily into passion.

And sweet Christ, he could see the inside swell of her breast where the silken wrap gaped in loose folds. Shadows and the color of sweat cream shifted with her every breath. Powder pink nipples, he remembered. Until they darkened beneath the attention he lavished.

A bolt of pure lust coiled through his body, igniting his blood like a match to oil. He leaned in. That traitorous pulse pounded a tympanum's rhythm along the side of her neck—the only tell he'd yet found. Otherwise she held still and waited, daring him as much as he challenged her.

Miles brushed his lips against the flawless skin of her throat. She still smelled like Viv, but darker, hotter, bathed in the scent of sun and earthy perfume. He'd only stolen the briefest contact when he'd kissed her nape. Now he wanted more.

Mouth open, he kissed her again and flicked out his tongue, indulging in her salty taste. He lingered there, nipping little bites along that taut tendon, up, up, to the elegant curve of her jaw. With the tip of his nose he traced back to her earlobe, then suckled that sensitive flesh. She gasped softly—bloody hell, just enough invitation. *Take more. Demand what they both craved.* Blood pounded in his ears and in his cock. His lungs had stopped providing his starved body with oxygen. He squeezed the armrests until the tiny bones in his hands threatened to explode.

"Tell me to go," he whispered against the skin he'd wet.

She swallowed—and hesitated. "Go."

With a curt nod, Miles straightened. Her pupils were wide, her plump mouth slightly open. *Thank God.* He'd have dropped to the floor in a melted heap had she remained unaffected.

"Good evening, Lady Bancroft," he said, then closed the bedroom door behind him.

Eight

*V*iv broke her fast at Chloe's side, with the young woman propped on fluffy pillows covered in fine, pale pink cotton.

"My lady, I'm embarrassed and—"

"Enough," Viv said gently. She buttered another piece of bread, topped it with strawberry preserves, and handed it to her maid. "I've endured the company of far less genial patients. Trust me on that score. Besides, if I stay here with you, I can delay becoming properly acquainted with the names and personalities of our household staff."

"Are you anxious, my lady?"

"Not anxious so much. Overwhelmed, perhaps. The enormity of this whole venture." Viv licked a bit of jam from her fingertip, only stopping herself when that flick of tongue reminded her of Miles's kiss. "But, one step at a time, yes? And that goes for you."

"How do you mean?"

"I'll have hot water brought in for your bath. The rejuvenating properties of such a luxury cannot be underestimated."

"Oh, my lady, I couldn't. The basin is fine." Her sapphire eyes were still clouded with turbulent emotions, but at least she ate and talked. The frightening catatonia of the previous days had, thankfully, ebbed.

"Believe me, sinking into hot water this morning made every agonizing minute of travel worth abiding."

She'd even dozed lightly after scrubbing her skin with a bar of lemony oil-and-glycerin soap. That she'd dreamt of Miles had been no surprise—not after her fitful night reliving his open-mouthed kiss. A whispered plea for more had been *right there*. Sitting on her tongue. Demanding to be said. To be left wanting by her husband was generally a dread she reserved for matters of the heart, not the body.

Suddenly parched, she finished her tea with a hasty swallow.

"Anyway, Chloe, I insist. After you've cleaned and dressed, you'll be as eager as ever. I just know it. You simply *must* be as revived as I am or else how will you keep up with my unfashionably boundless energy?"

Chloe tittered softly, her smile shy. But then, with a gratifyingly familiar gleam, she asked, "And may I use your bath salts, my lady?"

Viv spontaneously hugged her maid. "Yes, you silly dear. But only if you lie abed today. Promise me."

The girl crossed her heart. "Promise."

A lightness in Viv's chest banished some of her dark doubts. If her maid was up to resuming her little requests—for a piece of lace, to borrow a hair comb—then she would be fine. Chloe was a good girl, a loyal companion, and a tireless worker. But she enjoyed life's little fineries. Often she had been reprimanded by housekeepers and mistresses for such an unforgivable foible, but Viv enjoyed her boldness. Any young woman able to ask for what she wanted should be honored for having made the effort.

Perhaps she admired the trait because Viv herself had never managed it.

She dressed, requiring Chloe's help only to secure her corset and the back of her hunter green waistjacket. She flounced her green and white skirts, replete with trimmings and lace that now seemed ostentatious. No matter. If she intended to succeed in Kimberley, she needed to make the role her own. Part nobility. Part entrepreneur. Her custom-fitted Parisian ensemble was necessary armor.

"But you *must* let me do your hair, my lady. A simple bun will not suit. Not at all."

Before Viv could protest, the young woman had scampered out of bed with the vigor of a child after too much cocoa. She tugged her own waist-length brown hair into a quick plait, then joined Viv where she sat at the vanity table. Chloe worked steadily with pins, curls, and irons. An absolute magician of fashionable coiffure. Her mood seemed to improve. Every observation she had yet to speak—about the docks, the raid, the town—streamed forth in a reassuring stream of chatter.

"All finished, my lady."

A blonde coronet of artful curls topped Viv's head, woven through with shimmering ribbons that matched her ensemble and brought out the green in her eyes. Hearing her maid so improved had lightened Viv's mood, but Chloe's skillful concoction made her feel like a real lady again.

"Oh, Chloe. Just . . . perfect. Thank you."

"You're very welcome."

"Go rest now," Viv said once more, rising. "Enjoy your bath and take your meals in here. I'll make sure someone sends you a bit of cake or the like. That sweet tooth must be indulged, at least for today."

Chloe giggled.

"Tomorrow we can return to normal. And I'd love your company when I investigate what this town has by way of shops and culture."

Feeling delightfully refreshed, Viv made her way to the kitchen. The corridor was decorated with ivory flocked wallpaper, with wainscoting and crown moldings in that same distinctive pale yellow wood. A thick dark green carpet runner padded her steps. Although no pictures yet adorned the walls, vases of dried flowers decorated various points throughout the house: the landing of the front staircase, the foyer, a little writing desk in the main parlor. Airy lace curtains fluttered at each window, through which gentle gusts ushered in the dry morning air.

Past a study, a smaller parlor, and the staff's quarters, Viv found the kitchen simply by following her nose. The scents of some roast or maybe a salty stew mingled with fresh bread. The noise, too, gave away the room as the busiest in the manor.

"Ah, my lady," said a woman with a distinctly Kentish

accent. "Good to see you up and looking so well. I'm Mrs. Shelby, the housekeeper."

"Thank you, and it's lovely to make your acquaintance."

Mrs. Shelby stood no taller than Viv's collarbone, but she flounced through her domain with a sprightliness that belied her age and weight. She wore a starched dress the color of spring grass and a faultless white apron. Her hair, like a nest of copper and silver filaments, was pinned high atop her head. Skin beset by wrinkles in the usual places— around her mouth, at the corners of her eyes—remained soft. She must have been very pretty in her youth. Now a mature woman, she exuded a confidence and spirited cheer that Viv appreciated.

"This is Louise, the cook," Mrs. Shelby said. "My son, Jamie, is the lad who brought in your bathwater. He keeps the stables and helps maintain the house."

"We have horses?" Viv asked.

A half-eaten apple in his hands, Adam leaned against the end of the butcher-block table where Louise kneaded dough. "Lord Bancroft finally broke down and bought a pair of matched fillies and a barouche last week—in anticipation of your arrival, my lady."

"What had he been using?"

Adam flashed a grin. "He prefers . . . walking."

The notion of Miles walking from place to place struck Viv as unbelievably comic. This from a man who'd once ordered his carriage brought around so that he needn't walk from their town house to a solicitor's residence some ninety yards distant.

"Unbelievable, I know. But he's . . . changed." Adam shook his head and blanked his expression. "And of course, Mr. Shelby is sleeping."

Mrs. Shelby clucked over the cook's shoulder, apparently unpleased by the progress of Louise's bread-making. "My husband," the housekeeper said. "He stands guard at night, so he won't be up and about until after supper. He helps with the more difficult chores that Jamie can't perform."

Miles had done all of this? In just a few short months? Bad enough that he had behaved like some avenging hero. He had also found some deep reserve of perfect decorum, even hiring the right people for household tasks.

She should thank him. And even that urge was surprising. All of this was just so . . . *unexpected*.

And she hated the cowardly cringe pulling at her insides. How difficult should it be to thank one's husband? Immeasurably so, when she'd been the one to initiate their estrangement, and when she'd been set so firmly in the habit of believing him a wastrel.

Yet she'd managed, during those quiet moments after the way station attack. His actions had been so astonishing, so heroic, that her appreciation had been easy to express. Perhaps if she learned to praise what little good he managed, she would encourage him to take her feelings into consideration as well.

"Where is his Lordship?" she asked Adam.

"Gone to the Ford Inn, actually. I hadn't realized he was up and about."

"What for?"

"No notion. Probably something to do with giving testimony about the raid. As a nobleman, his word may hold more weight."

"So terribly honorable, what His Lordship did for those coaches," Mrs. Shelby said. Louise grunted her agreement as she hefted four loaves of dough into the oven. "It's been the talk of Kimberley since you arrived, my lady."

Viv wanted to sit down. This was too much. Miles had become a saint.

You don't know him.

She felt compelled to set the record straight, with far fewer rose-colored impressions. This version of her husband was unforgivably cruel, making her feel what she hadn't dared in years: hope.

Although words of protest edged forward on her tongue, she could not give them voice. To be honest, Viv didn't know who he was either—or at least who he'd become in the Cape. And she was hardly so callous as to dispel this fairy tale on the off chance it wasn't a fiction.

Her heart gave a little flutter. She *wanted* that fiction to be true.

"Otherwise," Adam said, "you both have an appointment at two o'clock to meet with Mr. Pieter Smets. He'll introduce you to the workings of the clearing house and show you the books."

Viv blinked. "And how was that managed on such short notice?"

"By paying his manservant incredibly well." He paused, his smile faltering. "How is Chloe?"

"Much improved. She'll be up and about tomorrow, I assure you."

"Good." Viv caught a glimmer of something unsaid on the man's deceptively youthful face, but it disappeared too quickly. He was nearly as agile of mind as his master. "Lord Bancroft left a note asking that you meet him at the Ford. Shall I have Jamie hitch the carriage for you, my lady?"

"Yes, please."

Twenty minutes later she accepted Adam's hand up into the carriage. Just before young Jamie set off, she couldn't help her curiosity. "Adam? His Lordship walked to the hotel, didn't he?"

"Yes, my lady, he did."

Inside the lobby of the Ford Inn, businessmen sat on fat leather chairs, their heads permanently crooked into the folds of their newspapers. Trails of cigar and pipe smoke lifted toward the ceiling as if from small campfires. Viv paid them only cursory notice. Her attention was immediately snared by Miles.

He leaned against the concierge's desk, his posture comfortingly familiar in its negligence. As were his garments. Good gracious, they were in civilization now—or what passed for it this far out on the Karoo. He wore the world's best clothing with silent disdain, much like his title. Although the midnight blue wool suit was classically handsome, he ruined its impeccable cut by leaving the coat unbuttoned. His sloppily tied ascot meant he had attempted the task of dressing without Adam's help, but the bright white silk accentuated the vibrant caramel color of his tanned skin.

The heathen of their inland journey had been scrubbed clean but not tamed. Any of his peers in London would have been startled, even appalled by his appearance. And yet his grace, his manners, his aristocratic lineage were evident in every polished movement.

Viv couldn't look away.

Inhaling, she waited until her breath bunched like cotton stuffing in her chest. Memories of how he'd kissed her neck—and how he'd claimed her mouth by the way station—flooded over her in a rush of hot, sticky sensation. She found herself touching the side of her throat, hoping in vain to rekindle that fire. But her kid leather gloves felt nothing like his warm, firm, assured lips.

She didn't need this. She certainly didn't want it.

Just another challenge to overcome.

With a refinement borne not of blood but of dedicated years of practice, she crossed the lobby as if meandering through Buckingham Palace. Facing her future in-laws for the first time had been a cause for nerves, as had making polite excuses for Miless's failings.

Or languishing in a French prison while her mother awaited the day of her execution.

This was nothing.

Miles noticed her approach. She expected him to straighten and hold his tall, firm body over hers in that harassing manner of his. But he merely bowed. "Good morning, my lady." Then he addressed his shorter companion. "If that will be all, Constable Mansfield?"

"Yes, thank you for your assistance, my lord."

"Good. Lady Bancroft and I have business to attend." He offered his elbow. "Shall we?"

They left the hotel and strolled together along the raised plank sidewalk. Only then did he lean near enough to whisper. "I had to get you out of there."

"Why? Something dangerous?"

"Oh, yes, Vivie. *Me.*" His breath warmed her cheek. "You look incredible. I was having crude ideas about hotel room trysts. Best we stay out in the fresh air."

Then he winked. There in the street in the middle of the day, he had the temerity to look her discomfort in the eye . . . and wink.

Flattered and aghast, both, Viv could only stare at his chiseled profile as they walked. No hat today, which added to his roguish air. His thick hair was due for a cut. Coffee-brown locks streaked with gold curled at the base of his neck and rested along the upper edge of his starched collar. Viv curled her fingers into a fist, fighting the urge to dive down to his scalp and tug. Hard. To kiss him. To revel in the light bronze stubble along his chin and proud jaw.

He was doing this on purpose, as always—mingling propriety with secret overtures.

But for all of his skill at cards, he did not have the patience for tact. His plan was simple enough to read: get her to give in and beg for an end to the thirty-day reprieve. But Viv had plans of her own. Next time Miles threatened her with kisses, she'd kiss him right back. She would make his thirty days as much torture as possible before handing over control.

At least the ill-fitting saintliness the servants had tried to bestow no longer squared. He was the same man, no matter how many trips he took by foot. Her sense of triumph at having been proven right was brought low by an unexpected whisper of disappointment.

"No rejoinder, my dear? I keep baiting you in the hopes of catching something. Perhaps a tasty bit of vitriolic wit?"

"Fresh out of vitriol."

"You can't give me the silent treatment forever."

"I can if you insist on taunts instead of civilized conversation."

He grinned. "Fresh out of civilized."

Viv looked him up and down, affecting her least impressed expression of disdain. "So I see."

Maybe she'd been naïve in entering their marriage with hopes of companionship and mutual respect. She coped as she always had, focusing on what she possessed rather than what she lacked. Her belly was full, her gorgeous gown was new, and Miles had given her a thirty-day reprieve. By then she might be better able to stomach giving him what he demanded—without losing another piece of her foolish heart.

Kimberley was busy in the throes of midday, bleached beneath the sun and swarmed over with the bustle of business. In this part of the city, where shops and patrons did their best to re-create fine metropolitan living, only the distant, dull, metallic thud of a thousand pickaxes hinted that they weren't strolling through London.

That reminder of the challenges they faced returned

her balance. Miles would continue his games, but that was the cost of his partnership. She could endure anything for twenty months, especially if it guaranteed security for the rest of her life.

She cleared her throat. "The house and the staff are all lovely. I'm impressed."

"Mr. Nolan had a significant hand in the arrangements, I must admit."

"I'd forgotten his efficiency."

"He likes revealing himself that way on occasion, but it always winds up to his advantage. Deuced frustrating."

"I'm glad he agreed to accompany you."

They came to a stop in front of a modest storefront when he finally looked at her. "Viv, are we on good terms?"

She hesitated. Trust was out of the question, but could she believe that he wouldn't abuse this tentative closeness? She smiled as pleasingly as she knew how. "What terms?"

"Oh, you're determined to remain so very *polished*. There's little I can do to alter that until we're alone." He looked up at the painted sign hanging above the store's front door. "And although this bears the Christie name, it's hardly private enough to call home."

Viv followed the line of his gaze. The sign read Christie Diamond Brokerage House.

A feeling like the tingle of static on a bright winter's day joined hands with her curiosity. No matter her low birth, she was a Christie. This was her burden. Her right. Her unparalleled opportunity.

Miles opened the door to the brokerage and motioned

for Viv to join him. They stood together in a vestibule bounded by two doors—to the street outside, which he closed firmly, and to the inner sanctum of the business. With the city noises muffled behind wood and glass, she and Miles shared the sudden, close quiet of that little entryway. Metal bars crisscrossed the second door like a prison cell.

She shivered. Diamonds. They were a curse of suspicion and fear that no one discussed.

"Can we say that our terms are . . . good enough?" she asked.

"No, because they're not. But I need you to trust me. At least in business."

His seriousness, so unaccustomed, made her take notice. A knee-jerk urge to object was tempered only by his gravity. Had he been jesting or, God help her, winking once again, there would've been no end to her protests. But this felt alien and threatening. Those metal bars told Viv that, more than the success or failure of her contract, cooperation could mean their literal survival.

"Tell me more?"

"Nothing yet, I'm afraid," he said. "This place is going to take a few more weeks to discern. There are new players in town—men I haven't yet met. We need to know where we stand before we proceed."

"You can talk to them, yes? At the Kimberley Club?"

"Yes, I plan to. But I need you to do your part as well. For example, I cannot take tea with the other rich matrons and wives. They might be more . . . forthcoming if they've heard anything about business matters."

"Hardly," Viv said, smiling. "I suspect that a woman entrusted with a business secret would clasp it all the more tightly for fear she wouldn't receive another."

Miles took her hand and gave it a squeeze. Such a restrained measure. Viv couldn't decipher its meaning. Agreement? Amusement? His face held no clues. The lips that had touched her throat with such delicate, demanding intimacy tightened into a stern line.

"Can we agree, then, to share our responsibilities?"

"Divide and conquer." She was breathless now, unaccountably excited.

"Exactly."

That excitement reflected back at her. A fierce gleam flashed in his eyes, matching his wild, captivating manner of dress. An untamed aristocrat, just as he'd always been, but this time fueled by undeniable purpose—a purpose she shared.

"Then . . . yes. In this we are in agreement."

"Good." He pulled a pair of keys out of his inside breast pocket. "Now, Lady Bancroft, would you like to become better acquainted with your business?"

Nine

*M*iles *unlocked the vestibule door* and entered ahead of Viv. The scents of ink and inexpensive cologne were made more pungent by the sun streaming through west-facing windows. But wrought-iron bars stood at attention behind each pane of glass, casting tic-tac-toe boards across the simple plank wood floor. It seemed as much innocuous office as cozy prison.

The lead appraiser stood from his neat rolltop desk and approached. He wore the demeanor of a whipped dog. Miles suspected it came from endless days stooped over a counting table with a glass pressed to his eye, but also from having to tell men that their diamonds contained minute, value-leeching flaws. He was a man entirely on the defensive.

"Lord Bancroft, you are returned to us at last," he said, his vowels nasal and his consonants clipped. "I heard tell your journey was an eventful one."

"That it was. And I'm learning anew that Kimberley permits few secrets." Miles pulled Viv forward with a hand to her lower back. "May I present my wife, Lady Bancroft."

She smiled graciously. "How do you do?"

"Ah, Christie's daughter. Here in Kimberley! I am honored, my lady."

Miles looked on while the man offered a stilted bow. "My dear, this is the head of our appraisal team, Pieter Smets of Antwerp."

"The diamond capital. Excellent. And you'll be so good as to show us the ropes, Mr. Smets?"

The Belgian's silver hair was closely cropped, which accentuated his overlarge ears—ears that waggled distractingly as he spoke. "Right this way, my lady."

Smets led them past two of his hulking countrymen who played cards on a small round table. Shotguns were propped against their chairs. Heavy pipe smoke lingered around their heads like malformed halos. Viv's eyes had gone wide, her neck craning as she walked.

"More security," Miles said under his breath.

"Good Lord. It's a wonder anyone awakens in the morning. So many precautions against theft."

"My question is what size their salary must be to keep them from turning into armed thieves themselves."

"Every decision will reflect back to our profit," Viv said. "We'll need to examine every practice and expense we've inherited."

Miles had long suspected that part of her success in London was because of her father's cunning. Climbing the ladder of social acceptance was very much like acquiring financial capital and applying it with the right combination of tact, daring, and forethought. But to hear proof of her quick mind shot a fantastic jolt up his spine. More truths about the wife he barely knew—the truths she hid beneath a crown of radiant sunshine hair and a docile smile.

With a great deal of reluctance, he pulled his attention away from thoughts of green and gold and sweet cream skin.

The building was shallower than it appeared from the street. Smets's sleeping quarters were on the floor above, as were years' worth of business records, but Miles had never ventured upstairs. Putting off the nitty-gritty of doing actual trade—the mere thought of the word "trade" would have sent his aristocratic forebears into conniption-fits— had been convenient enough while awaiting Viv's arrival. Other than an introductory visit to the office some months previous, he'd happily put off the inevitable.

While wielding a whip and staring across the vast empire of workers, his ability to imagine success bordered on gifted. But he was a child in these mundane matters of business. By contrast, Viv had been raised with one of the century's great masters in the art of spinning gold out of straw. The Christies had maneuvered into the highest strata. Why not in Kimberley too?

Smets led them to a room the approximate size of a coach's interior. Little space for splayed elbows and no windows, but from each corner hung an electric lamp. An array of tiny drawers and cabinets lined one wall, all labeled with catalogue numbers. The remaining walls were painted white, which reflected light back toward a central table. Aside from jeweler's tools and a ream of paper, it was entirely covered in diamonds.

"Here is the heart of our operation," Smets said. "The sorting room."

A beatific look smoothed Viv's features. The electric light made white porcelain of her cheeks, lending an ethereal glow. Parted lips offered a sensual testimony to her wonderment—how Miles dreamed she would appear when anticipating his kiss.

"My God," she whispered, cautiously stepping toward the table. "Are these . . . all . . . ?"

Smets smiled. "All are diamonds, my lady, if your question is that. Even the worst specimens carry more value than rock. Here we determine that value."

She glanced at Miles, as if looking for confirmation of what she witnessed. He joined her on one side of the table. Two hundred stones, he guessed. Together in a heap on a swath of black fabric, they formed a priceless, miniature mountain. He wondered how tall and wide the pile of discarded slag would be, those inglorious rocks from which these beauties had been extracted. As tall as him? As tall as the ceiling? The manpower required to excavate such a mass of earth held him in more awe than the diamonds.

"These are not fresh stones, are they?" Viv asked.

Smets raised his brows, the motion of which, of course, tugged at his ears. "Correct, my lady. That's right, exactly."

"Fresh?" Miles asked.

"These stones have already been sorted once." She picked one up, holding it to the lamp at her left. A splintered rainbow sluiced across her face. She flashed a smile toward Miles, as if sharing a secret.

God, he wanted to know what it was. What would open her to him, to prompt that smile again and again?

"The mines are always padding their deliveries with pretty bits of quartz," Smets said. "We weigh the refuse and charge a fee."

"For wasting your time?" Miles asked. "I do like that."

"The task here is to sort the best gem-quality diamonds, called brilliants, and trade them to jewelers all over the world, where the stones will be cut and set. On occasion, we find other gems: emeralds, rubies, lesser stones such as amethyst. The remainder are carbons." Smets toed a bucket on the floor.

Miles and Viv peered inside. So close, he caught the scent of rosewater and talcum. Wanting only to bury his nose in the delicately arranged strands of her hair, he instead palmed a dozen stones and brought them into the light. All were odious, globular masses, mostly gray, some flaked through with the green of rotten bread.

"These are carbons?" Miles nudged one with his index finger. "How utterly uninspiring."

"Like coal, they contain the same chemical and structural composition as diamonds," said Smets. "Only these have not been compressed to the same degree."

"But they must have *some* value," Viv said.

Smets shrugged. "To some industrialists, perhaps. We have thousands of them downstairs. Some brokerages toss them out with the rocks."

"Then why keep them? Or why not charge for them like you do the ordinary slag?"

"The mine owners argue that their negligible value should offset the time we devote to sorting them." The appraiser's scalp shone pale pink from beneath the silver bristles of his hair. "It always seemed a minor point, so we have not pushed. We've collected them mostly in deference to your father's wishes, my lady. He never advocated disposing of anything that might yet prove worthwhile."

"Yes, that was Sir William," she said, her expression detached. "Hmm, no windows in here. Security again?"

"Yes, my lady. Security is—as you can well imagine—a priority. Until we match the product with buyers worldwide, they remain the property of the mines that deliver them here for appraisal. Each stone is counted and signed for." Smets nodded to the room's only door, which Miles noticed was made of a solid iron. "That door locks, and the walls are reinforced with sheets of metal. The most valuable stones are stored here, while awaiting shipment." He gestured to the wall of small compartments.

"May I see one?"

Smets unlocked a four-inch-tall drawer and removed a metal box. Lined with a scrap of dark blue velvet, it contained a diamond the size of an eye. Still rough, its beauty was not in its cut or setting, as with the stones in Viv's wedding band.

No, its beauty was in its potential.

"It's flawless," said Smets, his voice reverent. "When cut . . . I cannot even imagine its worth."

Viv took the diamond between two fingers and stared. Her eyes were heavy-lidded and naturally sensual, but the brain ticking away behind them was sharp, noticing every-thing. Apparently she was no longer so awed by the dazzling shock of their trade. Miles shifted his weight, knowing that shrewd look all too well—for she'd turned it on him count-less times.

"And what's our percentage for brokering a deal between the mines and buyers?" she asked.

Smets faltered for the first time. His gaze sought guid-ance from Miles, who conveniently turned his attention to dumping the god-awful carbons back into their ignoble bucket. No velvet for them.

Viv carefully placed the diamond back in its metal box and snapped shut the lid. "Mr. Smets, my father's name adorns this building and I am your employer. Now, if you please?"

Smets's manner had decidedly cooled. "We earn ten per-cent, my lady."

"And the other brokerage houses?"

"The same," he said, his tone as flat as a boy reciting his times tables. "Mines stay with mines, brokerages with brokerages, diggers with their kind, Africans with theirs. No one breaks rank here, my lady."

She made a little sound that would have signaled an outright rebellion of opinion had she done so at a London tea. Smets hardly noticed it, while Miles only grinned. His beautiful, determined wife was having ideas. So was he, sud-denly aware of his hand's proximity to her thigh.

God, if he could turn that deft mind to matters of sexual gratification . . .

"Don't you think, my lord?"

"Hmm?"

The corners of her mouth tightened, the only hint of her displeasure. "I said, don't you think we should examine the ledgers? And I would very much like to learn more regarding the difference between these stones and the ones stored in buckets."

"Certainly," said Miles. "Assess to your heart's content."

Smets smiled, seemingly accepting the comment as Viv had: a husband condescending his overly interested wife. Her eyes' delicious mix of green and gold—that beautiful hazel—darkened with stormy malice intended only for him. But he had meant it as truth, and Mr. Smets needed to be dealt with.

"I appreciate your taking the time to explain all of this to us," he said. "We'll provide as much assistance as we're able, without getting in the way unnecessarily."

The man flicked a glance toward Viv. "Thank you, my lord."

And now for the challenging bit.

Miles drew from deep within his ancestral heritage and affected his most aristocratic conceit. "My lady, would you wait for us in the lobby?"

He bowed slightly, a polite yet glaring dismissal. But with his eyes, with the whole of his being, he urged her to trust, to remember what they'd discussed.

Her jaw held all the softness and warmth of a block of ice. Her gaze fired cannonballs. But she nodded. With her back straight and chin high, she glided out of the sorting room. Poise and unflappable grace seemed as innate to her as the delectable curve of her lush lower lip.

Relieved that Viv had consented, he faced off against Smets. "As for my darling wife, I would ask that you humor her interests."

"Humor?"

"She fancies herself a protégé of her late father and at times harbors . . . well . . . untoward interests." Miles stripped his words to a whisper. "But I think it's a bit of a ruse, you see. Girls and pretty stones and all that."

"Ah." The tension that had misshapen the man's shoulders suddenly eased. "I understand, my lord. She will be welcomed here."

"My thanks, Mr. Smets." He offered his hand, which Smets shook vigorously.

They returned to the lobby where Viv stared into an unknown middle distance. He needed to get her somewhere private. She would not explode. Vivienne Bancroft *never* exploded. But she wouldn't forgive him until she understood his motives.

"One last question, if you please," she said.

Carefully neutral, her expression revealed no hint of intrigue. Instead she appeared as vacant as a wine bottle at midnight. Miles could've sang for how happy he was.

She wasn't furious. She was playing along.

"Of course, my lady," Smets replied, his attitude now like that of a doting parent. He should've known Old Man Christie had been a taskmaster, expecting only the best.

"You mentioned many of the security features here in the office, the metal and the signing in." She waved her hand as if the details escaped her. "But what's to prevent men such as yourself and these fine card-playing gentlemen from, well, misbehaving?"

Smets paled.

"There seem to be so many arenas for graft, undervalued gems, et cetera," she continued, all things empty-headed and lovely. "Oh, but don't believe I ever thought such a horrible thing about you."

"Of course not," Smets said with an uncomfortable little laugh.

Viv offered a dainty shrug. "I was simply curious."

The Belgian stood before them on two legs, but he seemed to have shrunk by a good three inches. His fingers petted each other in an agitated fist. "Well, my lady, the last man in my position was sent to prison for eight years after he was convicted of just such . . . activities."

"Prison," Viv said. "Well, my lord, that does explain a great deal, doesn't it?"

"Indeed."

Smets relaxed somewhat. "And the last bodyguards to cross your father, my lady . . . they were hanged."

Once they'd emerged onto the street, Viv could breathe again. She had much to work through—diamonds and violence and her maddening husband.

"You did that on purpose."

They resumed a walk that was, to all outward appearances, perfectly artless. "Yes, I did. But I would count the encounter as a win, wouldn't you?"

"Divide and conquer."

"Naturally," he said with a glib smile.

Initially she had been upset at his condescension, with the decision to trust him coming after a silently fought battle. But no matter what he had been before, Miles would not jeopardize their chances.

"Good. Then what concessions did you wrest from Mr. Smets?"

His shrug was that of a bored gentleman. Strange how she kept forgetting that he was one. "You'll have the run of the place. Learn what you can. Just refrain from appearing too competent. I can only throw him off the trail so long. Show off that capitalist intellect of yours too frequently and you'll need more than simpering smiles to misdirect him again."

"He wasn't taking me seriously." She stopped. Rather than stall foot traffic along the sidewalk, she approached a dressmaker's window and affected perusing its frilly wares. "But why do you? Take me seriously, that is?"

Miles stood at her side, merely a man with his wife as they took in the selection. "You threatened to leave me once," he said, his voice oddly airy. "Do you remember that time?"

Memories rose up to flutter like caged birds attempting flight. "Yes, I do. The night you were so intoxicated that you slept in the gutter outside our town house."

"And I was there to greet your friends when they called in the morning." He sounded amused, but a quick glance revealed that the tendons along his jaw had tightened. Rather than conceal, the bristles of his stubble accentuated that small tick. "I imagine my behavior must have mortified you."

Was that an apology? The shivering relief in her stomach whispered that it might have been. "It did. And I said I would leave you if it happened again."

"It never happened again, but you left anyway."

"For other reasons. Learning where you'd slept after the Saunders' ball, for example."

"It wasn't what you think."

"A pity you were too intoxicated to explain."

"Granted." He cracked his thumb knuckle against his palm. "But the point remains, Vivie. I take you *very* seriously."

"I asked that you refrain from calling me that."

"You asked, yes."

"Miles." She stared through the window, her gaze fixed on a hem of Swiss lace. But her neck was flushed and her heart raced. "Why are you doing this? Truly? You know how it will be when we've accomplished our goal."

"You looked at that diamond—the obscene, monstrous one—and I saw your brain working. All of those calculations and possibilities. *That's* the enthusiasm I was talking about."

Her enthusiasm. Only Miles could set her alight with dread and shame and anticipation by using a single word. He had never been so two-fisted with her before: one hand stroking her pride with his confidences and esteem, the other hand reaching beneath her skirts. He was a much crueler version of the man he'd been in London.

She would do well to remember that, no matter their shared purpose.

"So you will have your way while it's still yours to have?"

"I've always enjoyed when we're in agreement," he said. "I hear tell that helps make a marriage happy." He caught her chin and tilted her face away from the store display. "I haven't had a drink since leaving New York. I miss my cigars like I miss rain. And soon I'll enter the Kimberley Club and refuse both vices—repeatedly, I'd wager, and to the detriment of my perceived manhood." His nostrils flared around each measured inhale. "And you insist on appreciating my reasons? It's all very simple, really. Shall I remind you?"

Viv nodded as an excuse to wrench away her chin. But he'd stolen her words, numbed her tongue, shattered her capacity for argument. She could only stare into his earthen eyes, where fury and lust roiled together in a primitive dance.

He was going to kiss her. Middle of the afternoon. A public thoroughfare. Her back against a dressmaker's storefront. And she didn't care.

Head angled, he blocked out the sun and shadowed her gaze. For the briefest moment she could see into him, through him, as if all his secrets were hers to read. All she found there was desire. For her. A giddy rush shot up from her toes. She felt charged with electricity when their lips finally met.

Viv's moan was instantaneous. Wanting turned to *having* in just that short span. Firm and patient, he was a dream lover made real. His tongue slipped along the line of her bottom lip and urged her to part for him. Open to him. She did, welcoming that gratifying invasion and the sudden shock of his taste. Hot, masculine—he breathed and pulsed and feasted, just as she did.

Strong fingers enveloped her wrists and held them fast at her sides. How had he known? How had he suspected that her next impulse was to dig her fingers into his sun-touched hair and drag him closer? She wanted his chest crushed to hers, their bodies acting out every depraved whim. Yet he kept her hands immobile. Only mouths in this kiss, this silent war.

So she gave it all she had. Diving more deeply, Viv luxuriated in the banquet of textures—the slick inside of his lower lip, the rough surface of his tongue, the hard scrape of his teeth.

But then he was gone.

Back straight and tall, he held his jaw at such a disdainful angle. Lust still sparked in his dark eyes, as did an animosity that she would've expected to see reflected in her own. His deep, shuddering exhale did as much to stoke her feminine fires as had his kiss. He was raging inside. Just who was the winner of this particular encounter? Viv could no longer tell. All she knew was that the hollow between her legs ached to be filled, yearning for the satisfaction Miles had always been able to provide.

But the hollow in her heart knew any such relief would only be temporary.

"Vivie, my darling," he said, his voice low and jagged, "you have twenty-nine days."

Ten

After his first formal supper with Viv, Miles decided to forestall dining together. He wanted no more part of forced conversations and averted eyes. Kissing her had been just as astonishing as he remembered. No, *more so*. He couldn't recall many times they had kissed without alcohol staining his tongue.

Now he had twenty-six days to earn her trust. And at that moment, he didn't trust himself to keep his hands where they needed to be. What a torture, this task of not touching. If that was what dining together meant, then he would kindly decline. Permanently. He'd rather skin himself with a butter knife and make Viv watch.

That evening he intended to take supper at the Kimberley Club. He and Adam strode along the plank wood walkway.

"There is a logic to it, isn't there, my lord?"

The setting sun took the day's warmth with it, as autumn overtook summer. "What's that?"

Adam grinned. "The walking."

"What was it Wordsworth said? 'A respite to this passion, I paced on with brisk and eager steps.'"

"Wordsworth never walked in Cape Colony after dark."

Adam eyed the city's secretive corners, where bold, wild dogs slunk in from the desert to forage along the outskirts of town. Birds added their melodies to the air, and in the far distance, the grunting call of a large animal sent a strange shiver up Miles's forearms.

"A rhinoceros?" he asked. "Or perhaps it's one of those massive wildebeests that put Spanish bulls to shame."

"Or a lion."

"Nonsense. Although, there is a certain thrill to living in a place where being *eaten* is an actual possibility."

Adam grimaced. "Thrill isn't the word I'd use."

Young shadows stretched sideways across the road. Soon the changing shift at the Hole would provide an exchange of men—diggers going home, guards heading down to work—but few other people walked after dark.

"Let's call my impulse toward exercise a fair alternative to pugilism."

His quirking grin was all too predictable, but Miles never held that against his manservant. From Adam, predictability was like having a firm, steady wall at his back. Dependable and unflinching. "Feeling the urge to punch something, my lord?"

"Kicking would be fine, too."

The urge had raged within him for weeks, like a lad throwing a wild tantrum. And why not? After all, he could do just short of murder and still retain his title. Kimberley could take nothing from him, while providing the unpredictable vigor England never had.

His rebellion of choice was to flaunt what so many others yearned to acquire. In London, that commodity had been respectability. Here, where fortunes could literally be picked up off the ground, he possessed what so many rich entrepreneurs envied: heritage. A noble bloodline. And connections as thick as a wall of ivy. So he paid little heed to neatness, and he walked—but not to become the talk of Kimberley. Let them try to negotiate with a man who seemed capable of wasting so much. Then they would never grasp what he truly valued.

"And my role tonight, my lord?"

"Eyes and ears, as always. If the disparity between my appearance and my status is any indication, I assume that the major players will not be readily apparent. Which of these fat cats has a wallet to match his talk and reputation? And which sly snakes are waiting to strike? That's what we must learn, and quickly."

A faint trace of sweat lined his collar when he arrived, the only proof of his ungentlemanly mode of transport. The large, rather exotic club, with its high gates and wraparound verandah glowing with a dozen gas lamps, looked particularly ostentatious. Most buildings in Kimberley admitted that the plateau's harsh conditions would be their eventual ruin. Not this one. Its girth alone proclaimed that it was a thing of wealth, grandeur, and permanence.

"Adam, do you have any idea how much money is at stake in this venture?"

"No, my lord."

"Just over two hundred thousand pounds sterling."

Adam's pale blue eyes widened, then he whistled low and long. "And here I thought you were just in it for her."

Cutting his manservant a sharp look, Miles fought a grimace. "No need to be *that* bold with your counsel. But yes, Vivienne figures into my intentions, just as her maid figures into yours." A grin was easy to indulge upon seeing Adam's amazement. Rarely had Miles been in a position to take the patient man by surprise. "You'll earn five percent of whatever I do, which means you can marry young Chloe in high style, if that's what you want."

"Your word, my lord?"

"My word," he said, offering his hand. "Now go find what dirt lurks beneath all this frippery."

With two fingers to his brow in a mock salute, Adam strode on ahead where he would join the other valets for gossip, gambling, and cheap gin. The perfect place to learn what even Miles could not.

Carriages came and went outside the entrance gate, disgorging men in all their evening glory. Miles observed their arrivals from his place across the street, momentarily donning the cloak of anonymity he'd worn at the way station. As on that day, he prepared to do battle.

In the coolness of the fading day, Viv stood in her so-called garden and surveyed the work that needed to be done. Must everything in Kimberley be such a tremendous challenge? But after the many shocks and surprises she had endured since disembarking at Cape Town, she was happy to be back among familiar tasks.

This certainly wasn't her garden in New York. Would wisteria grow here? Or lilac? She wanted blooming flowers and fragrant scents, but she hardly knew where to begin. What would grow in this climate? Perhaps the town's only bookshop, which she had visited to purchase industry trades and newspapers from New York and London, would have a guide to local flora and fauna. From what she'd observed, however, activities that didn't pertain to mining held little interest for the citizens of Kimberley. The entire population was obsessed.

She felt on the verge of joining them. Learning about the native environment might take the edge off her rabid thirst for answers. She had seen a small antelope-like creature only a few minutes before, and bugs of all kinds roamed the soil. Especially spiders. Which were useful? Harmless? Poisonous?

But starting completely anew was one of her specialties. Entering a French prison with her mother and leaving it an orphan, only to be adopted by William Christie. Or marrying Miles and undertaking the colossal task of winning over London. Those had been changes. This was merely a matter of reading and applying new knowledge. Insects and plants and little antelopes would soon have proper names, and she might even be able to think of the manor as her home.

Playing house. With Miles.

No, she was simply resuming her love of gardening. To forget him, if anything.

But how could she? Right at that moment, he was at the mysterious Kimberley Club, doing God-knew-what in the name of business. Likely, he did what he wanted in the name of his own pleasure.

She hoped that wasn't true. He had been the one to suggest a divide-and-conquer strategy, which was perfectly viable in practice. Only, it meant trusting him. He had never been reliable, unless it came to disappointing her quiet hopes. With the town's most powerful entrepreneurs cloistered in a men's club, her ability to conduct financial affairs on an equal footing would be radically curtailed. On the docks and at that marauded way station, she'd needed Miles because he was a man. He could protect himself with wit and words and, if necessary, with his fists and a whip. Now even backroom negotiations fell within his domain. Part of her had been unwilling to believe the extent of her dependence.

Frustrated, she tugged off her gloves and knelt in the center of the twenty-by-twenty-foot patch of ground. The modest plot of land was bordered by a whitewashed wooden fence. There, beneath the gleaming white manor's grandeur and high, sloped roof, she would have shady cover in the morning. That would mean ample time to work before the sun became too strong overhead. By midday, any plants she cultivated would thrive in full brightness. A perfect arrangement.

The previous owners apparently hadn't thought so. They had given up on any attempt at maintaining order. Weeds and tangled vines covered her to the waist, and she couldn't tell the cultivated plants from the wild ones. The odd bloom, so rare now with autumn's early push, seemed a useless achievement. But that was how to proceed. A little at a time. Small victories.

Oh, how she had missed tending her plants, nurturing the floundering ones to health and bringing the healthy ones to full splendor. Turning this patch of land into a garden was within her purview, unlike the challenges of the business, which would demand all of her concentration with no promise of results. Diamond prices were slipping. Everyone knew it. No matter how many times she had looked at the books over the past few days, she reached the same conclusion: the brokerage was failing.

And Viv had no idea how to stay solvent. That they could fail after investing an eventual two years of hard work was enough to squeeze her heart in a vise.

Perched just east of town on a slight rise, the two-story manor house overlooked the whole of Kimberley. Neighbors along that same rise were all mine owners, brokers, and bankers, having scouted and claimed the grandest views. Only if she held very still could she detect the constant rattling drone of metal chipping away at rock. It was always there, ceaseless, but less intimidating from such a distance.

At least she was standing in a derelict garden, not dragging rocks out of the ground with her bare hands.

I will not fail.

Although the light was fading, she scrubbed her fingers into the soil. Cool. Sandy on top. A hint of water lurked just beneath the surface—the last vestiges of the summer rainy season.

A noise caught her attention. She stood upright, hands behind her back as if caught without gloves by her strict governess. "Who's there?"

"Mr. Kato, my lady." He stepped away from the shadows at the base of the manor and into the purpled light. "I didn't mean to frighten you. Forgive me."

His skin was so impossibly dark. The bright whites of his eyes glittered. Something about his features or his expression combined to offer the impression of mirth. He was on the verge of chuckling, and Viv felt the oddest impulse to be offended. By an African.

"I'll forgive you, but only if you tell me why you did not announce your presence."

"Because you are an English lady touching the earth. You took me by surprise."

"As you did me." She brought her dusty hands forward. Dark crescents of dirt lined her nail beds. "Do few English women you know—how did you put it? Touch the earth?"

"None that I have ever seen."

"Are you Zulu?"

"Yes," he said, his voice impossibly deep. "Half, at least. My father was a Dutch farmer. I took a name from my mother's people."

Another bastard. *Like me.* Although she would never admit to such a connection, she felt one instantly with this man so unlike any human with whom she'd ever spoken. Much of her experience with him had been of an impersonal nature. He was dutiful and silent, like a painting in the background. Now she was seeing him as if for the first time.

That had been happening quite frequently in the Cape. Miles had opened her eyes to more than just his true nature.

"How do you know English so well?"

"If a Dutch father is never a part of his son's life, that son has one of two choices. Love all things Dutch—the mystery of a missing parent. Or rebel against it." He grinned then, almost laughing at himself. "I chose the latter. Working in Cape Town for a few years helped as well. Lots of English there."

"But the lure of diamonds . . . ?"

"Perhaps. Or maybe just the lure of something different." He nodded toward her. "I think you know that feeling. His Lordship, too."

"I wouldn't say that at all. I miss my home."

Mr. Kato approached the whitewashed fence and leaned against the gate. Perhaps decorum kept him there, which set him apart from Miles. Then again, Miles had clout and influence to spare. He could burn down the Houses of Parliament and come out of the escapade unscathed. This man, this half-Zulu man who bore whip marks on his back, had no such authority to squander. Like Viv, respectability might be all he had.

"Many people here miss their homes," he said.

"I can imagine. So far away from England and the Netherlands."

Mr. Kato smiled. "And KwaNongma and KwaZulu. Some from even farther away."

"I'm sorry, I don't know those places."

"Much to the east. People from many tribes were lured

here, just like the working men from your countries. A better life." He shrugged, remarkably calm when discussing the sweep of fate across so many varied cultures. "I came to dig for the stones, but soon I was not allowed to lease the land. Then I was an overseer. But soon that was not allowed either. Cape Town seemed better for a time. I wandered. Now that I have returned, I know I will wander again. For now, this is home. That's all home can be."

His quiet words invited a new melancholy into her heart. Viv breathed more gently for the first time in days. She had time. And in the spring, she would transform this small corner of Kimberley into her own paradise. As with all things, hard work would make it happen. Her father had taught her that, but Catrin, her stepmother, had been the one to show her the enjoyment of one's endeavors. She had never believed in work simply for its own sake, or for the sake of material gain. If one chose to support an opera company, one attended the premiere. If one chose to plant a garden, one was afforded the privilege of basking in the bright, sweet blossoms.

Perhaps in all the clamor of arriving in Cape Colony, Viv had lost sight of that simplicity. Yes, she would work hard, and the goal remained a long way off, but there would be little rewards along the way. She knew it.

"Do you know anything about plants, Mr. Kato? Or the insects that thrive here?"

"Some, my lady."

"Please," she said, opening the gate. "I should like any place to start."

After a silent assessment, he nodded once and joined her

in the garden. The spot where she had knelt was nearly the only patch of open soil in the entire enclosure. "These are weeds," he said. "See their sharp leaves? You can tell by the smell like pepper, but I do not know its real name."

Viv looked around and found most of the garden infested with the prickly invaders. She would need gloves after all.

"But this." Mr. Kato knelt next to an inauspicious shrub about one yard high. The plain white shirt he wore stretched across his wide back and seemed to glow in the orange and blue twilight. "This is a sugarbush. Protea, really."

"It doesn't look like much." The leather leaves were dull green. Nearly black bark covered its stumpy trunk and spindly branches. "Does it bloom?"

"Not this one. Well, not yet. It needs years to firm its roots before it can be beautiful. And some grow tall as acacias before they open their first flowers." He looked up at her from where he knelt. "We cannot rush these things. But then the spring comes and the colors come. It will be worth it, my lady. In time."

Her decision made, she said, "Mr. Kato, I understand that my husband hired you for matters of business."

"That is correct."

"Would you consider extending your duties to helping me here?" She knitted her hands together. The new soil did not feel so unfamiliar now. She would adapt and firm up her roots, too. But Mr. Kato only frowned. "Unless, of course, you think the work menial or meant for a woman. I wouldn't want to insult you."

Somewhere during their conversation, she had stopped

thinking of him as an African or even, more specifically, as a Zulu. He was a man, just like any other. And most men had inordinate supplies of pride. She knew even less about his mother's culture than she did about the plants surrounding her ankles. Viv frowned slightly. The last thing she wanted to do was demean him so soon after just having made a tenuous connection.

"I would be happy to," he said at last.

"Then why the hesitation?"

"Because once again you have done something I have yet to see another Englishwoman do."

Rather than correct his assumption that she was, in fact, from England, Viv concentrated on the mystery of her behavior. "And that is?"

"Talk to me without fear in your voice."

Viv exhaled with a tremulous smile. "Perhaps that is because I have known fear, Mr. Kato. And you look nothing like it."

He grinned at that, stood, and shook the dirt from his plain homespun trousers. "Miss Louise made pie."

Wearing a smile she hadn't expected, Viv followed the large African up the back porch stairs and into the manor. Sure enough, Louise had made three berry pies. She sat with Mr. Kato, Chloe, and the other servants and ate as she had always wanted to as a child—until her stomach was full and content.

Eleven

*M*iles *knew what it was* to enter the most exclusive establishments in London, Paris, and New York.

He had grown up among people who knew how to take luxury for granted. Pampered people in pampered lives, teaching him how to squander without thought. People for whom deprivation meant missing a Season or foregoing a fourth hunting trip to a distant cousin's Lake District grounds. If money ever became an issue, there were always eligible sons and daughters to be matched with bourgeoisie looking to step up a rung or six on Society's ladder. His marriage to Viv had been just such an arrangement, designed to keep his father's earldom solvent.

Thus it meant little to climb the wraparound verandah of the Kimberley Club, where men in fine silks and this year's suits sat in small groups around tables inlaid with precious stones. Mild lantern light burnished faces hanging with heavy jowls, affecting suntans that the wealthy tried desperately to avoid. Pipes, newspapers, and tumblers of liquor were abundant, as if they came standard with admission.

Here, unlike the best salons in Mayfair, the only measure of exclusivity was money. Those who could afford to become members were permitted entrance. The diamond aristocracy.

Strolling toward the entrance, Miles inhaled the pungent mix of burning tobacco and hair tonic, newspaper ink and rich leather. He missed some of the finery, but not the shiftless hours lost to gambling and half-remembered nights. Since his arrival, he had become too focused on Africa, the business, and Vivie. He would have been with her at that moment, in her bed—bloody hell, inside *her*—had that been an option. Instead he would play his part. But he did so now with purpose.

A drink would've been nice, though. And a cigar. But she trusted him so little.

He would honor his promise.

"Excuse me, sir, but this club is for members only," said an officious little man. Slightly built and not even as tall as Viv, his fat sideburns sat like caterpillars on his cheeks.

Miles added an extra dollop of Eton to his words as he said, "You must be new."

The caterpillars twitched around a contemptuous sneer. "I'm Morton Crane, personal assistant to Mr. Neil Elden."

"Ah, just the man you're going to introduce me to."

Crane sneered as he took in the lax state of Miles's suit. "If I might have your name, sir?"

No matter his dislike for the more tedious and restrictive aspects of the nobility, Miles very much enjoyed being able to reveal his title to men such as Crane. The ultimate trump card.

"My name is Miles Warren Durham, 9th Viscount Bancroft. As for character references, you might consult my father, the Earl of Bettenford. And when he tells you that I'm a sorry, ridiculous sod unfit for human company, then perhaps my wife's position at the head of the Christie Diamond Brokerage House will suffice. Now send for Mr. Elden so that he might apologize on your behalf."

He tipped his silk top hat and brushed past, leaving Crane and his caterpillars in a fit of apoplexy.

A starched attendant escorted him to a vacant booth. Its dark supple leather embraced Miles and whisked away some of the tension he'd been hoarding. While secluded, the booth's location allowed every opportunity to see who came and went. He grinned to himself, then waived away a waiter who offered to bring him a drink.

Other club members eyed him with that familiar combination of curiosity and decorum. The revelation of his purpose and background would be welcomed but never actively sought. After private inquiries, those same men would smile upon their next encounter. The high-class subterfuge made him spitting mad, in part because he was an active participant in the same stultifying rules, the same trite dance.

He drummed his fingers across the polished tabletop, its wood gleaming with a pale yellow cast. God, he'd known his boredom was slipping dangerously close to complete insensibility, but these past few days made a mockery of all he thought he knew. What he'd already experienced in Cape Colony shone a glaring electric light on the tried-and-true ways of merry old England, revealing ever-widening cracks and scurrying cockroaches. Any endeavor to re-create those same ways here, in a pockmarked wasteland, seemed even more ridiculous—here, where men changed their destinies by unearthing diamonds the size of strawberries.

Maybe that was the appeal, knowing fate was not set in Kimberley. Fate for him, most recent in a procession of spendthrift viscounts and monstrous earls, had been set since birth. For a second time Miles could claim the opportunity to make himself and his future into something unexpected. Viv had been his first revelation. She'd shown him that life was none so predictable.

A fair-haired man wearing immaculate evening dress approached Miles'ss table, his gait and posture assured. Built more like a plowman than a banker, he maintained an expression poised in a place of neutral friendliness. He greeted other club members with casual nods but didn't slow. Youth and rough good looks were to his credit, but new money was new money. White, straight teeth and hair tonic would never disguise that fact.

"You must be Lord Bancroft," he said, extending his hand when he reached the booth. "I'm Neil Elden, your servant."

Miles stood and bowed, leaving Elden's hand hovering uselessly in midair. The man must have recognized the extent of Miles's displeasure because he adjusted his ascot and offered a conciliatory smile.

"I'm on the Board of Directors here at the Kimberley Club," Elden said, "and I make a point of personally welcoming our distinguished members. Forgive me, but I've been away in Cape Town on colonial business."

Usually one for glib replies, Miles took a rare cue from his father and checked the urge to fill the silence that followed. The Earl of Bettenford would've swallowed his own tongue—or the tongue of a three-days-dead hound dog, for that matter—before making social interactions more comfortable for commoners. One only had to look to Viv and Miles's wedding as an example: the aged earl, nearly bankrupt but flush with aristocratic pride, had refused to drink when Old Man Christie lifted his glass. What an auspicious start *that* had been.

If Miles were to maintain the appropriate impression of wealth and entitlement, he needed to cultivate that same callousness.

"Please forgive Crane," Elden continued. "He protects this place with a zealotry that deserves its own place of worship. We knew you'd arrived in town, of course—this community is too small for privacy. But, well, appearances can be deceiving."

"Indeed." Miles offered a wide, impervious grin. "Then let's start again, shall we?"

Elden slid into his seat with no show of relief; he'd expected to be forgiven.

"And your wife is the new manager of Christie Brokerage, is she not?" He signaled the bartender, then pulled a cigar case from his breast pocket. Miles declined his offer. "The rumor mill here churns out as many tall tales as the mines produce diamonds."

"Yes, she's been afforded management of the Christie."

"As that I own a controlling stake in the Lion's Head

Mine, I am one of your most loyal suppliers. I should like to be apprised of any significant changes to the business model."

"Changes?"

"Changes that may affect my revenue-yield."

"I see," Miles said. "And I should like the opportunity to come into an industry and learn its pace before being pressed for details. Forgive me if I ignore your curiosity. For now."

The man blinked, a show of surprise that gratified Miles. Good. He considered it fair return for the half-truths Elden conjured. Something didn't add up.

A waiter brought a bottle of scotch. Elden played the gracious host, pouring two glasses and sliding one to Miles. Then he lit his cigar and settled back against the stuffed leather bench. "I like you, Bancroft."

"I can hardly believe that you do. But that's no skin off my back because I don't like you either." Miles circled his finger along the top of his tumbler. He grinned. "At least not yet."

Elden laughed, but the wariness in his expression was just what Miles had wanted to see. Keeping him off guard might provide time enough to discover why he grated on Miles's nerves. The oily, rehearsed cadence of his speeches? The earlier assumption that he would be acquitted of any social offense? Or that by any accepted yardstick, he appeared a perfect gentleman?

Miles didn't believe in perfect gentlemen.

Especially not when Elden was so obviously self-made

and grasping at every opportunity to keep the power he'd amassed in Kimberley.

"Well, aren't you the interesting chap? No matter, Bancroft. I'll await official news from the brokerage. I can be patient. And you're welcome here, as you well know. We can't afford to let the public think that we're anything less than a unified front."

"How's that?"

"Kimberley is a bizarre little wart, as you've probably assessed." He exhaled smoke, providing Miles with a sudden understanding as to why Viv detested the things. It wasn't just the smell and the ash, but the arrogance—the theatrics of it. "We have Africans working alongside proper Englishmen." He smiled. "And women running brokerage houses."

"Apparently."

"Society here is a muddle of broken rules and ignored conventions. The least we can do is establish a place of refuge for those of us who deserve our luxuries and our privacy."

"Interesting," Miles said. "It appears to me that you pick and choose."

"Oh?"

Miles pushed the tumbler of scotch toward the center of the table. "My father clings to the old ways, you see. He's a snobbish prig that way, but his title endows his opinions with more weight than those held by commoners. To his thinking, your use of the word 'we' in any context would be cause for offense. And he'd drive a stake through his own heart before taking his scotch with a new money aspirant."

He stood and matched the brittle, mirthless smile Elden

wore. "Now," Miles said, "there are a few new faces here tonight that I do not recognize. And since I'm no such stickler for my father's petty conventions, perhaps you'd be so good as to make my introductions?"

Viv wasn't consciously waiting up for Miles. No, that wouldn't do at all.

But when he arrived home well past midnight, banging open the front door and slamming into his suite across the hall, his dramatics did nothing to disturb her sleep. How could it when she had yet to close her eyes?

Instead she sat propped against her headboard, reading a pamphlet on gemstone grading standards. The lamplight on her bedside table wavered with the puff of a breeze. Outside, cooing quail and guinea fowl—native fauna Mr. Kato had helped her identify—added to the sounds of dry, swishing leaves and the clicking needles of acacia trees. And always the hum of insects. Day and night, they created an unsettling symphony of nature in all its beauty and peril.

She had been resolutely setting the pamphlet aside, ready to unfurl the mosquito netting, when Miles knocked on her bedroom suite door.

Knocked. Not pounded like a bored drunkard looking for sport.

Curious, she smoothed her nightdress and touched the cap that concealed her hair. The high neckline and tiny buttons would keep her covered, but no amount of fine linen would keep her safe. Though loath to admit it, her body yearned for his. Her mind could concentrate on little else.

The hypnosis he managed over even her most determined efforts was just as frustrating as stuffing her brain with fresh terminologies.

Her stepmother, Catrin, had charmed her otherwise abrasive father through a combination of humor, bustling energy, and firm tranquility that Viv desperately envied. She felt no such calm as she crossed on silent feet. Thick carpeting absorbed her nervous energy and tickled her soles.

Upon opening the door, she found him standing as recklessly as her imagination had promised. He pushed past her and closed them in together.

But always with Miles, the truth quickly overwhelmed what meager fantasies she permitted.

"You *reek*," she said.

He yanked open his ascot, ditched his collar, and undid three buttons, as if purposefully sinking to her lowest estimations. "I spent the last six hours in a club where the men drink like syphilitics and smoke like bonfires on Guy Fawkes Night. Of course I reek."

Suddenly all she could see was skin—his neck, his forearms, a flash of flat, hard belly as he yanked one shirttail free of his trousers. He raked his hair into snarled disarray, deconstructing what remained of his gentlemanly mien.

He settled on the high-backed chair next to her bed. His spread-eagled legs and lax dress mocked the chair's dainty floral print and prim construction. He owned every space, no matter how diverse. The world would conform to his standards, never the other way around.

"What I mean is that you've been drinking."

"No, I have not. Not a drop. Not a cigar." He wiggled his eyebrows. "And not even a single whore."

Viv flinched. "Then why act this way?"

"So I can prove it to you."

"Pardon me?"

"You wouldn't believe me if I'd come home as somber as an undertaker fresh from the Queen's funeral." He let a lazy, antagonizing smile shape his mouth. Viv watched, enraptured, as he touched his tongue to his lower lip. "Admit it."

"I'll do no such thing. Men who are sober come home and go to bed. They do not barge into their houses as if storming the Bastille."

"Men who are married generally have the option of going to bed with their wives, but I defy that convention, too. I'm an original several ways over."

"And how am I supposed to believe you?"

Miles stilled. He hadn't been moving, per se, but the energy he gave off vibrated around him like a cloud of bees. At Viv's question he peeled his long, negligent body out of the chair and strode forth until her back bumped the closed bedroom door.

"This is about trust, isn't it, Viv? I understand. I do." He touched the pulled thread embroidery banding her nightcap and smiled softly. Then he propped both hands flat on either side of her head, forging a cage with his body. "But by that rationale, you must let me establish trust before you can accuse me of breaking it."

"We tried that once."

"Let me try again."

He absorbed oxygen and common sense. Viv wanted to dig her nails into something to relieve the tension snapping in her chest, but the nearest thing to claw was Miles. His forearms, she thought, with their dark hair and sinewy new muscles. No careful restraint this time. She craved a kiss that meant hands and arms and whole bodies.

"What do you have to offer, my lord?" She had wanted to come across as haughty but her words were too breathless. She sounded like an ingenue negotiating a peck on the cheek with her first suitor, not a fully grown woman setting the terms of a seduction.

"You could make inquires at the club. Poll the waiters and the barmen, if you like. Ask that snake Neil Elden what an aristocratic snob I am for having refused to drink with him." He grinned. "I admit, that was actually a rather enjoyable bit of restraint on my part. But of course, men cannot be trusted, and perhaps they would all be lying for me."

"Wait, you spoke to Mr. Elden? What is he like?"

"Conceited. New money. Quite handsome. Better watch yourself, Vivie. He could turn your head."

"I have *never* strayed."

"Neither have I."

She laughed in his face. "No matter what means you have in mind for proving your abstinence this evening, you could *never* prove that. Stumbling out of a whorehouse is damning evidence to your discredit."

Rather than grimace, Miles tilted his head to one side, his expression pensive. "It all goes back to trust, Viv. I said as much. A little at a time, I should think."

She much preferred his teasing—so much easier to rebuff than unexpected sincerity. But neither did he deny the behavior she had accused him of perpetrating. Old disappointments battled with the better man he seemed intent on becoming.

"So, asking those at the club is off the calendar," she said. "How will you do this thing?"

He leaned closer until she could smell his breath. She strove to concentrate, to detect whiskey and smoke there, but she was too busy trying to ignore how near his mouth was to hers. "You're going to kiss me," he said, his words a delicious, rumbling promise. "Like you did in the street and overlooking the wide Karoo. And you're going to enjoy it just as much."

"Hardly."

"You are. And you're going to use that delectable pink tongue of yours and taste me."

Viv shivered. She looked for any means of escaping his mesmerizing ease, but her legs wouldn't move. Her knees had turned to porridge. The temptation he offered was as old as time—but it was not forbidden. He was her husband. They had been betrothed with all the romance of a business negotiation, but in the eyes of God and man, they were wed.

She could have him. If she wanted.

But that would be the beginning of the end. The respectable stability she had aspired to for so long would never be hers.

"I will do no such thing," she said thickly, though unable to look away from his lips. So close now.

"You will. And when you taste nary a drop of whiskey nor a hint of cigar smoke, you'll have to believe that I've kept my word."

"Tonight, perhaps."

"Is that an invitation, my dear? Because I could come back again and again." He placed the gentlest kiss on the apple of her left cheek. "And again." Then the other. "Until you believe me."

Viv closed her eyes. Oh, but he had always been able to deliver such pleasure. His voice, the scent of him—apparent now under the clouding smoke on his clothes—conspired like an opiate to muddy her thinking. The promise of another stupefying kiss was even more tempting. She breathed past a hot ache that radiated out from her belly. Only the wall held her upright.

"Vivie," he whispered against her mouth. "Kiss me."

Twelve

You promised me a month."

Miles grinned against his wife's mouth, half out of abject pleasure—the manic thrill of anticipation—and half mocking himself. They were bargaining over a kiss. Yet another simple, charged, *erotic* kiss. What a farce. Yet he'd never been more intoxicated by the chase.

"I heard no such protests the other day. In fact, if I recall correctly, I needed to hold down your hands so you wouldn't undress me in the street."

"Stop it. You promised!"

"One month, yes," he said, "until I climb into your bed or drag you into mine. Or perhaps we won't make it to a bed at all. We'll be so desperate for one another that any surface will do. But that doesn't mean we cannot negotiate other . . . pleasures."

"Leave me be," she said, her plea a breathy whisper.

He pushed more boldly into her space, his forearms tight, his cock hard and impatient. "You started this. Now prove me wrong, if you're so blasted confident in your appraisal. Find me steeped in scotch and smoked like a cod."

"No."

"Coward."

The gold in Viv's magnetic hazel eyes had brightened, overwhelming the softer green. A severe frown and compressed lips lent righteousness to her expression. An angry valkyrie. She simmered, puffing quick breaths from her nose. Miles didn't know if she was preparing to kiss him or hit him.

Just touch me, Vivie.

He half believed that when she did, she did so out of spite—simply to surprise him.

She tipped her mouth upward and dove in. No timid touch. No hesitant exploration. She gripped his forearms, nails gouging his skin, and kissed him like an invasion. Any talent for breathing escaped him. She was bolder than he remembered, her tongue more aggressive, her lips more assured. Denying each other this beautiful heat seemed a capital crime. He should taste her hot essence and feel the generous blending of their bodies every night. Every fresh dawn.

It would never be enough.

Miles kept his hands planted firmly on the wall bracing her back, lest he whisk her into bed. Yet again, no hands. What an exquisite torture. Instead he devoted himself entirely to their kiss, foregoing the distractions of breast and hip and thigh. This was Viv, his wife, the one he'd lost. And she'd given in. He would never tire of such a gorgeous victory.

She tilted her head, deepening her attack as if daring him to relent.

She should have realized how close dares came to gambling. This exhilarating kiss mimicked the thrill of outplaying an opponent, finding crevices of weakness and spreading them wide. Miles gave up on the futility of not touching her. With quick fingers to aid his questing lips, he glided down the row of buttons that fronted her nightgown.

Three. He would permit three buttons.

Expecting Viv to stop him with each unfastened pearl, he revealed the buttery soft skin of her throat, then the hollow at its base, then the gentle upper swell of her breasts. He kissed her with an open mouth, greedy for the sweetness of each new treasure. Soft moans and her clutching hands urged him without words and tunneled through his best intentions. Another seed pearl slipped free of its buttonhole. With the strong sweep of his tongue, he worshipped one perfect nipple. Viv arched on a gasp. She found his hand and pressed it against the delicate weight of her left breast.

Such an unexpected invitation.

Miles suckled until she writhed beneath his intensifying licks and nips. That sensitive flesh beaded against the softest touch of teeth. He palmed her breast with one hand and grabbed fistfuls of linen with the other, yanking the material up, up, toward her thigh. Sliding beneath that diaphanous fabric was as easy as nuzzling his way to her other nipple. Only the thin cotton of her drawers separated the questing tips of his fingers from the hot welcome he would find between her legs.

Was she as wet for him as he was hard for her? Needing to know, he cupped her mound and pressed his index finger between her concealed lips. Viv's hands tightened in his hair. He should have winced at that sharp pain, but he was too busy relishing her madness, her need, her body's undeniably slick response to his attention. He smiled against the under slope of her breast and licked upward, all the way to the sensitive spot behind her ear.

"Now feel how much I want you," he rasped.

He grasped her backside with both hands. Bodies flush, he ground his aching shaft against her hip. He could take her right there, banging the door off its hinges for anyone to hear. Let them listen. He and Viv made incredible music.

But her muscles had seized. She became utterly motionless, no matter the quivering hum of desire he felt coursing through her still. Barely more than a whisper came her plea, her command: "Stop, Miles."

He could have lingered, his forehead pressed to hers, their exhales mixing as the world returned, but he needed a quick withdrawal. Break away. End this *now*, before he went back on the word he needed her to trust.

He straightened completely and looked down. What he saw nearly thrust him to his knees.

Viv's eyes were dark, hungry, ripe with passion. Drowsy lids made her appear even more vulnerable, more sensual than ever. Her secrets and her lust were equally shadowed by burnished gold lashes. The tender flesh of her rosy, parted lips was slightly swollen and red from his stubble. A high blush stained her cheeks as if with the juice of a berry.

She was delicious, so tempting, and stricken by a look of wonder that left him humbled.

The eager fingers that had tangled in his hair slackened before retreating entirely.

With a heavy shudder, Miles wanted to throw up his hands and stalk out of the room. Why? Why did she hate this so much?

Or was it him? The question hit him like a brick to the skull. Had he really damaged her regard with such relentless skill as to engender true hatred?

He couldn't remember. There existed huge swathes of time that had been simply . . . erased. Drinking, gambling, an abiding boredom—they were a curtain over whatever initial hope or sentiment she had brought to their union.

Rather than let Viv's indifference get the better of him, he made a show of examining the crescent-shaped gouges along his forearms. Her mouth became a thin white line. The becoming blush drained away. Her wonder was gone, as was any residual anger. Now came regret. He could've dictated the turn of her passion, even after all this time.

Nothing had changed.

"Satisfied?" he asked.

She swallowed. "Yes."

"Hardly. Neither of us are."

He ushered her away from the door and opened it, allowing himself only one glance back. She stood three feet away; he would need to take a step to touch her again. His pride wouldn't permit it, not when crows of doubt feasted on his confidence. What if some things couldn't be fixed?

"Forgive the intrusion, Lady Bancroft." He bowed, his back stiff and his chest aching. Not to mention the pulse throbbing in his cock. "Good night."

"Lady Bancroft?"

Viv looked up from her ledger to find Mr. Smets standing in the doorway. "Yes?"

He smiled as if to say *I'm humoring you.* After nearly two weeks she'd become accustomed to it. "You asked that I retrieve you just before three o'clock. That would be now."

"Ah. Thank you, Mr. Smets." She indicated the journals and account books open on the table. "Will you leave these as they are, please? I'll return tomorrow."

"Of course, my lady."

Careful to keep dust from darkening the watercolor lilac silk of her day gown, she followed Mr. Smets down the stairs to the front lobby. James and Franc, the men who were as much a fixture in that room as the floorboards, looked up from their hand of poker and waved.

She stepped into an early April unlike any she'd ever experienced. The silvered twilight of days growing shorter put her more in mind toward Christmas. The seasons were backward but not unpleasant. Young Jamie Shelby would light a fire upon her return that evening. She would curl up with her manuals and notes, taking supper in her room. Avoiding Miles.

No matter. He was avoiding her, too.

The process of unpacking—establishing order in the midst of chaos—had kept her busy, almost happy. Very few of the items she brought from New York had been damaged by the transatlantic crossing. They layered memories and security over unfamiliar expanses. This town would be her home, at least for now. Then, every night, she expected the worst. But Miles behaved with perfect decorum. She couldn't have asked for a better arrangement.

Seething under the surface, ruining her satisfaction, ran twin currents that robbed her of breath and sleep and peace. Soon he would demand his reward. And she was disappointed that he hadn't done so already.

She dreamed of him every night, but rather than becoming more explicit, more arousing, her dreams left her hollow. He might kiss her on the forehead, then turn and walk away. Or he would press his lips to the back of her hand. That was all. Never the pleasure she craved, the closeness she would permit only in her most ridiculous fantasies. She awoke as restless as always, but a softer, impenetrable layer of grief left her shaking.

She could trust him again. Make that choice. A leap of faith to honor the man he seemed intent on becoming.

But dear God, such a risk.

On a hard shiver, she put Miles out of her mind and she set off toward Sileby's Tea Room. Walking through Kimberley had lost some of its novelty but none of its peculiarity. Africans claimed the same right to its sidewalks and markets as did women wearing Worth gowns to equal Viv's ensemble.

Granted, the Africans needed to produce work papers whenever stopped by a constable, and their permission to live within the city's confines depended on their employment. Failure to comply with either law meant jail time and expulsion from town. Without access to the diamond fields, those men would have no means of providing for families whose nomadic lifestyles had been almost entirely curtailed by mining interests.

The more she learned about her new residence, the less she liked it.

Upon arriving at Sileby's, Viv tugged the buff kid gloves buttoned at her wrists.

Make it look easy.

Whenever she felt uncertain, she remembered Catrin's words. Such a kind, dear counter to her father's bold demands and thundering ambition. Together, they had made quite the team, with Catrin smoothing over with polite decorum what Sir William's wealth could not. It's never easy, Catrin had said. *But you can make it look that way.* She'd repeated them often throughout Viv's life, when lessons in deportment and language became such a trial, or when missing her real mother burned like hot embers on her skin.

Viv opened the white French doors and breezed inside. Few things in life changed. Perhaps only the scenery. From Paris to Kimberley—with New York and London in between—she had become a practiced pretender.

Despite a small glimmer of apprehension, this appointment with Lady Galeworth was no great challenge. Viv hadn't traveled in vaunted circles since leaving England, but she had no fear of forgetting her way. If Miles's mother, the late Countess of Bettenford, had not spotted Viv as a little French urchin, no one would.

If anyone ever did, not even Sir William's name or wealth would protect her.

"May I help you, ma'am?" The striking young hostess wore a functional white gown and apron, the lace of which matched her cap.

"I'm Lady Bancroft. I have an appointment to take tea with Lady Galeworth."

"Of course, my lady," she said, switching easily to the proper form of address. "This way, if you please."

Viv followed her through the tea parlor, catching details like pieces of a distant melody. The wildness of the previous few weeks made Sileby's calm manners and elegance too pretty to be real. Fine bone china clinked as women set cups to saucers. Light streamed through a dozen beveled windows along the parlor's street-facing west wall and danced through gauzy curtains. The strong, comforting scent of freshly brewed tea and warm scones teased Viv with memories of security.

This is where she wanted to belong. Such opulence had been her privilege while her father yet breathed and while she'd lived as Miles's wife. Long days of pouring over registers and learning the diamond trade would pay off. Enduring this redoubled loneliness while sharing the same space as Miles . . . that would pay off, too. It had to.

"My lady?"

The hostess presented Viv to Lady Galeworth, a woman in her middle fifties. Steely gray hair was piled and circled in a way that made her head look ready to topple. Strings of a four-tier pearl choker nearly covered the sagging skin of her stick-thin throat, and a fat, perfect diamond dropped from the bottom strand. The ostentatious necklace screamed a contrast to her black mourning gown. Watery deep brown eyes watched Viv with unconcealed curiosity.

Well, that was different. Viv couldn't have located curiosity in Miles's mother had she used a compass and a divining rod. The countess had seemed to decide that ignoring the reason for Miles's marriage to a wealthy woman of indeterminate bloodlines was the best course for all involved.

But Viv had persevered, eventually earning the woman's respect and even a few kind words. "She conducts a rather tidy household" had been like benediction—certainly harder to earn than the respect of this baron's widow.

"Lady Bancroft, the pleasure is mine," the woman said. "Trudy, tea, please."

Trudy bobbed a curtsy before exiting. Viv eased into her seat and surreptitiously adjusted her bustle. The table was laden with a selection of dried fruits and petits fours. "Thank you for the invitation today. I appreciate your taking the time. I'm still a newcomer to Kimberley."

"Tush," Lady Galeworth replied. "We do what we can to make our stay here bearable."

"Have you been here long?"

"Nearly five years. Impossible to imagine, but it's true. My younger son owns the Galeworth Mine now, since my husband passed on in January."

Trudy returned with the service, poured the tea, and departed without a word.

Lady Galeworth frowned throughout the whole encounter. With an agitated wave of her hand, she seemed to dismiss the entirety of Sileby's and everything beyond its walls. "The sooner we return home, the better. We'll sell our claim and be done with this nightmare."

"What can you tell me about good Society here?"

"Well, that there isn't enough of it." Lady Galeworth munched on a buttered scone and touched her diamond whenever she wasn't fussing with her food. "There's an annual winter gala in August, and the holidays always bring a flurry of calls and social events—although, it never feels like Christmas. Hot and miserable is what it is."

They lapsed into silence as Lady Galeworth ate. Viv drank tea, but she disliked the woman's negativity and found herself short on topics for conversation. She fell back on old habits. "And what of charitable associations, such as those in London? Do ladies here offer aid to the poor or the workers?"

"Perhaps some do." The way the dowager wrinkled her nose explained just what she thought of the idea. "The men and women who come here to work are eager for quick money. They're a prideful bunch with no notion of how to behave properly among their betters."

"Surely they can't all be so terrible. I met a lovely family on the train." With some trepidation, she wondered how Ike and Alice Penberthy had fared since their arrival. Alice would've had no home waiting for her, no servants, no security, while Viv's only duty on that day involved cajoling a pompous old woman. "They seemed hard-working and eager to make a life for their boys."

Lady Galeworth narrowed her liquid brown eyes. "Did they?"

Viv knew a note of hostility when she heard it, and rarely did it need to be so strident to catch her attention. "Of course. They deserve that opportunity if it's available, and our industry—why, Her Majesty's very empire—requires dedicated laborers."

"You are American, aren't you, my dear?"

My dear. Not *my lady*, as was proper. Quite the slight. The baroness's five years in Kimberley must've made her feel quite the grand lady, rarely matched in wealth or status.

Today she was not only matched, but exceeded.

Viv drew her spine to its straightest, most rigid height. "I was raised in America, but my parents were both proud British subjects."

"Your *adoptive* parents."

"Of course," Viv said past the burn of anger in her throat. However, this bitter old crone needed a lesson in manners. "But I don't remember my adoption being an issue when I spoke to Queen Victoria. She's a magnificent woman, really. So generous with her wisdom and perspective. A true credit to our fair sex."

"You've spoken with Her Majesty?"

"On my wedding day," Viv said casually.

Lady Galeworth shaped her lips into an O. "I've only ever seen her from afar at various gatherings. To have actually shared words with the great lady herself, that must have been such an honor."

Viv relayed the most impressive details of the encounter—from Her Majesty's clothing to the blessing that followed—as if it hadn't been one of the most torturously anxious moments of her life. Now she fashioned it into an anecdote to impress a petty minor noblewoman.

Suddenly she understood a little more of Miles's disdain for the entire farce. In London, so intent on fitting in, she had ignored the sycophantic haze that choked every conversation.

The baroness dabbed a napkin at the corners of her puckered mouth. "So after such a grand time in London, what brings you to Kimberley?"

"My father, Sir William, owned the controlling interest in Christie Brokerage. By the terms of his will, I was appointed its manager."

Thin silver eyebrows lifted to comical heights. "You manage it? How is that possible?"

"I am under contract to do so, but by no means do I actually oversee the work." Her tone suggested complete shock. Let people believe what they would. She wanted no enemies among bored widows likely prone to gossip. "My husband, Viscount Bancroft, is delegating the details. I am but a figurehead, although I do enjoy looking at the diamonds. Such beautiful wonders!"

"Aren't they though?" Lady Galeworth stroked her pendant. "Completely intoxicating."

Testing the waters, Viv leaned closer. "But not everyone

can afford our indulgences. Surely you can understand my sympathy for women in reduced circumstances. They are here against their will, much as we are."

"I suppose," the baroness said. "There is a small women's auxiliary, but it is in woeful disrepair. As I mentioned, few of these people actually deserve our sympathy. We really must band together against the miners' demands."

Although Lady Galeworth's callousness made her stomach churn, Viv kept up her sweet smiles. "Oh?"

"The mine owners pay comparable wages in order to keep the workers from holding out for more. Any relenting on that point would foster an anarchy of greedy salary demands. It's us or them. Little room for sentimentality."

Viv smiled privately, realizing that the baroness knew more about her son's business than she initially let on. "Ah, well. Lucky thing I have nothing to do with that world."

As Lady Galeworth chatted on about the best dressmakers and hatters, Viv realized the source of her amused thoughts. She was bored and, quite frankly, unimpressed. This was the societal victory she'd worked so hard to attain? Mundane banter with a self-important old biddy?

She missed sparring with Miles.

A headache sprouted across her forehead. What a ridiculous turn of events. But there it was—the hunger for a greater challenge. She remained fascinated by the man he had become since their separation. Someone . . . *other*. Intriguing. Still dangerous, but perhaps worth the risk.

"Oh, my, I hadn't realized the time." She smoothed her interruption with a flutter of apologetic titters. "I really *must* dash, your ladyship. But I would very much like to invite you to take tea with me at the manor. Please say you'll come."

Lady Galeworth's spidery fingers touched the back of her hair. "My lady, I would be honored. Truly. To receive an invitation from a woman of your standing—now *that* is proper society!"

As Viv left the parlor, she stifled a sigh. Already something had shifted inside her. When had the refinements of a good, secure life actually *bored* her? How was she to process that surprising revelation? At least she had left the influential Lady Galeworth in a state of rapturous awe. Now Viv needed time to think . . . and perhaps a little more time with Miles.

Thirteen

Miles crawled out of the claw-footed tub and dried his body. The hour hand had barely crept past the nine. He used to slither home at dawn and sleep until early afternoon, as if the habits of the aristocracy constituted an entirely different species. *Homo sapiens nobilis.* Kimberley pounded with the sense that a minute left sleeping past sunrise would produce a missed opportunity. London, for all of its bustle and enterprise, had never affected him that way.

The fragrant morning air sluiced across his damp skin until every pore prickled to attention. Water dripped from the tips of his hair, sprinkling along his forehead and down under the plush collar of his robe. He grabbed the towel and indulged in a deep scrub down to his scalp. Adam had already left for his morning rounds. Behind-the-stairs espionage, they'd dubbed it.

Feeling restless and aroused, Miles padded the short distance to his bedroom window. The burden of the business was a terrifying responsibility. But the misery of living so near to Viv and not having her—that was eating him alive. His skin pulled away from his body when they stood together, aching to be nearer. The anticipation was rendering him less than human, an animal trapped in a box and left out in full sun. Suffocating.

Down below, she stepped into view. Sunlight transformed her into a golden angel. Rich, buttery skin and, dear Lord, a figure that promised both the bliss of heaven and the wicked sins of hell. Miles appreciated the shape women's fashions produced, with plumped breasts, tiny waists, and padded bustles. All very artful. But he'd strip her bare at the merest nod of permission, indulging in the curves God, not a dressmaker, had bestowed.

Everything would change after they made love. He would purge her from his system and be done with the wanting that crept toward mania. To hear her begging and gasping for his every sensual attention would be just the balm to his wounded pride. Then, money in hand, they could part ways. His younger brother, Thomas, already had three strong sons. Their noble line would continue.

So Miles would be free. Free to . . .

Bloody hell, he hardly knew anymore.

Viv was his wife. But he could've no more barged into her room, demanding her surrender, than he could jump off the edge of a building with the expectation of flight.

Artless thief—she'd stolen some part of him, something careless and vital and assured. Soon he would take it back.

A knock sounded at the door. Miles quickly made himself decent and found Chloe standing in the corridor. "Yes?"

"Good morning, my lord." She knotted her hands at her

waist but managed to keep her voice even. "My lady has asked, if you are amenable, that you break your fast with her."

Surprise kept him mute. Surely it must be some game. She would try to wiggle her way out from the terms of their arrangement. She would argue, or even worse, don a patently false smile that hid everything but her disappointment in him.

Or maybe she just wanted to share breakfast.

This is about trust, isn't it, Viv?

Time to put that to the test.

"*My lady, Louise says breakfast* is ready."

Weeks of familiar chores had set Chloe right as roses. And although neither would admit as much, she and Adam spent their spare hours together. They both had a fondness for history that left Viv scratching her head and smiling. She envied their easy conversations and furtive glances. They were new and tentative, yet happy—no matter that their cautious romance blossomed in the most unlikely soil.

But her maid's happiness didn't temper Viv's nerves. "And what of my . . . invitation?"

Loneliness had soaked into her like water into a sponge. Never had she felt more isolated, not even during those first few months after arriving at her father's house—a place of new language, new faces, new expectations. She'd cried herself to sleep every night, until Catrin had taken to singing her lullabies and Alex read to her from a book of mythology far too big for his ten-year-old hands.

Now she was too weary to cry, haunted by the fear that she'd brought all of this on herself. Blaming Miles had become less gratifying than it once was.

Chloe smiled shyly. "His Lordship accepted your invitation, my lady. He's waiting in the sunroom."

Nothing outrageous, and certainly nothing to justify her pulse's sudden jump. Just an ordinary breakfast. After all, they had business matters to discuss. But it felt like a leap of faith rewarded. Maybe regular conversation would help her shed the ache she carried like stones in her heart.

"Thank you, Chloe."

After passing one last glance over the garden, she turned toward the house.

She found Miles in the airy sunroom, his gold-tinted head bent over a broadsheet. His breakfast of toast, dried fruit, and cheese went untouched. At irregular intervals he used a pencil nub to scratch something onto the curling pages of a ledger. Why hadn't she ever realized that he was left-handed? Noticing that detail would be like awakening beside him and studying whorls of dark hair across his chest—fascinating, strangely sinful, and almost more intimate than she could bear.

Watching him became her privilege as a nervous heat radiated from her belly. He made a quiet noise of disapproval and propped his chin on his fist. The pose was reminiscent of a schoolboy fitfully working over his sums. But as he pressed tense fingers against his temples, he was a man again—a man working to the limits of his endurance. Did he have a headache? So soon in the day?

Her throat tightened and her thighs felt as flimsy and weak as meringue. As far as Viv could discern, he'd stuck by his promise to forego his standard complement of vices. Upon returning from his visits to the Kimberley Club, he was always sober. Adam had let it slip to Chloe that Miles never gambled. And he slept every night in the room across from hers.

Not that she dared challenge him on the subject of vices again, not after the last time. Their kiss had ripped her apart. The idea of upholding her end of their bargain left her shaking, nervous, and tingling with an anticipation made of both dread and pleasure.

Who are you? And how long will you stay?

He was Miles, Viscount Bancroft. Whatever his current fascination with Kimberley, he wouldn't be captivated for long. The alternative, that he'd made a serious commitment to the mine's success, *for her*, was terrifying—a far greater leap than simply sharing breakfast.

"Viv?"

She blinked and his face came into focus. Sunlight from the eastern windows streamed over his shoulders, lighting him from behind and casting the details of his aristocratic features in shadow. But his chocolate-dark gaze missed nothing. A knowing smile eased across his mouth. *That* was Miles, all insolence and expectation.

Then it was gone. He finished with his paper, folded it into a haphazard pile of wrinkles, and set the ledger aside.

"Come sit," he said, all business. "We have much to discuss."

Viv took a seat and Chloe bustled in with a fresh pot of tea. She offered a reassuring smile but hastened away as quickly as possible.

"You frighten her, I think," Viv said. She poured tea for them both, then assembled a plate for her repast.

"Do I frighten you?"

"Hardly."

"Uh-huh." He spiked a piece of cheese with a small fork, devilishness sparkling across his expression.

Walking everywhere—that odd, ungentlemanly habit he'd cultivated—had honed his physique. His tan had darkened. Shaving seemed to slip his mind for days at a time. Every night, he arrived home with his ascot askew. Viv had lost track of the times she wondered what it would be like to help him undress at the end of such trying hours, to remove that silk and bare his throat to the fading evening. He would taste of salt and dust. His quiet, throaty moan would be an invitation to feast.

She took a hasty sip of tea.

"Careful there, Viv."

Rimmed with lashes far darker than his sun-touched hair, Miles's keen brown eyes laughed in return, making her blush for such foolishness—and because her thoughts weren't foolish at all. Far from it.

Yet he would end any given encounter with a single word from her lips. He always ensured that she was equally culpable in their trysts. That she hadn't stopped him on so many occasions forced her breath to quicken. He thought it was liberation—unleashing a matched passion. But she couldn't possibly match his passion if he remained unable to give her security.

"I have some interesting news," he said.

Viv used the excuse of swallowing another sip of tea to collect her thoughts. "Oh?"

"Yesterday afternoon, I walked Mr. Kato to the Hole and presented him to the heads of our mining customers. He will provide security for couriers delivering and retrieving diamond shipments from the brokerage. But with the common harassment of Africans, no matter their employers, I needed to impress my will upon them personally."

"Did it work?"

"We'll see, but I have no intention of letting them determine our policies."

"I feel better knowing that men of our own choosing are on the payroll."

He smiled, dark eyes dazzling in the morning sun. "Precisely. Which brings me to my news. Mr. Ike Penberthy has yet to secure adequate employment. The recent slump in prices means the mines aren't hiring as many skilled workers. Even if they could use a man who knows rocks and the like, they won't foot the cost."

"So it's not just us." She sighed and pushed her toast away. "Everyone will suffer if pricing trends continue."

Miles nodded soberly. "I wanted to ask how the books look to you."

He always took her estimations seriously. They *were* partners, fully and devotedly—at least with regard to the business. Was that so terrible? Why spoil it with dreams of more, the kind that teased her as she slept? The backs of his hands were dusted with a light spray of fine, dark hair. She wanted to fold her own hand over his and stroke that hair with her thumb, just to see if it was as soft as she imagined. Another lonely pang tightened in her chest.

"Viv?"

"Oh, the books. Yes. Anything in particular?"

"I don't know if we have means enough to offer him employment, or even a job for him to do. And I don't want it to seem so menial as to be insulting."

The tightness in his voice revealed a level of sympathy Viv hadn't thought him capable of mustering. He *felt* for Ike Penberthy, a clever man with pride and a family to support—a man he never would've noticed had they remained in London.

Impulsively Viv squeezed his hand, giving into the temptation to touch. Nothing more. But how could she not? She understood his sympathy and was moved by it. "We have enough. And with his experience, we're likely to benefit immeasurably."

Miles flicked his eyes—eyes that burned amber in the morning sunlight—toward their clasped hands. He frowned as if trying to recall the last time she'd touched him voluntarily. She couldn't remember either. He disengaged and cleared his throat.

Viv looked away. She was feeling too addled and off-center to make sense of her disappointment.

"I'd like to pay his wife a visit to make sure they're coping," she said. "Perhaps their baby even arrived by now."

"Not alone, please. Take Adam or Mr. Kato."

The grave timbre of his voice made her uncomfortable. Any reminder as to the dangers of their new home had that effect, stealing the security wrapped around her in their sunlit nook. It was all outside, those hazards and filth. But if Alice Penberthy could stand it, fighting for the sake of her boys and her new babe, the least Viv could do was visit.

"I promise," she said.

"Good. Then tell me. Where do we stand? Exactly?"

She couldn't help but sit a little straighter, as she always had when her father valued her abilities and judgment. But with Miles, she could not deny an undercurrent of deeper need. His obvious respect for her mind gave her the smallest hope that one day he would respect all of her wishes.

Unfortunately, she could not give him news to complement the warmth in her chest.

"We are utterly at the whim of the market. Even our best plans could be felled by one good strike outside of the normal rate of excavation. The market would be saturated with new stones and prices would crash. Last year, floods took out two mines and production halted for months. What if they had been our clients? Such extremes would send us beyond the reach of even the most generous creditor." She sighed heavily. "We lack stability. The whole business is built on speculation."

"Sounds more like poker every day. It's a matter of who flinches—and who lets that fear be seen. What of the carbons Smets mentioned?"

"From all I've read, they're nothing more than slag." After

finishing her toast with raspberry jam, she tapped his ledger. "And this?"

"These are the going prices for all of our supplies. Everything is extortionary. The shareholders have set out our operating budget, and I'm not sure it will be enough to see us through the year." He shoved the papers aside as if the very sight turned his stomach. "Your father should've acquired a dry goods company. The best money will be found in the ability to supply those hopeful souls who keep digging."

He sank back into his seat and closed his eyes, hands laced at the top of his head. He looked weary. *And he's a viscount*, Viv reminded herself—a man whose sole pursuits had been, until recently, those of a hedonistic variety.

"What is it?"

The grin he wore made fun of his own failings. "My brain is not built for all of these numbers."

"But you're doing wonderfully." To her surprise, the words came without hesitation or flattery.

He had lovely eyebrows, dark and thick yet perfectly shaped. They dipped in a curious frown. "You're in earnest."

"Yes," she said, her voice tight. "I am."

"Good. Then I know you aren't humoring me when I ask about the books."

Now it was Viv's turn to frown. She always assumed him simply too . . . fickle. What interest would the Viscount Bancroft truly have in figures and accounts payable? But never once had she doubted his capacity. Even during the worst discord of their marriage, he had always been an avid reader and a quick wit.

"Not humoring, my lord," she whispered. "Admiring."

Miles moved slowly—slowly enough to let her back away—but Viv welcomed his palm at her nape and the inexorable way he brought their mouths together. Feeling amicable and open, she accepted his kiss. Not a punishment or a dare. Just satisfaction that they were in this venture together. All of it.

His lips moved with purpose. He countered her moves to fit his hot mouth more securely over hers. Large, graceful hands at the back of her neck stalled any avenue for retreat, but she had no intention of backing away. Not before she had sipped her fill of this marvelous closeness. The public room they occupied, the servants who might walk in . . . she couldn't bring herself to mind. Miles was kissing her. And she only wanted more.

Almost without sound, he pushed back from the breakfast table and sank to his knees, their mouths never parting. In fact, he took the kiss deeper—all tongues and aggressive breaths—as he settled between her legs. Arms made powerful by certainty wrapped around her upper back and bowed her down, down to his level, until the starched lace of her bodice crushed against his shirtfront. Her softness. His hard strength. Viv shivered. Her breasts ached. Her whole body—craved more.

She brought her tongue into the fray, stroking his lower lip. Miles moaned at her acquiescence and pulled her flush. Tension that had been gathering between them snapped her skin and tingled in her blood. This was Miles. Every dirty thought, every wicked impulse, every denied need—he was their personification. That she'd staved him off this long seemed impossible to believe.

Her traitorous heart had settled upon imagining him much more heroic, which was absurd, even dangerous. But perhaps she could be safe if she just let their bodies come together. If this is what they needed to endure one another's company, they would have it. Hope and trust and emotion could be locked away, leaving only the elemental fact that she desired her husband.

The slide of her palms along his jaw was no longer enough. She wanted a glimpse of the body he had forged beneath the African sun. Shoving her hands inside his suit coat, she found a soft cotton shirt warmed by his body. His second moan urged her on. Viv became a twister over an open field, laying waste to the woman she'd worked tirelessly to become. A quick tug on his ascot, his collar, his buttons, and she pushed the fine white shirt over his shoulders.

Miles looked toward the ceiling and swallowed. Such an incredible view—from his taut throat to his flat, ridged stomach. She eased off her chair and knelt with him, belly to belly, and stripped him from the waist up. With her fingertips, she traced the pattern of dark hair around his flat nipples, along his defined pectorals, and down to where it arrowed out of sight. Never had she seen him so bronzed, so robust. Even the pink scar along his collarbone reminded her of the startling violence he'd brought to bear for her protection.

She dug deeper. Nails scored his skin.

Dear God, what am I doing?

Touching. Needing. Scraping every inch of flesh she wanted to lick, then tracing those marks with her tongue. No longer so uncertain, she ran the outside of her hand along the front placket of his trousers. He hissed softly as she traced the hard line of his erection. Bolder, she took gentle hold and squeezed.

He yanked her hand away and pushed her back. His nostrils flared wide. His lips were slightly swollen. Wet streaks over pale red scratches crisscrossed from his collarbones to his lowest ribs.

I did that.

Miles blanked his expression. He stood without preamble, helped her to her feet, and gathered the pencil, ledger, and newspaper. His clothing came next, as if gathering those personal items was just as casual. "Will you dine with me this evening? We can discuss what comes of our meetings with the Penberthy family. And I have an idea for the business. I'd like to share it with you."

How was his voice so remarkably calm? Viv felt ripped open. Her knees barely held her weight. The beat of her heart echoed in her ears and at the apex of her thighs.

"Yes," she managed to say, still dazed. "That would be . . ." She swallowed. "That would be nice."

"Good. Say, the Ford Inn? I'll meet you there at eight."

"All right."

"Well, then." He exhaled tightly. Tension warped his wide bare shoulders. The strong line of his jaw was shot through with stiffness. At least he offered those clues, even if his demeanor was as polite as . . . well, as polite as she'd always desired of her husband.

"I'm off to the Hole to meet with Barnaby's overseer," he said. "We get more slag from them than anyone else. I'm tempted to raise their fees. And then, of course, I must con the Board out of a few more pounds to meet our day-to-day needs." He shook his head. "Uncomfortable business, all of it."

And with that, he departed. Viv sank onto her chair. One silver cufflink caught the sunlight moving across the carpet. She picked it up, although sensation in her fingertips was blunted. Someday soon it would happen. There would be no stopping. She only hoped to protect her heart from what her body so recklessly demanded.

Parched and dizzy with desire, she picked up her cup of cold tea and drank it down to the dregs. Unlike when taking tea with Lady Galeworth, her hands would not stop shaking.

Fourteen

Convincing Ike Penberthy to accept employment at the brokerage hadn't been as difficult as Miles imagined. Two weeks without steady work would do that to a man . . . and his pride.

Make him desperate.

Make him shake and shiver at having a taste of what he desired.

Miles escaped the memory of that morning's heated encounter, just as he had when speaking before the brokerage's Board of Directors. After sweet-talking them with his most effective snake charmer's smile—the one that Viv alone seemed able to resist—he'd gone straight to find Penberthy. As a general rule, Miles put little stock in formal education when push shoved against experience. After all he'd gone to Eton and didn't trust himself to properly tie an ascot. But Ike Penberthy had both. Ignoring such a valuable asset was as wasteful as leaving that pile of carbons to languish in the brokerage's basement.

The niggling idea in Miles's mind would not be quiet.

He walked the silent Cornish miner to the office, intent on making introductions and showing him the ropes. The day was downright chilly—the first cold snap Miles had experienced in the colony. But rather than turning thoughts toward his own slight discomfort, he supposed that the miners in the Hole would eagerly welcome the relief.

As he unlocked the vestibule door and ushered Penberthy inside, he wondered when he had become such a do-gooder.

"Good morning, my lord," Mr. Smets said, rising from his desk. "I didn't expect you to visit today. Your charming wife is more often our company."

"My charming wife is paying social calls this morning."

"Ah, probably for the best."

Miles made sure to take offense on Viv's behalf. She'd been pulling her hair out over the bookkeeping. Money came and went with the irregularity of a bat's flight path. He had ideas and charm and influence, but she had the brain for minutiae he sorely lacked.

He greeted James and Franc where they sat dealing out yet another hand of poker. Did they ever actually work? No, their work was simply maintaining a dependable presence. Few would harass the Christie office as long as their rumps were settled and their eyes intent on a string of five new cards—although the old urge to sit for a hand made him edgy.

No. Focus.

"Mr. Smets, this is Ike Penberthy of Cornwall. I have a special task for him."

"Of course," Smets said, shaking Penberthy's hand. "Your wish is our command."

Now it was Miles'ss turn to find offense. To say he was unused to subtle barbs would be a lie; the nobility made an art form of such means of communication. But he *was* unused to being on the receiving end of sarcasm from a commoner. Deference was generally the order of the day. Although the Cape was Her Majesty's colony, it most certainly was not Britain.

"This is not a whim or a charitable endeavor, Mr. Smets, no more than your position within this firm. I will remind you to watch your manners, sir."

"My apologies, my lord," he said with a quaver to his voice. "Anything I can do to make Mr. Penberthy welcome, please let me know."

"I require only two things from you this morning: a pen and paper, and an escort to wherever you store the carbons."

Smets's eyes bulged slightly. "The carbons? Whatever for?"

"Questions, sir, were not on my list of requirements. Now, if you please?"

The appraiser led Miles and his guest to the basement. Penberthy was like a child who stayed silent and small so as not to attract the attention of a cruel headmaster. That had never been Miles; he'd hurl a spitball or test a fresh new curse word, an ongoing experiment to determine how long his status would protect his backside. Viv had been the first person to stand up to him since his voice changed.

"Paper and pens are upstairs with the bookkeeping,"

Smets said upon unlocking the basement door. "Shall I show you there, too, my lord?"

"Quit simpering, Smets. I want obedience, not slavering. And I'll find the paper myself." He held out his hand for the basement door key, then made a brushing motion. "Off you go. I'll inform you of Mr. Penberthy's responsibilities before I take my leave."

Smets offered a hasty bow and departed. Penberthy was smiling.

"Amused?" Miles asked dryly.

The blond man shook his head. "It must be like magic, being able to do that."

"Pull rank?"

"Yes."

"Absolutely."

They passed through the door and down two more steps to a dark crawl space. The air was replete with cool dampness. "I know where I'll be spending next summer."

"You could sell tickets, my lord."

"If diamond prices keep tumbling, that may be our only recourse." He found a lantern and lit the wick. Like a geological boil, a four-foot pile of carbons swelled up from the center of the tight room. "Well, well. I wasn't expecting quite so many. But this is a boon."

He held the lantern with one hand and scooped up a fistful of carbons with the other. Penberthy extracted a jeweler's glass from his pocket and leaned in to take a look.

"I knew you'd prove useful," Miles said. "How did I know that?"

Penberthy grinned. "You're an astute judge of character?"

"Only across a card table. What do you see?"

Bringing a single carbon close to the lantern, Penberthy squinted into his glass. "I'll need more light to see much of anything, that's for certain."

"You'll have it."

"High-quality carbons, though, my lord. That much I can say straightaway."

"What's the difference?"

Penberthy hummed under his breath, made some grunting, appreciative noise, and then nodded a few times. "Very good indeed. Gem-quality brilliants are graded and valued on their color and clarity, but that says nothing about their durability. They're exceedingly hard, of course, but a glancing blow can crack them along tiny fault lines."

"No good for industry."

"Correct."

"And these?"

"Durable, my lord. Not just hard but with fewer fault lines than I've ever seen. These would grind away slowly, not cleave in two. Some in the Cornwall schools suggested their use for mining, but nothing ever came of it."

Miles examined the carbons he held with a new eye. He couldn't see what Penberthy saw. Instead he pictured something else entirely: a future.

And he had an idea of how to harness it.

"I want you to take your time with this, Penberthy. Sort them by whatever grading system you see fit, catalogue quantities, et cetera. You'll work until the project is complete, or until we run out of funds to pay you."

Relief drained the man of tension. He shook Miles's hand with happy vigor. "I'll get to work right away, my lord."

"Good. I'll find you paper and light."

Miles climbed the stairs in the dark, the image of Penberthy's face still in his mind. The man was relieved, excited, grateful. The job not only suited his talents, but he would have work for weeks. His family would not suffer. That Miles could bring about such a match of individual and purpose leant a queer rhythm to his heart.

The responsibility Penberthy shouldered for the welfare of his wife and children must be crushing. Miles swallowed twice just thinking about it. For all of their ambition, he and Viv would fare well even if they fell short of Old Man Christie's posthumous dare. Her siblings might offer a hand, as would members of his extended family. Worse case, his vote in Parliament would always carry a hefty price tag. Their pride would suffer as poor relations, but they would never know hunger.

If Viv stopped long enough to consider her options, she might admit the same. Her determination stemmed entirely from a desire to leave him again. Permanently this time.

Miles stopped on the top step, shuddering, as if this were the first time he had actually contemplated such a thought. Viv would leave. Or he would leave her—his original plan for revenge. But after what they had shared that morning . . .

It felt like a new start.

"Mr. Smets." Miles was a little breathless upon returning

to the ground floor, but it had nothing to do with physical exertion. "Four more lanterns for Mr. Penberthy."

"Yes, my lord."

"That's more like it."

Miles took the steps two at a time to the upper story and found the bookkeeping room. Leather and stale air reminded him of Christie's library. What had Gareth called it? *A polite dungeon.* This cramped office barely warranted even that denigration, hardly bigger than a closet. He tried to imagine Viv sitting here for hours on end, every day, her delicate neck craned over dusty old volumes and ledgers. To his surprise the scene came easily to mind.

Then he played out a fantasy: he would come to her by surprise one afternoon. Her fatigued eyes would light up upon catching sight of him in the doorway. He would rub the back of her neck with gentle, calming strokes, easing the stiffness. Making love would be a tricky endeavor, what with the cramped space and the men downstairs. But they would manage well enough, whispering and shushing each other like naughty young people evading a chaperone.

Even in such an inauspicious place, his thoughts turned to her.

He checked his watch and found the hour just past two. So much time to fill before their plans for supper, but so much to do.

Out of curiosity as to Viv's labors, he sat at the lone chair and opened a ledger. Her handwriting, neat and distinctly feminine, ornamented the page. But the figures were all business.

Diamond prices.

In fact, diamond prices chronicled by week all the way back to the early part of 1874, when Christie had either established or acquired the brokerage. On a second page waited a set of calculations whereby Viv had predicted their eventual profit or loss based on different variables, as well as their probabilities. Had Christie realized his daughter's capacity? Never one to miss a bargain, Miles suspected that he had.

Their predicament was all there, outlined in Viv's proper script. She had said the market for brilliants was erratic, but he'd never seen the outcome of that volatility with such precision.

He found the paper and pen for Penberthy, gratified that Smets had secured four more lanterns for the crawl space. Then he bid everyone a good day and headed to the bookstore. His niggling idea would not be quiet.

Jamie Shelby hitched the carriage. While Mr. Kato quickly gobbled a hunk of buttered bread for his lunch, Viv tucked a red-checked cloth over the gift basket she'd packed for the Penberthy family. Like Miles's concerns about offering employment to Ike, Viv mulled how to word her offer of aid. The last thing she wanted was to wound Alice's pride.

Viv's own mother had refused charity when it came at too great a price to her dignity, a contrast to her profession that had struck Viv as absurd, even at a young age. To her eight-year-old brain, food was food and coal was coal. Her clamoring stomach and frozen toes had cared not a whit as to which strangers brought gifts, nor as to their motives.

"Ready, my lady?" Mr. Kato asked.

"Certainly."

They boarded the coach with Jamie holding the reins. He was a large boy for eleven years, with thick bones and a neck that would only increase in girth and strength as he matured. Mr. Shelby wanted him in the mines, but their spirited housekeeper refused to entertain the idea until Jamie turned thirteen. Even then, she'd said on many occasions, why send a boy into the Hole when he had perfectly respectable—and frankly safer—employment with Viv and Miles? Jamie's thoughts on the matter remained unknown; the boy hardly ever spoke. But far from being unintelligent, he was observant and quick to perform his duties.

The carriage rattled through town, subjecting Viv, Mr. Kato, and Jamie to pits and wheel ruts enough to loosen teeth.

She grimaced. "I can understand why Lord Bancroft has taken to walking. They'll have electric lights in town before paved roads."

"Not everywhere," Mr. Kato said.

"No?"

He hesitated, squinting ahead toward the downtown's business hub. "Never mind, my lady. It was impertinent."

"I insist. Speak freely." She tilted her bonnet against the sun and tried to catch his eye. The man could be nearly as evasive as Miles, hiding a great deal beneath a crafted exterior. Brawny and dark as midnight skies, he still caught her off guard by using proper address and words like *impertinent*. "You know how new I am to this place. I wish to know all I can—the good and the bad. The last thing our household and our business needs is to shrink from facts we deem too embarrassing to hear. Please, Mr. Kato."

He glanced skyward as if the answer might fall down from the tarnished blue. Shifting on the bench opposite, he took a breath that expanded his wide barrel chest. A rifle sat across his lap. Viv should have taken comfort in that measure of security, but like the bars on the brokerage house, it was just another reminder of the danger.

His indecision made her somewhat uneasy. He was an African, yes, and an employee. But he was also a man trying to do right by her. The line between wanting protection and independence was so very thin.

"Town planners decide which improvements to build," he said quietly. "Those improvements benefit only the rich. Very simple, my lady."

"But I should think security in the shantytowns would be a priority. Maybe then we would all have fewer locks on our doors and windows."

"Why waste funds on workers whose wage demands and strikes put the industry at risk?" Mr. Kato shrugged. "On the other side, why live in squalor when businessmen spend more on a week's liquor than diggers earn in a year?"

"How did you learn all of this?"

"I told you my history. Briefly."

"Yes, but not every miner and not even every overseer, aside skin color, makes such observations."

"I like being underestimated, my lady. I suspect you know something of that."

The sun was already dipping toward the west when they arrived. Mr. Kato helped Viv down, then directed Jamie to take the carriage back to a more suitable area of town.

"Be back for us in an hour," she said to Jamie. "No dawdling."

Viv and her now-silent guard walked away from the pitted road and into the shantytown just east of the Hole. At first the conditions weren't so rough. Although corrugated tin walls would do little to keep out the cold come winter, they appeared in good repair and free of filth. Women formed loose knots of community, chatting over their cooking or mending, watching one another's youngsters— but almost entirely segregated by color. Of course, they eyed Viv's progress, but they were neither hostile nor rude. Simply curious. She caught a few awestruck remarks about her gown, made of functional dark red muslin and cut for practicality. Compared to the women who watched her, however, she was dressed like Queen Victoria.

But the modest conditions didn't hold. As they made inquiries and pressed into the heart of the shantytown, a stench gathered and pressed into her nose. Unwashed bodies. Gutted animals. Human waste. The shacks on the outskirts at least looked upon wide-open spaces and permitted access to fresh air. The walk to dispose of refuse was considerably shorter. The inhabitants of these inner hovels could not claim even those scant luxuries.

Mr. Kato stood close. "My lady, are you sure?"

"If she can stand living here, I can stand an hour's visit."

But her stomach was an angered nest of hornets. She wanted to remove a handkerchief from her bag and stem the tide of foul odors. Yet even here, perhaps with more need for comfort, women gathered to share conversation and repetitive chores. Their gazes followed Viv with ever more covetous stares. She certainly wasn't going to hide behind a swatch of linen, insulting them to boot.

Tensing her back until the muscles between her shoulder blades cried, Viv kept walking. She may as well have been traveling back in time, her every step erasing another day until she was once again a terrified eight-year-old.

I'd forgotten what it smells like.

Other long-buried memories struggled out of dark and distant corners: seeing her mother quickly cover her body with a robe after a sponge bath, but not so quickly as to hide the bruises on her hips and upper thighs; the scent of different men's cologne on the linens they sorted for wash day; the feel of Viv's first kiss when one of her mother's callers had cornered her, his tongue like a hot snake in her mouth.

Mother had beaten him with an iron pipe until the police arrived. They'd arrested the man, yes, only to arrive at the end of their shift to demand payment in tandem.

A shudder kicked through her torso. She fought for breath. Mr. Kato was there to steady her balance, but her will to move had slipped away.

"Lady Bancroft?" came a feminine voice. "My, my, I thought that was you."

Viv shunted her ghosts aside with as much force as her

mother had used when wielding that pipe. A quick inhale brought the shantytown back into focus. She gently pulled free of Mr. Kato's concern and greeted Alice Penberthy.

Soon they sat together inside the Penberthy's one-room shanty. Ike had done well to make it as secure as possible. Shredded paper insulation daubed the cracks and crevices. A small cook stove provided heat, and a neat stack of timber lined the wall opposite the door. The stack took up valuable living space, but Viv knew full well the price of wood in Kimberley. There was a reason Ike Penberthy kept a rifle loaded and hanging above the bed he shared with Alice.

The new baby, a healthy, tiny girl named Samantha, lay sleeping in a cot fashioned out of a fruit crate lined with a beautiful floral quilt. David and John were out playing, making Viv wonder how far they traveled and what they saw of life out in the shantytown. By their age she'd already seen far more than her scant years could interpret.

Alice settled on her stool, smoothing her skirts and fussing just once with the strands of loose hair at her temples. She gave a timid smile and poured tea.

"I've come because I wanted to see how you and your family are faring," Viv said. Then more words spilled out of her even before she could think. "And because I want to help."

Fifteen

*A*lice's *eyes narrowed with obvious* caution. "How do you mean?"

Viv cursed her lack of tact. The conditions of the slum had called to her on an elemental level. *Help them all.* Yet . . . how?

A flicker of her uncomfortable conversation with Lady Galeworth provided the answer.

"I've heard it said that there is—or perhaps *was*—a women's auxiliary to help those wives, mothers, and widows who have fallen on difficult circumstances."

Alice regarded her with intense frankness. Bearing the scrutiny, Viv calmly sipped her tea, noticing the lack of sweetness. When was the last time she'd taken refreshment without sugar? The twins' nurse had laughed at her the first time Viv tasted it, there in the Christie brownstone, even going so far as to add more just for the amusement of her amazed reaction.

Seeing the woman's doubt, Viv continued her pitch. "I noticed clusters of women throughout these shanties, all of them gathered together to share the work and childcare. That's what I have in mind, but on a much larger scale."

"Many hands make light work, and all that?"

Cynicism didn't sound right coming from Alice, but then, Viv was remembering the woman she'd met on the wagon train. This woman was . . . harder. Her eyes held little of the same spark or vigor. And after only two weeks! How would she appear after a year? Or five? What would happen to the family she and her husband had uprooted?

"Something like that, yes," Viv said quietly.

"Wouldn't that be nice."

She thought the phrase sarcastic, but Alice's face revealed a flash of wistfulness. "It *can* be done. There exists an element of this population that dearly wants to be seen as worthy. I can turn that into generosity."

"By playing to their sense of guilt?"

Viv offered a rueful smile. "Not so much that as to their ambition. After all, what's an entrepreneur? They want to be ladies and gentlemen, but few here know exactly what that entails. I'll foster a sense of what I learned in London. No grand family goes without pet projects."

"Sounds like a lot of work, my lady."

"Initially, perhaps. But then we make it self-sustaining."

"Is . . . Do you think that's possible?"

"I don't know."

Alice dipped her gaze. "At least you're honest."

Viv finished her tea and decided to stop treating the woman like a specimen beneath glass. She would either be a magnificent general or she would flat-out refuse.

"But you need to take the lead on this, Alice. Can you do that?"

After carefully setting aside her cup—porcelain, beautifully painted—Alice stood. She knitted her fingers together in a ball, the first time Viv had seen her agitated.

"We left a lovely little flat in Camborne. Tiny, or so I thought at the time. But neat and sturdy. Ike had bigger dreams for us." With a glance toward her newborn daughter, she inhaled. "His Lordship came round today to talk to Ike. What was that about?"

Viv smiled despite herself. Long-standing impressions of Miles had altered so greatly that the news came as no surprise. A warm varnish of emotion settled over her heart. No matter what other failings lurked for Viv to find, he would do right by this family.

"Offering him a job, I believe."

"But . . . why help us?"

Standing, Viv took the woman's hands in her own. "My father and I weren't close in the traditional sense. He was not a man to tolerate sentimentality. But I asked him once why he had decided to found an academy for immigrant children. Why *these* fifty students, when there are thousands roaming the streets?"

Alice's expression had taken on the hopefulness of just such a child. "And his reply?"

"He said, we have to start somewhere."

In that moment he had revealed a great deal. His relentless financial ambition had been birthed by deplorable conditions Viv would likely recognize. Never before or after had she felt as close to the remote man who had fathered her, abandoned her . . . then rescued her.

"We can start here, then," Alice said quietly.

"I think so." After one quick squeeze, Viv released the woman's hands. "I'll be back in a week. If you need anything before then, send word with your husband when he comes in to work." She ushered Mr. Kato inside, where he deposited the gift basket without word or fanfare. "Good day to you, Mrs. Penberthy."

"And to you, my lady."

She turned to leave before Alice either refused or cried; she looked ready to do both.

Fifteen minutes later, Viv and Mr. Kato emerged from the shantytown. Her corset permitted no deep breaths, but she did her best to clear the stink from her lungs.

"You did well by her pride," he said.

"My husband is still a better judge of people than I am." She blinked, wondering why she had revealed such a personal observation to an employee.

Mr. Kato grinned. He had the most brilliant white teeth and eyes that crinkled almost shut when he smiled. What a singular human being. "Maybe, but he is not . . . subtle."

"No, he's not."

She forced a smile, but in truth, she felt lightheaded. No matter her success at helping Alice, the cloud of thick memories refused to dissipate.

She was walking away from a slum. She had done so before, slowly, with the progress of years. Never had the contrast between her childhood and her new life jammed so tightly in her chest. An unclean feeling made her skin itch. But why? The good she would do for Alice and other such women was rare in a city that judged worth only by carat weight. But Viv didn't need to live in a shack, sleep on an infested mattress, or bathe a newborn babe in putrid water. Her boots claimed more and more ground until she was nearly running. Breathless, as terror scratched in her throat, she dreaded an invisible hand poised to drag her back to hell.

A fancy open-air carriage rumbled to a nearby stop. A coachman in livery more suited to Mayfair sat on the elevated bench. A blond man wearing a fine top hat opened the half-door and descended. He was well-groomed, thick-limbed and sported a walking cane. His clothes were immaculate and fashionable, and he kept a neat mustache.

"How do you do?" he said, tipping his hat. "Forgive the intrusion, but are you by chance Lady Bancroft?"

"I am."

"Oh, what luck."

He offered a courtly bow. Viv hadn't seen its equal in months. But she also saw the hours of practice behind it—the same slight hesitations she had worked for years to erase. Whatever his airs and dandyish clothing, he was no aristocrat. "I'm Neil Elden. I've had the honor of meeting with your husband."

"Yes, I recall."

What she recalled was Miles offering a few crude details. But compared to the filth of the slums, this man was positively angelic. Furthermore, she recognized in him another self-made soul. Someone who had escaped.

"A pleasure to meet you, sir."

Mr. Elden smiled benignly. "The pleasure is mine, I assure you."

He had fair skin that wasn't sallow and blue eyes that weren't overly bright. A rather ordinary man, actually, but one who held himself with such confidence as to exude the impression of good looks. Her father had been such a man—straightforward and aggressive, winning people with his command of what so many envied: pure ambition.

"My lady," Elden said, "I understand that this is quite forward, but I wonder if you would take tea with me? I was just on my way to Child's."

Child's was a tearoom more frequented by men of business who preferred crumpets to cards and gin. Women dined there, too, as did those who couldn't afford the Kimberley Club's high membership fees.

Jamie Shelby arrived with his carriage. Adam sat with him on the driver's bench. "Just catching a lift home, my lady. Are you ready?"

"In a moment, Adam."

"Purely business," Mr. Elden said. She felt him pressing the advantage of her hesitation. "As I understand it, you are the manager of Christie Brokerage, are you not?"

"I am."

"Then I should like to get to know you better. Perhaps our partnership might benefit."

Adam made a nearly imperceptible noise, like a mouse being strangled. "My lady, you have plans for this evening, do you not?"

Viv stilled. Plans?

Ah, yes. Supper with Miles.

Dear God, what had she been thinking in agreeing to his request? Some mania produced by that torrid kiss—a kiss that had nearly become something far more dangerous. In the sunroom!

Now the prospect of dining with him only added to the unease she'd battled back when walking clear of the slum. All through supper, he would stare at her in that unnerving way, daring her with his eyes. Beneath the table, he might even touch her calf with the toe of his shoe or, as he had during many a dinner party, he would lay a hand on her leg, his fingertips grazing the sensitive flesh of her inner thigh. Bite by bite, course by course, he would leave her aroused, eager, and unable to resist.

Two weeks remained before she would make good on her promise. Such a dinner might be as much a torment to him, but Viv needed time to hide her heart. It was far too vulnerable to him right now.

"I would be happy to, Mr. Elden. Adam, can you see Jamie and Mr. Kato home?"

Adam's expression tightened. "And what should I tell Lord Bancroft?"

Even as she took Neil Elden's hand and stepped into his carriage, Viv recognized her decision for what it was. She was running. Plain and simple. The shantytown had addled her so thoroughly that her knees still jittered. At that moment, she wanted to take tea with a self-made gentleman who didn't burn her from the inside out. Something uncomplicated and refined.

She would endure the consequences later.

"Tell His Lordship that Mr. Elden and I have much to discuss."

Miles stomped up the porch steps, refusing Mrs. Shelby's offer to have a bath drawn. "Not now," he growled, feeling vulgar and surly.

She's at tea, Adam had said. Much to discuss. With Neil Elden.

Smacking his fist at regular intervals along the hallway wallpaper, Miles yanked at his ascot until it hung limply at his throat. Upon reaching his door he rested his head against the cool wood.

She hadn't come. He'd waited at the Ford, but she hadn't come.

Once, long ago, they'd done the impossible. They'd made absolute magic, and that magic had scared him witless. She blamed him for the petrified missteps that had followed, and rightly so, but neither had she found the courage to see if they might make it happen again.

No. He was being ridiculous, letting her whims get the better of his pride and patience. Had he actually been contemplating earning her respect? What a mockery. And he was an even greater fool for not having pressed the physical advantage of their reunion. It was just sex, after all. A fever to be burned out of him.

Especially when she chose tea with Neil Elden over dinner with her husband.

Miles pushed away and crossed to her door. He pounded out three succinct knocks. "Let me in, Viv."

Rather than talking to him through a crack, she let the door open wide and stepped aside, silently inviting him in. "I thought you'd want to see me."

The bruised tone of her voice and the direct way she confronted the topic tempered Miles's righteousness—tempered, but did not erase.

He closed the door. The frustration he couldn't ignore twisted his gut. The urge to forego his promises, march right over to the Kimberley Club, and drink until he couldn't stand rode him like a cruel master. Why was he trying to obey her dictates when she had so little inclination of bedding him, let alone with the passion they'd once shared?

He liked to think that she gloried in reminding him of her decision to leave, such as abandoning him that evening, but he honestly believed that she rarely revisited the topic. She held such power over him, an unnatural power borne of an infatuation he'd never wanted to yield. Yet she still considered him some no-account gambler whose thoughts began and ended with the pursuit of pleasure.

He hadn't been that man since departing for the Cape.

"And how was tea, my dear?" he asked, looming over her where she sat on a chaise.

He might have expected some other reaction, maybe anger or shame. Instead, with her flaxen eyebrows drawn together, she studied him as if deciphering a dead language. "Tea was just tea."

"With that Elden chap."

"Yes," she said. "He stopped on the street to introduce himself after I visited Alice Penberthy. He wanted to talk business at Child's."

She was as pale as the white damask on which she reclined. Only her irises—so dark as to nearly obliterate the flecks of green—and her unnaturally red lips, worried and chapped, lent color to her face. Had she been this tired for two weeks?

"And you preferred that to dinner with me."

Her jaw tightened. "I'd quote you the number of times you chose another hand of poker over a meal with me, but the number eludes me. Delicate feminine brains shouldn't count so high."

"So this is punishment? At least have the courage to admit as much."

"Call it what you will. I choose to call it managing connections of a different sort. In business, the flattery of a woman can be just as important as the competition of a male rival."

"Mocking my aid, my lady?"

"No, simply reminding you of our agreement to divide and conquer. We're a business arrangement, remember? Our marriage has been little else."

He crossed his arms and looked down at her. None of it helped. She had him strung too tightly. The blazing sense of betrayal was more than he would've thought to expect. How did a man prepare for a pain he'd never experienced?

"Lord knows you've displayed similar sentiments in the past," he said. "I should be grateful, perhaps, that we're only discussing tea and a missed dinner engagement rather than your departure for another continent."

She flinched. "Don't play games."

"Does that bother you, Vivie? You cringe at any reminder that we are, in fact, *wed*."

"It never should have happened."

He aligned his fists together, knuckles to knuckles, and pushed until the bones cracked. "You truly believe that?"

"Yes, of course I do." She hesitated. "You don't?"

That limp frown eased off her lips and her seductive eyelids lifted slightly. She looked . . . hopeful? With a start, Miles was reminded of how she'd regarded him during the first few weeks of their marriage, full of a childlike faith that had slowly dimmed.

Moving with a slowness that sat at odds with his temper, he sank to one knee. Her hand in his felt like a branding iron, hot skin swathing the fragile skeleton and tendons beneath. "You deny what we had. How?"

"What, exactly, did we have, Miles? Your insolence and your vices?"

"I gave up my vices, remember?"

She edged backward, her cheeks glowing pink. "We made love behind a stairway, for God's sake. Like *heathens*."

"You enjoyed it."

"Like an addict enjoys opium. You never gave me a choice! And then to learn where you spent the night afterward. Did you think I wouldn't find out?"

He grimaced. "That was a mistake."

"Just like our marriage. God, Miles, every one of Society's

rules I'd labored to learn—you ridiculed them and coerced me into breaking them right along with you."

The room was too hot. His blood surged as if trying to escape his skin. But her words sank in, despite how staunchly he wanted to focus on the physical. He had never intended his mockeries toward *her*, but toward the stultifying society in which he'd been raised. Had she really been so resentful of his scorns and petty rebellions? So . . . frightened? He wouldn't have believed the daughter of Sir William Christie frightened of anything.

He traced a finger down her cheek, then pushed a tendril of hair behind her ear. "You laughed with me, Vivie. You sank into the most beautiful sins, right there with me—as my wife, not some harlot. Why this resentment of the good we shared?"

"You never let me *breathe*. I was always waiting for the next embarrassment you'd foist upon me."

"But we're changed people here. I don't know what to do with myself, my head buzzing with ideas and impulses. That isn't me—I know. But it's like a dare I can't walk away from."

A wobbling smile fought to curve her lips. "You said that once about me."

"True then." Smoothing his thumb along her bottom lip, he dipped inside to find a trace of moisture. "True now."

That same look of wonder was back, but rather than flashing like the strike of a match, it lingered. The hard set of her hazel eyes softened, glittering with tears she would deny. So he didn't press. Instead he held fast as if his next intake of air depended on utter stillness.

"I cannot fathom you," she whispered. "You treat nothing with respect—no fear, no worry. How? What kind of person can just laugh at that which terrorizes everyone else?"

"A lucky person?"

"The money is all I want, Miles. My parents had no noble blood to give me, so money is all that will keep me safe. I have nothing else."

"For now, at least, you have me."

She looked away. "I don't know what that means."

This wasn't proceeding as he had imagined. He'd wanted revenge and shouting and maybe seduction. Instead she was peeling back layers of need that had nothing to do with her body.

"Well, then," he said, pushing her vulnerability away with both hands. "Good thing we still have our deal. At least one day I'll have what I want from you. For now, a kiss. Show me you mean to give me what I deserve."

"No," she said, the word grinding out of her throat.

Miles found either side of her trim waist with his hands and dragged her flush against his chest, legs, groin. "Come now, Vivie. Show some of that backbone I know you have and we'll both enjoy this a lot more."

The tilt of her jaw promised more fight. "I will not."

"Careful. Dares are very much like gambling, and you know how passionate I am about long odds."

He dug his fingers into the soft flesh along her hip, her softness matched only by the ridge of steel that kept her backbone immobile. Yet her gaze had taken on a sleepy laxness, a silent invitation. She licked the lush swell of her lower lip—swear to God, just to taunt him. Miles bit back a groan. He yearned to punish her for the turmoil she swirled into his life. He wanted to grind his erection against her mons. More dares. More proof that they shared an undeniable passion.

He trailed his hands up, up to her breasts and cupped the gentle swell along each side. He continued until he could lace both hands behind her nape. With patience that belied the stormy fervor of his pulse and the hot insistence of his erection, he plucked a dozen pins from her hair. Silken blonde curls draped down around her, tickling the backs of his hands and forearms. The scent of rose water and Viv splashed over him. Twining his fingers into those curls, he forced her to look up, to refuse him eye-to-eye if she would refuse him at all. Her breathing had gone heavy and fast. Color stained her cheeks like a sunburn.

"Kiss me, Vivie." He paused. His need to know would ruin everything, but it was just that: a need. Greater than desire. Certainly greater than his pride. "Unless Mr. Elden has already left you satisfied."

She flinched. "That's the second time you've insinuated that I'm capable of being unfaithful. Liars always suspect their own dishonesty from others. Perhaps the same goes for adulterers." Lips pursed, expression unyielding, she pulled his hands from her hair. "Get out, Miles."

He straightened. The bones of his spine seemed to creak as he did, protesting the distance his mind forced between their bodies. He could tell her—*Vivie, my love, I never did.* But she was hardly in the mood to hear the truth, and he needed to decide what the bloody hell he truly wanted from his wife.

Sixteen

*H*e'd smelled of fried meat and stale ale. The food stench made her hollow stomach contract. Viv's mouth watered, but she was going to vomit. His lips had been like two wet slabs of fish pressing against her cheek. His snaking tongue pushed into her mouth.

Then her mother—she'd swung a pipe. The metal made a spongy sound against his ribs. He'd bellowed and raged until she hit him again, square on the face.

Viv awoke screaming.

Disoriented in the dark, she struck out and screamed again when her fists met flesh. Hands were grabbing her, holding her down. She flared to life once more. Her feet kicked and her body bucked with a terrified energy she didn't want to control.

"Don't touch me!"

"Viv, good Lord—Viv! Wake up!"

Strong hands held her shoulders until the last embers of her dream went cold. And all the while a low, beguiling voice eased her out of that realm of old fears and hideous memories. "Come back to me, Vivienne. Come back. Calm down. It'll be all right now."

Oh, God. Miles.

What had she said? What did he know?

Frightened for entirely different reasons, she laid her hands over his. Her heart wouldn't quiet. "Miles, I'm here." She tried to swallow, but her throat was lined with gravel. "Stop, please. I'm awake."

She lay on sweat-damp sheets and shivered. Collecting her thoughts was like chasing dandelion fluff. She'd never catch them all. She only knew that her nightmare was back, a memory from her childhood made slow and viscous.

Miles had pulled her from it. Three days on from their fight, having barely spoken—that mattered not at all. He'd heard her cries and he'd come to her.

"Wait here."

He lit a single oil lamp on her bedside table. Wearing only a white nightshirt, he crossed the bedroom on bare feet. Viv soaked up the unexpected intimacy of his appearance. When was the last time she'd seen his heels? Or the dark hair dusting the backs of his calves? The curve of his taut backside seemed almost entirely new, as were the rounded caps of his shoulders. Miles poured water from the pitcher on her washstand, first fortifying himself with a drink before returning to her bed.

Chloe opened the door connecting their rooms. "Are you all right, my lady?"

"Fine, Chloe. Just a bad dream."

"Oh! My lord!" She tightened her shawl around her body and dropped her gaze. "I didn't—That is . . ."

"Back to bed with you, now," he said softly. "I have this."

She bobbed a quick curtsy and fled.

The mattress dipped under his weight as he sat. Again, that intimacy. Her husband was coming to bed. In a deep, desperate part of Viv's heart, no other dream existed.

Her terror transformed yet again. Whatever he had overheard would be incoherent nonsense. She could still keep her secret. But what about the sweet, warm reassurance that he had rescued her from the terrible black? Miles as . . . her champion?

No. That was impossible.

Yet her feeling of security didn't dissipate. In fact, he intensified it by cradling the back of her head and pressing the glass to her lips. She drank greedily, heedless of the water spilling down her throat. Only once she'd finished, her thirst sated, did Miles use the bed sheet to dry her chin and neck.

How was she supposed to resist tenderness? Any number of coy innuendos and sidelong leers—easy to deflect. Years of practice had fortified her against his usual methods of seduction. This was entirely new. A tiny flicker of hope flared to life.

The mattress shifted.

"Good night," he said, voice low and gruff.

Before she could doubt, Viv found his hand in the pallid lamplight. "Stay. Please."

His hesitation became a rushing sound in her ears. The

thump of eager blood. The morbid fear of rejection. *Not now, Miles. Not like this.*

How could she bear the next few weeks, few months, if he disappointed her again?

A soft half smile shaped his mouth—lips so finely carved yet so perfectly masculine. "Shove up, then."

Viv nearly gasped her relief. She shimmied a few inches from the edge of the bed to make room. Miles eased back the covers and slid inside. His bare feet brushed hers. She flinched.

"Easy," he said. "Your invitation. Your rules."

He wore his nightshirt and she her fine linen nightgown. The intimacy of lying torso-to-torso, leg-to-leg, however, was as shocking as any sexual act they'd ever shared. More shocking was her body's reaction. She simply became a part of him, softening like butter on hot toast.

Strong arms circled her with assured power, yes, but without the intimidating sexuality she'd come to expect from his embrace. Long-boned fingers remained in neutral places—flat, still, comforting. Warm lips rested gently at her temple. His pelvis made no untoward advances. The thrill of safety was as profound and unexpected as watching Miles use a bullwhip. This was a man who could take care of her.

Would it be so wrong to forget the past and start from that moment?

"Are you going to tell me about it?" he asked.

"No."

Being so near to him, wearing his body like an extra skin, she could feel the way his breathing changed. She had expected fervent excitement. Instead, he simply exhaled. He sounded . . . tired. Maybe even frustrated.

"I would've surprised you had I chosen to confide," she said. "Isn't that true?"

"Absolutely." He petted the damp hair back from her forehead. "And in a moment or two, you'll remember some reason for why I shouldn't be here. Then I'll go."

A sob bubbled out of Viv's throat. The resilience of his vital arms and the breadth of his chest offered a place of refuge. Deep, heavy sobs kept coming, lunging out of her body. Through it all, Miles held her.

He was steadily dismantling every truth she'd come to believe about him, about their marriage, working with the confidence of a hypnotist. If she had any sense, she'd do just as he suggested: tell him to leave. Lock the door. Throw away the key.

Because none of it is real. None of it will last.

But as her sobs eased and his hands remained civil and soothing along her back, Viv lost her will. He lulled it out of her with the patience of water and earth. This was too much beautiful comfort to deny.

"Viv . . . were you raped?"

She raised her head. The lines on the inside of either brow tightened as he frowned. Those lovely, dark brows. Troubled. For her sake.

Although she wouldn't tell him everything, she could mollify his curiosity—not entirely for his sake, but because his sympathy was threatening to break her heart.

"No, I never was."

"And your father, he didn't hurt you?"

"No. Not ever. Well . . ." She offered a wan smile. "Not with obvious intent. He frightened me. He was hard and exacting. But I always assumed he must care a little."

"Why is that? Because he took you in?"

"No, because he never compromised. He wouldn't have given me his name if he hadn't wanted me to have it."

For long minutes he was silent. His left hand rested on his stomach outside the covers. He twirled his wedding ring. Thinking, thinking.

"Then, this dream?"

"Miles, you know I was adopted. I was eight. That means I spent eight years in places I don't want to discuss." She shivered and dove back into the refuge of his arms. Weathering his scrutiny was far easier when she didn't have to look him in the eye. "Being here," she whispered against the smooth heat of his cotton-covered shoulder, "being here brings it all back. The conditions. The struggle to survive—it's all right here to see. Does that make sense?"

"Yes." He was stroking her upper arm now, hypnotizing her once more. "I think it does."

Miles left her bed before dawn, but not before staring down at the fan of golden hair that spilled across her pillow and the soft curve of her cheek. An elemental craving sped his heart. Unlike those initial weeks when he'd convinced himself that his interest in Viv was purely sexual, he was under no such delusions now. Not after holding her as the last tremors of a nightmare shook her body. Not after hearing the fear in her voice and wanting nothing more than to sweep it all away.

As a gambler, he understood his weaknesses as well as he knew that twirling his ring was his tell. When there wasn't an ante to be won, he hardly enjoyed looking such weakness in the face—hence the convenient oblivion of his vices. But he was no longer that man, and the stakes of this game were the highest he'd ever wagered. The time had come to be honest.

He was in love with his wife.

As if that news did not shake the very foundations of his life, he returned to his own room, finished his morning toilette, and broke his fast. Something precious would have been ruined had Viv awoken in his arms. Instinctually, he knew it just as birds knew to migrate. She had not been herself last night, but likely as close to her true self as he had ever witnessed.

Although their conjugal relationship had yet to resume—and it would resume, one day, if Miles planned to remain sane—he wouldn't have traded these last few weeks for a pound of brilliants. Forget Neil Elden and forget their fight. Kneeling with her beside the breakfast table had been one of the most singularly erotic moments of his life. So near to his temptation.

And last night, screams fueled by unknowable nightmares had yanked him out of his sleep. She hadn't fought when he closed his arms around her. Just the opposite. Sweet Christ, she had *asked* him to stay. The wonder of their closeness was as marvelous as a ball of blown glass, and just as delicate.

That she wouldn't confide in him should have been a minor concern. But the need to know prodded in his brain and somewhere near his heart. What was she so afraid of?

Funny. Sipping the liquid off the last dregs of his tea, he'd never considered that the dream might be pure fantasy. He knew—his gut knew—that her nightmares had been conceived in life.

Maybe he would talk to her about it. They had become so much closer, but he hesitated. Again, that idea of blown glass. They would shatter with the least little jostle. In previous years, he would have avoided such concerns by topping up his tumbler of Hennessey and seeking out a game of chance. That morning, however, he had more reading to do. Not the Romantic poets his father so detested, but a mining and drilling pamphlet Ike Penberthy had lent him.

Miles needed to understand it, because his idea would not be quelled. Daring and untested, it would be the key to proving himself to Viv.

Two short weeks after her nightmare, Viv accomplished what she could to combat it by founding the Auxiliary.

Or, the beginnings of it. Right now it was little more than a plain, bare warehouse made of corrugated tin. She had Neil Elden to thank for that. His enthusiasm about the project reminded her of Sir William's decision to found a home for orphan children. It heartened Viv to think that such men existed in the world. They built themselves from nothing and gave back in return. Her father would have been satisfied with the results.

But so much work remained.

"This is marvelous," Alice said, her voice soft as a church-goer.

Together they stepped through the threshold. Alice carried her newborn daughter in one arm while David and John ran through the warehouse's cobweb-draped shadows. Two windows at the front and back of the building provided its only light, but it would serve their purposes well.

"I'm envisioning rows of cots on one side." Viv swept her arm to the left. "We could designate an area to care for young children, with rotating volunteers to assist in their care."

"And for the remainder of the space?"

"What we discussed before: a laundry, a quilting circle and seamstresses, a food kitchen. So many men are here without families. Tasks such as cleaning and mending their own clothes can become a forgotten chore. We can provide those services."

Alice nodded. "That will help attract some of the widows from the slums."

Knowing all too well the boundaries of a desperate woman's pride, Viv added her affirmation. "I promised you that from the first. It's a business, not a charity. Women in need will register their names, children, and skills. Whether they wish to volunteer details of their circumstances should be left to their discretion. My hope is that none should need to stay for more than a few weeks. Just long enough to find suitable employment, or to return to their families elsewhere. But some of the best may sign on permanently, as you see fit."

"Me, my lady?"

"Absolutely. I cannot accomplish all of this and manage my business, too."

A smile quirked across Alice's lips. She still wore the haggard fatigue of a new mother, but her skin had taken on more color. Dark hair was neatly combed and bound in a bun. The brightness of her wide green eyes made for a lovely contrast. Even the strains of her family's circumstance no longer dimmed her quiet, earthy beauty.

"From what I hear," she said, her tone teasing, "your husband controls the brokerage. No lady of quality would attempt such a feat."

"You're quite right. The word I intended was 'household,' of course. Manage my household."

Mirth danced in Alice's eyes. "Then I hope your household is a raging success, my lady."

As did Viv.

Once, bolstered in large part by her new title, she had thrived on the glittering spectacle of high society in London. The challenge, as always, was to become one of them, with rewards beyond compare. Delicate stemware, mannered conversation, beautiful gowns, and glittering jewelry were the creature comforts she desired, symbols of the security she so desperately needed.

And yet a new restlessness covered her like a contagion. Few at Sileby's or Child's wanted to address the issues that had come to dominate her waking energies. She could not discuss her involvement in the brokerage's management, and no one wanted to examine Kimberley's obvious disparities.

The only impressive quality about diamonds was the effort applied toward their excavation.

From across the warehouse, one of the boys shouted as loud as he could. Both laughed at the echo and continued the game. Baby Samantha fussed, obviously displeased by the interruption to her nap. Alice only smiled indulgently. "Nothing to be done about boys and that energy."

Balancing the books was not the same as caring for flesh and blood. That responsibility made Viv's heart clench. She'd given up on the idea of children of her own. At that moment, however, the full force of an unexpected longing washed over her. The problem had always been Miles. The would-be father to any of her children was himself no more reliable than a toddler, and with far greater capacity for betrayal.

The previous two weeks had left her depleted, she realized, as tears pricked behind her eyelids. Sparring with Miles, securing funds for the Auxiliary, and maintaining a nearly obsessive hand in overseeing the brokerage—she wondered how long she could keep up that pace.

As long as it takes. All three endeavors were too important to forsake.

And the most daunting challenge remained. Two days left before her reprieve came to an end. Miles would make love to her. She craved it as much as she dreaded the repercussions. The one night spent wrapped in his arms had yet to let her go. Every evening she wondered if her nightmare would return. And she wondered if he would come to her again if it did.

"My lady, are you well?"

With a blink, Viv donned a placid smile. "Of course. But I have much still to attend today."

Alice chuckled. "With your household, yes. All the more reason to turn this over to me." She bounced her baby girl but managed to stand straighter, pride showing in every petite inch. "You've done more than enough. I have plans to make and women to speak with. I *can* do this."

"Yes," Viv said with a smile. "Yes, you can. Gather the women you need."

"Africans, too?"

"I hadn't even considered the idea. Will white women take shelter with African women?"

Alice shrugged. "It would be a test of their pride, I suppose. I hope most will. There are just as many tribal women who have lost their men. It doesn't seem Christian to leave them to the worst fate."

Viv thought of Mr. Kato and his surprising depth. With only a few conversations, he had convinced her that the commonly held beliefs about African intellect and humanity were grossly misinformed. "I agree with you wholeheartedly. *Any* woman, Alice."

"Good, my lady. I'm very glad you share that opinion. Living here . . . It has been an eye-opening experience."

"That it has. In the meantime, report to me with lists of supplies, and I'll keep pressing the right individuals for their investment and support. Otherwise, this ship is yours to captain."

"That's quite a thrill. I'll be honest." Alice appeared more hopeful now, more like the stalwart pioneer wife she'd been on that first fateful coach journey.

Despite knowledge that decorum would forbid such a gesture, Viv hugged Alice as she would have her only sister. Missing Gwen pressed against her fatigued eyelids, so she took brief comfort in this other woman's embrace.

"You know where to find me. Anytime at all."

"Hopefully not *any* time at all. Even with the children, Ike and I still make time to remember why we married."

Except you likely married for love. I married for status and the exchange of assets.

Despite her customary defense, Viv could not ignore the redoubled flutter in her stomach. Two days. She hoped he would be fast, cruel, thoughtless. But such crass behavior no longer suited Miles. She much more feared that he would be considerate. He had always been a seductive man, able to find the fiery, wild side she did not like to admit. Passion would be just another reason to find him irresistible.

And she was already on the verge of loving him again. The man she swore to leave for good had taken up permanent residence. Where could she go so that his memory—the need for him—would not follow?

With one last goodbye, she left the Auxiliary and walked home. Despite her fatigue, she needed those few minutes to collect her thoughts and force them to make sense. But walking to Egypt wouldn't have provided time enough. She arrived home far too quickly, the tip of her nose bit by the autumn cold. Perhaps later she would take out her frustrations on a few weedy yards of her garden, preparing for spring.

She wished in vain that she could discuss her confusion. Maybe the demons would not seem so daunting once dragged into the open. But she could not talk about this with Alice or anyone else. It was a private war, no longer against Miles but within her own heart.

Seventeen

hey rode in the coach, which made the
evening unusual to begin with. Viv petted the back of one
hand with her thumb. Her neck was sore, a continual point
of tension, and her throat ached, always swallowing back
emotions she could barely restrain. Miles, as had become
habit, stared idly across the space between the opposing
velvet-covered benches of their barouche.

The thirty days was up.

They'd put one foot in front of the other for one month.
Her standing in local society was secure, hailed as a benev-
olent angel who fought to keep the cutthroat diamond
industry civil. The Auxiliary would not only help desperate
women, but it aptly disguised her active management of the
brokerage. Every connection she made on behalf of charity was one she tucked away for Miles to strengthen at the
Kimberley Club. Divide and conquer.

At least that aspect of their agreement worked smoothly.

Miles was distracted by something, some idea, but he
had yet to share it. That lack of confidence nettled under her

skin, although she understood her hypocrisy. Trust. Always back to their lack of trust. Instead they exchanged the bare minimum of facts, as if each were engaged in a transaction with a pawnbroker: eyes averted, language terse, neither coming away with exactly what was desired.

Tonight it would come to an end. Viv was nervous. *So* nervous, but also unaccountably eager. She desired her husband now more than ever. The part of her that knew the risks was stridently outvoted by the promise of languorous, delicious loving.

Jonathan Montgomery, whose mine was co-owned by Lady Galeworth's son, was hosting a dinner party for the best and brightest citizens in the city. Of course Miles and Viv were invited. The evening offered a magnificent opportunity. Viv had done all she could with the books. Every possible penny had been pinched. Now it was about charisma and connections—the Bancroft name, where it held even more clout and celebrity than in London.

Strange. She simply accepted that Miles would do his part to sway opinions and foster goodwill. Not once during the evening's tense preparations did she assume what she would have when traveling to a Mayfair event: that he would drink to excess, gamble, and generally court scandal. That man had not returned since the afternoon in her father's library.

She wanted something daring and bold and so terrifying as to dissolve her insides. At night, alone in her bed, quakes overwhelmed her as she huddled into the duvet, remembering his musk, his kisses, the roughness of his stubble. And she shivered with desire for his body's warmth. Man and woman. Coming together as she knew they could, with such explosive power.

Would taking a chance be any worse than wanting it so badly?

"We're quiet this evening," she said, surprising herself at the impulse to fill the silence.

He raised an eyebrow. "I would be more surprised if it were otherwise. No doubt you await a reunion with the esteemed Mr. Elden. It's been days now, hasn't it?"

Viv didn't know how to react. Yes, she'd taken tea with Neil several times, as she had with any number of their clients and backers. Always she did so with the broker-age and the Auxiliary in mind. He was a charming man, in possession of all the good things one could expect from an entrepreneur with aspirations toward even greater suc-cesses.

Miles's dislike had been a sticking point from the start—the only matter of business where they actively disagreed. To hear his snide question made her feel clammy and unclean, as if even speaking to Neil constituted some betrayal of her vows.

"He wishes to be my *friend*. And an ally in this venture. Surely you can understand that."

"Vivie, he's a two-legged reptile."

"I cannot believe that," she said. "You do him an injustice. This is pure aristocratic snobbery talking. How can you possibly understand what it is to admire a man born to nothing, yet who has achieved so much?"

"He's a bounder and a cad." His elegant shrug, wrapped in halfheartedly donned eveningwear, dismissed the man. "I've known plenty. Fleeced a few. Wondered if I was one. But I wouldn't trust Neil Elden as far as I could throw him."

"Stop, please."

"There won't be any stopping when we're alone tonight."

"But you can give me the time until then. We both need to concentrate."

He sank back against his bench, posture oddly defeated. "Or admit that this has all been a mistake."

Viv flinched. "What did you say?"

"You have a good footing here now. I'm sure you'd do well enough on your own. Say the word and we'll leave it."

"Leave it?" she croaked

"I'll walk away and you can earn your fortune."

Her stomach clenched in pain. She'd experienced that same sick feeling all through her childhood, faced with never having—or worse still, losing—what she wanted most. A home. A safe place. This man, the man she'd vowed would never control her again, still held the power to help her earn that safety or see it dissipated forever. She would lose her greatest ally and her most stalwart source of influence.

She would lose *him*. Lose Miles. When at that moment, she wanted to strip off his crooked ascot, bare his skin, kiss his neck. Lick and taste and hold on forever.

The coach came to a stop and Miles looked away, dismissing her with that confident noble mien. Rarely was she on the receiving end of his highborn condescension. The slight stung, but the pain of their marriage was born of a thousand tiny cuts.

Adam opened the coach door and greeted his master with a bright smile.

"Shall we?" Miles was smirking. Had he been holding a lit cigar and a tumbler of cognac, he would've been a dead ringer for the man she'd married.

And she'd let herself fall in love with him all over again.

Viv exhaled and swallowed another mouthful of inexplicable hurt. She took his hand and stepped out of the carriage. This is what she'd wanted, what they'd bargained for. A partnership. Sex in exchange for influence and acumen. And it was entirely wrong.

Make it look easy.

But denying her heart? How long could she keep up that charade?

Montgomery's residence was a bloated town house in the middle of the central business district, as if he couldn't bear to be away from reminders of his success for even the span of a night's sleep. Footmen adorned with what appeared to be a family crest—as if Jonathan Montgomery's family had been respected for generations, not just a handful of years—stood outside the front entrance.

A majordomo announced their arrival. "Lord and Lady Bancroft, of London."

Viv wanted to rub her arms where gooseflesh had sprouted under her sleek evening gloves. Was that who she was? Ever? Still?

"So good of you both to come," said Montgomery, shaking hands with Miles. He wore his silver hair like a helmet, slicked back with pomade. His muttonchops were full and wiry. Narrowed eyes contrasted with his welcoming smile, as if he couldn't quite shake the habit of viewing all of humanity as a business deal to be concluded. "And Lady Bancroft, you look radiant. I'm pleased you're here."

She expected a word from Miles, something irreverent and flippant, but he merely smiled—an expression to accompany comments regarding the weather. What if his threat in the coach hadn't been idle? Was he really giving up on them? An attendant took her wrap and she shivered.

Miles joined the men. From across the room Viv noticed that he held a glass of sherry but never drank. His low, easy words—so different from the terse tone he'd used with her—bridged the parlor's distance. That relaxed voice warmed her blood and made it difficult to focus on the gathering of matrons.

"And what is this workhouse you've established?" asked Frances Goode, a banker's wife from Dorset.

"It's hardly a workhouse, Mrs. Goode," Viv replied. "It will shelter women in times of desperation, certainly, but they will earn their stay and retain their sense of worth."

"I fail to grasp the difference, Lady Bancroft."

Did women dislike seeing proof of their vulnerability reflected in the faces of those sisters in need? While Viv did what she could to battle back old nightmares, others merely thrust their heads into the sand and admired the lovely view.

"A workhouse implies destitution and charity," she said. "The widows of Kimberley have lost husbands in the Hole or to illness, but as with any woman of proper morals, they want to maintain their dignity. Honest work ensures that, while the Auxiliary will provide a safe haven for them and their children."

"I suppose the alternatives would be much worse," Mrs. Goode said with a sniff. "And the jails are already so crowded as it is, what with the renegade blacks and union whips."

Viv sipped her tonic water. "I would hardly call spending six hours in town without a work permit cause enough for the term 'renegade.'"

Lady Galeworth joined their conversation, her face a map of disapproving wrinkles and parchment-thin skin. "Don't mind Lady Bancroft, Frances. If she wishes to occupy her time with those riffraff from the shantytown, so be it."

Viv's smile was in sound working order. "I suppose the alternative is running a business. And we couldn't have that, now could we?"

Content to end talk of the subject with that rejoinder, she maintained a steady stream of acceptable chatter and gossip. But her patience was sorely lacking. Thoughts of the business kept her sociable, while thoughts of Miles made her fretful and eager to seek him out. At last she could no longer stand preening among the perfumed, bejeweled queens of the colony. Viv strolled the parlor and examined the fine array of paintings adorning cream flocked walls.

Neil Elden met her while she stood before a particularly nice Dutch landscape. Was it by Bruegel, or just an exquisite copy? In Kimberley she never could be sure.

"Enjoying yourself?" he asked.

"Quite."

He smiled as if he understood exactly what that brief reply signified, but he didn't contradict. Neil's full lower lip balanced the neat blond whiskers of his mustache, and a light application of pomade slicked his hair. He looked quite dashing in his eveningwear, but he still wore it with the puffed stance of a man showing off his latest treasure. Her father had behaved that way with particularly fond acquisitions, from prime hunting dogs to pocket watches. Perhaps that was the biggest distinction between new money and old—boasting versus taking for granted.

Viv did neither. What did that make her?

"I wish to ask you a question regarding Christie Brokerage."

She lifted her brows. "Oh?"

"Is it true that your husband will begin trading in carbons before the close of the year?"

This was new. She assumed Miles's interest in carbons had been to humor Ike Penberthy. But to trade them? The brokerage had never attempted it. What money could be squeezed from such useless stones?

"I've distanced myself from the tasks of the brokerage," she said coolly, with no intention of giving away her secrets. "Society in Kimberley has proven rewarding enough."

"And your good works."

"Exactly. If you wish to know more about the direction of the business, please ask His Lordship." She felt strangely uneasy in what had previously been charming company. "Out of curiosity, Mr. Elden, why would trading in carbons concern the Lion's Head Mine? Wouldn't a stable bottom line benefit everyone involved?"

His mustache twitched around a quick smile. "My lady, the purveyors of high-quality gemstones should not deal in such low materials. The prestige of the house would be reduced. It smacks of a certain financial desperation. And you wouldn't want suppliers to doubt the viability of their chosen brokerage."

Viv's mouth had gone dry. If there had been a more politely delivered threat, she'd never been party to it. Across weeks of tea and conversation, he had always been perfectly cordial. She had taken to assuming he shared the same entrepreneurial spirit as had her father, but perhaps that did not guarantee Sir William's more generous, honorable qualities.

When the majordomo announced seating for supper, Neil offered his arm. Viv glanced at Miles, but he was busy allowing two bankers to run off at the mouth, his posture as negligent as the arm he draped on the massive marble mantel.

Had he really made plans to sell carbons? The figures she'd compiled during the weeks up in the brokerage's cramped bookkeeping room suggested few scenarios for success, even if the gem trade remained volatile. What plans did he have for a mountain of rocks in the basement? But rather than doubt her husband's judgment, she found herself scrutinizing Neil's so-called concerns. Something did not add up.

"Have no worries about my husband, Mr. Elden," she said, taking the man's elbow. "I'll speak with him."

"I appreciate it, my lady."

She wasn't her father's daughter for nothing. Neither had she navigated a lifetime of social obstacles by being unobservant. As she and Mr. Elden entered the dining room, Viv put faith in her gut impression: her concession was exactly why he'd approached her.

And she didn't appreciate being manipulated.

Repeatedly stabbing a carving knife into the back of his hand would've been a more satisfying way to spend the evening. The woman Miles was promised to bed before dawn ate supper at Neil Elden's side. That the seating had been a coincidence was beyond his ability to entertain.

Stuck between the vile, stringy old harpy Lady Galeworth and her slack-faced son, a fat bachelor with a penchant for off-color jokes, Miles was in hell. The food was tasteless and the water completely unsatisfying. Instead he drank in the sound of Viv's voice, chasing its dips and rises with far more dedication than he followed the tedious conversations that swam beneath the ceiling of cigar smoke. One endless month of *not having* Vivienne had cleaved a split in his brain.

Frustration and boredom plagued him through the interminable dinner. He accomplished the bare minimum with regard to involvement. Drinks with the men afterward held just as little interest, except that he kept his ears open to possible industry gossip. The entrepreneurs in this town were as competitive as they were uncouth— braggarts, all of them—which meant the ill-mannered lot divulged more secrets than a fishing vessel spilling its catch on the docks.

Preserving the mystique of the nobility was Miles's obligation and birthright, one he had gloried in ruining. But gambling was all about holding one's cards close. He knew how to keep his mouth shut.

Their words and posturing blended into an aural backdrop. Viv was with the women in the other room and he wasn't with her. They would drive home, inflicting hideous silences on one another. And then they would finalize the last terms of their bargain: how to make love without feeling.

Goblins would've been more welcome company at that moment, but Elden's appearance was more genuinely hellish. *Talk of the devil, and his horns appear.*

"Good to see you, Bancroft," the eel said.

Miles made a noncommittal noise, unwilling to rouse the energy to offer a proper greeting. Instead he applied his imagination to how satisfying it would be to crack his fist against Elden's cheekbone. What would happen? He didn't seem the type to punch back. Likely he kept hired muscle for dirty deeds that he considered beneath his newly elevated station.

"I appreciate your permitting me the pleasure of your wife's company this evening," Elden continued, perhaps not realizing what a clear invitation his words were to violence. Miles set aside his tumbler of tonic water and squeezed a fist until the knuckles in his left hand cracked. "She really is the most amazing woman, and yet nothing above her station."

"Her station?" Miles asked.

"As a woman. I was worried, initially, when you both arrived in town. We all were. Christie's decision to place her in charge was a point of contention for myself and the other suppliers. Any active role on her part . . . well, no one was pleased. Not in so many words, of course." Elden slammed back the last of his liquor. Then like a cat embarrassed by a misstep, he smoothed his palm over the hair at his temple. "But she seems a keen sort of woman, properly versed in matters of decorum. You've done well keeping her in line."

Had Miles been in a jovial mood, he would have laughed. Keep Viv in line? Not only was that impossible and quite the opposite of their true marital roles, it meant their discretion was paying off. Elden didn't suspect how deeply she was involved with running Christie Brokerage. "Indeed, she is my most daunting challenge," he said dryly.

"That's why I had no qualms investing in her women's project. Something to occupy her."

Miles regarded him as he would a specimen jar containing a preserved tapeworm. He'd seen such a thing, once, at a curiosities exhibit in New York. He'd been both fascinated and revolted that such a creature existed. He could respect new money, in a distant way like admiring a bird in flight— an achievement he would never share. Sir William Christie had been such a wonder. But Neil Elden was not the self-made paragon Viv seemed to believe of him. Something about the man did not ring true, even among the falsities of such a dinner party.

A dissection for another time. At the moment he

wanted to establish one particular boundary with unflinching clarity.

"I would appreciate, Elden, if you left me the task of occupying my own wife. Wouldn't want to strain our business relationship, would we?"

"Is that a threat, Bancroft?"

"It's Lord Bancroft to you, my good man." Miles grinned at the indignant flare of Elden's nostrils and edged into his space. The ability to look down at his rival, both socially and literally, held a distinct advantage. "And that was most certainly a threat. Stay away from my wife."

Miles turned to go before the urge to belt his opponent became too great to stifle. The thick pulse in his ears submerged every sound. He made his apologies to Jonathan Montgomery, then departed through the front door, leaving Viv to endure the final hour amid diamond-decked females.

Having tapped deep into a wellspring of aggravation, he hardly trusted his ability to restrain it. Rather than dragging Viv home and risking irreparable harm by claiming his reward, he simply needed to take a walk.

Eighteen

Viv couldn't find Miles. Using polite inquiries to mask her burgeoning anger, she discovered that he'd left the party an hour earlier. But why leave her behind? On the night when they were to consummate their marriage anew? In years past, she would have assumed that he had ducked into some private room for an all-night card game—or worse. She could not count the number of times they had attended a function together, only for Viv to ride home alone.

But the heat sizzling along her nape suggested this disappearance was even more sinister. Perhaps this was checkmate in an elaborate revenge, where a new, tempting version of her husband softened her heart, crumbled her defenses, and left her wanting. Embarrassed. Broken.

It wouldn't happen.

Adjusting her wrap, waiting for Adam to bring around the coach, she gloried in the steel reinforcing her spine. Whatever petty games Miles wanted to play, she would rise above them—perhaps with enough resolve to overcome her renewed fascination. How could she possibly love a man who thrived on such whims? Her heart was too precious to leave in such careless hands.

The coach eased around the corner and came to a stop before Montgomery's palatial residence. Adam stepped out and made a face. "Where is he?"

Viv matched his confusion. "I thought you took him home already."

A flicker of something—guilt? sheepishness?—briefly eclipsed his concern. "I spent the last few hours in Chloe's company. I haven't seen him since I dropped you both here."

"He probably went for a walk," she said. "You know how he can be at functions such as these."

Adam didn't appear convinced and neither did Viv's words convince herself. Short of grabbing a lantern and searching the streets, she had little recourse but to climb inside the coach and return home. Old humiliations haunted that solitary carriage.

She recalled his quiet words, spoken just before their arrival. *Perhaps this has all been a mistake. Say the word and we'll leave it.*

A halfhearted rain to match her mood spat down from the sky by the time Adam returned her safely home. She dashed indoors, hoping Miles was there. She stood before the door to his room. Never had she ventured inside. The first knock was tentative, but she tried again with more resolve.

He did not answer.

Hands unsteady, she opened the door and crossed the

threshold, feeling like an intruder in her own home. The scent of him—bergamot and plain glycerin soap—breezed over her, sparking impulses through her senses. She tasted his insistent lips, felt his hand caressing her inner thigh, and recalled the relaxed sprawl of his big, beautiful body after they'd made love.

His bed was draped with a dark blue duvet. Matching curtains lined the windows, creating the impressions of a sensual cave, a place of refuge and intimacy. Part of her was intimidated and more than a little furious, but she still wanted to explore it, be part of it.

Be with him.

Rather than torture herself with what they did not share, she returned to her room and closed the door. She tossed her evening gloves on the foot of the bed. Her hair came next, as pin after freed pin released pent-up tension. The mental image of Miles doing that for her, sinking his fingertips down to the scalp and massaging away the subtle ache, was almost clear enough to believe. But the truth was more lonely. Just her own hands. Just the wish he would, for once, honor his promises.

She nearly laughed at herself. That evening's seduction had not started as a promise but as a threat. Something akin to disappointment had settled around her heart. Although she feared Miles would prove as fickle and insensitive as always, she had also hoped . . .

No. Even in this seduction, he was determined to play games. She wanted stability, not the caprice of a man used to indulging every stray impulse.

With a huff, she turned toward Chloe's room. The sooner she was out of her evening gown and asleep, the sooner Viv could put this monstrous night behind her.

A shadow on the balcony moved, stopping her heart. But then Miles stepped into view. She muffled her shock with both hands over her mouth.

"No need for that, Vivie." He lounged shirtless against the frame of one open French door. "After thirty days of waiting, I want to hear you scream."

All of her frustration and confusion became a physical force. She launched herself at her husband. Miles caught her wrists as she flailed against his chest. The strength of her anger was no match for the casual potency of his body. He restrained her with an ease that should have been frightening. Instead, as he brought her hands behind her back and held her still, she felt only a rush of desire.

He finally kissed her, and she was more than ready. Miles reversed their positions and pressed her back against the doorframe. Hard wood behind her. A harder body pinning her there. Too far gone for shame, her only thought was for more. She wanted him bruised and bloody after all he'd done, warping her life. She could kiss him that hard. The urge made her strong and reckless.

"We have all night," he said against her throat. "I even sent Chloe downstairs to sleep. No need to rush. No need to be silent. Give me what I've earned, Vivie."

"If you talk to me I'll toss you out right now, our deal null and void."

He pulled back. His mouth tightened and his brows

dipped into a fierce frown. He seemed angry, yes, but also . . . dashed?

Never. The man wanted sex and he'd get it. She hadn't promised a meeting of the heart—just her enthusiasm. He'd long ago closed off the opportunity for anything more than the physical and had no cause to appear so disillusioned now. She had said her vows with every intention of being a good wife. That he'd missed his chance was not her burden.

"Damn you," he rasped. "Damn us both."

He hooked her under the legs and hauled her into his arms. Viv was tossed off balance, finding purchase with her hand on the hard, smooth curve of his shoulder. She clenched her fingers, then found his throat. Imitating the kiss he'd placed along her neck—oh, so many weeks ago— she opened her mouth and tasted him. His skin was peppery, hot, and smooth. He tipped his face to the ceiling. Tension made ropes of the defined tendons along his throat.

His arms didn't tremble as he walked her to bed, even though his whole body shimmered with energy. So strong now. She remembered seeing him on the Cape Town docks, wondering about his new physique. Then, kneeling before the breakfast table, she'd seen the proof, how his more vigorous daily regime added lovely, lean bulk to his long aristocratic frame.

Now she could see the whole of him. She admired his chest, arms, neck, all thicker with carved muscle. The half-light of a pair of taper candles accentuated the deep shadows of his pectorals, the ridges along his abdomen, the casual bulge of his biceps.

No wonder she was shaking.

"You're staring." His voice was as elemental and rough as she felt.

"And you're talking again."

"Undress and that will no longer be a problem."

Viv swished her hair over one shoulder and turned away, presenting him with a maid's task. He stepped close, warming the length of her back, and took the hair from her hands. He twisted it into a single rope, then placed delicate, feathering kisses along her nape. One quick tug pulled her head back, her crown flush with the hollow where his shoulder joined his torso. Viv closed her eyes as his kisses—nipping at her ear, throat, collar—became more aggressive.

"Miles," she whispered.

"Soon."

Once again he swept her hair aside. His nimble fingers unfastened the hooks of her gown. With that expanse of silk pooled around her ankles, he started on the stays and tapes of her corset. She inhaled deeply, relishing that sudden return to meaningful breathing.

Still at Viv's back, he slipped his hands—fine bones wrapped in rough skin—beneath her corset as she inhaled, taking hold of breasts that rose to meet his palms. They moaned in tandem, his mouth nuzzling her temple. His body enveloped her, hands and mouth and the tall, sure height of him. His erection, like a hot pipe, settled firmly between her buttocks. He glided his palms down, taking the corset with him until he could fling it to the floor. A quick tug relieved her of her chemise.

He turned her and trailed graceless kisses down her throat, down her chest, until he nipped gently at one nipple, then the other. Teasing was likely his frustrating intention. He wanted her mindless and crying out his name. Viv had no hope of keeping that from happening, especially when he cupped her mound and slid two fingers between her private lips. Dampness seeped through her cotton drawers. Then he abandoned all pretense and slipped his palm down her stomach, under the cloth, touching her where no other man ever had. And still he continued the gentle assault on her breasts, caressing the heavy sweep of flesh beneath. His tongue rolled and roiled over one sensitive peak. He suckled before blowing softly on her erect bud.

"My gorgeous girl," he whispered there.

The rush of his breath over her bare nipples cooled Viv's fiery blood, ushering in a surge of panic where mindless pleasure had been. Goose bumps sprouted on her lower back.

Stop.

The word formed on her tongue and dissolved there like sugar. Again she tried. But their mouths met as Miles's fingers kneaded her backside, his thick penis goading where her body craved. Soon he would press inside, just where his fingers had swirled her wetness across slick skin.

Viv's panic exploded, but not because she feared her husband. Not even because she wanted to refuse the pleasure he offered and demanded. No, she feared that she would back out, deny him, turn to ice—long before finding the release that teased and enflamed her.

She spoke against his roughened jaw. "Don't let me stop."

He arched her backward, bent low, and sucked the tender spot where her neck met her shoulder. His teeth grazed that sensitive skin. Viv gasped and thrust her hips. After one more quick nip, he whispered, "Do you want to stop?"

"Yes." Her hands were in his hair now, dragging him back to that wanton breast. "But no . . . no, don't stop."

Miles tugged her drawers as he worked down her body with tongue and teeth and firm, determined lips. All along her belly he pressed hot, wet kisses. "Then I won't let you. No stopping, Vivie. Not tonight."

Ah, that name. It sounded appropriate now—the name he'd given her when they shared these moments of need and release. She expected his mockery to reappear, but nothing came. Only more glorious kisses and the delicacy of a man enjoying a sensual banquet. Viv could only revel in the shimmering electricity of his touch.

Miles unfastened his trousers and pushed her back to lie on the bed. Then he followed. Determined hands separated her thighs. Before she could think, before she could close her knees, he nudged the head of his thick shaft against her opening.

Every second slowed. His face had taken on a primal cast, full of dark places and darker thoughts, so very like her husband and yet entirely new. Brown eyes were midnight black, his mouth severe with concentration. Sun-streaked hair slipped down across a forehead already damp with sweat. He slowly entered, not ravaging but stretching her inch by inch, as his searing stare measured each reaction to that most intimate caress.

Viv melted. This wasn't the fighting and anger she'd expected. This was a bliss so sweet that tears pricked her eyes. This was dangerously *right*.

His taut strokes accelerated, his lean hips rocking her back, deeper against the mattress. Viv's climax had been gathering for days, weeks, months—ever since he strode into that distant library and draped his arm around her. You are mine, his body had said. Now he proved it, withdrawing and pushing deep in a rhythm that built like scalding steam inside her skin, trapped, readying to explode.

"Vivie," he ground out. "Vivie, look at me."

She wanted to shut out the sight of his strong torso over hers, shut out whatever she might find in his expression, but that would be a betrayal of this closeness. Made brave by the pleasure liquefying her muscles, she caught his gaze and held it. A quick flick of her tongue over her bottom lip pulled another groan from him, his fierce control disintegrating into more powerful, jerking thrusts. She hooked her heels along the firm rise of his buttocks, riding crests of heat and heady power.

The tingling need became too great. She clenched her eyelids and sank into her climax. Jewel-tone lights fired in the darkness. She spun away, blown apart by a quivering that would not relent. Her cries sounded foreign and erotic as pleasure became a violence in her blood. Miles's mouth was at her ear, filling her distant mind with darkly whispered words.

"Vivie. God, Viv." A shudder rippled through him, radiating out from where they joined. His body surged with a final thrust.

Slowly, as slowly as he'd entered her, his arms relaxed. He nestled his face along her throat—not kissing, just folded there.

Long, languid moments later, Viv lay on her side with her head tucked close to him. His hand traced idle circles on her bare hip. She watched his chest lift and lower as his breathing returned to normal.

Even while nude Miles conducted himself in the same irreverent fashion, his legs splayed just where they'd dropped after rolling off her. The crook of one elbow covered his brow. Hair—at his armpit, down his chest, between his legs—mocked any notion of modesty. He was a man sated, relaxed, at ease with all that he was and all he did. Viv envied it as much as she resented it, knowing that if the Queen herself happened upon their bedchamber at that moment, Miles would do nothing more than peer up at her and grin. Worse still, he'd expect Viv to brazen out the situation, too.

"You're thinking, aren't you?" came his abraded voice—a low, deep voice saved for the most intimate conversations.

"Yes."

"I don't think you should."

But she couldn't stop. Too many fears and memories leeched the moment of its wonder. She'd worked too hard to make use of the opportunity her father had provided by adopting her. Becoming Society's idea of a wealthy heiress—and then a proper viscountess—meant lesson after lesson in biting her tongue and hiding the coarse habits that had helped her survive. No one ever saw who she truly was.

Being with Miles . . . He knew. She could feel it when he touched her, stared at her with that unrelenting intensity. Whatever he had yet to unravel, he would do so with time. Worse than being vulnerable to a man she couldn't trust was being found out by him. What would Miles, Viscount Bancroft, think of her childhood in a French slum? Her deepening feelings—no matter the folly—meant hiding her past with even more diligence.

Lying there atop the duvet, growing chilly now, she wanted to hide away again before it was too late. Before she confessed everything, including her love.

"I think you should return to your room."

The hand at her hip stopped its caress. "Do you?"

Viv swallowed. She could still taste him on her tongue. Why did that make her want to cry? "We never agreed to . . ."

"Go on," he said after a time. "Finish."

"We never agreed to any more than what we just did."

"If you believe you can buy another year and a half of labor and sobriety with a single romp, then you shouldn't be let anywhere near a business. The market doesn't work that way."

Her heart had been beating quickly, as it always did when in the midst of a confrontation, but now it kicked like an angered mule. A prostitute. The word remained unspoken, but Viv felt the shame of it nonetheless.

How had she become anything more upstanding than her mother? What they'd done amounted to nothing more than bartered services. How good she felt, how connected they'd been—what did that matter?

She'd wanted his mouth on her breasts and on her neck. She'd wanted his body joined with hers. In the aftermath, however, she only felt sticky. Unclean. Their sweat smelled stronger, less like the intoxicant it had been only minutes before. His arm around her might have been the pinch of metal chains for all the comfort it provided.

"Just an exchange," she whispered. "You wanted to make this into a bargain, and that's what it was. How else am I supposed to feel?"

"How else was I supposed to get you back in bed?" He tensed, his expression an unreadable mask. "You *left*, Viv. Hard to convince my family and our friends that all was well when you lived on another continent."

"Define 'all is well.' Because I heard the rumors of your behavior all the way in New York." Viv sat up and hugged her knees to her chest. "Out, please."

At first she didn't think he would obey. He lay there—as sickening, as intimidating, as beautiful as ever. Then he flung his arm away from his face and skewered her with a cold look. Silently, radiating anger, he slid out of bed and grabbed his clothes off the floor. Viv wondered if he had the audacity to walk across the hall that way, naked and holding rumpled eveningwear across his sculpted chest and slim hips.

But no. He shrugged back into his shirt and trousers with more finesse than a man ever warranted, especially when he seemed savage enough to rip through the seams. For all her modesty and shame, Viv hadn't moved. She couldn't. He was leaving and she was watching him go. She'd told him to. Would he stay, even now, if she changed her mind?

But the fear of asking kept her silent. Survival was enough. To desire more was a guarantee of disappointment.

Viv compressed her lips, fighting tears in earnest now.

Miles stood before her—disheveled, aloof, exceedingly sexy. He was toying with his wedding ring again. When he noticed too, he smiled like a snarl. "What a farce." Hard eyes raked over her naked, huddled body. "This wasn't a single engagement and you know that. I'll be back tomorrow evening, Vivie. Count on it."

Nineteen

Avoiding an inevitable confrontation with Viv, Miles sat in the study and flicked the dry tip of a fountain pen. The only window was open, although that luxury would not last much longer. Autumn was growing chillier by the day. Much like every other aspect of his life, he had no idea what to expect from the next change of season. Outside, probably in the herb garden, Louise and Mrs. Shelby were bickering about what to prepare for dinner. Birds and chattering insects gave voice to the foliage.

He should work. Or *not* work. Both constituted a decision regarding his future. Instead he stared absently at a stack of wage statements and mail, as erotic glimpses of the previous evening conspired to leave him aching. He sank his head back against the padded leather and closed his eyes. Viv, stripped and glorious—as enthusiastic as he ever could have wanted.

His hard cock pushed against the confines of his trousers. He reached between his thighs and rubbed the ache created by such heated memories. Her breasts thrusting up to meet him. Her gasps keeping perfect time with her determined hips, taking every inch of him.

Just an exchange.

That stark appraisal of their encounter cooled his arousal as if with a splash of iced water. He'd tried bullying and coercion, bargaining and guilt. But even if it killed him, Miles was ready for something new. To keep making the same mistakes would guarantee their ruin. Success would mean having Viv. All of her. Keeping her. For better or worse. And because he never backed down once committed to a wager, he refused to contemplate failure.

The handwriting on one of the letters caught his attention—the fine, perfectly straight neatness of it. And then the return address: Colorado Mining Company.

Curious, he opened the envelope and quickly scanned the contents.

"Viv!"

A quick search of the house revealed nothing. Eventually he found her in the plot of ground she, Mr. Kato, and Chloe had prepared for her personal garden. The three worked at clearing out tangles of plants, while Adam gathered the dead remains and hauled them to a future bonfire at the base of the bluff. All that remained in the plot was cleared, cultivated soil and a few shrubs and vines. Miles had even less of an aptitude for horticulture than most pursuits, but he would gladly watch Viv work at her favorite hobby for the rest of the afternoon.

She knelt in the dirt with bare hands, patting a lump of earth around the base of a plant she'd just watered. Her hair was loosely bound in a knot at the back of her neck. Silvery blonde tendrils curled around her ears and temples, while darker strands poked out from her nape and trickled down her back. The brisk air pinked her cheeks and the tip of her nose. She wore a cherrywood-brown dress that he didn't remember, one without adornments or fluff. But it had to be hers. No other woman's gown would so perfectly fit the sidewinding curve of breast to waist to hip.

And buttons. A whole row of buttons down the proud arch of her back. He toyed with the papers he held, his fingers craving an expedition. He would become an explorer, baring her back to the dark yellow light of the afternoon. He'd never been a man to imagine sex out-of-doors; there were far too many sumptuous places to take one's pleasure. But he had the sudden urge to bow his body over hers, there in newly tilled soil gently warmed by the sun. He would take her from behind.

Adam noticed his presence first, as he returned to scoop up another wheelbarrow full of floral refuse. The man's quick eyes and slight smile missed nothing. "Good afternoon, my lord," he said with a nod.

Uncomfortably aware of his public arousal, Miles clasped one wrist at his waist. The letter hid his erection. "Good afternoon, all. Working hard, I see."

Still kneeling in the dirt, Viv pushed a hand against her lower back and arched. The artless motion thrust her breasts against the restraints of her formfitting bodice. Miles could only swallow thickly and trace the curve of her bosom. His heart was an engine pump set to maximum capacity. A twinge of fire licked inside his veins.

The letter. Yes.

"Chloe, Adam, why don't you take the coach for a ride around town? I insist. Mr. Kato can drive you."

Chloe's face lit with innocent pleasure. Her gaze jumped immediately to Adam before the skin along the bridge of her nose turned a sweet blushing pink. Adam's posture revealed a slight embarrassment that Miles decided he deserved for being so cheeky in his observations. Mr. Kato grinned at the whole scene. He walked away shaking his head and muttering something in an African tongue. If he was chagrined about the strange ways of British courtship, Miles shared the sentiment. So much ritual and nervous posturing. He wanted no pretty words or simpering blushes—just Viv. Again. Without the anger and distrust that burrowed between them like worms in an apple.

He waited until the garden was empty save for his wife, then closed the wooden gate behind him. Power and purpose fused in his blood. They weren't made of glass. They wouldn't break. He wouldn't let them.

She stood as he approached and dusted off the dirt from around her knees. Her palms and fingertips were tinted by the soil.

"No gloves?"

"Not yet," she said. "I'm still making friends with this ground."

Miles inhaled when he was near enough to smell her, all warm woman and the dusty fragrance of that exotic land.

Her hazel eyes, first beset with mild confusion, flicked down the length of him. That keen gaze caught and held at his groin, where he remained maddeningly hard.

Had Viv made any comment about his aroused state—speaking in a teasing way, her lips tipped into a sneaky little smile—he wouldn't have been able to control himself. His body would've interpreted any hint of willingness as an engraved invitation. Dragged, hauled, or pushed to the bedroom, he would've convinced her to trade garden chores for an afternoon of decadent pleasure.

But she was still Viv, after all, and surrendering to passion had never been her great skill. Once there, in that place of questing and giving, she was a marvel unlike one he'd ever hoped to find. Getting her there, however . . .

Her lips parted on a quiet exhale. She licked the lower one until it glistened. Was she nervous? Baiting him? Good God, he could hardly tell up from down. Angry with himself and at their whole tightrope of a marriage, he wanted to curse. Or kiss her until they knew nothing but seeking and taking.

"What's this?" she asked, nodding to the papers he held.

Miles stared at the letter he'd received as if seeing it for the first time. All of his frustration faded. He hadn't come out to the garden to make love to Viv. No, he'd sought her out because the letter he held was the key to their future.

It hardly seemed possible. He had been ready to kiss her. Viv saw it in his widened, fathomless pupils and the defiant twist of his mouth. That much she expected after the explosion of passion they had shared the night before. She had even expected far worse, that their renewed intimacy would give him permission to speak or behave inappropriately in front of the help.

None of it came to pass. Miles remained a perfect gentleman, despite the wool trousers clinging to his undeniable erection. Jaw clenched, breathing roughly, he backed away and released her from the spell of his dark, silent yearning. But upon awaking alone in her room—her inner thighs sore and his scent clinging to her skin—Viv had admitted the truth.

She no longer wanted to be released.

How easy it would have been to awaken together at dawn's soft light, turning a night of angry passion into a morning of slow exploration. She had told him to go and she regretted it.

She'd resolved to be grateful that he did not press. Now she was simply . . . aching. The tension between them was like a geyser. Violent bursts and scalding bubbles gave way to periods of quiet, but the pressure always built anew.

He broke the mood by smiling. She shivered. Could a man make a dare without words? Viv didn't know about other men, but Miles could. He said nothing and his stance didn't shift in the slightest. Yet Viv understood exactly what that smile meant. *I know what you were thinking.*

Once she would've been appalled. Now she simply wondered why he wouldn't act on what they both wanted. The barrier of their bargain was gone. He could demand her acquiescence at any time.

"Come to the study," he said, his smile tucked away. "We have business to discuss."

He turned smartly and strode back toward the house. His long legs made quick work of the distance between her little garden and the back porch. Black trousers contoured to his firm backside. She could not help the picture in her mind—all of that taut flesh, there for the taking.

She dragged in a deep breath of bracing air and found her center. He meant business. Their partnership. Thoughts of wicked smiles and firm backsides and *want* had no place in her head.

She followed him to the porch, then kicked the dirt off her sturdiest boots with more force than was strictly necessary. What she really wanted to do was hit something, bite something, scratch her nails deep into . . .

"*Stop it.*"

And now she was talking to herself. Good God.

Once indoors, surrounded by the bustling sounds of Mrs. Shelby, Louise, and Jamie clanking around the kitchen, Viv let her eyes adjust to the dim light. She had no cause to be so edgy.

"Tea please, Mrs. Shelby," she said after washing the earth from her hands. She took a considerably long time, making sure that every fingernail was scrubbed. "I'll be in the study with Lord Bancroft."

"Of course, my lady."

Viv found him hunched over the account ledgers. He flicked a pencil up and down against the hard leather cover. "You seem very animated," she said as she sat in the chair opposite. A functional desk guarded the netherworld between them.

"Here." This time she accepted the papers he foisted in her direction. "It's from Franz Framholt, a German inventor in the employ of the Colorado Mining Company."

"That sounds familiar. It isn't one of our clients?"

"No, one of the companies your father was so good as to own a portion of before he passed."

"They contacted us?"

"No, I wrote to them in December, hoping a little name-dropping might inspire grounds for a business arrangement—grasping at straws, really. I had no idea what might come of it."

Viv frowned at her husband, trying to peek inside that devilishly unexpected brain of his. He had been thinking ahead to their success since *December?* She'd spent the holidays in Newport with her brothers and sister, their conversations decidedly manic in light of the tasks awaiting them. She had given no consideration to the notion that Miles would be doing the same. Planning. Making sure they would not fail.

"What does he say?"

"Mr. Framholt is their chief engineer with a special interest in creating more efficient mining equipment. Look at the second page." A boyish smile made him appear years younger. The stark yearning that had overpowered them in the garden was nowhere to be found. In its place was an emotion like joy.

She blinked away from his magnetic eagerness. Mr.

Framholt's handwriting made her hands cramp in sympathy. Every line was a precise ode to horizontal, diagonal, and vertical, every arc as if rendered with a tiny compass. She had never seen more exacting print, not excepting mechanical type. On the second page was printed a schematic.

"It's labeled in German. What is it?"

"A drill bit."

"How would you know that?"

"Certainly not from any great knowledge of drills. Or German." He retrieved a pamphlet with bent corners and yellowed pages. "But I do read rather well in English."

"You always did enjoy books."

"Not all books. Just the Romantics to annoy my father." He winked. "But this is as far away from Shelley as intellectually possible. Ike Penberthy lent it to me, as well as his time in deciphering the cryptic thing. Turns out Mr. Framholt is simply expanding on existing drill designs, but tipped with diamonds. Carbons, actually."

Viv went still.

Miles looked like a man ready to burst for the secret locked inside. "You see it, don't you, Vivie? Carbons. Which we have piles and piles of."

"Wait here."

After hiking her skirts and practically running up to her room, she returned utterly breathless. Mrs. Shelby had delivered the tea service, which waited atop a waist-high bookshelf. Miles, however, remained in his chair, elegant hands laced over his flat belly. The study's tiny lone window and warm tones lent a richness to his coloring. More tan.

Eyes darker. Hair that intriguing mix of coffee and gold. He smiled softly when he caught sight of what she held.

A ledger of her own.

"I knew it," he said. "I just *knew* you'd have the other piece of this puzzle. Give me the good news."

Excited now, thrilled even, she didn't hesitate in joining him on his side of the desk. Only then did she realize how secluded they were, and how lovely he smelled. Some warm peppery soap. Clean but spicy and exotic. The study was at the far eastern end of the house, and it shared only one common wall. Lock the door. Draw the single curtain. Fling the ledgers aside.

The desk wasn't large, but it would hold them both.

"Here," she said, her throat chaffed. "See? Year after year, carbons have remained a stable commodity. In fact, their worth has actually been increasing."

"If Mr. Framholt is able to patent this design, we'll be sitting pretty." He worked lean fingers through his hair until it stood out at the temples. "Miners across the world will use it to dig their iron and gold out of the ground. Coal and oil, even."

A slow, awed smile worked across Viv's face. The tension—that other tension, one that had nothing to do with Miles and everything to do with the war between success and failure in Cape Colony—drained out of her body. "Drill bits tipped with our carbons."

"And because the vendors and appraisers in Europe don't want the things, we could sell directly to the miners and manufacturers."

"More of a profit to us."

"Exactly. No sweeps and variations in the pricing. These will be ugly, practical little stones—stones that no one else yet sees as valuable."

Viv leaned in to get a better look at Mr. Framholt's design. Nothing changed. It still made sense. It still meant a future.

"This . . . Miles . . . I . . ."

"Hm?"

"I am so very impressed. You . . . took a chance." She shook her head. "That's not my strong suit. I've been so busy looking at the books, trying to make the figures add up. Never once did I imagine a solution outside of pinching pennies. You thought on a grander scale."

His levity had eased, replaced by the unfamiliar contemplative expression he'd worn for weeks. "I simply couldn't let go of that pile. How could they be worthless? They're still just as hard, just as durable. We can put them to use and save this company."

"Save ourselves."

"My primary objective, yes."

Viv sat on the edge of the desk, her knees trembling. "Miles, I'm relieved. I'm *giddy*. This is just marvelous. I . . . I'm so proud of you."

She stopped and swallowed before she lost track of language all together. It started with the simplest touch—just Viv smoothing a disheveled thatch of hair that guarded his ear like a thorn bush. His hair was so soft, even the stray flecks of wiry gray.

But then the simmering heat sparked.

"Now kiss me," she whispered.

"If I kiss you right here, Vivie, I'm not going to stop."

"Oh?"

"I think you know exactly what I mean." He banded her hips with splayed fingers. With that wide span he was able to hook his thumb around her pelvic bones and dig his fingers into her tender backside. His expression determined yet mischievous, he squared her body with his. She sat on the desk. He stood between her knees. And he pushed her back, back, until she stretched along the top of his clutter. "I think you know that if I kiss you, I won't stop until we're both satisfied."

A wicked thrill coursed from her heels to her scalp, then back down to settle as a wild pulse between her legs. "Is that true?"

"Yes, my lady," he said, grinning. "Very true."

"But your papers? Your ledgers?"

"All very much suited to being flung to the floor." To demonstrate the point, he tossed a stack of mail aside. Viv covered her mouth, giggling, as she watched the fall. "Now you try."

She swept her arms wide. Sheets of paper fluttered to the ground like October leaves in Central Park. So far away. But she didn't want to be anywhere but right there.

"See? Easy." The twist of his lip, which could be so cruel when he wanted to appear a callous, flippant rogue, softened to something closer to wonder. He traced the slope of her brow, the curve of her cheek, the round point of her chin. "You are a beautiful woman, Vivienne."

He straightened, and for a moment Viv feared he might actually walk away. Instead he locked the door to the study, then shut the room's only window. He resumed his spot between her legs and leaned over her. Their noses almost touched. She could lick the stubble on his chin—if only she were bold enough.

She was.

The rough texture sent a delicate shiver from her tongue to every other nerve in her body. "I thought you were going to kiss me."

"You asked."

"Miles, please. Kiss me." She began to unfasten his neckwear and the buttons that covered tempting male skin and hair and muscle. "But you were right. You shouldn't stop. Not until we're both satisfied."

Twenty

Viv took Miles's hand and descended from the barouche. Lady Galeworth's marble mansion was one of the few buildings in the world entirely lit by electric light. The strident yellow glow from fifteen external lamps imitated the sun, again dazzling Viv with the wonder of that fascinating new technology. It was invaluable in the brokerage's sorting rooms, but almost overwhelming when applied on such large scale. She was reminded of her father's enthusiasm for the industry that would emerge from electricity. Some considered it a fad or fashion, but Christie Holdings would've capitalized on the possibilities had its namesake lived.

And whenever her thoughts expanded outward toward the larger reputation of her family name, she thought of her siblings. Dear Gwen had been so terribly scared, even angry at what she saw as their father's betrayal of her future as an opera singer. Gareth had been his practical, cynical self, but even his anxiety had been easy to read. And Alex—to be ushered toward such a new and unpredictable life with a young son in tow. How were they all coping? Having posted a dozen letters of her own, she waited daily for replies that had yet to arrive.

"They think that by one day lighting the entire town with electricity," Miles said, squinting slightly, "Kimberley will be the envy of the world."

"Until ambition outweighs taste, that won't ever be the case."

"And which do you prefer?"

"Whichever will get us that reward and the right to choose our future."

"*Our?*"

Viv licked her lips intentionally. A week had passed since making love in his study, and each night since had been filled with passion that bordered on mania. Knowledge it would happen all over again simmered under her skin with heated promise.

Another more lasting future, however, remained difficult to imagine. "Perhaps," she said softly.

Immaculately groomed, he seemed to have made a genuine effort to look his most commanding. For appearances? For her? She hardly dared guess his motives, only admired the result. Hair combed back from his face caught the electric light, shining bronze and blond against lustrous chocolate. The sensual curve of his lips offset the hard lines of his jaw and cheekbones. Not even on their wedding day had he looked more handsome. In the set of his shoulders, the tilt of his head, the quirk of his half smile, he was a confident man. Such a *powerful* man.

Her man?

Carriages released their passengers and were shunted out of sight. Viv hadn't seen the likes of these footmen since leaving London, right down to the powdered wigs and gold braid trim on their livery. She discreetly examined the décor. No expense was spared, from the immaculate statuary to the ornate crystal chandelier just inside the foyer.

Miles offered his arm. "Shall we?"

Nerves fluttered in her stomach. A ball was so much more special than a dinner party. Here, they would dance and dance. She nearly giggled as they made their way through the crowded mansion. Less than two years before, she'd abandoned their life in London *because* of Miles'ss behavior at just such a gala. Now she awaited every touch that promised more. Even taking her wrap and handing it to an attendant, his mischievous eyes said he hadn't lost interest. If they'd made love every time she caught that familiar flare of heated longing in his gaze, she would never leave the house.

They stood at the top of a wide double staircase that led to the ballroom. The Galeworth mansion was built on the side of a slope, resulting in a lower story that was also at ground level. The walls were made almost entirely of floor-to-ceiling windows, which meant that every resident in Kimberley could see the brightly lit party. Every glittering jewel. Every imported Parisian silk gown. If they listened closely enough, they might even be able to hear the quartet as it began a lively waltz. Viv couldn't help but think that the architect had done it purposefully.

"If you leave my side tonight, I'll come find you," he whispered against the side of her neck.

A shiver danced up to her scalp and down between her shoulder blades. "Oh?"

"Because you look breathtaking, Viv. Every man here wants you. Don't ever doubt that." He tightened his hand at her waist. Half caress, half possessive tug. "But I want you more."

"Do behave."

"Hardly what your expression says. Would you like me to interpret what I see?"

A blush warmed her skin down to the cleft between her breasts. "Yes."

"A woman who wants to be kissed."

"Is that all?"

He brushed his mouth across hers, just the barest touch. "Hmm. Doesn't seem to be. At least not that sort of kiss. We both desire more, don't we?"

"What do you mean? We've already been doing . . . more."

The tips of his fingers danced along her upper back, where her gown revealed bare skin. A gentle tease. A wicked tickle.

"May I make a request, Vivie?"

"And what is that?"

"I want to spend the night with you. All night. A real seduction, Vivie. You and me. Exploring. Completely open. No more of these furtive bursts of passion, where neither of us can look the other in the eye come morning." He traced the bones of her spine until he cupped the base of her skull.

His breath was warm against her cheek. "I want to see you bathed in gold when the sun rises."

Another hard shiver. The scene he painted with hushed words was too evocative to deny. She could not refuse, but neither could she boldly leap to answer his request for more intimacy.

"You're terribly sure of yourself this evening," she said, hoping for a lighthearted tone. But all she felt was awe. He could turn on his charisma like one of those electric light switches. Tonight he blazed.

With a scant smile, one that hid all the secrets of their evening yet to come, he offered his arm once again. "We need me to be."

"Yes, but now let me interpret your expression. If you keep looking at me that way, you'll never have the chance to meet Mr. Rhodes or the colonial governor."

He lifted his brows, lips quirking around a suppressed smile. "I can resist you long enough to do my job tonight, Lady Bancroft."

"Can you, now? Even with thoughts of me bathed in golden sunlight?"

"If you want to tease, we can tease." He brushed up her ribs until his thumb caressed the underside of her breast. "But I ask that you don't make a mockery of something I requested in earnest."

"Miles . . ." She arched her neck to catch his gaze with hers. Troubling, the idea that she could push him too far. That she could hurt him. She would need to think about how he had been affected by her departure for New York. "I'm sorry. I won't do it again."

He shrugged. A genial expression layered over any deeper sentiment, disguising him as thoroughly as grease paint on an actor. She knew that process well, but rarely had she seen it of him. By letting him inside her defenses, she was learning the difference between the viscount and the man she'd married.

What a terrifying, thrilling gift.

"Come now, my lady. We have work to do."

Even as she basked in the sensual jolt created by their conversation, she wondered if he would want her just as much had he known the truth of her origins. She doubted he or any other man in the room would—at least not as a wife.

With an agitated sigh, she accompanied Miles to greet the usual crowd: Mr. and Mrs. Goode, Mr. Montgomery and Priscilla Lumley, his mistress, and Lady Galeworth and her son. Strange how Viv had such difficulty remembering the man's name, especially since it was his name on the contract between the Galeworth Mine and Christie Brokerage. Lady Galeworth was simply too domineering to permit anyone an opinion. Even Mr. Haverstock, the banker who had abandoned Chloe in that long-ago burning carriage, skirted the edges of their exclusive cluster. Viv made a point of ignoring the toad.

"Lord and Lady Bancroft," Mr. Goode said, extending his hand. Miles quirked a haughty eyebrow, but shook anyway. "Delighted to make your acquaintances at last. Business in London has kept me away."

Montgomery harrumphed. His grand mustache twitched. "Nothing in London but relics covered in cobwebs."

Miles's fingertips tensed at Viv's waist, but his expression maintained that bland neutrality. "Some of us manage to shake the cobwebs off," he said evenly. "They would appear none too attractive under these electric lights."

"Why the shuffling of feet, my friends?" Neil Elden asked as he joined the conversation. "Lord Bancroft is a valuable asset to our community, as is anyone who brings the prestige of the old guard to our fair venture. Any businessman who doesn't see the benefit of such connections isn't looking hard enough."

"And the prestige of this event is incomparable," said Montgomery's mistress. Miss Lumley was a pretty, bird-like young woman with a turned-up nose and marvelous blue eyes. Rumor had it that she'd crawled up from the Boston docks to achieve her current place of dubious standing, but judging by the fat, flawless brilliants weighing heavily on her earlobes and the way Montgomery never left her side, she'd made the very best use of her assets. "I'm quite in awe of the company we keep here."

Viv smiled but couldn't help noticing her mistake. Ignoring the splendor was the surest way to let everyone else assume one belonged among it. She felt a charitable impulse to save the woman from further embarrassment, but she was too busy navigating the currents of dislike radiating between Miles and Neil.

The latter made the task more difficult when he offered

Viv one of the two glasses of champagne he held. "No, thank you, Mr. Elden."

"Then I suppose a dance is out of the question, too," he said quietly.

Right there. Within earshot of Miles.

"You suppose correctly." As a distraction against the violence she felt in her husband's taut body, she made a show of admiring Neil's suit coat. "Is this new from London?"

"Paris, actually. Just arrived this week. I'm quite fond of it already."

She flicked her gaze to Miles, practically able to see a snappish retort straining to be let free of his beautiful mouth. But Neil had already moved on, complimenting Miss Lumley's earbobs—his conversation as animated as a hummingbird's wings.

Ever since Miles's warnings, she could not relax around Neil. Had she been so deceived, believing him a self-made man in the image of her late father? But Sir William Christie had never played games that involved neither profit nor acquisition. His tolerance for complimentary chatter expired after only a handful of minutes, relying instead on blunt words and unmistakable commands. Viv would've preferred even his displeasure to Neil's frivolity.

The entire evening had taken on an element of tedium, just like afternoon tea with the town's finest society women. When had the tinkling of polite laughter and the clink of fine crystal begun to sound so foreign and contrived? She'd longed for this sort of refinement for as long as she could recall, even before she knew such magic existed. But it was just that: magic. It wasn't real. Behind the smiles and the exquisite silks lay ambition and fear as desperate as her own. And just as she'd attended the ball as a means of furthering her business interests, so had everyone else.

Although she feared that Miles's cynical view of Society was clouding her own, she had come to believe that his interpretation was much clearer, more honest. But where did that leave her, a woman whose past was best left entirely obscured?

Dizzy, she made her excuses to the small gathering. Miles accompanied her to a small alcove. He tipped up her chin with two white-gloved fingers. "What is it?"

"I hate these lights."

"Lies from my Vivienne? Very unbecoming."

"I need a moment, nothing more. Just to catch my breath." She smoothed her palms down his silken lapels. Not once since arriving in Africa had she seen him so resplendently dressed, and yet all she wanted was to strip each layer away to indulge in hot skin and dense, sturdy muscle. "Please, do what you must to maintain our appearances."

He peered deeper. Lit from behind by the electric lights, his cheekbones appeared stronger, his eyes hooded and dark. All she could see clearly was the pearlescent shine of his teeth as he indulged in a lazy smile. "Very well. But remember what I said, my dear. I'll come find you."

Despite her misgivings, fearing the worst should he find out the truth behind her nightmares, she returned his smile. He had opened her body, showing her unimaginable pleasure. Now he wanted more vulnerability. She could hardly do that and expect to keep Viscount Bancroft as her husband. Her hands shook slightly as he kissed her knuckles. He caught that, too, frowning slightly.

To prevent him from probing, she said, "I'll be here, Miles. I promise."

"Lady Bancroft, whatever are you doing alone?"

Neil Elden arrived at her side as if conjured by a shadowy spell. The urge to pull away from his presumptuous closeness was instant, when she had once considered him a friend and ally. The support he continued to muster on behalf of the Auxiliary was remarkable, which meant Alice was well on her way to opening its doors to Kimberley's most desperate women. Yet goose bumps sprouted on the inches of bare skin between her evening gloves and the sleeves of her most decadent red silk gown.

"Yes, just a moment free of business and politics. I can only bear so much before I lose the threads."

"Here, drink this." Neil pushed a crystal of claret into her hands.

She sipped the sweet red wine and smiled halfheartedly. "Thank you."

"I don't suppose we could have that dance now? Your husband is quite occupied with matters of greater significance."

Wondering at Elden's choice of words, she very much doubted that Miles would consider dancing with her insignificant. "No, thank you. I'm not quite up for the exertion."

Not with you.

But Neil's face had taken on a harder look. He reached out as if readying to stroke her face, then hesitated. Viv could only watch, removed from her own body, as he tried again. The touch of his fingers against her cheek made her jump. Mouth open, a predatory keenness had crept into his blue eyes.

"Mr. Elden." She backed against the wall. Only her glass of claret acted as a tiny shield, promising a red wine stain. "Stop, please."

"I have no intention of doing so."

The threat in his tone stole the fear from Viv's spine and replaced it with anger. "Get away from me."

"I will. But I'm only going to tell you this once, Lady Bancroft. You will regret it if you go ahead with this scheme to sell carbons."

"I have no idea what you're talking about."

"Do not think to insult me with some vapid protests. Say what you like to the others, but I suspect you know a great deal more about the workings of your father's business. You either make the decisions, or you influence that noble braggart of yours. You are as much a partner in running Christie Brokerage as you are a married woman." His hand cupped the back of her neck. Like a velvet rope, his touch was soft but no less restraining. "I rather think I forgive him on that score. I imagine your kind could be rather . . . persuasive."

Her *kind*?

"Mr. Elden, I insist that you let go of me, right this instant."

Rather than comply, Neil's expression darkened. He yanked the glass of claret from her hands. A few drops of red scattered across the lapels of his new suit coat. The crystal clattered to the marble floor. Viv looked around frantically but found no one. The alcove she'd chosen to find a moment of reprieve and privacy kept them shielded from the main body of dancers.

I can always scream. If he goes further, I can scream. But he won't. He wouldn't dare.

"Don't fight this, Viv," he whispered, so close now. "Change that business model or I will find out exactly who you are."

Her sputtered protests meant nothing as he leaned in to kiss her. He smelled of the spilled claret and cigars.

Maybe that cigar stench was what freed her. Cigars meant Miles and the way he used to batter and abrade her will to resist. But that was a long time ago. And no matter Miles'ss teasing aggression, she'd never actually feared him. Loved, hated—never physically feared.

But she feared Neil Elden. He touched his lips to hers, igniting the fury of the nightmare she'd once lived. Viv's frozen body finally responded to her mind's frantic pleas. She pushed against his chest and slapped him clean on the mouth.

"I said *no.*"

Her chest hurt. The palm of her hand hurt. And her pride was a wreck. She'd fooled herself into believing that her father was a reflection of all self-made men—the opposite of Miles'ss behavior in London. Something better, more honest in a world constructed of polite lies.

Neil smoothed his mustache. "I tried to warn you because

I admire you. You've clawed your way up from nothing, just like I have."

"We have nothing in common, Mr. Elden."

His meticulously pale skin had taken on the pink cast of a man losing his temper. "That's what I intend to disprove."

Viv threw back her shoulders. Her head ached and every muscle along her spine had turned to rock. "You do not want to make an enemy of my husband. The business arrangement between the Lion's Head Mine and Christie Brokerage will be irrevocably damaged."

"Believe me, Lady Bancroft, it has been already."

She spun away from him, tripping blindly toward the ballroom, seeking someplace public and well lit. Her neck itched where he'd touched. She wiped her lips with the back of her gloved hand. The skilled quartet had moved on to a lively minuet, but it all sounded like the lowing of cattle.

A hand touched her arm and she nearly shrieked. Her heart stuttered.

Just as he promised, Miles had found her.

Twenty-one

Over the previous few weeks, Miles had come to understand the delicacy of Vivienne's expressions. She possessed no fewer than eight different smiles, seven of which expressed emotions other than joy. Embarrassment. Chagrin. Derision. The last one—the one he liked best—shaped her lips right then. Genuine happiness. She was glad to see him.

Fire and fear mixed in his chest. He wanted to stand up taller and run away at the same time. She had such control over him. When had he ever thought otherwise? He'd peel off his own skin for her.

The musicians ended their frothy minuet.

He bowed and when he kissed her hand, he lingered. He turned her palm up and placed a second kiss on the inside of her wrist. Were he in command of the entire world, including women's fashion, he would ban bustles, corsets, and evening gloves. The leather, warmed by her body, was a poor substitute for skin. But her radiant red gown was undeniably gorgeous. The deep scarlet made her hair brighter, her eyes greener, her pale skin even more lustrous. Silver embroidery shimmered with each movement, until he could see her pulse as it rippled down her body—her heart creating waves in a river of red.

"You have impeccable timing, Lord Bancroft," she said, that smile still molding her strawberry-pink lips. "I was just ending a most unpleasant conversation with Mr. Elden."

Something had happened, tightening Miles's chest. "What did he do?"

Hazel irises darkened and her hand tried to flutter away. "Ask me to dance."

Miles caught her fingers, kissed them, held them. The quartet had started a piece by the younger Strauss. "Will you waltz with me, Viv?"

Couples began pairing off. She watched them go with a strength of longing that Miles had rarely seen. Always torn between what she wanted and some other darkness he couldn't identify, let alone remedy. He'd thought it ambition or even the need to live up to her father's expectations. But if Viv's sleeping hours were diseased by nightmares, he needed to reconsider. Some piece of her was still hiding.

"It's been . . ." She dropped her gaze. "It's been such a long time since we waltzed."

"It has."

Memories of the Saunders' long-ago gala layered over them—not like the quartet's sweet melody, but as a discordant screech. Yet despite Miles's fear that a brick wall would thrust between them once more, Viv's smile turned rueful. "Shall we try to rewrite history, then?"

"Just a new chapter, my dear."

With more haste than he would've admired in another man—but damn it all, he didn't want Viv to change her mind—Miles led her to the dance floor. He encircled her body and pulled her near, his fingers possessively splayed between her shoulder blades. And they waltzed.

Moving in time to the music was natural and familiar. Their bodies found a place of unison, rising and falling, spinning and twirling. He led and she followed, which was fact enough to leave him more excited than the dance. Color and light spilled like paint along his peripheral vision. Conversation and music layered over the pulse in his ears.

"You're smiling," she said.

"That sounded like a question."

"One can never be certain with us."

"That has been our wont, hasn't it? Blasted unpredictable."

A frown creased between her flaxen brows. "I suppose it can't be helped. We bring out the worst in one another."

"Funny." He pulled her closer. "I was just thinking that we bring out the best."

She appeared a little dazed, a little shy. Miles wanted to crawl into her thoughts and live there until he could interpret her mysterious reserve. What would he find? Did she feel anything for him at all? More likely he was a monumental fool, the likes of which the British aristocracy had yet to survive.

They finished the dance and started straight into another. He was reluctant to let the moment escape. Still, some matters simply outshone all others. Apparently dread and an uncomfortable tickle of jealousy were, at present, stronger than desire.

"Tell me now, Viv. What happened?"

"He kissed me."

Miles stubbed his toe, then tightened his grip on Viv's upper body to keep from taking them both down. To her credit, she kept the rhythm and yanked him back into step.

"Saving your renowned subtlety for more worthy peers?" he asked through clenched teeth.

"Best to say such a thing bluntly."

"I might beg to differ."

He gulped a mouthful of hot air, tasting a hint of ozone from the electrical lamps. The room seemed jaundiced then, bathed in that unnatural yellow light. Or maybe the idea of Elden's tongue pressing into his wife's mouth put him in mind of disease. Miles certainly felt capable of retching.

"Did you enjoy it, then?"

"No! Of course not."

"There is no 'of course' about it, Viv. We're back to that measure of unpredictability. I can no more judge your appreciation of Elden's sexual advances than I could predict whether you'll accept my proposition."

"Which . . . proposition?"

"As to where you'll sleep tonight."

Soldiers prepared for incoming cannon fire with less anxiety than Miles as he awaited her reply. He pushed at Viv because she could push him to the point of ruin. He'd been close once, so very close—and he hadn't loved her then. With no trust and no faith, they had no future. Those were the stakes.

"Yes," she said simply. "I would like to sleep with you tonight."

Miles stopped dancing. It was either that or take an irrevocable tumble the next time she lobbed another verbal volley. He avoided swirling couples and walked her off the floor.

They wound up tucked behind the ostentatious staircase. "Well, this is nicely reminiscent," he said dryly. "Now, explain. Everything Elden did."

"For some reason, he doesn't want the brokerage to sell carbons. When I told him I wouldn't be intimidated, he kissed me. It wasn't . . ." She made a sour face and crossed her arms over her stomach. "It wasn't one of passion. He means to intimidate us."

Miles closed his eyes as red dyed his vision. "By threatening you? Viv, I'll have him arrested."

He remembered the wagon master he'd fought there on the Cape Town docks, and the Boer raiders who'd attacked the stagecoaches. Would that dealing with a human snake like Elden were so easy, so physically satisfying. Nothing short of garroting the man would completely quell the steaming rage in Miles's veins. But no. He may as well have been back in London, tangled by the polite conventions of money and politics.

"No need for anything so dramatic," she said. "He promised we'd be sorry, but nothing more specific. In the meantime, don't you think we should discover the real reason he's so against our new business model? The idea his dislikes are based on its lack of prestige doesn't ring true."

Her eyes twitched to take in every nuance of his expression. He'd never quite felt so much like an exotic beast. No matter the tidal pool of nausea swirling in his gut, he appreciated one plain fact: she cared what he thought.

"Yes, of course." Miles, however, needed other answers. "When you described this . . . *encounter*, you seemed disappointed. Why?"

"I admire that entrepreneurial spirit—the ability to rise above one's birth. Perhaps because that's what I admired about my father. But they are nothing alike beyond their rise to fortune." She shaped her lush lips into those of a prim spinster. "I most certainly did not enjoy it."

"Good."

"Good? That's all you have to say?"

He stalked nearer. Viv retreated one step, then two, until she pressed against the back of the staircase. A rush of memory overwhelmed Miles, mingling with a possessive turmoil that left him shaking and light-headed. They had a history with staircases.

"What more would you care to hear? That I want to remove the man's heart for violating you?" He slid his hands down along either side of her breasts, his thumbs flicking over the nipples hidden by layers of red silk and lace. Her lips parted. "Or that the idea of your mouth touching another man's turns my stomach hard and hot as a lit coal?" When his hands reached her waist, he pressed his groin against hers—not so much an expression of lust but a claiming of territory." Or perhaps that I refuse, *absolutely* refuse to share you with anyone else?"

She swallowed. Any minute now, the past and present would collide in her mind.

"You're being very generous with me."

He blinked. "What was that?"

Viv offered a lopsided smile—a new one he'd never seen before. He quite liked it, although the way it twisted his heart was probably more dangerous than being caught making love behind a staircase.

"You haven't mentioned how you've kept your word ever since we arrived," she said. "And you have yet to say 'I told you so' regarding Mr. Elden's intentions."

Miles let out a heavy sigh. He bracketed her face in his hands and kissed her softly. "I told you so," he whispered.

Her hands tightened on his biceps. She made a little pleading noise in the back of her throat. If they didn't leave in the next three minutes, he'd crawl under her crinolines and smile as history repeated itself.

But Viv wouldn't allow that. Not again. She had the poise of an angel—something he'd been too stubborn and conceited to recognize before. And that majesty was as much a part of her as her wit, her flawless skin, and the green and gold in her eyes. The passion she was capable of rendering was as valuable as her burgeoning trust. He was responsible for protecting it, not flailing at her dignity until she succumbed.

With an effort that left him more dazed than their waltz, Miles stepped away from his wife. His blood fizzed and popped. His ears rang as the distant quartet's melodies turned muddy. His body demanded release, but he refused.

"Miles?"

Her hands were molded flat against the costly white marble, as if bracing against a fierce wind. But the only storm was inside his wife. The animal flare of her nostrils and the tight tendons along her throat revealed her blustering turmoil.

Miles waited. He would have all of her or nothing. That had been his gamble from the very start. Only now did he understand that fully.

She stood away from the wall and laced the fingers of one hand through his. Heat and promise and fear mingled in her decadent gaze. But no matter the challenge, she'd always been a brave woman.

"Miles, take me home."

Viv sat next to Miles in their enclosed coach. Their knees touched. She could move away—anything to put an end to the seductive closeness they'd discovered. But she didn't want to see it end. No matter what tattered ghosts remained come morning, they would be naked, loving, sleeping entwined tonight. There was only darkness inside the coach, but Viv saw the next few hours so clearly.

Then why wasn't she frightened? The jittering feel in her limbs wasn't fear. It was delicious anticipation.

Waltzing with him, wrapped in his firm, skilled hold, had been her every secret fantasy made true. She should have been appalled at her behavior, when her pelvis fitted so snugly against his, but she'd only wanted more.

Viv pressed gloved palms against her flaming cheeks. He didn't say anything as he took one of her hands in his. Slowly but without hesitation, he turned her wrist upward and began unfastening the tiny row of buttons.

"Miles," she breathed.

"Shhh. Close your eyes."

But she couldn't. The white leather of her gloves glowed faintly, while Miles'ss agile fingers offered a dark contrast. The buttons undone, he peeled back the oppressive leather and exposed her skin—first one wrist, then the other. Soon. Soon he would do the same to her dress and her underclothes.

But not soon enough.

She yanked back her hands and stripped off the gloves. The leather dropped into the darkness around their ankles. She shifted on the bench until she could face her husband, this man who ignited her from the inside out. With her fingers naked and trembling, she brushed her knuckles along both of his cheeks. His lips moved, but she couldn't hear what he whispered. She leaned nearer, the crinkle of her silk gown sounding inordinately loud.

"What did you say?"

A hint of moonlight shimmered over his eyes, like the watery reflection of a lake. The volatility she felt was staring back at her. "Kiss me," he whispered.

"Is that what you said?"

"Nearly."

Viv cupped the sides of his face. "Tell me."

"I said, please." He turned his face and kissed one palm.

She shivered. "No, you didn't."

"I said, I want you."

Miles eased her backward until her shoulders braced against the side of the coach. The scent of him, all peppery soap and sun and starch, sped her pulse. But he didn't touch her. Needing that connection, Viv slid her fingers into his hair and tugged. He winced, then grinned.

"Try again," she said against his lips.

"I said, Vivie, I can't breathe. Don't you know that, my darling? I can never breathe when we're together."

"Neither can I."

He pressed a chaste kiss on the end of her nose. His hands fit perfectly into the curve of her waist, then journeyed around to find her backside. Strong fingers fought past the layers until he could squeeze flesh, pulling her thighs apart. Viv gasped. The insistent thrust of his erection nudged against her belly.

"I said, are you scared?"

"Terrified," she said.

"But you're still here. You haven't pushed me away. Why?"

Her face glowed hot. The skin between her legs was hotter still, so slick and ready. "That was our agreement, wasn't it?"

He flinched. "This is just obligation, then?" Although he kept his tone light, his fingers radiated tension into her thighs and buttocks. He breathed with short, shallow breaths through his nose. "I see. If that's how it must be . . ."

"Miles, kiss me properly."

"No," he whispered. "Do you know why?"

"Why?"

"Because I'm tired of chasing you. It does in a man's pride, you see. Pulls it to shreds."

His pelvis flexed. With slow, maddening strokes, he mimicked entering and withdrawing, rubbing his swollen shaft against her hot center. Her drawers were damp. Wet cotton rubbed against that sensitive skin. Viv was strung between agony and white-hot pleasure. She breathed his name and matched his rhythm. Her hips tipped up with his every grinding push, meeting him, inviting him. The friction teased and stretched and sparked, so near to what her body craved. So very near—but so frustrating that she pounced.

She kissed him. Hard. Teeth and lips and tongues jammed together as she took out her frustrations on his firm, luscious mouth. Miles grunted. He tightened his hold on her backside and rubbed his smooth cheeks against hers as they fought for a better angle. He tasted just right, her husband, this man she wanted more with each hot inhale. He was the passion she had never known with anyone else. He was promises kept.

Only when her head thumped against the wall of the coach did they part. Viv panted. Miles's hands still held her lower body in the most exquisite cage of raw need and beautiful brawn. They regarded each other, still and suspended, with only the noise of wheels along the gravel and their own rough breathing to color the silence.

Miles swallowed. "Do you want to know what I said? Truly?"

"Yes."

"I said, come to me." He eased a lock of hair off her forehead and followed it to her ear. Such tenderness. God, he was impossible. "Because I wasn't lying, Viv. I don't want to beg or bargain anymore. If you want me tonight, you must come to me. Come to stay."

He sat up and resumed his seat. With a swift hand down either sleeve, he smoothed his evening suit back into place. Only the way he shifted slightly on the bench gave away his body's discomfort. Was he still hard? If she slid her palm up his thigh, would he open his knees for her, invite her as she had?

The thought made Viv shake. Her mouth felt cottony and her tongue swollen.

But worse than the unspent passion whirling through her muscles, glimmering just beneath her skin, she considered his words. She'd always assumed that only her pride was at stake, as he wiggled and wormed past her defenses. She'd never considered that her rejections might affect him the same way.

And dear God, she'd left him. Twice.

Miles wanted her. She'd come to rely on that fact. But one day, after one rejection too many . . . what if he no longer did?

With a jolt the coach came to a stop. Miles jerked the handle and swung the door outward, not waiting for Adam. He jumped down to the ground.

She bent at the waist and grabbed her gloves, then went about slowly tugging them back into place. But the fire in her blood refused to ease. She finally accepted his hand. Her knees wobbled as she stood on solid ground. The light of an external lamp lit his face from one side, exaggerating every plane and ridge in strong shadow. Adam flicked the reins and drove the coach back toward the stable, leaving Viv alone with her husband.

Husband.

Not lover. Not master. Not any of her mother's faceless customers.

"Why does this have to be so difficult, Viv?"

Because you don't know me.

He didn't know the terror and the hunger. He didn't know the putrid smells and the sound of abused mattress ropes, or the screams of the mad and the damned, all clutched behind iron bars. He didn't know and he never would.

With desperation layered atop desire, she looped her arms around his neck. She kissed him again—hard, hot, questing. She held on, eyes closed tightly, her tongue memorizing the taste of him as if for the last time.

Twenty-two

*M*iles stood on the walkway and kissed his wife. But despite the wicked, needful fire in his gut and the ache of his impatient erection, he didn't devour her.

She devoured *him*.

Such a gratifying reward, one he tried to savor. So he kissed Viv, but with the restraint he'd never known he could muster. Her tongue invaded and his retreated. Her hands grabbed at his hair and his shoulders, while his remained fixed at her lower back. He was being worshipped by a stubborn, mysterious slip of a woman and he didn't want to miss a single sensation.

Viv angled her head to kiss more deeply, stoking the flame of his need. He would let her determine the pace—for the sake of his pride, yes, but also to let her discover how shattering it could be to lead, to demand, to take. He needed a partner in all things, even in his greed.

His own eagerness could wait while he soaked up hers.

That amusing noise of frustration returned as she pulled away. "Why are you doing this?"

"Simply awaiting orders, my lady."

"Orders?"

"Your sexual demands. I will obey your wishes, but I will not anticipate them." A thick strand of golden hair had unfurled. He tugged it, then let the curl spring back against her cheek. She looked wild and delicious. He breathed her rich rosewater scent and spoke against her temple. "Trust, Vivie. I'm yours for the taking. I promise. Tonight, you decide *everything*."

Her gaze fastened on his mouth, as if the sight of his lower lip had become more fascinating than a hundred perfect gems. "Very well. Your bedroom. Now."

She tugged his hand, practically dragging him toward the house. He followed her across the threshold and up the stairs, watching the swish and sway of her bustle. The magnificent red gown had likely made her the envy of every woman at the ball, and the object of every man's desire. But the lush creation had served its purpose. He wanted her free of it. Soon.

No, her pace.

Bloody hell, he was a madman.

Down the corridor, she opened the door to Miles's bedchamber and shoved him gently inside. The click as it closed sounded like a promise. Safe there, tucked together away from the rest of mankind, she laid her hand flat against his chest, right over his heart. That light, warm pressure accentuated how quickly it beat.

"I'm through second-guessing what I want. At least for tonight. But . . ." She swallowed, her eyes rimmed with the slightest shimmer of tears. "But I'm going to need your help."

Miles held very still. She had the potential for such authority and aggression, but doubts could make her skittish. He wanted none of that hesitation between them when their bodies came together.

"How so?"

"Have you ever had infinite choices? Have you ever sat down at a dinner party only to learn that you can have any meat? Any dessert?" Rather efficiently, she went about lighting two candles, one on either side of his bed. No matter what she said about choices, she had obviously pictured certain details already. His room, lit by a gentle glow. "I wouldn't want to make a mistake—request Yorkshire pudding with pheasant and a side of mint sauce and custard."

His lips twitched, beginning to glean her meaning. "But what if that is, in fact, what you want?"

"I wouldn't want to look a fool," she whispered.

Her desolate expression made Miles want to hold her. Not make love to her. Just hold her. Ah, God, this had not been about sex in ages. Maybe it never had been so neatly sordid. Their hearts wouldn't let go.

"Would it help to know that anything is possible here? With just us? Mint sauce and all."

"Don't tease, Miles. Not about this."

He shook his head slowly, his gaze never wavering. "No teasing. Here, just you and me and *anything*."

"I . . ." She wiggled the second candle into its holder and joined him in the middle of the room. "I would prefer . . . choices."

"Marmalade or butter? Beef or lamb?"

"Trifle or fruit. Exactly."

He touched her cheek, stroking from the soft crest to the hollow below. Such a strong, lovely creature existed nowhere else in the world. What he wouldn't do for this woman. The possibilities tightened a vise where his lungs had been. "Very well. Choices it is."

"Where do we begin?"

"With me."

Her smile flashed. The derisive one. "Naturally."

"Would you like me clothed or naked?" He loved how her lips parted in reflexive shock—just before she licked them. "Do you want me completely nude? You can see me, touch my skin, kiss me where you choose. Or shall I undo my trousers and have you in my evening suit?"

"Naked."

He nodded, affecting a businesslike manner. "Will you do the honors or me?"

"You."

"Will you watch me?"

"Yes."

Her eyes were wide and luminous. Miles wanted to sink into them, into her, but he had a task to attend. If he could manage. She was worth the effort of traipsing across Africa and learning what he could about mining and drill bits. Offering the use of his body for her exclusive pleasure should be nothing by comparison. Yet his pulse thundered and his breath burned. She was going to break him apart, and he was her willing victim.

He pinched the ends of his silken ascot and pulled. The first step to becoming entirely hers.

Viv backed against the bedpost, her hands behind her, gripping it fiercely, but she never looked away as Miles disrobed. Coat, waistcoat, shirt—only her flared nostrils and intent stare gave away her desire as he bared his chest. He kicked off his shoes, then stripped off his socks, trousers, underclothes.

He was breathing rapidly. Rarely, if ever, had he felt so exposed, especially when her heavy-lidded gaze widened as she caught sight of his erection. No matter her reassurances, Viv could walk out and leave him naked, aroused, greedy. In such a scenario he didn't trust himself not to beg. She'd be the end of him if she ever made that discovery.

"Now you," he rasped, his body hot despite skin bared to the cool bedroom air. "Naked or clothed?"

Viv was sucking on the tip of her index finger. "That's an interesting mental picture, is it not? You, ah, as you are—and me still dressed."

"Interesting? Or arousing?"

"Both. It's a matter of power, I should think. The woman is usually nude."

"Vulnerable."

"Exactly." She toed off her slippers. "But I want to breathe. Help me out of my gown."

Miles met her at the bedpost. She could shift her hand and touch his pleading cock. "Quickly or slowly?"

"Must every aspect have choice?"

He dared to slide his palm up her sleek arm. "To do it properly."

"Slowly, then," she said. "Very slowly."

"And may I kiss your skin as I reveal it to the light?"

Viv lifted her hands and gracefully unpinned her hair. With a few quick flicks of her wrist, she tossed her head. Silken gold streamed around her shoulders. Miles inhaled her rosy scent.

"That strikes me as what *you* want," she said. "Is that true?"

"Yes."

"I thought this was about what I want."

He swallowed. "It is."

Viv trailed a finger down her neck, then to her bust line, just inside the lacey edge. Miles imagined taking that same journey with his tongue and groaned.

"All this time," she said, her voice as dark and sweet as wine, "you've done your level best to make me desperate. Did you know that? You wore me down until all I could do was *need*."

She laid both palms flat along his flanks, her fingers splayed. Miles couldn't help it: he thrust. But his rigid shaft didn't find the hot slickness he craved—only cool, crisp silk.

"Viv, what are you doing?"

"I never saw that you were just as desperate."

She pushed against his chest and stepped clear of him. As if kicked by a horse, he couldn't take a breath. "Vivie?"

"Lie down."

"What?"

"You heard me, but I'll say it again. Lie down."

Miles relaxed the hands he'd balled into fists. He lay down on the bed, as if condemned prisoners facing firing squads now did so from a horizontal position. His body remained throbbing and hard, his cock upthrust and demonstrating even less pride than he did.

"I've changed my mind," she said.

His heart thudded out an extra beat. She was going to leave him. She was going to walk out—her hair unbound but her gown still clinging to her perfect curves—and Miles was going to crumple. He'd gambled and he was going to lose everything.

Somewhere between their waltz and the door to Miles's bedroom, Viv had won the hand. After all, she'd never witnessed a more erotic sight. Miles lay sideways on the bed with his hands behind his head. His legs dropped over the side, bent at the knee—legs so long that the soles of his feet rested flat on the floor. He wiggled his toes as if impatient.

Instead of turning toward the door, she joined him at the bed.

"That is allowed, isn't it? Changing my mind?"

His jaw muscles bunched. "Yes," he ground out.

"Good. Because I've decided to leave my gown on after all."

The tension eased from his face. She was intimidated, yes, but she was going through with this. What more glorious challenge had she ever faced? Not only did the notion of returning to her room strike her as cowardly, it smacked of genuine stubbornness. The relief he'd shown upon hearing her reassurances helped remind her that she wasn't alone in this risk.

He needs me.

But oh, how her heart guttered and raced. And breathing . . . she'd catch her breath sometime after dawn.

With a daring that was as unfamiliar as it was liberating, Viv slowly lifted her skirts until she grasped the waistband of her drawers. She kept her eyes on Miles's mouth the whole time. Such a decadent thing, his lower lip—masculine in its shape and surety, but soft, full, even beautiful.

She remembered that night, so long ago, when Miles had seduced her with depraved words before kissing between her thighs. The pleasure had been swift and fiery. Her climax had overtaken her so quickly, almost as soon as it began. Afterward, she couldn't look at his mouth for weeks, ashamed of her behavior. And wanting it again.

But right then, free of her damp cotton drawers, Viv knew what she craved.

The trick would be asking for it.

She clamped her knees along the outsides of Miles's spread-eagled legs. He pressed back, challenging her, smiling that knowing smile. The taut muscles of his thighs bunched. His skin was golden in the lamplight, dusted with hair as dark as his eyes. And all the while his thick, proud erection stretched toward his belly button.

He gave a little thrust, his buttocks barely contracting.

His arrogance *always* returned. The only way she'd found to counter it was to take him by surprise. He expected her shyness, just as he expected that her desire would win out. How much more conceited could one man be?

No matter that it was true.

But when she spoke her desire aloud, wielding it like a weapon, she could level him.

"What, no more choices?" she asked.

"This position didn't strike me as one with too many options."

"No?" She leaned over, permitting a generous view of her cleavage. "You simply expect me to hike my skirts and climb aboard?"

"I wouldn't say no."

"Of course not." Viv laid her hands on either side of his nipples and stroked all the way down, slowly, her fingers rigid, until she reached his thighs.

"Again," he said, breathless.

"Oh, but this isn't about you, remember?"

"Viv."

She licked her upper lip as if swiping away a last bit of cream. "Very well."

With her nails this time, she repeated the long, languorous caress. The rounded flesh of his pectorals gave way to the thump, thump, thump of each rib. She watched, fascinated, as his stomach muscles contracted, followed by another small thrust of his pelvis. Down past his groin, scraping his outer hips, she didn't stop until she was clawing deep into the hard bulk of his lean thighs. He'd always been overwhelming. Some combination of character and carriage made him larger than life.

And at that moment, he belonged entirely to her.

Viv slowly wrapped her hand around his erection. "Choices, Miles?" She squeezed.

He gasped. His hips pulsed off the bed. "Fuck me or kill me."

"No, that's not the way of it." She leaned near enough to rub her lacy décolletage up the length of his legs, until her mouth hovered above one flat, dark nipple. She licked. Then she repeated her full body exploration, trailing her tongue down to the thin, satiny skin between his belly and his groin. Knowing how tender that swath of skin was on her own body, she kissed him again, mouth open, then sucked.

He grabbed the back of her head.

Viv lifted and pushed him away. "Don't touch."

"You're doing this on purpose."

"Yes."

"Damn it, Vivie." But to his credit, he grabbed two handfuls of royal blue duvet instead of her unbound hair.

"Tell me you aren't enjoying yourself." Her mouth was within inches of the heavy erection she still petted and stroked. Nothing smelled the way Miles did—the masculine salt of his arousal. Nothing grabbed at her deepest, most shocking urges like that primal scent. "Tell me this isn't what you wanted."

He didn't reply with words, only a guttural growl of frustration. He still wore a smile; it simply wasn't so smug now.

"I think," she said, "my next choice should be about kissing. Don't you?" If he could still feel something so subtle, he'd feel her breath along his hot shaft. "So many choices. Who should kiss whom? And where? And how deeply? How am I to decide?" With a quick flick she touched her tongue to his swollen head. "Come now, use that clever mind of yours."

"In my mind, I'm already inside of you."

"Concentrate, Miles. Kisses."

"You kissing me. There. Kiss me there."

"That's not a choice," she said, her voice throaty and raw. "That's a command."

She shifted so that her wet center straddled one of his muscular thighs. Maybe leaving her dress on had been a mistake. Her corset left her even more light-headed. She felt like a sleepwalker acting out a potent dream.

"Not so easy, is it?" she asked.

"What?"

"Giving up control. You like it, no matter your penchant for gambling."

He thrashed his head to one side. "It's just a game."

"I don't believe you."

"It is. Have you ever done what you're taunting me with right now? Certainly not with me."

"Doesn't mean my thoughts never strayed." She petted his thick shaft, then rubbed up and down with a rhythm that he quickly matched, hips gyrating. "But you've said it from the start. This is about trust. You have to believe I'm here to give you pleasure. And I have to believe you won't use my wanton impulses as future ammunition."

"Do it, Vivie."

"Because I want to," she whispered, smiling softly. "Not because you told me to."

She took him into her mouth.

Miles cried out. His hips lifted. His thigh ground between her legs.

Viv had transformed into another person—maybe no person at all, but rather some creature that amused herself by torturing naked men.

Not just any man, though. This one. This one whose shaft pressed into her mouth, whose essence salted her tongue as she swirled and licked. Her heart slammed against her ribs and filled her ears with a fast cadence. As her adversary more often than her lover, Miles had never engendered confidence enough to act on such a bold intimacy. But now she reveled in the task. He groaned with every touch of her tongue, every deep plunge that pressed his hard rod deeper, thrusting even as she bobbed her head. The power of taking so much of him into her body, in this new and wholly erotic way, was even more heady than his kisses.

Miles had given up on the duvet. Instead his hands found her hair. He guided her strokes, silently instructing her on this delicate art. Then clever fingers edged beneath the border of her gown, finding flesh, finding her nipples, rolling them, tugging. Viv sucked hard to remind him who was in charge. He didn't stop. In fact he pulsed his thigh between her legs in what could only be a deliberate torment.

She withdrew with a laugh, then made a grand show of wiping her mouth and adjusting her bodice. Miles looked absolutely murderous. His hands clenched and opened, useless at his sides. The leashed potency of her man stretched out before her, waiting for her, aching for her, leveled the scales of power between them. She needed him, but oh how he needed her, too.

"I think I got that all wrong," she said. "You're supposed to be kissing me."

"Where?"

If he thought that was going to shock her, he hadn't been paying attention to the last half hour. Viv yanked yards of splendid red silk above her knees and crawled onto the bed. Straddling him at the waist, she bent low and licked the blunt, roughened contours of his chin.

"First here," she said, touching her lower lip. Then she stroked her thumb along his. He caught the pad between his teeth and suckled. His hands found her naked backside and began kneading sensual circles.

God, he was handsome. Her heart flipped over just watching him. The cut of his cheekbones, the slope of his brow, the piercing beauty of his dark brown eyes. She touched his temple, feathering back hair that had turned gold, as if the sun needed to make him more irresistible.

Rather than wait for Miles to comply, she retrieved her thumb from between his lips and dove into a deep, probing kiss—unleashing all of her frustrations.

When air and time abandoned her, she pulled up and took a deep, shuddering breath. "No. That's not it either. See how badly I've managed this?"

"Woman, I am going to make you suffer for this."

"For a gambler, you're a terrible liar."

"Normally this doesn't happen at a card table."

"Shouldn't do, no."

She crawled forward until she framed her husband's unyielding torso with her knees. When she'd positioned her pelvis near enough to his face, she made a show of slowly, slowly bunching her scarlet skirts. His eyes widened. Finally, with her most private place revealed, she exhaled slowly. The dizziness was going to steal her words. But she forced it aside and stared him down.

"Kiss me, Miles. Right there. I dare you."

Twenty-three

Although his control was only going to last another few seconds, Miles gloried in what he'd wrought. Viv was the most erotic, the most blazingly beautiful woman he'd ever imagined. Thighs the color of cream straddled his chest. Private curls as pale as her hair shone silvery-gold in the candlelight. A goddess, a witch, she had ripped out his heart and seemed intent on ruining his mind and body, too. But for all the power he'd ceded—forcing control into her hands like a weapon she barely knew how to aim—Miles was a happy man.

He was also a man on the verge of spilling his seed as would an inexperienced lad.

Briefly, he closed his eyes. She'd been strong enough to ask. He'd be strong enough to give her what she wanted, his own body's needs be damned. But closing his eyes barely grounded him. Viv's woman's scent intoxicated him. Her rasping breath was a siren's call. And his hands at her backside, pulsing, clutching, was as much to release his own tension as to arouse his wife.

"Miles?"

The doubt in her voice did more for control than any attempt to block her out. Even now she was afraid of committing some social faux pas that would garner ridicule. He saw it in the way she nibbled her lower lip and how her hands were slowly going slack, lowering the silken curtain of her gown. Her mouth was somber, not soft and breathy.

"No mistakes, Vivie," he said softly. "Not here. Now be a dear and keep those skirts out of my eyes. I don't want to miss a glimpse."

Her quiet exhale cleared the path for a return to passion. Her smile was almost grateful, grabbing inside his chest and twisting.

He didn't want gratefulness and he didn't want doubt. He wanted her crying out his name.

With a surge of strength Miles reversed their positions on the bed. Viv was beneath him, her thighs wide. He kissed her then, beginning with her bewitching mouth. He nipped and nuzzled until she laughed. He intensified the kiss, just his mouth over hers, exploring, mating tongue to tongue. His fists he kept tangled in the wild beauty of her unbound hair. She gave him her sighs and her restless noises.

But kissing was simply dry kindling on a fire that already glinted and roared. Miles edged down her neck and soothed tense tendons with each stroke of his tongue. Further down he reached the rounded swells of her breasts and indulged himself only briefly, just a few kisses, until the idea of stroking his shaft between those two full mounds threatened his frayed control.

Like finding an oasis, he finally reached her feminine center. Pale skin glistened and her thighs shifted in a restless dance. He hooked his arms around those limbs, stilling her. He lowered his mouth and tasted.

Viv cried out, then sighed deep and long.

She was honey and heat, sex and whiskey, melting his mind in a vat of sensation. Miles swirled his tongue and found the rhythm that made her whisper his name over and over. Her fingers threaded through his hair, tugging him closer. He kept his mouth pressed firmly against her flesh, his tongue sliding across that most sensitive bud. The moment, when it came, lifted her hips from the bed. Her hoarse gasp echoed through his room.

He had no more to give. His erection was a force of nature now, making demands that only Viv could satisfy. With his elbows still crooked behind her knees, Miles lifted his body and drove into hers. His own cry was guttural and low. He thrust hard, harder, rutting like something mindless. He knew better, but he couldn't stop. Dimly, with his sense of hearing blunted by the drum of his heartbeat, he heard Viv gasp once again. Her inner muscles clenched the length of his shaft and her fingernails clawed deep into his buttocks.

A pinwheel of pleasure set fire to every nerve, sparking and flashing from head to heel. He grunted, came, and collapsed with a breathless groan.

Minutes later, roused from the black by the swirl of Viv's gentle petting along his temple, he struggled to make his bones and muscles work in concert.

"Is this a little gray here, Miles?"

"Me? Never."

"I like it."

He found himself praying then, although what deity might listen to a wastrel like him remained a great unknown. *God, don't let this end. I'll be good. I promise.*

Slowly he pulled off of Viv and rolled clear. She looked wanton, wicked, all rumpled silk and untidy hair. A bite mark he didn't remember inflicting was a dusky pink crescent on the upper slope of her breast.

"Will you leave?" he asked.

"I said I wouldn't." Her eyes widened. "Not tonight, I mean."

"Of course. One romp doesn't mean forever, does it?"

He regretted it as soon as he said it. Unresolved bitterness wouldn't let him keep a civil tongue.

Viv's smile, however, seemed inclined toward reconciliation. She pushed off the mattress and held out her hands. They stood belly to belly, gazes lost in one another. "It doesn't have to," she said softly. "But it could. If we want it to. We make the rules, remember?"

Miles stood gobsmacked as she turned her back, once again offering the intimate task of removing her gown. Laces and tapes and buttons eventually gave way to the damp cotton of her chemise and long naked legs. He wasn't above indulging his imagination once more as she bent over the head of the bed and drew back the covers. Her backside was a work of art, one made even more erotic by the rose-hued finger marks he'd put there. But then she was gone, swallowed by yards of sumptuous sheets.

Miles wanted a drink. Needed it. He didn't think it possible to need anything after having just experienced such a satisfying encounter.

I love you, Viv.

What would she do if he said it aloud? Would she smile like she had when waltzing? Or would her brows lift and her eyes go wide, that expression of polite distance he'd come to dread?

"Aren't you cold?" She'd poked out of the bedding just enough to extinguish the nearest candle.

He shook free of his languor, blew out the other candle and slid into the bed. Her body was smooth and warm. Sleek limbs melted over his like chocolate in the sun, just as she had after her nightmare. Only now they were sated and completely nude. A faint trace of moonlight limned every surface.

Slowly, he exhaled. This *was* enough. For now. They had come so far and had months left in Kimberley. He'd be the man she needed, no matter how long it took.

"What will we do about Elden?" she asked, her breath soft across his chest. "He won't forgive my slap."

Quiet laughter rumbled out of his throat. "You slapped him, too?"

"I did."

"That's my girl." The intimacy and possessiveness of that statement struck him afterward. Only, Viv didn't stiffen or pull away. She snuggled more deeply into his embrace. "We'll deal with him in the morning. Think nothing more of it tonight."

But still she didn't sleep.

"Something on your mind, Vivie?"

"Mmm."

"Now's the time for it. You have my undivided attention."

She propped her head on one arm and gazed down at him. Her face was made of shadow, her hair of silver. "What happened the night of the Saunders' gala? After we finished?"

"Will you believe my answer?"

She swallowed. "I'll try to."

Miles stared up at the ceiling. He curled her to his chest and held her slender shoulder a little too tightly. She petted his chest hair and breathed softly against his throat, her mouth nestled there. This was harder than he'd expected, but he would not hide what he felt. Not anymore. If he was asking her to trust his reply, he needed to honor her with the complete honesty she deserved.

"You scared me that night," he said into the darkness. "Every challenge and every dare, you leveled me with a look. Just . . . bored of it all, even after we'd ravaged each other behind the staircase. I knew it then, that you were at the end of your rope."

She had gone still as a hunted rabbit. "And where you woke up?"

"The Duke of Hereford's youngest son suggested a round of cards. It seemed at the time like the perfect escape route. Why take you home and risk everything by making it a real marriage—working hard for what we wanted—when I could be as useless as ever? Cards led to more drink, and drink led to a house of ill repute. It also led me to being sick and falling unconscious on an extremely tacky purple velvet settee. I awoke after noon and even in such a state, I wondered if you would be gone when I got home."

She kissed the notch between his collarbones and dipped her tongue inside. Surprised heat shot from head to toe. "We had no trust."

"Now you're the one being generous tonight, Vivie. I gave you no reason to trust me. That was the way of it."

"But then we were apart for so long and . . . I wouldn't. That is . . ."

"Are you asking if I've been unfaithful?"

She nodded silently.

He was thankful then—thankful for whatever latent sense of honor had kept him out of any other woman's bed. He was thankful because he could tell Viv the truth.

"I swear it," he said, his voice low and calm. "There's been no one else, not even when you had cause to assume the worst. I recited my vows carelessly, yet those vows have bound me. I was many things, Vivie—drunk, irresponsible, obnoxious. But I've never been unfaithful."

She let out a long exhale that sounded very much like the relief he felt. "Then what do we do?"

He stroked her upper arm as if she were the one shivering. But it was Miles who quivered on the inside. They were on the cusp of something new. New could be good, just after it finished being petrifying.

"I want to change. I want to be the man you can depend on."

Viv looked down at him from amid a halo of pale tangled hair. She was Venus personified, a living goddess that fate had decided might be his. What a ridiculous fool he'd been, waiting so long to be worthy of her.

"You've kept your side of the bargain admirably. More than I could've hoped. You *have* been the man I could depend on, when no one else would've dared." Slim fingers worked down his chest, following the line of hair toward his groin. Firm, beautiful breasts pillowed against him in an unashamed display of her body's lush bounty. "Tell me it wasn't for my enthusiasm alone."

He slid his hands into that lush curtain of hair and brought her face near. Against her lips he whispered, "It was for you, Vivie. *All* of you."

Their mouths met just as she found his member with a sure grip. His erection surged in her hand. Blood and hope and relief spun together. He fused them in his kiss and rolled his breathtaking wife onto her back.

"Then maybe," she said between gasps, "it's time to start again."

At the sound of rustling papers, Viv opened her eyes. Frankly, it wasn't how she had imagined greeting the morning. Ideas of Miles nuzzling her awake and making love to her in the sleepy half haze of dawn had been more probable—and more enjoyable. But he was sitting up in bed reviewing notes from a stack on his bedside table.

Had he often done as much studying as she did? A warm shiver of happiness tickled up from her belly. Only, he saw the world in distinctly different ways. Learning those ways would be a joy for the rest of her days.

A future. They had talked of a real future.

That happy tickle threatened to turn to fear. So much could still go wrong. She no longer doubted Miles, but her own worth. If he discovered the truth of her birth . . . Would he want her then? It was all well and good for a nobleman to cultivate a reputation for vice, but could he bear to know that his wife had been born to such a dismal life?

The chance was worth taking. She peeked up at him through half-lidded eyes. His sun-touched hair was tousled. A serious expression shaped his mouth, his jaw, the corners of his eyes. The gathering dawn caught the brown of his irises and lit them with a sensual golden fire. Barechested, he radiated that effervescent combination of physical strength and confidence. Perhaps she should have been startled by the faint scratch and bite marks that revealed the path she'd traveled from his throat to his groin. Instead she grinned at herself. He was her territory to claim.

"When you're done consuming me with your gaze," he said dryly, still examining the papers in his lap, "I have something to show you."

Viv giggled and buried her face in the pillow that carried both of their scents. Man and woman together. Husband and wife. At that moment, she knew she would do anything to keep him now—and that meant keeping her secret, too.

Miles caught her by the shoulder and rolled her onto her back. "I mean it, Lady Bancroft. My brain can only sustain a train of thought for so long, especially when presented with such a delectable alternative."

"What alternative might that be?"

"Worshipping you from head to toe until neither of us can think ever again."

A hot jolt settled beneath her sternum and wet her inner thighs. That he could manage such a thing with words alone was only intimidating in that he used his mouth, his hands, his glorious manhood to even more potent effect. "I like the sound of that."

"Yes, but not exactly the makings of a profitable company. Come figure this with me."

"You really are determined on this point, aren't you?" She sat up and dragged the sheet with her, covering her breasts.

Miles eyed the move with obvious disdain. "If I'm the naked object of your unabashed appreciation, I demand reciprocity." He tugged the bedding down until her breasts were fully exposed. "I could become a dedicated entrepreneur if this is how we conduct our morning meetings."

Although she blushed as furiously as humanly possible, Viv remained still. Her nipples tightened, from both the slight chill and his blatant stare. She snuggled against his side, curious now what would be so interesting as to hold his attention, even when making love was the alternative.

"These are Adam's notes about what he's discovered among the servant class," he said. "That's where I began, because I remember him mentioning something about Neil Elden and the Opsberger Brothers' Brokerage. Turns out he held a position on their board of directors and bought them out last year when their loans came due."

Viv perked up, their nudity briefly forgotten. "He owns another brokerage? But still does business with us? That doesn't make any sense."

"Worse than that. He owns *three* brokerages."

"And no one knows this?"

"Well, he's made it deuced hard to follow. Covert stock exchanges, silent partnerships." He offered up various snippets of proof: business records, company statements, and Adam's meticulous notes. "But the process is always the same. He sits on a board of directors until, by chance or by force, the business falls into disrepair and he gobbles it up."

"How did Adam manage all of this?"

"I don't ask. Better that way."

"Well, obviously Elden intends some sort of horizontal monopoly."

Viv wished she had a daguerreotype of Miles's baffled expression. She stifled a chuckle to save his pride.

"Explain, my dear," he said with a tight grin. "Show me what your father stuffed into that brain of yours."

Feeling powerful and cheeky, she slipped out of bed and collected Miles's clothes from where they'd been discarded the night before. His puzzled expression only increased, but he seemed to be enjoying himself. A naughty smile tipped the corners of his sinful mouth. "Or tidy up the room while completely naked," he said. "That works, too."

"Both." She laid out his clothes on the bed, from socks to top hat, in the shape of a man. "Now, imagine that all your company sells are complete suits. How many customers will you have?"

"For complete suits? Nothing else? Probably not so many."

"But those who *did* make purchases would bring in a great deal of revenue. My father and another Scots rival of his, a man named Carnegie, believed you could do this with business. Own every aspect of production. In this case, outfitting a man. Carnegie has ambitions to do it with steel. Own the coke, the ore, the railroads, the refineries—so that the price of the final product is his to determine." She shrugged. "It goes vertically, top to bottom."

"Like this suit." Pausing, he pulled back the covers and urged her to climb back into the warmth of his bed. Viv complied eagerly. She wrapped around him, soaking him in, while his hands found her backside and her breasts. All over. Every inch just . . . his.

"But Elden is only buying up brokerages," he said.

"So now imagine your clothing shop only sells ascots. In fact, it was the *only* business in the whole of Kimberley that sells ascots, because you've bought out all the competition. You could charge any price, and a man who wished to wear a complete suit would need to pay it."

"Cecil Rhodes is determined to own the entire Hole. Perhaps Elden sees the future. The only way he'll be able to compete is to determine which diamonds make it to Europe, and at what commissions."

"Then he needs rid of us."

"Well, that certainly isn't going to happen."

Viv stopped petting his chest. Her fingers rested in the spaces between his ribs. "I feel like such a fool."

"About what?"

"Elden. You're a much better judge of character than I am."

Miles kissed her hair, then rolled her back and gazed down. She could fall into his earthen brown eyes and live there forever. She would be safe there now. "I think we both saw what we wanted to see," he said. "I saw an ambitious, successful, passably handsome man spending too much time with my wife. What conclusion was I left to draw but an uncomplimentary one?"

"And me? What explains that I was willing to think so highly of him?"

"Because you miss your father."

He held her when she shivered through a sweep of unexpected grief, then made love to her when she ached for more. Never once did she doubt he would do just that.

Twenty-four

"And here you can see the best-quality carbons. There are literally thousands, my lord."

Ike Penberthy sat across from Miles in the upstairs office at Christie Brokerage, explaining the results of his weeks spent cataloguing. Columns of notes regarding size, quantities, and grades lined sheet after sheet of paper.

Miles assumed by default that Penberthy had assembled a similar system in the crawl space for keeping the piles neatly ordered. He was simply that meticulous, but not in Smets's grating, submissive way. No matter what nerves he might feel in presenting his findings, Penberthy did not fidget with the brim of the hat he held in his lap.

"Excellent work."

"Thank you, my lord."

No fawning or excessive sense of indebtedness. Another good sign. He had combed his hair, trimmed his curly blond beard, and dressed neatly for this meeting. More than mere grooming, he held Miles's gaze with the confidence of a man who knew his worth. Once given the opportunity to prove himself, he had done so with gusto.

Miles no longer thought to pay him well because of some altruistic concern for his wife and family. After all, there were literally thousands of people in Kimberley living with similar burdens. No, this was about honoring a job well done.

"I want you to consider assuming control of this new wing of our business's model," he said. "Smets obviously does very well with the brilliants, but you would be in charge of the carbons. All decisions about their market value, how much to pay the mines for what they sell— this would be your domain." He peered at the man, judging each reaction. Wider eyes. Nostrils that flared over a quick intake of air. But also a straighter back and shoulders that squared to assume new weight. "Do you think you can manage?"

He asked the question even though he already knew the answer. Penberthy nodded once and said, "Yes, my lord. I have no doubt."

"Neither do I. Now, Lady Bancroft tells me that the flat above Westmeade's Milliners is available to let. I suggest you prepare Mrs. Penberthy for the task of moving your children and belongings there."

"Moving . . . ?"

"Of course. Your new salary will be more than adequate, I assure you. And from what Lady Bancroft tells me of the work your wife has accomplished for the Women's Auxiliary, she deserves better accommodations as much as you do." Rather than endure a round of profuse appreciation that would do neither man's pride any good, Miles raised his eyebrows. "Well then, we both have work to do."

Penberthy stood, his hands a little less steady now as he smiled. "You have my gratitude, my lord."

"And you have mine. You've earned this, and I intend to rely on you to the point of beastly tedium. Good day to you, man."

Penberthy departed, his steps almost imperceptibly lighter. Miles grinned to himself. But the tasks of the day remained. Viv had charged him with drafting a formal letter to the Board and their key suppliers. Any mining company that didn't appreciate trading in carbons would be released from obligation at the conclusion of their existing contracts. They were gambling that enough time would pass for them to prove the viability of Miles's idea.

The task of formally winning them over would be an arduous one. He needed to bring to bear every shred of aristocratic authority, maybe even make a few promises— Parliamentary promises. A letter here. A suggestion there. Just the hint of favor from a man such as his father might be enough for most of these rags-to-riches entrepreneurs.

Except for the likes of Neil Elden. That would require more . . . aggression. Miles and Viv debated long into the night, every night, regarding how to neutralize their biggest threat. Ideas from bribes to intimidation to fraud inquiries came to naught. Miles argued for a preemptive strike, while Viv maintained the need for subterfuge. Let Elden reveal his plans first. Their debate would surely continue, but always they ended on the best of terms: sweating, panting, and completely sated.

He was beginning to *adore* business.

So, yes, Miles had his work cut out for him, while Viv did her part by greasing the wheels with the usual gaggle of influential matrons. A very full afternoon. But in his mind, he was still at breakfast. Oh, the way she'd teased him with sideways glances. She'd taken an inordinate amount of time slathering butter and jam over a thick slab of fresh bread, then nibbled and licked and slowly devoured her breakfast in a manner that he could only describe as sexual.

The minx.

No wonder he couldn't see straight, couldn't think straight. He would begin a new sentence, then remember how Viv's inner thigh muscle had tensed when he put his mouth on her, the way she would sigh and relax as the initial shock gave way to slow, building pleasure. He'd begin adding a column of numbers, then feel the hard pressure of her heels digging into his lower back. Her body always welcomed his every stroke, no matter how hard, how deep.

A blissful homecoming.

They had turned a corner. Miles could see a real, lasting marriage. So close now. Soon, after they solved the business's problems and he could promise her the future she deserved, he would declare his intentions once and for all.

So what was he doing in the cramped little office in the brokerage house? He should be at *their* house. To spend another moment away from her was a monumental waste.

Miles rubbed his eyes. He scratched the back of his neck.

He stood and paced the tiny room, which was like pacing the interior of a hatbox. With as much bearing as he could muster, he glared at the account ledgers and the unfinished letter.

"Give me one good reason," he said.

But the truth of it stared back, a festival of ink scratches and paper piles. He would do his duty. Work first, then play. How novel.

Mumbling curses under his breath, he loosened the hangman's noose that Adam still insisted on calling an ascot. He yanked it off and returned to his desk.

"Very well," he said. "You win. But I don't have to like it."

"Throwing in your hand so soon, Miles?"

He turned in his chair and found Viv at the top of the pinched little stairwell.

She looked especially beautiful, despite the telltale circles beneath her eyes. He smiled at the sight, knowing he had kept her up too late. Her luminous hair was a plaited halo, topped with an elegant emerald bonnet that did marvels for the precious green flecks in her irises. A sleek beige silk gown molded to her body—a body he wanted beneath his once more.

Would the sight of her ever refrain from stopping his heart? He didn't want to see the day when it did. To take something so exquisite for granted would be as great a waste as spending time apart. She held herself with such mystery. He'd become so enamored of her that he no longer wondered where his pride had gone to. He was, quite simply, *hers*. Every other consideration paled.

"My, my, aren't you the sneaky one," he said, rising. "Checking in on me?"

She remained poised at the top of the stairs. "Do you need checking in on?"

"Absolutely."

"Up to mischief?" Her smile quirked as she said it.

"No, in truth. Not up to much of anything."

"Having trouble concentrating?"

Her lips bowed around a private smile as her gaze traveled down the length of him. She took her time, lingering, lighting him on fire with that slow perusal. She was most definitely teasing him again. It was like becoming accustomed to a talking cat.

He cleared his throat, then reached for the glass of water on his desk. "You could say that, yes."

"I can relate."

Removing her hat and gloves, she breezed into the room as if she hadn't just used her eyes to undress him. With a grace she couldn't shake if she tried, she sat lightly on the edge of his desk. A hint of sugar fused with her warm scent. Perhaps she'd had a scone or another sweet treat with her tea.

"You see," she said rather airily, "I simply couldn't marshal the wherewithal to follow those silly conversations. So much gossip, about which I could really care less."

Miles edged closer until they sat side by side. Their hips touched. The heat of her body eased over his. "Preoccupied?"

"Entirely."

"May I inquire where your mind preferred to tarry?"

Mischievous passion did a little dance across her expression. "In your bed."

His jaw had dropped. What manner of gentleman gaped? Perhaps one whose wife insisted on startling him to the point of mindlessness.

"And what," he said, his voice rough, "do you find so interesting about that particular piece of furniture?"

"I like how it feels. I never suspected that a piece of furniture, as you so astutely pointed out, could be so . . . entrancing."

He traced a line from her cheek down to her jaw, then along the silken column of her throat. The hot pulse in his veins intensified, thrilling through each limb. "Do go on, my lady."

She glanced down at where he touched. "Only if you do."

Miles grinned. He outlined the slope of her breast through the worsted silk, still just one finger, until he gave into the urge to cup, to knead, to claim. She moaned softly and arched into his touch. Even beneath layers of clothing, her nipple pebbled against his palm. "You were saying?"

"Hm?"

"About my bed."

"The mattress is soft. Yet it provides marvelous . . . support."

"Support is quite necessary, you know," he said. "For the back, in particular. When you sleep."

"I wasn't thinking about sleeping. Your bed smells like you. Makes me wonder why I've denied us for so long."

"You know why." He touched her cheek. "But we can put that behind us now, all the mistakes and mistrust."

She looked toward the floor but not before Miles caught the blush tinting her cheeks. Was it something he'd said? Or just a small reminder that she was terribly new to this sort of play?

Viv stood away from the desk. She nudged his knees apart with more boldness than he would've imagined, then stepped into the V of his open legs. The gentle pressure of her hands on the outside of his thighs urged him to draw her in close. Miles watched for any sign of resistance.

She still came to him willingly. Of her own initiative. He could almost believe it now.

His heart was a clockwork bomb in his chest, ready to burst. He tensed the muscles of his inner thighs until she fit flush against his body. But the way she arched slightly, pressing her bosom against his chest—that was all Viv. Time slowed until every nuance of breath and motion became a ballet of seduction. She smoothed her hands up his torso, lingering a few extra beats when her fingertips brushed across the fabric concealing his nipples.

Her boldness reminded him that his own hands had fallen useless to his sides. Like discovering the perfect tool for the job, he cupped her nape with one, her lower back with the other.

Her lips parted. She licked the lower one.

Miles wanted to kiss her like he wanted to keep breathing—or breathe again, one day, when the shock and wonder had worn off—but he was enjoying her initiative too much.

They were so near that the warmth of his own exhales fanned off her face and back to his. "How far will you go today, Vivie?"

"Farther than yesterday."

"That's enough to build a future on."

"Yes, it is."

Their bodies had already become reacquainted, pressed together from knee to chest, and now their mouths played eager games. Miles tasted the bitter sweetness of the tea she'd swallowed. He no longer gave a damn about artful curls and coils as he dug his fingers down to her scalp. Pins pinged as they hit the floor. He luxuriated in that silky softness as the scent of her, so much more potent now, unraveled his control.

He squeezed his legs tighter. Her slim body fit against his, bringing her stomach, tightly bound in a corset prison, right against his aching groin. He would find no relief there, but he ground against her anyway. A little moan vibrated out of her and into him. He answered by taking the kiss deeper, pushing his tongue inside. She'd given permission. Now he would have all of her.

Banging footsteps climbed the stairs at a frantic pace. Viv jumped out of Miles's arms and away from the desk—their would-be bed. The change was too sudden for him to absorb. Why were his arms empty? Why weren't they still kissing? The ledgers would wait as they made love. He was certain of it.

But Mr. Kato's appearance at the top of the stairs forestalled any hope of an afternoon tryst. Viv's face was bright red. The bodice of her gown was rumpled, the lace crushed. Her hair was a glorious mass of snarls. Even then, at the height of what should have been her embarrassment, she merely smiled as if greeting a preferred acquaintance. The strength she had always applied to the most demanding social situations radiated from her now—brazening out even the most compromised position.

For him? Dare he believe it possible?

Miles grinned past his disbelief. Even so, they'd still need a lock for the door at the bottom of the stairs.

"Lord Bancroft."

The urgency in Mr. Kato's voice broke through Miles's haze. "What is it? What's wrong?"

"Come quickly, please. Constables are downstairs with Mr. Elden. He's demanding Adam's arrest."

Viv's head spun as she watched Miles snatch up his whip. "Arrest him? On what grounds?"

Mr. Kato smoothed a hand over his shaven head, expression solemn. "That I do not know, my lady."

Quickly following the men down the stairs, Viv didn't have time to rearrange her hair. She used her fingers to comb through the worst of the tangles, then clapped her bonnet back atop her head. Good enough for now.

Adam arrested? This had the potential to get ugly—just when she had been relishing an otherwise thrilling encounter with Miles. Her happy fantasy, simply being with her husband. Trusting him with all she craved and imagined and needed. Perhaps she should have been embarrassed by

Mr. Kato's interruption. She would have been in years past. But if Miles promised to be her partner in all things, she had no reason to fear. He would protect her reputation as much as her body and her heart.

That she believed such a thing now, without reservation, lit her with joy. But what if Elden went through with his threats to uncover her past?

To bring those secrets out into the open . . .

Nothing she had accomplished as a woman of good society would matter. And without quality connections, she would be unable to make her father's venture a success. A whore's daughter in charge of a diamond brokerage? No businessman with higher aspirations would forgive such stigma, not without being offered discounts too deep to bear.

Doing her best to keep her panic out of sight, she shunted those fears away. Miles held one hand while he gripped the coiled whip with the other. He strode to the ground floor and found Adam panting, his hands clutching Mr. Smets's desk as he caught his breath. James and Franc stood at the door with their rifles ready. Mr. Kato joined them. Shouts clamored in from the street.

No one would get in. For now.

"What happened?" Miles asked.

"Got caught in Elden's office. Take these, quickly." Adam handed over a wad of papers, which Viv tucked out of sight in one of the desk drawers. "Elden's outside with six of his armed bodyguards, Mr. Mansfield, and three additional constables. James and Franc held them off just long enough for me to get inside."

"Mr. Nolan, please stay here with my wife." The determined set of his jaw was one Viv had never known when they lived together in England, but it was all too familiar in Kimberley. He was going to intervene. The thought tightened a fist around her heart.

She was dreaming. A bad dream. Worse than the echoes of old nightmares. He would walk into danger against a man who held a mile-wide grudge and a strong reason to see them fail. "That's not fair."

"Little of this is."

"Wait!" She grabbed his arm. "Miles, think about it. Any man will be less likely to pull the trigger with a woman at the center of an argument."

"Absolutely not."

"I can talk to Elden. He'll listen to me. He likes to think he can manipulate me, so let him try. We *cannot* let him have Adam or those papers. Whatever they contain is obviously worth all this commotion. We can make some sort of deal." Tears cast a watery curtain over her vision. She sniffed and blinked them away, straightening the brim of her bonnet. "I'm not leaving you, Miles. Not this time."

He gripped the hilt of his whip and bit his back teeth until his jaw muscles bulged. "You'll stay right with me?" he asked at last.

"Right with you. I promise."

Twenty-five

The crowd had bulged to two dozen men. Immigrant, entrepreneur, and African alike jostled for a better view of the ad hoc proceedings. Across the street, a fair distance away, women had gathered as well. Just beneath one of the brokerage windows stood a boy of maybe thirteen who must have wanted to see the action up close. His upper arm was stringy with lean muscle and long bones.

Viv caught his attention, then asked, "How much money will you make watching this through the bars?"

"Nothing, ma'am."

"Exactly." She pulled a coin purse from her pocket and tossed him a silver half crown. "That's a down payment. Go find a surgeon. Tell him Lady Bancroft will pay you each a month's wages if you bring him here."

The boy's eyes widened. He stuffed the coin in his pocket and took off running toward the hospital.

Despite a stomach full of watery fear, Viv joined the men at the front door.

It's never easy, but you can make it look that way.

She took Miles's hand and they walked outside together. Shoulder to shoulder, with Mr. Kato just behind, she stood with him before their well-heeled opponent. James and Franc fanned out on either side, their weapons raised.

"Ah, my lord and lady," said Elden. "Just who I expected to see here, although I am rather impressed you brought her along, Bancroft. Quite the devoted little wife you have."

"Quite."

"Would you mind awfully, Mr. Elden," Viv said sweetly, "if your people put away their guns? Then our men could as well, and everyone will breathe easier as we talk."

He grinned tightly. "Of course, my lady. Anything for such an esteemed woman."

A flash of fear made her skin bristle. What was that tone of voice? That gleam in his eyes? But he signaled his bodyguards, and Mr. Mansfield did the same for his constables. Miles put his hand on Franc's rifle and said, "Enough now. Time to see if words will work instead."

The hulking Belgian hesitated. "My lord?"

"I have little else by way of skills to recommend me. Let the fault be his, if any shot is to be fired."

"Not the most reassuring scenario," Viv grated out. But Franc and James did as their master demanded.

"Now what seems to be the issue, Mr. Elden?" Miles asked. "Surely we can resolve any dispute you have with my employee."

"You're certain of that? Because it seems to me your

man is guilty of theft and needs to be punished accordingly. There's very little to dispute."

Viv angled the brim of her hat against the sun. She noticed how Miles kept his body between hers and the bulk of the crowd, while still permitting himself a clean line of attack against Elden. But good heavens, if he threw a punch—would anyone keep from firing?

"Theft of what, if you please?" she asked.

"I don't need to answer to you, Lady Bancroft, no matter your title. Your man is guilty and I'll see him whipped for his crimes."

"I'll see you whipped first," Miles said, deadly soft. "I even came prepared."

Viv yanked on his wrist, holding him as she would a leashed attack dog. Her restraint wouldn't last long. "Sir, Mr. Nolan is paid exceptionally well. I know because I find that His Lordship's generosity borders on indulgence. Why would he have reason to steal? Surely you've made some manner of mistake."

Elden crossed his arms. His smirk sent a shiver up her back. "No mistake. And if you'd like to discuss how your brokerage conducts research on its competition, I'll be more than happy to. Your choice."

Miles had calmed, at least for the moment. His brain was a beautifully devious device. "I think we both know discretion is best for all parties involved. Unless you'd like to reveal certain . . . acquisitions."

She released Miles's arm and stepped nearer to their enemy as he blanched. How had she ever seen anything different in looking upon such a smug, scheming rat?" "No need for that sort of talk, my lord. I'm sure Mr. Elden will be willing to come to an arrangement."

Interest darkened his icy blue eyes. His pupils grew larger. "An arrangement? Of what sort?"

Viv wet her lips. "Let's send everyone back to their afternoon's activities and we'll come to terms."

"You don't dictate this matter, my lady."

Miles affected his most haughty tone. "Come now, Elden. Street-side is not the place for negotiations between gentlemen. You do believe yourself a gentleman, am I right?"

Elden's top hat shaded much of his reaction to the jibe, but Viv felt confident that Miles would soak up every detail. After mulling his options, Elden spoke briefly to Mr. Mansfield. The constable eyed all the participants with some mix of resignation and suspicion. Viv had no doubt he was capable of being a good man, but it had yet to be seen whether he could remain one in the face of Kimberley's rampant bribery and the free flow of diamonds.

"Very well," Mansfield said at last. "I know my place here. Men, we'll leave these citizens to settle their own differences. As for Nolan"—he pointed toward the front door—"he doesn't leave town until all parties are satisfied. But the first shot fired will end my willingness to let you regulate yourselves."

The constable and his men herded the onlookers away from Christie Brokerage. Miles said something hushed to Franc and James, who aided in keeping the citizens back and away. Only Mr. Kato remained, as did two of Elden's bodyguards, as the interested parties entered the brokerage house. Adam was nowhere to be seen, perhaps having taken shelter in one of the upstairs rooms—or even in the crawl space filled with carbons.

But at least all weapons had been removed or holstered. At least no one would be harmed. Viv finally felt as if she could breathe, although the negotiations had just begun.

"So, my lady," Elden said. "You've had your way. Now what?"

"What charges do you propose against Mr. Nolan?"

"Eustis here caught him sneaking out of my office. I want to have this building and his person searched to assure nothing of value was taken."

Viv scoffed. "You can hardly expect us to open our doors to you for a random search of all *our* paperwork."

"He's a thief and should be jailed. And the both of you should be labeled as the worst sort of scheming competition."

She glared at him from beneath the brim of her bonnet. "And what of the Opsberger Brothers'? Or Fellman's? Or any of the other brokerages you're quietly acquiring? What of the means you've used to pressure them into selling? Your reputation could suffer terribly if we reveal to the community what we know."

A tic twitched below his left eye. She hoped very much that Miles was taking notes. "What do you propose?" he asked.

"A poker game."

Whether or not he caught Elden's flicker of hesitation,

Miles must have understood her meaning. His bearing changed. Gone was the belligerent for whom wearing a whip seemed a natural complement to his lean physique and intimidating height. His posture turned negligent. His face softened. In his place was the man she remembered from so long ago. At that moment, Miles, Lord Bancroft, appeared as bored as if he'd spent the afternoon watching Viv's garden sleep through the winter.

"Come on, then, old chap," he said, his voice eerily casual. How *did* he manage that? "A few rounds of cards will make this much more, well, civilized." He waved a slack hand toward Elden's bodyguards. "Truly, is this how you conduct legal matters in the jungle or wherever this is? I cannot remember the last time we solved anything by brawl on the floor of Parliament."

Elden scowled at the affront. "All right, what are the stakes?"

"For a start, you'll pursue no further charges against Mr. Nolan." Viv lifted her chin and looked the man up and down. "After that, you have yet to agree to the terms of our new business model. I want your full cooperation."

This was a tremendous amount to lay on Miles's abilities, but she took the chance. If it failed, the gossip would be so loud that they'd certainly never need to advertise again. Christie Brokerage would become notorious, just before Neil Elden bought it out from under them.

She turned to Miles. The tender lover she'd given herself to the night before was in there somewhere, behind that smirk and those vacant brown eyes. God, no wonder she'd never been able to know him. He'd never shown her. The choice had always been his, a façade to keep or discard—as much a pretender as she ever was.

"Are you game, my lord?" she asked, her brows lifted.

"For you? Always."

"And for a few hands of cards?"

"Oh, that will do, too."

"You, Mr. Elden? Cards? Or would you prefer to see what violence and intimidation do to your reputation?"

He pinned his narrowed gaze on Viv. That same slinking sensation crawled down her legs. Had they been on a battlefield, she would've ducked. Something was coming. He bared his teeth in an expression caught between disgust and desire, turning her stomach.

"I'm not the one who should be worried about reputation, Lady Bancroft."

When Viv flinched, Miles struggled to hold onto the blasé mannerisms that had once been as much a part of him as his skeleton. Elden was slandering his wife. Even a man less observant of body language would be hard pressed to miss how the color drained from her creamy skin.

"Hardly the place for defamation," Miles said. "Even if such low behavior would be my assumption for you."

"You do enjoy pulling rank on us commoners, don't you?"

He matched the man's cold, disdainful smile. "Comes with the title. You should ask the Queen for one. Very useful. At the very least you should earn a knighthood for this grand, ugly enterprise you have going here. Quite an achievement in the name of the Empire."

"You mock what lines your pockets?"

"Maybe that's the difference between you and me. You *need* to believe in it while I . . . well, I don't need it at all." He clapped once. "Now then, I'm bored of all this drivel. Are we quite finished?"

Elden again turned to Viv. The pinch of her mouth had been a debonair grin only moments before. Now she seemed to be holding down a flood of bile.

"We never agreed on what I will win." He flashed Miles a grin. "Because I *will* win."

"Hardly."

"I fancy something exotic, actually." He leaned nearer to Viv, as if examining each and every pore. "French. A dancer, perhaps. Don't you find that idea exciting, Bancroft? Long legs. Flexible. Shameless."

Miles popped his knuckle. "Out with it, man."

"What do you say, my lady? Is a whore's daughter willing to wager herself?"

Without thought Miles hurled a quick punch. His fist connected with teeth in a satisfying crack. Elden bellowed. Blood smeared across his cheek from where he wiped his split lip. Not waiting for the man to recover, Miles threw another pair of quick punches. One to the ribs. One to the breastbone. Wheezing, Elden dropped to his knee, then slumped to the ground. His cough was sickly wet.

A sharp blow to the skull sent Miles down, too. Viv screamed, like a high-pitched explosion within the brokerage's close walls. He caught a glimpse of Mr. Kato holding her out of harm's way as another cracking pain lanced across his nerves—this time a boot connecting with his left kidney. He rolled and hacked his whip across the wooden floor. The leather coiled around his opponent's leg. With a sharp tug, Miles hauled the man to the ground, where Franc and James had already subdued Elden's other guard.

"We can continue," Miles said, holding back a groan as he stood once more. Viv folded against his side. Her fingers gently assessed the wound at his temple. "And let our men do what they were hired to do, namely to protect this business from violent intruders. Or we can proceed with my wife's suggestion of a card game."

"Your *wife*." Elden spit blood. "Ask her, Bancroft. I dare you. Ask for the truth about her birth—the truth my private investigator in New York discovered. Then be willing to stake the entire brokerage and that million-dollar bonus you're so set on winning." He grinned, revealing red-streaked teeth. "Oh, yes. I know about that, too. I won't settle for less. And if you touch me again, so help me God I'll have that pompous grin shot clean off your face."

"Glad you kept from claiming you'd shoot me yourself, because I could never take such a threat seriously. How did such a coward get to where you are today?"

"By taking down the likes of you, by any means necessary. You *disgust* me. Born to all the advantages in the world, yet you come down here to meddle where working men deserve to make their fortunes. *I* was here first."

"Mr. Kato would probably disagree with that rather strongly." Miles was shocked by the vehemence of Elden's vitriol, but not by its presence. Much of his own past behavior had the potential to turn his stomach if he lingered there too long. But at present, he was not the man spitting up blood and cringing at the prospect of more. "Threatening a peer, however, is not the cleverest move. I politely suggest you get out of our building."

"Noon tomorrow at the Kimberley Club."

"Agreed."

"But don't bring your wife, no matter that our stakes bear her family name." Elden pushed to his feet, righting his coat and scrambled hair. His ascot and stained shirtfront were lost causes. "We don't make exceptions even for women of *good* society, let alone the likes of her."

Miles restrained his violence—not because of any particular strength, or out of respect for a downed opponent making his retreat. No, it was because of Viv. She held his gaze so steadily, chin lifted only a shade. No blushing or fuming. Her eyes held no emotion other than fear. She looked like a woman who expected the very worst.

Fear. When she should have been furious at Elden's insinuations.

James and Franc earned their keep, prodding Elden and his men back outside. Mr. Kato quietly asked, "Should I bring the carriage around, my lord?"

"Yes, please do. And find where Adam hid himself. If rumors of all this nonsense make it to Chloe before he does, she'll take it none too well."

Viv's expression remained a strange combination of blank and imploring. "You're bleeding."

"Yes, and I have no idea why." Miles took her arm and tugged her discretely against his side. "Tell me what the bloody hell is going on."

"Please." She cleared her throat and blinked rapidly. "Let me wait until we get home. Not . . . not here. Please, Miles."

She smelled of roses, as always. She was still Vivie. *His* Vivie. But her unfathomable exchange with Elden made him doubt that claim.

A headache pounded across his brow, but he felt ready to do violence all over again.

Twenty long, tense minutes later, the carriage delivered them to the manor. Chloe happily greeted Adam with a hug that clearly signaled their intentions as a couple. Only at that moment, when his own confusion was a bright burn in his mind, did Miles realize how well the girl had adapted to life here. She had a roof over her head, a steady wage, and a man who cared for her deeply. Did the rest have to be so complicated?

Chloe's expression, however, turned cloudy as she caught the mood of their small party. Quickly glancing toward Miles and back to her mistress, she only bobbed a curtsy before dragging Adam indoors. Jamie arrived to help Mr. Kato with the horses, which only left Miles and his wife.

Like a man condemned, but uncertain of the crime for which he'd been convicted, he trudged upstairs and followed Viv to her chambers.

With even the balcony shut to keep out the strengthening cold, the closed bedroom door sealed them in together. Miles felt dusty and unclean among her lovely furnishings. His knuckles ached. His temple banged out a ragged pulse, and a twinge of fire licked up his lower back. A distinct tug in his right bicep and shoulder was testament to the beating he had delivered, as was the raging rush in his veins.

Perhaps that was just dread.

As Viv slipped off her bonnet, she revealed the hair he'd so delightedly tangled in the upper floor of the brokerage. Only an hour earlier they had been prepared to make love over a desk strewn with ledgers and papers. But that moment seemed long ago. Or maybe he was reminded of years past, when their marriage had always been this cold. The woman he had made love to for weeks now—glorious weeks that promised a future—was nowhere to be found. She simply hung up the bonnet as if his heart weren't being pulled apart by silence.

He grabbed the nearest cloth from her washing stand and held it to his temple. "Tell me." Just two words, sticky and difficult to voice.

"It's better left unsaid. Believe me, Miles. You don't want to know."

"Don't you dare assume what I want." He stalked toward her, combating his worry with anger. "Or maybe you would rather I learn from Elden? Snake that he is, he would be glad to rub my nose in whatever dirt you're hiding. Call me a traditionalist, but I'd rather hear personal matters in private. That means from you, my dear. Straight from that pretty, exasperating mouth of yours. Now tell me who you are."

"And if I don't?"

"Then I'll be the one leaving. For good."

She stilled, her expression devastated. "You'd end this?"

"Not because I want to. God knows I don't—and now I'm telling you, too. But I refuse to endure a marriage where we cannot trust each other, where we keep secrets that inflict quiet harm. That was our downfall the first time we tried. Not anymore." He cupped her face with one bruised hand and kissed her as softly as he knew how. "Please, Vivienne. Trust me."

Twenty-six

*D*ark emotions bound her as firmly as Miles's strong hands. Terror led the parade. Her past would no longer be a secret. Fear of the consequences skittered down to her numb fingers and cold toes. Their tenuous marriage had survived so much, almost in spite of their worst efforts. She had no doubt this moment would herald its end. Limbs weak and shaking, she looked upon his desperate, stricken face. He *would* leave.

What could the truth possibly do to make it worse?

"I have my father's eyes," she whispered.

"Your father's . . . ?"

A deep breath didn't relieve her nausea, but she found the strength to speak. "William Christie was my father. My real father. The next time you see my siblings and I together—we inherited our eyes from him."

"Why the ruse? The adoption?" An *a-ha* expression moved over his tired features. "You were illegitimate."

"Yes."

He lifted her chin and would not let her look away. "Such

a distinct hazel, my dear. I'd never noticed. But then, who would? You were supposed to be adopted. And who better to adopt you than the man who'd sired you?"

Viv sank onto the foot of the bed and spoke to the swirling rose motif in the carpeting. "My mother was a Parisian actress, a singer, dancer. She was beautiful. Lauded. She always believed he loved her. This was just after the death of his first wife. Alex was but two years old. My father was still young. He left Alex in London with family and went to Paris. To drink. Perhaps to forget."

"In your mother's arms."

She nodded, dimly aware that he'd given up standing in favor of a place next to her on the bed. He lowered the cloth from his temple; the bleeding had stopped. Her stomach clenched at visible proof of his pain, just when she thought she couldn't hurt any worse.

"Four months later, he was done forgetting. He left without a kiss goodbye. She never knew why. She was pregnant, stubborn, and prideful." Wiping tears from her cheeks, she said, "If I could ask one question of her now, it would be why she never told him. Knowing she bore part of the blame was the only way I could forgive his leaving. He hadn't known— not until the end."

"Those were the years you didn't want to discuss."

"Yes. That's how I grew up. A bastard daughter of a woman who turned to prostitution. Her . . . patrons came to the flat. I became quite familiar with the nuances of her trade. The sounds. The smells."

"Christ, Vivie."

"Mother became sick. She had the consumption. I believe she must've written to my father before . . . before . . . *it*."

"It?"

"I was asleep." She clamped her eyes shut, but the horror of that night, of her dream, followed her into the dark. Miles stroked the unbound hair at her nape and she flinched. But his touch seeped through the blackness, not erasing the quivering fear but holding it at bay. "He must have waited until she went to relieve herself or wash. He crept behind my curtain and kissed me."

"One of your mother's customers?"

"Yes," she said, the tears thick in her throat. "That was my nightmare, you see. He would kiss me, hold me down. Mother attacked him with a pipe. Beat him. And he died."

"She killed him to save you."

Viv nodded stiffly. "The police came, of course, and they offered to take care of the situation if my mother serviced them both . . . while I watched. She refused and was arrested."

His arms circled her shoulders. The warm cotton shirt that clung to his broad shoulders smelled of dust, sweat, and a faintly metallic tinge of blood. "What happened to you?"

"I went to jail with her," she said simply. "I had no one else. She'd wanted me to run away, but I wouldn't let go of her hand. No words in our language can explain what prison is like—the damp and cold, the infested food. Mother never gave up hope that my father would arrive in time. I'd been eight years old and didn't know any better. So I believed, too. And I waited for him to come make it better."

"He never did."

"His people found me six weeks later, but they were too late to save my mother. She'd already been hanged for murder."

She couldn't stop shivering. Maybe she never had, not following the last time she'd seen her beloved mama's face. Resolution had mingled with panic as the guards led her away. Viv had concealed echoes of that raw, vulnerable moment ever since, one that felt like fingernail chewed down to the quick.

"I hated my father," she whispered. "I blamed him for her death. His first lesson was that terrible hurt could come from placing faith in the wrong people. But he took me in, he and Catrin. They adopted me. He'd already founded Crittenford Academy. To say he'd plucked me from the ranks of those immigrant children wasn't so difficult."

"Do your brothers and Gwen know?"

"Yes. Our secret."

Miles frowned slightly. "I remember Gareth once saying that you'd been a difficult child. I couldn't imagine it, not knowing the woman you are. But he clammed up after that, as if he'd revealed too much."

"Nothing he said would've done justice to the hellion I was." She rubbed her forearms. "I spoke only French. I knew nothing of etiquette. Sometimes I stole bread in the middle of the night. It took me years to believe that I would always have food." The shame and wordless terror of those months quickened her breathing, as if she were still on the verge of being caught and punished.

"Gwen and the boys, they did their best to bring me into

their fold. The twins wouldn't leave my side—particularly Gwen, like a little blonde shadow. Alex read me myths and fairy tales at bedtime. And poor Catrin, she endured the years when I reminded her that she was *not* my mother. All the while she taught me what I would need to enter proper society. And my father . . ."

"You *did* forgive him." Miles stared at her with such burning force. "How? How did he win your devotion after such a poor start?"

"Years of high expectations, if not blatant affection. Steadiness. Predictability. He had such confidence in my abilities. Eventually I decided I could be what he expected of me—better than the circumstances of my birth."

"But you wound up with me." He stood and began to pace, fingers pressed against the place where Elden's bully had kicked.

"The others rebelled eventually," she said. "Alex loved the stars. Gwen had her opera, with Gareth always so keen on guiding her career. It was almost their duty to antagonize Father and counter his wishes, whereas I thought to earn his approval by marrying into the nobility. I'd have enduring refuge, at last. Simple."

"That's why you were always so critical of me. I threatened to undo everything you'd worked to learn."

"Yes! And there is *nothing* wrong with respectability. Believe me, Miles, it's far better than being a bastard or starving in a prison where the rats ate better than we did."

"How disheartened you must have been," he murmured, almost to himself.

"Terrified, more like. I thought that one day the truth would come out and the vows we'd said wouldn't matter. Especially since . . . God, since we never conceived. You would divorce me. Or you would tempt me to ruin so that even hiding the truth wouldn't matter. I needed to find security of my own. I couldn't trust you with that."

Miles stopped his agitated pacing. He stood directly in front of her, his shins brushing her knees. "Look at me."

She nodded once, her heart cleaving in two.

This is it. This is goodbye.

She hadn't confided in him. Not about this. The stark fact nettled Miles in the vicinity of his pride. As always, their lack of trust revealed itself as the rotten core of their union.

But he had all the pieces now—to Viv and to why their marriage had bumped and busted like a three-wheeled carriage. Even his bruised pride would not let her lack of faith ruin what they shared. The last thing he wanted was to concede defeat, not when they could start afresh.

That meant revealing *his* nasty truths.

"Viv, would you like to know how I endured your leaving?"

He waited then, waited for her interest to overcome her trepidation. Finally she raised her face. His breath hitched. Tears plowed saltwater furrows down wan cheeks. Red rimmed her lower lids. Moisture clumped and darkened her eyelashes. Her lips were full, chapped and worn by nervous teeth. But she held his gaze, unable to bank her sparkling curiosity—the only brightness left in the woman he loved.

"You've always assumed the worst," he said. "Other women, debauchery, bankruptcy. But that's not how it was."

"No?"

"I spent that year drunk."

"Miles, don't jest."

"No jest," he said softly. "I didn't just lose an entire year. I threw it away with both hands."

Memories picked over what was left of his dignity. He couldn't recall anything specific, of course. Hennessey made it impossible to find those details, like sifting through ash for the words of a singed letter. But a cloying sense of failure and hurt layered over drinking rooms and gambling parlors and the anonymous floors he'd made into beds.

"I would drink long into the evening, then wake up and start again. Days. Months, even. All a blur. I created quite the grand scandal, which helped distract from the fact my wife lived across the Atlantic. 'Tending to her ill father,' I would say to anyone who asked. They never thought much past that thin excuse and how much money I could lose in an evening. That bargain for one third of your inheritance wasn't for show. Any cash I had disappeared." He shook his head. "I simply wasn't in my right mind, you see."

"But . . . why?"

He knelt and took her hands, kissing the knuckles of each. "Because you were gone. Whatever purpose I'd inadvertently found in being your husband—faults and all—was gone. I missed you."

Her mouth opened on a slow exhale. She whispered his name.

"When your father died," he said, hurrying on before he lost his nerve, "I knew that was the end. I still had no notion as to why propriety meant more to you than the passion we'd found, but it wasn't hard to see that I'd pushed you too far. You weren't coming back. An inheritance from Old Man Christie would end our marriage." A heavy breath churned out of his lungs. He was sore all over. "So I sailed to America. I wanted to be there, at least, to see the death throes. But when he gave you that challenge, Vivie, I was so thankful."

"I couldn't have guessed, not by the way you acted."

"Let's just say that I woke up thankful." He swallowed. "Your note . . . about Newport . . ."

"That I'd left you again."

"That's the one. In England, it had been easier to stay insensate. Otherwise I would've needed to admit I was the reason why you were gone. But there in New York, I woke up to a splitting headache and a second chance."

She regarded him for what felt like a decade. Her eyes, wide and clouded and wet, shifted to take in every feature of his face. Miles had never been so thoroughly probed and prodded, all without a single touch.

"And our wager?" she asked, almost too softly to hear.

"I tried to convince myself that it was all about revenge. I would bed you and have done." A sick laugh gurgled out of him, which seared pain along his ribs. "Yet that's not what happened at all, is it? The challenge of Kimberley and the brokerage—of you, all over again—has made me proud. I've never been a man with purpose, and imagine my surprise in learning that it suits me. Yet now . . ."

God, he wanted to touch her. Sumptuous blonde hair looped and curled around her jaw, her collarbones, her breasts. Rose water blended with her natural fragrance. Her chin quivered. He rested his thumb in its center and rubbed that quiver away.

"Tell me," she whispered.

"To be lied to all this time. Before, I wouldn't have trusted myself with a laundry list, let alone the details of your past. But in these recent weeks?" He bowed his head, resting the bridge of his nose on their entwined hands. "I was doing my best by you, Vivie. You know I've been trying."

She wrapped her arms around his head. Heavy tremors shook her shoulders even as she held him. "You *have* been. Miles, I am so proud of you. Do you hear me, my love?" She kissed his crown. "So proud to be your wife."

"Then why keep this from me?"

"I didn't want to lose you." Her voice broke. She swallowed again and pressed on. "When I was a child, I wanted food. I was hungry all the time. *All the time.* But my mother loved me so fiercely. It didn't matter that we had nothing to eat or that we were cold. Then I had my father's mansion and I could finally eat . . ."

"But your mother was gone. And now Catrin and your father, too."

At an answering nod, Miles eased off the floor to sit side by side on the bed. The mattress dipped, urging her body nearer. He let out a tight sigh and his eyes rolled shut when she didn't pull away.

"It was always a trade-off," she said. "Love or safety. To

ask for both . . . That sort of dreaming was meant for other people. I don't know if I can." She strangled an errant sob. "I'm terrified of losing everything and going back to that place. Do you see what Kimberley is to me? It's my nightmare brought to life."

A weight pressed on his chest. Another bowed his upper back, squeezing from both directions. But his determination, that strange sense of purpose he'd only discovered upon arriving at the Cape—it remained.

"You want love *and* safety."

"Yes," she said, her voice shredded. "And I'm not brave enough to ask for both."

He kissed her lips, softly, sweetly. "I don't see why not. You're the bravest woman I've ever known."

"I don't feel it. Determined, maybe. But never brave. Every time I walk into a room, either here or New York or London, I'm convinced someone will find out what I've been hiding. I'll be back in the slums and lost. Forgotten there, with no one to come save me."

Miles chuckled. He pushed her back against the bed, ignoring her slight protest and the stinging pain of his injuries. "You have that all so wrong . . . I hardly know where to begin."

He smiled more deeply at her flare of indignation.

"Hear me out," he said, curling his body alongside hers. "First of all, you *have* been found out. I know the truth now, Vivie. And isn't that a relief? Every room we enter together—you'll have an ally at your side who knows exactly how you think and what you fear and the amazing miracle of this life you've forged. Tell me that isn't a seductive secret to keep, just the two of us."

"It is . . . seductive. Intimate. Like knowing what secrets you keep hidden."

"Me? Surely not. I'm an open book."

"Of Romantic poetry and industrial drills." She touched his bottom lip. "Your gambling cohorts in Mayfair would be shocked."

He caught that delicate fingertip between his teeth and grinned. "Would do them good to see what wonders a wastrel can accomplish when he sets his mind to a goal. Then no more lies, my darling girl. The last thing I can endure from you is more of the same old patronizing rubbish I've endured my whole life. I want all of you—real and visceral. The worst and the best. Nothing else will do justice to loving you."

Viv smiled softly, her eyes wide, lustrous, and full of wonder. "You love me?"

"I am more in love with you now than I ever have been. Had I been a different man when we married, one you could confide in, perhaps all of this would've made sense. But . . . oh, sod it." He raised his head. "Say something."

"I love you, too, Miles."

The tight, fiery knot in his gut unfurled and cooled. The weight pressing between his shoulder blades lifted, as insignificant as steam. He hadn't needed her acquiescence or her enthusiasm in bed. Just her love.

"It is now of the utmost importance that I strip you bare and taste every inch of your skin. You do realize that, yes?"

Viv giggled and tried to get away, but she fell back laughing when he caught her around the waist. "You're a heathen and a cad."

"And you're a wanton angel. Hold still. Corsets are such a nuisance." As he unfastened her gown, he felt as giddy as a young lad. "Do you know what else you got wrong, my love?"

"What's that? Just bear in mind that I care very little for being wrong." She lifted her lush hair to give him better access. Miles couldn't help but kiss the downy-soft skin at her nape. Goose bumps shivered along her spine. Then he found the loveliest stretch of throat ever created.

"You must believe that you'll never go back there," he whispered. "You'll never be alone or forgotten again. Strong and capable and so deucedly stubborn, *you* won't let it happen. Neither will your family, and neither will I. Not ever, Vivie." She gazed up at him with awed reverence. Miles was sure he had never felt more powerful. "I promise."

Twenty-seven

*M*iles awoke to a slate-gray morning. Nearly winter in the south of Africa. But the season hardly mattered when the angel he was blessed to call his wife lay stretched naked at his side. Because of the snowy duvet, he couldn't see her curves, the delicate dips of waist and spine—not unless he closed his eyes and relived their passion. From the night before. From weeks before. Layer upon layer of satisfaction. But underneath the heavy down, her body curled around his like a vine climbing a trellis. Thigh and hip and breast, all topped by her cheek nuzzled against the crook of his neck. Slow, even breaths warmed him from the outside in. This was his woman.

And he would do anything to protect her.

Knowing what awaited him at the Kimberley Club, he slipped from Viv's arms. Adam not only helped him dress, but summarized the information contained within papers he had acquired from Neil Elden's office.

"You did well." At Adam's scowl, he asked, "You think differently?"

"I got caught. You wouldn't be facing this ridiculous situation if I had done my job properly."

Miles eyed his reflection in a mirror on the door of the mahogany wardrobe. "Appears you've dressed me to perfection. Job done."

"That not what I meant and you know it. My lord, I won't ask Chloe to wait for me while I serve a jail sentence."

"You won't see a day in prison. How on earth would I function without you?"

Adam smoothed the lapels of his practical navy blue coat and regarded Miles with his usual calm cordiality. "Even as young lads it was always thus. You would bludgeon me into some fool scheme or another. We never failed to get caught. I would stare in wonder when you slid out of whatever punishment was our due."

"Then why come here and risk your liberty on my behalf?"

"Because you're impossible to refuse. And I find it amusing when people underestimate you."

"You always were a peculiar chap," Miles said with a chuckle.

Adam matched his grin. "And because you always intervened on my behalf. You saved me from more whippings than I have teeth."

"As I will today. I swear it." He clapped a hand on Adam's shoulder and offered quiet reassurance with his gaze. "But now your task is much more arduous. Keep Viv occupied. Take her down to the Auxiliary to work with Mrs. Penberthy. Anything. But I don't want her anywhere near Neil Elden."

Adam nodded tightly before turning to refold a jumbled pile of ascots he had deemed inappropriate for Miles'ss attire. That he was capable of business intrigue and various means of warfare, as well as selecting the correct neckwear for any occasion, should have earned him a medal for patience and loyalty. The percentage of their eventual bonus would have to do. He, too, was staking everything on Miles'ss abilities.

Squinting into the pale winter light creeping through his bedroom window, Miles silenced his misgivings. This was no time to show weakness. If ever he needed to keep his blank, hapless gambler persona on display, it was now. Last night he and Viv had ripped the scabs off their floundering marriage and had done their best to bandage the wounds. They could heal now.

None of that had a place at a card table.

He bid his loyal friend adieu and climbed into the carriage Jamie had readied. Miles remembered the few weeks spent in Southampton before sailing to Cape Town, when he had cobbled together funds enough to finance their initial business costs. But he had been ridiculously lucky. The cards simply hadn't made sense. Opponents' stern faces had appeared just that way: stern. Unreadable. No flicker of the doubt or anticipation or relief that normally sang to him. What if part of his youthful daring had been liquor? Or knowing that he cared nothing about the outcome of any hand?

This was different.

This would be the game that decided their future.

Losing, however, was a certainty if he let those doubts

infect his game. He would not lose. Viv said she loved him, but he knew that only a secure future would make her truly happy. He wanted to give that to his wife. The life she deserved.

With the cold May wind in his face, and distant sounds of pulley chains, voices, and exotic animals in his ears, he climbed the stairs up to the Kimberley Club. Morton Crane and his caterpillar whiskers barred his entrance.

"Your membership has been revoked, my lord, by order of the Board."

"Assaulting a member of said Board likely has that effect. But I'm here to play cards. Mr. Elden and I made the arrangements yesterday—just after I punched him." Miles withdrew a cigar case. His fingers didn't shake. "Now inform him that our game is still on, if he's willing. If not, he can have the pleasure of personally escorting me off the property. I'll even resist, so as to make it more fun for us both."

Without waiting for Crane's reply, he strolled into the club. He sat at the same booth he had once shared with Elden. Stretching his legs, he nodded casual greetings to members who littered the darkened interior.

But he had a job to do.

How very like him that his job involved sitting in a luxurious men's club and smoking his first cigar in months, but one could not argue with the nature of things.

"So, you came," Elden said.

"Of course I did. You and I have unfinished business."

He casually lifted his eyes and smiled in the face of his handiwork. A bulge in Elden's lower lip was the size and color of a black cherry. His left eye drooped around a puffed bruise. Both cheeks were canvases for a watercolor collection of blue, purple, and nauseating green. Miles's only regret was that the abuse made Elden more difficult to read. He needed to see how truths and lies played out across his opponent's newly renovated features.

No doubt Elden was sizing him up the same way. To hide his lone tell, Miles slipped his left hand into his trouser pocket. Thoughts of Viv could hide there, along with his wedding ring.

Elden slid onto the padded leather bench opposite and poured two glasses of cognac. A pair of hulking bodyguards lurked nearby, taking seats of their own at another table. "I'm glad to see you're not the sort of aristocrat who would retreat from such a challenge."

"While I can only hope you're not the sort of underhanded slime who will stack the deck against me in your own club."

Anger showed in a faint tightening along Elden's top lip. "Too bad we're only playing for money and the brokerage. I should've enjoyed adding that whore's daughter to the stakes."

"My wife isn't chattel." Miles bit his tongue and tasted blood—something he could do, apparently, while smiling.

"Perhaps not now. But it must have come as quite a shock."

And there—that was what taunting looked like.

While Miles kept his voice calm, inside his pocket, he pushed his gold wedding band down to the bone. "Just because she never divulged it publicly doesn't mean my family wasn't in full possession of the facts." He winked. "In truth, it quite added to her appeal. She's exceedingly accommodating to my needs. I wonder if the law will be as accommodating to you when your secrets come to light?"

"That won't happen."

Miles took a long drag on his cigar. He'd gone without for so long that a cough threatened. "So let's cut straight to what we both want. One thousand pounds each to start and a one-hundred-pound limit. Should I bankrupt you, you sell all shares of Christie Brokerage and relinquish a quarter of your mine's profits for the next eighteen months. No matter what happens, you drop all charges against my manservant and hand over whatever foul proof you've collected about my wife's origins."

"And when I bankrupt you?"

He shrugged nonchalantly as his sleek, airy persona returned in full. Good. He'd been afraid he misplaced the blasted thing. "My conditions still stand with regard to my manservant and my wife. That's the cost of earning this chance to best a Peer of the Realm. Once we fulfill our contract and earn the right to buy Christie Brokerage, we'll relinquish it to you."

Elden sipped his cognac. "I can take it from you before then."

"But without the promise of that million-dollar bonus. You win this game . . . we hand it over. That leaves you free to concentrate on some other mark." He paused for emphasis. "You do have a million dollars to counter with, I assume."

Miles already knew the truth. He simply needed to see how defeat looked.

Elden flicked his eyes toward his bodyguards. "Of course."
Perfect.

For a long, long moment Elden simply stared. Let him look. There was nothing to see. Miles let his mind go to a very happy place, one involving Vivie and breakfast in bed. She hadn't yet permitted such experimental liberties. But if a man didn't have hope for the future, what did he have?

"Very well, Bancroft. Let's play."

Viv paced the width of the Women's Auxiliary, holding baby Samantha as Alice carried stacks of blankets. "Why didn't he wait for me?" she asked again.

Adam looked up from where he assembled the last cot, with Chloe nearby, linens in hand. His expression remained just as apologetic. "Kimberley Club is for men. And I don't believe he wished you subjected to Mr. Elden's taunts. He was trying to protect you, my lady."

"Protect me! Did he take his whip? Or a pistol? No. He didn't think to protect himself."

"Surely Mr. Elden wouldn't stoop to such measures," Alice said. "He helped make all of this possible."

Viv looked around at the bustling warehouse. A dozen women of all nationalities, colors, and ages put the finishing touches on the Auxiliary, which would open to its first residents the following Sunday. Several local businessmen and ministers would be on hand to offer the two most important blessings in Kimberley: those of commerce and God. Probably in that order. She could not deny that Elden's attempts to ingratiate himself with her, and thereby snuggling closer to ownership of the brokerage, had provided the foundation for this grand project. But other contributors, including each woman who worked beneath Alice's astute, patient eye, had also brought it to life.

"I am grateful for how generous Elden has been with his support. However, I cannot condone the methods by which he acquired his wealth." Viv smoothed Samantha's hair, which was as soft as the tummy fur of a kitten. "As for my husband, he still believes men behave by a certain code. But some don't play by *any* rules, let alone the sort an aristocrat would be privy to."

Her fingertips went numb.

Chloe looked up from where she tucked a sheet into place. "My lady? What is it?"

"Adam, where are the papers? The ones I hid in Smets's desk?" This time Adam did not appear apologetic; he positively blanched. "I hope you hide your emotions more completely around men, Mr. Nolan, because you're doing a dreadful job of hiding them from me."

"I gave them to His Lordship. They're locked in the upstairs desk in the brokerage."

"Summarize, if you please."

"Financial statements. His Lordship was only interested in what resources Elden could access during the poker game."

"I want to see them."

With her heart so fast and aching, Viv swiftly handed the baby back to her concerned mother. "Do you need Ike's help?" Alice asked.

"I should hope not." She swiftly hugged her friend. "Sunday we will open these doors, and both our husbands will be with us to offer their congratulations. Until then, we both have our work to do."

"As usual," Alice said with a wobbling smile. "Do be careful, my lady."

"I will. Chloe, stay here. Adam, with me."

They stepped out into the temper of a late-autumn gale, where loose dust kicked against her skirts. Hurrying, her breath came in gulps cut short by her corset. She ignored Smets's surprised welcome and climbed up to the bookkeeping room. Adam, close behind her, produced a key that unlocked a small desk drawer.

Minutes of anxious searching through the stack of jumbled papers yielded nothing other than what Adam had claimed: financial statements. But Viv had no time to gloat. Fear kept her searching.

A sliver of newsprint slipped from between two sheets of paper. Her eyes leapt over words chilling enough to freeze blood. "Obituaries," she whispered.

"Opsberger?

"And Malcolm, another former broker. One was found beaten to death in an alley, the other shot by an unknown assailant on the outskirts of town."

Adam frowned. "Elden acquired both of their businesses. I remember their names."

"Jesus," Viv rasped. "*Miles.*"

Only when she had reached the outdoors once again, those papers tucked in her skirt pocket, did Adam catch her arm. "I trust that you'll stay out of harm's way?" He grimaced, his fair features pink in the cold air. "He would hang me personally if you were injured."

"I promise. I'll find Mansfield. You . . . just keep him safe. Go now."

He hesitated. Maybe he knew just how difficult it would be to keep from intervening. Adam was a far better means of protecting Miles. At least that's what she forced her stuttering heart to admit as she watched her husband's servant stride toward the Kimberley Club.

Not so different from his master after all.

She mustered one more burst of energy—born of love and desperation—and ran.

Miles heard the commotion long before he saw Adam. His voice echoed through the entryway as he shouted at the guards. Never had the quiet, loyal man ever sounded so riled.

But Miles didn't let his face slip. With the confidence of a prophet, he flipped two more fifty-pound chips into the pot that already held five hundred. This would be the last hand.

"Seems we have unexpected company."

Elden's expression was tight and brittle. "No one else is allowed in the club. Get him out."

"You have your manservants. Why shouldn't I be allowed mine?"

"Is he the wretch who stole from me?"

"Stole what?" Miles asked, his demeanor suitably vapid. At least the unexpected visitor wasn't Viv. He signaled the dealer. "Two cards, please."

"Let him in, then." Elden wore a sour expression—no more than the twitch of his undamaged eyebrow. But Miles had learned the man's face as thoroughly as a hard lesson.

"Much obliged. And I believe the bet was to you."

Elden pushed the remainder of his chips toward the center of the table. "All in."

This was the moment. Viv trusted him. Adam trusted him. The whole future of the brokerage depended on his skill. After giving his cards another cursory look, Miles let out a dejected sigh. "Could be worse, eh? Adam, my good man. How goes?"

Not ten feet from the card table, Adam aimed a pistol at Elden's head. "Don't move."

"What is the meaning of this? Get him out of here!"

Smoothly, Adam swiveled the weapon to ward off Elden's bodyguards. "My lord, you might want to come away now."

"I was winning, Mr. Nolan."

"It's a trap. Constable Mansfield is being notified as we speak. Your whip is here on my belt."

Miles stood slowly, still watching his opponent's expression. He was reminded of that long-ago wagon master—beaten, yes, but not without the capacity for violence. Holding a whip felt much more natural now than a hand of cards, especially if what Adam claimed was true.

"Unless you wish to add a piratical scar to your appearance, I suggest you tell your bodyguards to remove their side arms."

Elden joined him in standing. "Weapons away, men." His expression was deathly smooth, his shoulders relaxed. That ease didn't change, not even when a dozen armed men filed in from the kitchen. "We've been accosted by brigands who will be divested of both their liberty and their property. Perhaps this was the best way to end our game after all."

Miles held his breath. Law and order would be wholly welcome, if only he knew who they had come to detain.

"Neil Elden, we're placing you and your bodyguards under arrest," came the voice of Constable Mansfield.

"On what charges? If anyone should be arrested, it's this viscount."

"On charges of fraud, conspiracy, and murder."

"That's preposterous!" As the bodyguards laid their guns on the card table, constables moved to secure Elden.

Miles lifted his brows and sought answers from his manservant. "Murder?"

"Her Ladyship found links," Adam said. "They deserve hearing out."

Warm joy spread through his chest. "And she didn't come for me herself? I feel I've made progress in a task I hadn't thought to undertake."

"Taming your wife?"

"Not in this lifetime, even if I wanted to."

"You don't care a thing about this town," Elden shouted as the police bound his wrists.

"I doubt even Kimberley brooks coercion and murder. And although I cannot speak for the rest of the nobility, most of us quite frown on threats. You made this very personal when you threatened Mr. Nolan. Oh, and when you kissed my wife. Don't forget that." With a casual flick of his wrist, he turned over his cards to reveal a full house. "Out of curiosity, what did you have?"

Elden shrugged off his captors with the dignity of a man born to wealth, not made by it. He turned over three queens.

"You didn't rig the last hand," Miles said.

"No."

"Well, I give you that much credit, at least."

"At least."

Miles saw a glint of silver and moved without thought. The whip cracked as loud as a gunshot in the close confines of the club. Elden shrieked and doubled over his bleeding wrist, which grew too weak to hold the small derringer he'd pulled from his sleeve. The constables who had briefly permitted his dignified turn of cards withdrew those niceties. They cuffed even his wounded arm and dragged him toward the front door.

Everyone in Kimberley would see him brought low.

A scuttle of relief did nothing to ease his pulse. He could be dead. Realizing just how close he'd come to losing everything—not just a fortune—caused his vision to gray at the edges.

"My lord?" Adam nodded toward the kitchen. "Her Ladyship promised to stay out of danger. She'll be back at the servant's entrance."

Thoughts of Viv halted his slide toward worse case scenarios.

"Would you be so good as to bring around the carriage? I should like very much to go home. All of this work, you understand . . . it's exhausting."

"Right away, sir," Adam said, grinning.

Miles stalked through the kitchen and down a flight of stairs toward a small wooden door.

The woman he met was Vivienne, Viscountess Bancroft, but he was still taken by surprise when she barreled into his arms. He smiled into her wind-tossed hair as she kissed his cheeks, his neck, his lips.

"Oh, God, you're all right. You're all right."

He tightened his arms. She seemed to need something steady. He was glad he could be that something. Then she launched into an explanation of the clues she had pieced together. In stunned silence he listened. The shock returned . . . then ebbed away. Elden was through. The brokerage was saved. And Miles held the woman he adored.

Could this be real? Now? Truly?

He touched a finger to her lips. She still vibrated in his arms, but he waited until he had her complete attention.

"Vivie, I don't know what we'll endure for the rest of our stay. The brokerage will thrive or fail. That bonus will be ours or it will slip away. But tell me I have you. After so many false starts and missed chances, tell me that you're my wife." With his hopes and his dreams right there for her to see, he said, "I love you, Viv."

"Oh, Miles, I love you, too." She flung her arms around his neck and held on tightly. Then she began to whisper words powerful enough to bring tears to his eyes. "To have and to hold, my darling husband. For richer, for poorer, in sickness and in health, till death do we part . . ."

Epilogue

*V*ivienne *stared at the portrait* of her father and softly smiled. A span of more than two years had done nothing to mollify his discontented scowl. The somber painting remained unchanged, as did the oppressive library. But Viv had changed. She'd turned herself inside out. A more contented, confident heart beat within her chest.

"Are you nervous?"

And she had Miles now. Together, with his skill and his unexpected ideas, he had discovered the key to saving the business. She'd kept the books, he'd wooed their clients, and Smets had appraised tiny piles of fabulous diamonds. But a steady trade in industrial carbons paid the bills—so well that Ike and Alice now lived in a house, not a hovel. Through all their hard work, Christie Brokerage was officially in the black.

They had *won*.

Elated as always by that thrill of victory, she found her husband standing by her side. Immaculately dressed, wearing a coal-black suit and an expertly tied silver-and-navy-striped ascot, he brought to mind the long-ago waltz they'd shared in Lady Galeworth's ballroom. It seemed Adam's engagement to Chloe had done nothing to diminish his efficiency.

Miles'ss tan remained vibrant after their long sea voyage back from the Cape, and the brilliant white of his sharply pressed dress shirt heightened his rakish coloring. A light slick of pomade·added the finishing touch to a man who was perfectly groomed, perfectly suitable. Perfectly breathtaking.

Only his eyes gave him away—dark eyes that made promises she couldn't wait to let him keep. She never tired of the way lightning sizzled outward from her belly, anticipating their next touch of skin to skin. She'd become brave enough to leave her fear behind, trusting this man, trusting what her heart and her body and her mind all declared. *I love him.*

She smiled. "I confess to being a little nervous, but not in the least like last time."

Chin lowered, he slowly shook his head. "Last time. I hardly care to think about that."

"Then let's not." She cast a final look at her father's stern expression, then eased into the safety of her husband's arms. "Now . . . well, now I'm more curious than anything else. Miles, what if Gwen and my brothers haven't fared so well? I cannot stand the idea of walking out of here with a million dollars if they leave with nothing."

His long fingers gently soothed the stiffness from her upper back. "I promise, Viv, your family will not go hungry. I won't let it happen." His dear features resumed their customary teasing. "But have a little faith. After all, *we* managed . . . and we were near to hopeless."

She laughed and pressed her cheek against his shirtfront, inhaling the warm, sharp scent of him—Marseilles soap and a dash of spicy aftershave. All very civilized. But she'd swear that the dry, yellow dust of the Karoo was a part of him now.

"What will we do after this? Do you wonder?"

"There's always Mr. Framholt," he said. "He insists there's money to be made in manufacturing his design. But he'll need financial backers."

"An investment opportunity? Intriguing."

"We'll make sense of it in time. But come now." Miles took her hand and led her to sit on the nearby settee. "I have a gift for you."

"A gift?"

"I find it a remarkably simple thing, darling, to spend your money." He produced a rectangular jewelry box wrapped in burgundy velvet. "Here. I meant to give it to you this morning, but, well . . ."

At the fresh memory of their decadent morning in bed, Viv sucked her lower lip. His lean muscles and bare torso had been her table as she'd indulged in chocolate-filled croissants and candied fruits. Afterward, starting with the crumbs at the edges of his mouth and working her way down, she'd licked him clean. Potent male had mingled with bittersweet chocolate and crystallized sugar. Only once Miles had given her the gift of his salty release had she stretched out on her back, gasping as he returned the favor.

"I distracted you?" she asked innocently.

An uncharacteristic blush tipped his ears. He cleared his throat. "Open it."

Viv pried open the spring-hinged box and blinked. Inside, nestled among folds of black satin, rested an exquisite bracelet. Intertwined circles of filigreed gold formed the links. A single rounded charm provided its only adornment. Only, it didn't twinkle in the light, nor did it shine with radiant color.

"A carbon?" She touched the slate-gray stone. It was smaller than her pinkie fingernail. Flecks of moss green and dull, muddy brown gave its surface an irregular texture. "I don't know what to say. It's . . . well, it's . . ."

"Ugly. Unforgivably ugly."

Viv giggled, one hand over her mouth. It truly was. Even the beveled gold setting couldn't save that charm from ignobility.

Miles edged closer, sharing her view of the unusual piece. "But Penberthy tells me it's one of the best he's ever examined. No weak crystalline structures, no cleaving plains. Immensely durable. When it comes to industrial diamonds, it's the highest quality that can be produced. Naturally, I had to have it."

His grin fell at the corners as he took her left hand. Somberly, he ran his thumb across the radiant diamond on her ring finger. "The man who gave you this gem—he didn't love you. It's utterly flawless but holds as little sentiment as the signatures on our marriage contract. The tools of a negotiation, nothing more." He inhaled deeply. "Vivie, that's not us."

"No," she said reverently. "We're hard work and trust, arguments, passion, mistakes. And secrets . . . all the secrets that make us special."

"Yes. Yes, exactly."

She looked on the globular gray carbon with new eyes. "Thank you, Miles," she breathed. "I'll find a way to explain it when fine ladies spot it on my wrist and make rude comments."

"Oh, dear God, woman. It's an *anklet*."

He knelt on the lush carpeting. Without waiting for permission, he grabbed her right foot and stripped off her slipper. Viv leaned back against the brocade settee and smiled as he fiddled with the delicate gold clasp.

Head bowed, his hair looked impossibly thick. "All that I am, I give to you," he murmured. "And all that I have, I share with you."

He'd spoken those vows years earlier as he'd endowed her finger with the wedding band she still wore. That he made the same vow again, now, with such a meaningful token of his love was more than enough to fill Viv's eyes with happy tears. His palms gentled along the meat of her calf. The lightweight gold links shimmered atop her stocking. With every movement the charm tip-tapped the inside of her ankle.

"I never meant it to be shared," he said, the words as intimate as a confession. He leaned over and placed a kiss atop her silk-wrapped shin. "It can keep company with your stockings." His sure, strong hands slid upward, cupping the backs of each quivering leg. "And your crinolines." He dragged the hem of her gown higher, feathering kisses as he climbed. "And your drawers." With his mouth hovering just above her thigh, his smoldering eyes met hers. "Something to be gloried in. Privately."

Those flashes of lightning in her stomach gathered, strengthening, scattering caution like a hot summer gale. She caught his face in her hands and pulled. With his body braced above hers, both of them half sprawled on the settee, she kissed him deeply. The library dimmed as she reveled in this man, *her* man, and the wicked, beautiful passion they'd found.

"Or perhaps not so privately," he whispered.

She furrowed her fingers into his very proper hair. Kissing again, she hooked a stocking-clad foot around his thigh and flexed, fitting his pelvis against hers.

"Vivie, enough." His words sounded choked and dry. "We should—"

"Oh, good heavens!" Alain Delavoir stood in the library's doorway, a portfolio tucked beneath his skinny arm. "I'll return momentarily."

The shame Viv expected to feel never came, only a naughty sort of humor. She grinned against her husband's mouth. "No, not at all," she said, half laughing. With steady movements she untangled her body from Miles and sat upright on the settee. "The fault is ours. Stay, please."

Once her clothes and hair were in order, she and Miles arose. A chagrined smile shaped his lovely mouth.

"I never would've taken you for bashful, my lord."

He leaned forward, for her ears only. "I despise interruptions."

"Ah, but now is the time for business." She reached up to retie his rumpled ascot. "What news of my siblings, Monsieur Delavoir? I've received but few letters and no updates of late."

"I have no information to add, my lady. You are the first to arrive."

She found Miles's hand and squeezed. Contentment washed over her, unlike any she'd ever experienced. But it wasn't quite enough. She needed her family to be as safe, as protected, as cherished as she was.

"In the meantime, this paperwork is for you to approve," Delavoir said.

Viv's hands shook as she signed the documents that transferred one million dollars into her name. She had not thought this moment would be so charged—more perfunctory than powerful. But the magnitude of her accomplishment washed over her in a wave of emotion.

Miles brushed a kiss against her temple. "Congratulations, my love."

She exhaled a heavy breath. So much work. So much to be proud of. And now, such a future awaited them both. "It was quite possibly the most difficult undertaking I'll ever attempt, but it was worth it. Even without the money, it would've been worth it."

"You both performed admirably." Delavoir smiled. Such an odd expression for his hawkish face, like seeing an undertaker laugh. "Now I'll withdraw until your brothers and sister arrive." He performed an exacting bow and turned to go. "Oh, my mistake. This is for you as well. From Sir William."

Viv accepted a folded, sealed letter. Even her father's scrawled handwriting threatened a new round of overwhelmed tears. She glanced up at his portrait, then opened the heavy stock paper. Miles stood behind her, his forehead bowed to rest on her nape, his fingers gentle on her shoulders. He was nearby, so close, yet giving her the privacy she hadn't needed to request.

The paper trembled as she read one final message from her father.

> *My Vivienne,*
>
> *If I could change one thing in my life, I would return to those months in Paris—or the fateful years that followed. I would have been your mother's champion. I have never been able to think of her without regret. Pride kept me from offering what she deserved, and you both suffered for it. Please forgive me, my daughter, for the pain you endured because of my mistakes.*
>
> *You have always been the most deserving girl, so quick and dutifully minded. I can only hope, as I pen this missive, that one day your husband earns your heart. He always struck me as a man in need of a challenge, and you, my dear, were the most challenging endeavor a father could undertake. To love you is to love untapped potential and the thrill of the chase.*

Perhaps in tackling the wilds of the beautiful, untamed Cape, you will discover that thrill together.

Be well, my exquisite girl, and be happy. You deserve both and so much more.

Your father,
William

"Good tears or bad?" Miles asked against her cheek.

"Good. So very good."

She turned in his arms and held on tight. A feeling of incandescent love enveloped her as surely as he did. The million dollars was nothing compared to the miracle of learning her father's true heart.

Only after Miles forced a gentle distance between them did he find a handkerchief and dry her face. "No more of this now, Vivie," he said. "Your family will be here soon. I'd rather they catch us in an indelicate position than see you crying." He kissed her softly. "Shall we wager as to whether Old Man Christie changed their lives, too?"

"Absolutely not. No more wagers between us."

"What then?"

Instinctively, as her heart had taught her to do, she found his dark brown eyes. Her amusement and happiness were reflected there, and in his guileless smile. "Only love, Miles. Love and trust and forever."

Author's Note

I have a special place in my heart for Viv and Miles—for their strength, vulnerability, and hard-fought faith in one another. I hope you've enjoyed their story of reunited passion!

To complete their happy ending, I knowingly took two liberties with history. Although patents utilizing carbons were issued at the rate of roughly twenty per decade between 1865 and the end of the century, the true value of industrial diamonds was not realized until WWI. Whether a brokerage could have profited by trading carbons as early as 1881 must be left to our willing suspension of disbelief.

In addition, the genuine Kimberley Club was established by Cecil Rhodes three months after Miles's poker game finale. For a time the club boasted more millionaires per square foot than any building in the world. Twice it was rebuilt following devastating fires. After various concessions toward membership throughout the twentieth century, women were finally allowed to enter through the front door in 1980.

Countless people's lives were bettered by the opportunities in Kimberley, but very little about the diamond trade has been flawless. In setting Viv and Miles's story in Cape Colony, I hope I have done justice to the balance between hardship and romance. As with all settings throughout history, both must have existed in Kimberley.

As always, I look forward to your comments! Please contact me by email at carrie.lofty@gmail.com. I also welcome you to visit www.CarrieLofty.com and to follow me on Twitter (@CarrieLofty).

Turn the page for a sneak peek at Carrie Lofty's next novel

Starlight

Coming soon from Pocket Books

One

Polly Gowan knew the overseers were looking for her. They always came for her.

She ducked her chin and concentrated on the mechanical arms swishing cotton into cloth. Adjusting the tension of the warp threads, she glanced toward the commotion at the north entrance to the factory floor. One of the overseers, a bulldog-faced man named Rand Livingstone with a taste for expensive clothing, consulted a ragged sheet of paper. A list of names, no doubt.

Christie Textiles had a new master, reported to be the son of the company's namesake. No one could admit to having met the man, so privately did he keep his own counsel. But a face-to-face meeting was exactly what Polly sought. Any information she unearthed about his methods and personality would aid the weavers' union, especially during contract negotiations. They needed to know their new opponent.

And she needed to stay clear of blame for last week's accident. Several newly delivered looms had been ruined in a small explosion, with three horses killed. Mary Worth had ruined her hand trying to save the poor beasts. Many believed it to be sabotage, including Polly. But the identity of the perpetrator remained a mystery. Far too many mysteries for her liking.

Livingstone may as well have been working from memory, so predictable were his persons of interest. Tommy Larnach, Agnes Dorward, and Les MacNider shuffled toward the door under armed guard. Other workers hustled to take their places at the looms. The day's orders still needed to be filled. Half the factory floor could be hauled to jail and that expectation wouldn't change.

When questioned by one of the enforcers, stout old Widow Ferguson pointed a gnarled forefinger toward Polly. But Livingstone was already pushing past workers, his sunken eyes fastened on his target. Yes, he and Polly were very well acquainted.

She banked her apprehension as if throwing water on hot coals. Her best defense was, as always, to be perceived exactly as Livingstone assumed. A little simple. A little cowed.

"Miss Gowan, you're to come with me." His voice box must have been damaged during his petty, miserable life. He perpetually sounded as if a strong hand clasped his throat. "You're on the list."

"Of course, sir." But she did not pause in her work. Threads whisked to form cloth—the mechanics of the loom nearly magic, except for the grit and toil and steam they consumed.

"*Now*, Polly."

She hid the shiver that came at his use of her Christian name. "Only finishing my quota, sir."

Livingstone yanked her away from the loom. Constance Nells eased into Polly's space, insuring that the work would not suffer. She deftly maneuvered three machines at once, aided by one of the apprentice weavers. A slight smile tipped Connie's lips, the only indication that she was amused, too. They had, after all, performed this ballet more than a dozen times. Just enough insolence, without inviting the full wrath of the overseers.

That Connie was also involved in union activities probably would have surprised the likes of Livingston. Studious, tidy, and quiet, with her two wee babes tended at home by her elderly grandmother, she hardly seemed the type.

But Polly . . .

Being the eldest child of Graham Gowan meant notoriety. His dedication to workers' rights spanned three decades. Polly's youth and gender would not protect her forever, especially if the masters discovered that she served as her father's right hand.

Livingstone prodded her in the lower back. He always touched her more than was necessary. Little pinches and grabs reinforced what damage he could do if the opportunity arose. Polly kept her eyes forward, her jaw fixed. The heavy pulse in her ears rubbed out the looms' thumping, humming clatter.

Out the front doors, she squinted against the pewter sky. Calton was hardly a pretty area on the most brilliant of days. In fact, spring's eventual sunshine would only make clear every crack in the tenement sandstone. But when licked by March's drizzle and cold, buildings stood as dark, hulking shadows amid the ghostly gray. No color. Very little hope.

She and the other suspects—for that's what they were—shambled toward a constable's wagon. But they wouldn't be dragged before civil authorities. No, with regard to factory matters, the masters may as well be God's representatives on Earth. Or Satan's.

That no one had yet met the devil of Christie Textiles was enough to make Polly shiver. How could she strategize against a man she had never met?

Her shawl offered little protection against the slinky

late-winter cold. Once inside the wagon, seated on a hard, shallow bench, she huddled closer to Agnes Dorward. The woman's age was completely indeterminate, a contradiction of smooth skin and gray hair. All Polly knew was that she had four grown children and had lost her only grandchild, a wee baby girl, to cholera during the previous autumn.

Agnes's closed eyes silently proclaimed her boredom with this routine. Polly shared her fatigue, knowing their destination would be Buchanan Street in the City Centre. All she could hope was that this time, the new Mr. Christie would be there to question them personally.

Les MacNider, however, was full as ever of piss and wind. "They haven't the right. They never do. And yet we let them herd us along like cattle to the slaughter."

"Ah, shut your flapping gums, Les." Hamish Nyman had been arrested at least four times for inciting political discord. He lit a rolled tobacco paper. That sweet, ashy scent quickly filled the enclosed wagon, tensing Polly's stomach.

"No, I won't," Les said. "Polly, take my back on this. Your father wouldn't stand for such abuse."

"He has and he would," she replied. "We all tell our stories, and then we go back to work. No harm done. And no masters the wiser. At least this time they have just cause. Someone really did sabotage those looms. We all know it."

Hamish's whip-thin disciple, Tommy Larnach, grinned

at her with the witless abandon of a simpleton. But sparks of intelligence shone from his eyes, as did the fondness born of their shared history. Some of it was very intimate. Not all of it was pretty. Once, back when they were children running loose in the alleys of Calton, Polly had seen him kick a stray dog to death. He'd grinned that exact same way.

"Beats working," he said. "Anything to keep from finishing my quota."

Les sneered. "You little pisspot. Do you think those demands disappear when we leave the floor? No, someone else takes up our slack. They work twice as hard while we have to defend ourselves against ever more suspicions."

"Their fault for being so upstanding," Tommy said with a shrug.

"Shut it." Hamish exhaled a long gray billow of smoke. "You'll wake the old lady."

"I'm not asleep," Agnes said, eyes still closed. "How could I be with the lot of you nattering on?"

Polly permitted herself a tight grin. They were unruly, thick-headed, bitter people, but they were *her* people. Even Tommy, as barbarous as he could be, would lie down in front of a team of galloping draft horses if it meant protecting union secrets. His limp was a testament to that when, half a decade earlier, at the mere age of fifteen, he'd taken the fall for her father.

The wagon chugged to a stop. Livingstone jerked the

double doors open, his hand on Polly's upper arm faster than she could have imagined. She stumbled to the pavement where flint-sharp ice crystals chapped her cheeks. Agnes emerged last, with Les helping her down.

The office for Christie Textiles was a modest affair when compared to some of the masters' grand places of business. Situated halfway down toward St. Enoch's Square, the squat four-story building resembled in shape and color the dull bricks used for its construction. Heavy overcast clouds leeched the walls of their deep red. A modest sign hung over the front door.

"The sign's been painted anew," Polly said to Agnes.

"New master. It's little Will Christie's boy, come home."

From nipping bites, Polly wore a raw place on her chapped lower lip. Her father's committeemen collected information like birds building nests. But what they had gathered about Alexander Christie did little to round out his image. Indeed, he was Sir William Christie's eldest child, born to an English noblewoman who had died during his infancy. Raised in London by his mother's family, the boy eventually moved to New York City when Sir William remarried a Welsh commoner. Now he taught astronomy at an American university in someplace called Rhode Island, widowed with one child.

But his personality, politics, and plans—even his appearance—were as opaque as the clouds.

"Home," Polly said, the word brusque. "He was neither born nor raised here."

Agnes shook her head. "He's got its blood in his veins, though. No denying."

"Masters are never new. He'll be a parrot for the one before him, and for the one before him."

Livingstone glared as he shoved them through the front door. "You two, quiet."

He and another overseer, Robert Huttle, flanked Polly as if she posed the most immediate physical threat. The skin along her neck shrank as if trying to escape. Four doors along either side of a short hallway were all closed. What manner of bookkeepers inhabited those concealed rooms? Did they know where the cotton came from? Where the cloth went? She merely stood at a machine all day, her eyes shriveling when she forgot to blink. Repetitive. Every motion, thought, day the same. Hunched clerks behind wooden doors saw more of the world from their ledgers and manifests than she ever would, though they might never appreciate their narrow cubbyholes with such imagination.

They arrived before a door at the end of the hallway. Livingstone opened it with a heavy iron key and pushed the detainees inside.

Polly had been inside that same office many times since her thirteenth birthday, when she and her father were suspected of writing and distributing notices about an upcoming rally. Only the humiliation of being proven unable to read had saved her that day—the day when she decided to do whatever she could to help the union.

However, she had never seen the master's office like this. A wall of new, empty shelves lined the eastern and western walls. The air still smelled of freshly cut pine boards and the alcohol sweetness of varnish. The oversized desk, always so imposing, was entirely devoid of clutter. A rich sheen warmed its highly polished surface.

All renovated. All expectant. But still devoid of the master she sought to meet.

If that remained the case, if Mr. Christie did not appear, then Livingstone's harassment and Polly's missed work would be for naught. Indignation boiled under her skin and left a sour taste on her tongue.

She sat beside Agnes, while the men stood. No one spoke. A thick press of tension gathered as did sweat along her hairline. But Livingstone would see it if she fidgeted. So she sat perfectly still, her fingers as neatly folded as the braids of a little girl on Sunday morning.

Ten minutes passed. Then another ten. The sweet varnish scent was overcome by the palpable reek of Tommy's anger and Les's indignation: sharp, bitter, hot. Both men radiated with energy, although she knew only Tommy would use violence. Les was a chatterbox and a reasonable thinker, but he was whippet thin, prone to a flurry of words rather than punches. Hamish lit another roll of tobacco, which threatened to send Polly's stomach over the edge. She swallowed fiercely to hold down the nauseated gurgle in her belly.

"Now where the hell is he?" Tommy finally shouted.

Polly flinched. Part of her feared what damage her first boyfriend was capable of rendering, but she was also pleased that at least one of them had finally spoken up. She would have, had her ambition to meet the new mill master not trumped her pride.

Livingstone lifted his truncheon. "Be quiet, you."

"I won't, you puffed-up prig. You drag us down here in the middle of a working day . . . to what? Admire an empty office? Sod that. I'm not staying."

Robert Huttle, with his overly wide shoulders and flattened face, barred the door. "You'll stay here as long as we say."

"As *you* say?" Polly asked. "Are we not here on the direction of the new master?"

Livingstone raked a filthy gaze down to her bodice, then back to her face. "Oh? Did I give that impression? So sorry."

Tommy's face turned the color of cooked beets. "You son of a—"

But Hamish and Les grabbed both of Tommy's arms before he could launch at Livingstone. Polly jumped up too. She placed her hands flat against his bony chest. "Not now, Tommy. Not here. Please. Do it for me."

"Do it for me," Livingstone mocked. "And you hope she'll do for you later."

Tommy spat to one side. "I beat you to her, you sniveling pig."

"Enough! I won't have my private business used as fodder for a shouting match." She turned her back to Tommy, confident he would do no worse than to ungallantly mention their shared past. "I suggest you either remand us to the nearest constabulary for questioning, present us to the mill master so we may address his concerns, or let us return to the factory."

Livingstone broached the space between them, with Huttle close behind. At her back, Polly could feel Tommy, Hamish, and Les tense. If she handled this without the right nuance, she would be caught between ten flying fists.

"You think you're in charge here, Polly?" Livingstone asked with that raspy nightmare of a voice. "With your fancy words and your da's sass?"

"No, Mr. Livingstone. Surely this was all some . . . mistake. Let us part as fellow workers who all draw sustenance from the same company." She significantly eyed the brocade satin waistcoat that peeked out of his greatcoat. "After all, our productivity means your prosperity."

His narrow eyes were nearly swallowed up by his

squint, as if he could look hard enough to read whether she spoke in earnest or in jest. *Look all you like.* She had not achieved her place within the union hierarchy by being easily read or intimidated. Still, she was very glad he could not hear her heart. That fast, traitorous rhythm would have clearly revealed her nerves.

"This was a warning," he said. "You can expect more of the same if we don't get answers about that explosion."

"We? Are you speaking for the elusive Mr. Christie?"

His gaze flicked away. Brief. But telling.

Polly edged into his space. He was a good half foot taller, but he held no power over her. Not at that moment. "You haven't met him yet, either. Have you?"

"No business of yours. Get out of here."

"Not until you tell me who has."

But Livingstone's moment of weakness had passed. He crossed his arms and stared down with bald-faced contempt. "Keep your head down, Polly Gowan, or our next meeting won't be so pleasant."

"My imagination has not that potential. Good day, Mr. Livingstone."

She brushed past him, ably dousing her disgust. Agnes joined her and the men followed, hounded by the echo of Livingstone's rasping chuckles. "Got to watch that young one, Huttle. Graham Gowan's daughter. She'll bite you as soon as speak to you."

Keeping her eyes forward was a challenge but Polly persevered. Yes, she had bit Livingstone. And she would bite his bloody finger clean off next time he tried touching between her legs. The insult was sharp enough to rouse Tommy again, but Hamish and Les did their best to drag him outdoors.

"Goddamn vermin is what they are," Les said into the strengthening wind. "Turning against their own kind like that. What evil, infected wombs did they crawl out of?"

"Enough of that gutter talk," Hamish snapped. "What's done is done." He nodded toward where the wagon was no longer tethered. "I suppose we're walking back. Will give Tommy here a chance to cool off."

Tommy hunched into his coat, his expression dangerous. "That bastard deserved my fist in his face."

"But I'm proud of you for withholding," Polly said. "The last thing you need is more trouble. None of us need it. Until we find out who sabotaged the factory—betraying us as surely as revealing union secrets to the masters—we must keep a low profile."

The men reluctantly nodded their agreement, which suffused Polly, as ever, with a sense of importance. They listened to her. They trusted her judgment. Perhaps it was the lingering effect of being Graham Gowan's daughter, but she rather fancied thinking that her own personality and quick thinking had something to do with the respect she had fought to earn. Respect was better than most girls in Calton received.

She intended, however, to do one better. The union would tear itself apart trying to find the identities of the saboteurs, while the elusive Mr. Christie hid behind his secrets. They could afford no more such pointless delays. Time to press her father's contacts a little harder. Surely someone would know who and where he was.

"You boys go on ahead," she continued, linking arms with Agnes. "We have an errand to attend."

Alex needed a break from the expense reports and informational pamphlets spread across his desk. Numbers of a distinctly commercial variety clogged his vision and his thoughts. There remained so much to learn. For the first time, he wondered how his father had successfully ingratiated himself into so many varied businesses. Had he really learned each industry as thoroughly as Alex was trying to learn the textile trade? Or did enterprises eventually come to resemble one another, so that the commodity no longer mattered?

No matter how his father had managed, Alex was not a businessman. The only way he knew to approach a topic was to study it from the ground up to the limitless sky—an aim made difficult because of Edmund's health.

The wet nurse he had recruited in Rhode Island would leave in three weeks to rejoin family in London. And he still had no reliable nurse. Even his contacts at the University of Glasgow had fallen short on recommendations. Every able-bodied woman in the city seemed to be employed in the factories. Those he had interviewed were either too young, and therefore woefully inexperienced to care for a boy with Edmund's needs, or so recalcitrant in their views on parenting that he feared their methods.

So he did what he was wont to do when the stress and strangeness became too much: he consulted his telescope. The largest and by far the most expensive piece of equipment he owned occupied a place of importance in his library, with the powerful lens pointed skyward. However, it could have been pointed toward a thick pile of muck for how often he'd seen the stars. Glasgow was enshrouded in a heavy layer of cloud and smoke that rarely abated. Thus, rather than ease his frustration and permit his mind to float along familiar, even comforting paths, he was only reminded of his significantly altered life.

He adjusted a dial, fiddled with a knob, and wrote a few notes on a sheet of paper. And he held still at the sound of knocks at his front door.

Curious.

The courier he used for deliveries to and from his shift manager had already made his two assigned daily visits. Alex had met his key members of staff during his first week in Glasgow. The men were educated, from good merchant families. He trusted them with the discretion he desired as he sought care for Edmund and secured his footing in the industry.

In an effort to conserve funds, he had hired a man named Griggs to act as butler, valet, and coachman. Alex's garments were never *quite* right, and the horses took a good while to hitch, but Griggs served as a rather respectable butler. The sound of his voice in the foyer, in heated discussion with a young woman, urged Alex to further awareness.

Perhaps an interview for Edmund's nurse he had forgotten?

"Miss! Miss, you cannot go up there."

"I insist. In fact, I insist on behalf of every person employed by Christie Textiles."

The sound of feet clomping up the stairs actually made Alex . . . grin? He shouldn't be grinning. But the resolute, heavily accented voice of a riled woman diverted him in ways he could not explain.

Rarely did he appreciate things he could not explain.

"You tell me if I'm wrong in thinking Mr. Alexander Christie does not live here." The door burst open.

Red hair. He was felled by a head of exquisite red hair. That the young woman also had a petite, lush figure only added to his bewildered amusement.

"I am Alex Christie," he said past his dry tongue. "And yes, I do live here. Now shall we hear your half of this unconventional introduction?"

Don't miss the sizzling
follow-up to *Flawless*

Starlight

By CARRIE LOFTY

Coming in mass market and eBook
Summer 2012 from Pocket Books!

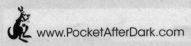

Get a Lesson in Love

with bestselling historical fiction from Pocket Books!

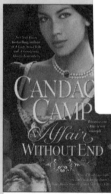